At seven n third pods, were both overdue. It was time for Clement to act.

"Captain Yan," he said in a commanding voice, "go to station red, repeat station red." At his call the CAC broke into a bustle of activity. Automatic alarms went off throughout the ship. Clement looked at Yan.

"Captain," he said, "can we go back into LEAP space and try to contact them?"

"We can, but that would leave the rest of our ships unprotected." She looked at him, deadly serious. "We should wait, Admiral. Those ships were with us every step of the way, and I find it highly unlikely they've simply vanished from the universe at our journey's end."

"We have other ships in the fleet that have LEAP reactors," Clement said. He made his decision and opened a direct com down to Nobli in Engineering

"Engineer Nobli, you will prepare the *Beauregard* for deployment. Get your techs down to the landing bay and warm up her reactor. We're going out to find our missing ships."

BOOKS
by DAVE BARA

Trinity
Trinity's Children

The Lightship Chronicles
Impulse
Starbound
Defiant

Standalone Novels
Speedwing

To purchase Baen titles in e-book form, please go to
www.baen.com.

TRINITY'S CHILDREN

DAVE BARA

BAEN

TRINITY'S CHILDREN

This is a work of fiction. All the characters and events portrayed in this book are fictional, and any resemblance to real people or incidents is purely coincidental.

Copyright © 2022 by Dave Bara

All rights reserved, including the right to reproduce this book or portions thereof in any form.

A Baen Books Original

Baen Publishing Enterprises
P.O. Box 1403
Riverdale, NY 10471
www.baen.com

ISBN: 978-1-9821-9298-3

Cover art by Kurt Miller

First printing, November 2022
First mass market printing, October 2023

Distributed by Simon & Schuster
1230 Avenue of the Americas
New York, NY 10020

Library of Congress Control Number: 2022029143

Printed in the United States of America

10 9 8 7 6 5 4 3 2 1

Dedication

I'd like to thank my former editor here at Baen, Tony Daniel, for his faith in this project. Thanks also go to Toni Weisskopf for taking over and especially Dave Butler for his feedback and wise counsel in getting this book to the finish line. When you work for Baen, you work for a family.

TRINITY'S CHILDREN

The old diesel-powered train made its way smoothly down the tracks, taking its few occupants from the only real metropolis on the planet, Ceta City, to the small settlement town of Meridian Station and other, more distant, near–ghost towns. It was a trip one of the passenger cabin's occupants had taken many times.

That occupant was a certain Jared Clement, once of the rebellious Rim Confederation Navy, and now, for the second time, in the Five Suns Alliance Navy. The difference this time was that he wore the rank uniform of a Fleet Admiral, rather than merely that of a spaceship captain. It wasn't a change he was entirely comfortable with, but it was a reality, and something he decided he would just have to get used to.

Sleeping gently on his shoulder was his adjutant and primary military and personal confidante, Tanitha Yan, now a captain of her own ship, the Five Suns Navy battlecruiser *Agamemnon*. The *Agamemnon* was the most advanced ship in the Five Suns Navy, currently nearing completion at the Kemmerine Station dry docks. *She's a beauty to behold*, thought Clement, thinking both of the ship, and of Yan. As much as he may have wanted it, their relationship had to remain platonic and professional because of the strict Navy protocols against fraternization, particularly in the higher ranks. Yan was special to him in many ways, but he wouldn't trade her value to him as an officer for the comfort of having her as his wife. Not yet anyway, but, maybe someday.

She snored gently and quietly on his shoulder as she slept, and he dared not move his arm, which was falling asleep, lest he wake her. Outside, the bleak gray landscape rushed by with no vista or natural feature of any interest. Most of Ceta was a flat gray and brown plain with just a minimum amount of low rolling hills and the occasional river or creek with sparse trees to break up the monotony.

A train going in the opposite direction, toward Ceta City, rumbled by slowly on the parallel track. It was packed full of refugees, families with grim faces and carrying all their worldly belongings with them. The outer communities were failing at an ever more rapid pace than the rest of the planet, and people were abandoning their farms and towns in droves, heading to the city looking for some sign of hope to relocate, either on or off the planet. Unknown to them, the potential "cascading failure event" of which the first Trinity mission was born was already in motion, and well ahead of its expected schedule. Ceta was growing barren, and simply couldn't support its already meager population anymore. It was the grim reality the Five Suns government faced every day, but refused to talk about, at least publicly. Clement was the front man for the fight, and he would rise or fall based on the outcome of the planned migrations from the Rim worlds to the Trinity system. It was a responsibility he took very seriously, and one that he felt he couldn't ignore if the people he loved were to be saved.

The passing of the refugee train left Clement feeling hollow. These were his people, and Ceta was the front line in a war of attrition that could lead to the total breakdown of Five Suns Alliance society; one planet collapsing, the people being forced to migrate to the next, followed by a second collapse . . . and so on.

The expert's best models showed the inner core worlds of the Five Suns Alliance collapsing within three decades, but personally Clement knew that timeline was unreliable. He believed it would be half that, if they were lucky, which was why the Trinity worlds were so critical to humanity's future. They were rich and bountiful planets, all orbiting a single stable red dwarf star. Perfect for colonization, and with only a small "native" population of humans, whose presence on those worlds was still a mystery to unravel. Clement's thoughts turned to that first Trinity mission, and his interactions with "Mary," a beautiful and carefree native girl on the planet designated Bellus. She had shown him the "Hill Place," an artificial construct built on a mountain that seemed artificial in its own right, reflecting a level of technology the natives clearly did not have. That was a place he wanted to return to, to seek the answers to its mysteries. At his core he was a man who wanted to explore. Now, he felt increasingly like a merchant ship captain stuck carrying cargo between two insignificant ports of call.

He turned his attention back to the bleak landscape of his home world as the train slowly rolled forward.

Ceta was a place no one in their right mind would want to live, but three generations ago Clement's great-grandparents had decided to stake a homestead out on this dreary plain, more than thirty kilometers outside of Ceta City. They had been poor, kicked off one of the inner Core Five Suns Alliance worlds for some minor violation of law, most likely tax arrears or a civil fine they couldn't pay. The story went that they had taken a judge's offer of a clean record if they agreed to relocate their family to the Rim. Much of the details of this story were unclear, and his father didn't like to recite it often, if at all. Clement thought that in some way his father was embarrassed by it, and didn't want it circulating outside of the family.

When he couldn't take the tingling in his arm anymore, Clement leaned in and gently shook Yan on the shoulder. This stirred her and she woke.

"Are we there yet?" she asked in a quiet voice, her eyes still closed.

He smiled. "Not yet, but close enough I thought I should wake you. Plus, you were cutting off the circulation in my arm, so if I wanted to save it I had to act."

She quickly pulled back and opened her eyes. "Oh god, I fell asleep on your arm? Why didn't you tell me? Did I drool on you?"

"No. And if I'm honest, I was enjoying the human contact."

She gave him a sarcastic smile and then smacked him in the bicep with her fist.

"See? I didn't even feel that. You've killed my arm."

"You're a liar, Fleet Admiral Clement."

He had no answer to that.

"How long was I out?" she asked, rising up and stretching but keeping her attention on him.

Clement looked at his watch. "About forty minutes," he said. "Just enough time to recharge the batteries."

"I think that train station potato soup knocked me out," she said, leaning back in her seat with a sigh. "Too many carbs."

"Umm," he said. "Ceta is not a place to come to if you don't like carbs, Captain. Keeps the people alive."

"Yes, that and the occasional musk ox steak," she replied.

He shrugged. "Sometimes we have to eat our work animals," he admitted as he rubbed out his arm.

"Not as good a cuisine as the Kemmerine Station food," she needled him.

"The steaks on Kemmerine are replicated protein. So are the prawns."

"Mm-hmm," she said. "Still, they're tasty."

"Cuisine is not something we on Ceta brag about," he admitted.

"Nor should you."

He shook his head at her. "This is the second time I've brought you to my family home, Yan, and yet you persist in making fun of my backwards little planet."

She turned her head to him and smiled.

"You're right," she said. "It's too easy to do. Not like when I took you to meet my family on Shenghai."

"Yes," he replied. "I couldn't really make fun of your family's estate and servants. It was hard to mock. And I didn't know your father was an oil magnate."

"Oil magnate? You make it sound like he's a criminal. He's just a businessman, and my mother is just a teacher."

"Just a businessman, and a teacher...in Advanced Particle Wave Physics. Sure. That's like saying my parents are land barons, not potato farmers."

"Isn't everyone on Ceta a potato farmer?" she said to him with her best "innocent eyes" look. But Clement knew better. Behind those eyes was the mind of a devious devil.

"Be nice," Clement said, waving his finger at her in a mock warning. "Some people grow wheat and corn."

"As I suspected."

He sighed, reflecting. "Why do you come on these trips with me, Yan?"

"Your mother likes me. She writes to me all the time, checking up on you, you know."

At this Clement grew alarmed. "My mother *writes* to you? About what?"

"Like I said, about you. She's worried about you."

Clement closed his eyes and sat back in the couch. "She wants her son to settle down and have a family."

"That's about it."

"And she wants that to be with you."

"Of course."

"But she realizes that's not possible, right? I mean, I am working hard to save humanity here."

Yan laughed. "I've explained that to her, but she's not buying it. She wants me to have your babies."

Clement opened one eye to look at her. "Busy saving humanity over here..." he said, pointing at himself.

"She specifically asked me to come and visit again, she

liked me so much the first time. And you don't exactly have a reputation with the ladies. So yes, as a mother, she's worried there will be no more Clements."

Clement closed his eye again. "After I get our colony established maybe I'll settle down on a patch of land on Bellus and marry one of the local girls. Have a dozen Clements. Maybe that Mary girl. She was pretty cute."

"I'm pretty sure she was more interested in me than you."

"Oh, I'm absolutely sure, based on your little tryst together at the pond. Still, a man can dream."

Their verbal fencing reached a stalemate then, and they both remained quiet the next few minutes while the train began its deceleration into Meridian Station. Yan started in on him again.

"Well, maybe, someday—"

"Not today please, Xiu Mei, not today," he said.

She sighed. "Please don't call me that," she said. "In my culture that kind of intimacy is reserved for married couples or permanent partners, of which we are neither."

Clement sat up then. "I'm sorry. I won't do that again."

"Thank you."

"And just so you know, I do consider us to be partners, of a kind," he said. She said nothing to that.

And now the conversation was truly over.

Once they were secured at the station Clement pulled their luggage down from the top rack and they made their way out into the dim gray-and-orange sunlight of Ceta. They waited alone at the train dock for about ten minutes until their scheduled ground car pulled up. Clement loaded their luggage in to the trunk of the car and then hopped into the passenger cabin with Yan. The old-style electric vehicle said nothing verbally, but a visual display panel showed their programmed destination as CLEMENT FAMILY FARM and set an estimated time of arrival of twenty-one minutes. Clement leaned back and looked at Yan sitting across from him as the car started to rock and roll on the rough gravel road.

"Ah, home," he said.

She smiled.

Clement's mother, Abigail, waved to them as their car pulled up in a cloud of dust and dirt outside of the large single-story ranch-style house. It was a common enough design on the planet, and not distinguishable in any significant way from a thousand others. Faded yellow siding with white trim paint completed the rural décor.

Clement got out first and hugged his mother, then extended a hand to Yan, who stepped out of the car and was also greeted with a hug. He unloaded their luggage, nothing more than overnight bags, and closed the trunk. Once he was clear of the car it backed itself up to the family charging station and plugged in to recharge, waiting for its next call.

The three of them went inside and Clement stored the bags at the doorway, then they went into the dining room. Yan and Clement sat down at the large table made of reclaimed hardwood while his mother disappeared into the kitchen and then returned with a setting of tea and scones. She poured for them and then sat down on the opposite side of the table, the large picture window looking out on the family wheat fields at her back. She looked out once and then turned her attention back to her son and his companion.

"Your father is still out on the far forty, claims he's checking for pests in the wheat crop, as if there were any bugs on this desolate rock," said Abigail.

"He's just like me," Clement said, taking a sip of the sweet tea, "he hates both arrivals and departures."

"He does at that," agreed his mother. "I've paged him. He doesn't have much excuse not to come now." She turned her attention to Yan. "I don't suppose our sweet-tasting tea is much to your liking, Tanitha."

Yan smiled as she swallowed. "It is very different to what I get at home, but equally as pleasing, really Abigail."

Abigail smiled. "I think I've had enough of the formalities between us," she said with a wave of her hand. "Just call me Abby. Everyone else does."

"Abby, then."

"I just call you mom," interjected Clement.

"Yes, and I only call him Jared Robert when he's in trouble."

"Which I imagine was quite often when he was growing up," said Yan.

Abby smiled. "Oh, absolutely. One eye on the ground and always one eye on the sky. Our young man here was never destined to be a farmer."

"I'm forty-five now, Mother, almost forty-six. I don't think that qualifies me as a 'young man' anymore."

"No, it doesn't," she admitted, then turned back to Yan. "So what does he call you? Tanitha seems very formal."

"He just calls me Yan," she laughed.

"Oh that's terrible! Jared you must do better than that!"

He shrugged. "She calls me 'Clement' most of the time, except for the occasional 'honey bunch.'"

"I do not call you 'honey bunch,'" said Yan, cocking her head and giving him an annoyed look.

"Oh, you two are bad! You need better names than that. Tanitha, what would you like to be called?"

"Well, actually, we were just having that discussion on the train," she said. Abby looked to her son, expectantly. He sat back, taking his tea cup and saucer with him.

"It did not go well," he admitted. "We're sticking with Yan and Clement for now."

"I'll just settle for Cletus," came his father's deep voice as he rounded the doorway into the dining room. He placed his hat on the hanging rack on the wall and then sat down next to his wife and across the table from his son and Yan. He was a big man with a bald head sprinkled with short white hair, and wearing his typical worn work coveralls. To Clement, his father was a caricature of the rural farmer. Cletus merely nodded at his son and Yan as he sat down.

"No hug for your son? Not even a handshake?" chided Abby.

Cletus shook his head no. "We both know why he's here." Then he looked at his son. "So, get on with it."

Clement put his tea cup down and leaned forward on the table. "The first colony ship leaves for Bellus in two weeks. I want you to be on it," he said.

"What, and leave all this?" said his father, gesturing wide with his arms.

"Cletus . . ." said Abby in a warning tone.

Jared continued. "I've reserved eighty acres of the most

fertile growing ground you've ever seen for you. A new modular home will be there and waiting for you, the most modern equipment you can imagine. Nearly anything will grow there, year-round. Fruit, vegetables, rice, grain, anything you can think of. And you can trade what you don't eat for things that you want. It's my own personal homestead. There's a freshwater lake within walking distance, stocked full of fish. It's the chance of a lifetime. You just have to tell me that you'll take it."

Cletus Clement looked uncomfortable, and shifted in his chair. He looked to his wife, who remained stoic, leaving the decision to him. Jared started in again.

"Mom, remember when you used to make strawberry jam and preserves? How long has it been since you were able to do that?"

"Nine years," she replied, looking down at the table. "Fruit won't grow here anymore."

Clement looked to his father. "And when was the last time you fished?" he asked.

"No need," he replied. "I can get what I want at the market."

"If they have any," his wife added.

Clement leaned back again. "It was the summer of my twelfth birthday. I remember it. The lake was gone the next year."

"You may be right," said Cletus.

"You know I am."

Now silence descended on the table. Yan and Abby exchanged glances, and Abby picked up the tea tray to take it into the kitchen. "Could you lend me a hand, Tanitha?"

"Of course."

"You can't leave," protested Cletus to his wife. "We haven't made a decision yet."

Abby stopped and turned back to her husband. "Well, I have," she replied, "the rest is up to you." Then she disappeared into the kitchen with Yan.

Now the two Clement men were left alone in silence for a good long while, then: "It's difficult to change your ways at my age, son," Cletus started.

"You're only sixty-six, Dad. Life expectancy, even on this rock, is a hundred and eight. You're not old, you only want to act that way. On Bellus, I can hire hands to do all the hard work. You can ride in the combine and just supervise all day, in between trips to the lake."

"You make it sound tempting, son, no question, but . . ."

"But what?"

His father hesitated.

"This is our home," he said. Jared stared at his father, who wouldn't look back at him.

"Our family had a different home once too, then we came here. But Ceta can't support us anymore, and Bellus offers us the prosperity of a lifetime."

"You keep saying 'us.' Do you mean the Clement family? If you don't settle down and have children soon, there will be no more Clements."

"With whom would I settle down? There's no time anyway. I'm busy trying to save as many of our people as I can."

His father nodded his head. "You could do worse than that lady in the kitchen," he said.

"I'm aware of that, sir. It's just not possible while we

still serve in the Navy. And right now I have no intention of leaving the Navy, and neither does she. I only brought her here again because she and mother are good friends." At this point he paused, seeking the words to reassure his father of the choice he wanted him to make. "There will be more Clements someday. Maybe not this year, maybe not for five more, but there will be more Clements."

Cletus eyed his son. "I'd just like to know that if I leave this place, I'd be going somewhere that I can leave something behind. A legacy, for my grandchildren."

Jared was very uncomfortable with the conversation, but he understood his father's concerns. "You will be, I promise."

"What about the natives? I've heard there are people there already. Will we be running them off their land like conquering colonists?"

Jared shook his head. "We have extensive mitigation plans in place. Bellus is full of untouched, bountiful land, enough for everyone. And the natives there will always be protected, always share in the bounty that the colonists produce, and they'll be free to live their lives how they want, either their way, or ours."

"So I won't be stealing from anyone?"

Clement shook his head. "No sir, that won't happen. And I can say that because I'm in charge of the program."

Cletus looked at his son. "You were never going to be a farmer, were you, boy? I should never have let you have that telescope." He shook his head. Jared smiled.

"I think my destiny was always somewhere other than here," he said, then extended his hand to his father. "Do we have a deal?"

"Do I have a choice?" said Cletus.

"No, you don't," came Abby's voice from behind him. Cletus turned and saw his wife at the dining room door, with Yan standing close behind her.

"I guess I don't," he said.

Then he reached out and shook his son's hand.

✵ **2** ✵

The trip back to Kemmerine was swift and efficient, which was something Clement liked to see in his command. It was something the Five Suns Navy had gotten slack on, based on his observations.

He had managed to get back to his apartment on Argyle Station and clean it out before he left the Rim, probably for the last time. He edited the pictures of his old crew, the ones with Elara DeVore in them, to delete her image, and printed new ones. He kept his Rim service medals and other personal items with him. What he carried off the station fit in a very small box, and for once, there was no whiskey in it. He found alcohol to be something he didn't have much desire for these days, and that was a good thing, and a needed change in his mind. He handed the box off to Yan to deal with the shipping.

His future seemed to be very much "out there," at Trinity, the three new and beautiful habitable worlds that promised humanity so much, not in his old, failing home. The Trinity worlds were a great, resource-rich gift to the Five Suns Alliance and its struggling colonies. A gift he hoped would stop the deterioration of Five Suns civilization permanently.

He arrived in his office on Kemmerine Station Wednesday morning precisely at 0800, seven days after he had left it to go to the Rim. The nineteen-hour sublight journey back and forth between Kemmerine Station and the Rim stars took its toll on him physically, and he had arrived home more than a bit "space-lagged."

He had changed the station's regular work shift earlier by an hour to increase discipline among his new recruits and to (hopefully) motivate them to be more precise in their work. Precision was important, he felt, and he wanted to demonstrate that quality, so regardless of how he felt personally, he felt it was important to show up on time and set the example.

He sat down at his desk, which had been swapped out from the old one that DeVore had when she was in command here, and logged in to start his day. As someone who had betrayed him and the Five Suns, and clearly would have taken his life at the Battle of Trinity if she could have, he wanted as few associations with DeVore around him as possible. The fact that they were former lovers during the War of the Five Suns only complicated things for him, emotionally.

He paged Yan as he shuffled through his messages and updates. She arrived a few moments later from her own office on the other side of the floor.

"Sir," she said by way of welcome.

He looked up from his morning reports and coms and across to the box of mementos from Argyle Station sitting on the corner of his desk. "Thank you for having this box delivered here, Yan, but I really don't want these things in my office," he said.

"Oh," she replied, surprised. "I thought you'd want all of your military awards in one place," she said, nodding toward the half-filled display case on the near wall. It had his Five Suns Navy awards and plaques, things he had received in the last eighteen months in his role as Fleet Admiral for the Kemmerine and Rim sectors.

"I appreciate the thought, Captain, but I would like to keep my history as a rebel separate from my role here as Fleet Admiral. No point in mixing the good memories with the bad," he said, turning his attention back to his monitor.

She nodded slowly. "I see. I'll have one of the yeomen from the pool remove it. Where should I—"

"Just send it to my quarters, please," he said, meaning the small one-bedroom flat he had in the officer's wing of the station.

"Of course sir," she said formally, and swept the box up off the table. "I assume our 0900 meeting is still on?"

"Unless I see something in these reports that changes things, that's a yes, Captain," he said, looking away from her and down at his desk.

"Sir." And with that she was gone, moving quickly out of the overly large and ostentatious office and into the reception area.

Promptly at 0900 Clement came through the doorway of the conference room to find his reports all waiting for him. Yan was at his right hand, as always; Colonel Gwyneth and Fleet Commander Gracel represented the station's old-guard commanders; and a promising young officer named Harry Samkange was there from Station Services, a vital cog in the ship-building and refitting process for the Kemmerine Fleet. Clement looked around the table, seeing Gracel and Gwyneth with their gray hair, and then Samkange, a young man just under thirty of African descent with dark skin and hair. There was a sharp contrast of nearly forty years in their respective ages. Samkange was ready for a command of his own, but he had proven invaluable as the refit and construction manager for the new fleet, so for now, that decision was still there to be made when Clement wanted.

The room itself had formerly been part of the large, open expanse of the office that the previous occupant had preferred. Clement was much more conservative and had ordered the conference area enclosed with walls to allow for more privacy, and also just to break up the massive office layout. The ostentatious unused space could have accommodated fifty cubicle stations or even good-sized offices for all the senior ship commanders. As a man who had been forced to fit inside the confines of a rebel gunship for most of his career, he had developed a distaste for wasted space. He made a note to talk to Yan privately about including the fleet captain's offices in the next round of facilities updates. For now, though, he was focused on getting the most out of the facilities that he had up and functioning right now.

"I think we'll begin with the construction and refit report, Commander Samkange," he said as he sat down, still carrying an owly look on his face. He had no coffee, so Yan slid a cup over to him along with a croissant from the meeting supplies on the table. He ignored both her gestures and said nothing.

Commander Samkange started in. "The retrofit program is nearly complete, or at least Phase One is. We have twelve functioning destroyers now with operational LEAP drives and the gravity wave displacement units for inertial dampening in normal space. We couldn't manage to get the gravity-shield generators installed, though; the ships are simply too small for those to fit."

"As we suspected," commented Clement.

Samkange nodded before continuing. "We've had better luck with the light cruisers as they have enough room to install both the LEAP reactors and the full gravity-systems generators, so they'll get both the inertial dampening effect and the defensive shielding benefits."

"Excellent," said Clement with a hint of a smile, then he reached out and took the first sip of his coffee.

Samkange looked at his admiral, concern etched across his features at how the next news would be received. "There is one side effect of these refits, though, sir. We only managed to get six of the cruisers fully outfitted. The other four had to be cannibalized for parts and critical systems."

Clement winced slightly. "I knew that was a possibility, but I was hoping for eight running ships from that group."

Samkange nodded. "That was our goal too, sir. We did the best we could, but in the end these ships were just too outdated, and we had to make some tough decisions."

"I understand," said Clement, taking a bite of his croissant now and downing it with more coffee. "As long as we can get good captains and crews for them, I'll be happy."

"I used to command one of those vessels," commented Gwyneth.

"As did I," said Gracel. "They were the pride of the fleet back in their day."

"Things change, Amanda," Clement said to her, "sometimes faster than we want or imagine."

He turned back to Samkange. "What's the status of The Beast?" "The Beast" was the nickname they had all given the *Agamemnon*, the only truly modern ship in the fleet. She was a huge battlecruiser with a complement of more than fourteen hundred men and women, two hundred of them Marines, and the fleet's flagship. She had every bell and whistle imaginable, including double LEAP reactors and six gravity-field generators, three for inertial dampening and three gravity-wave projectors for defense. Her ordnance capability was enormous and her belly was full of weapons.

"She's ready for her final pre-mission trials, Admiral," cut in Yan, who was, after all, *Agamemnon*'s captain and rightly proud of that fact.

"You'll see to that schedule I assume, Captain?"

"Already drawn up, sir," she replied with a smile, picking up her pad and throwing the schedule com to Clement. He let that sit for the moment as he read the report.

"Very good, Captain Yan." Clement returned his attention to Samkange again. "And how is the gunship program coming along?"

"Still about a month out from rolling the first one off

the line, sir, but once we get to full production we should start commissioning two a month out of the factory." Clement had ordered forty gunships just like his old ship, the prototype *Beauregard*, to be built. They would be the fastest in-system ships in his fleet.

"What are you going to do with all those gunships, Admiral? Hold a lottery for who gets to command them and use the money to trim out your fleet?" said Yan, pulling his chain.

Despite himself Clement gave a small smile to his chief adjutant. "That's a good idea, Captain, but actually I have other plans for that particular fleet."

"Such as?"

"Well, we're going to take the current five prototypes that we have in service, use them for patrol of the Trinity system, in case any unwanted visitors show up," he said. "Then we'll use the new ships to do the same in Kemmerine, the Rim, and even sell some to Virginis sector if they want them."

"Good plan, but why patrol the Rim? Everyone's going to be leaving soon enough to migrate to Trinity, right?"

"That's wishful thinking, Yan. No doubt some of the population will stay behind, it could be as much as ten percent, and we'll keep Argyle Station open for just that eventuality. Plus, we don't want anyone else moving in on those planets. They're kind of strategic."

"Don't want to give any errant Earth Arks a beachhead in the Five Suns?"

"Precisely, Captain," replied Clement.

Clement turned next to Amanda Gracel. She was clearly somewhere in her late sixties age-wise, with flowing gray hair and a wealth of experience. She was a good officer, if from an older generation than Clement and certainly older than Samkange and Yan. Clement found her helpful as an administrator and would almost certainly use her in one of his future commands, in some capacity.

"Commander Gracel, how is the recruiting and planning going for the civilian transport ships?" he asked.

"Very well," she said, smiling. "We've secured ten military transports from the Virginis and the Core sectors and the conversion to civilian transports has gone well. Each transport will have the capability of moving three thousand migrants and most of their belongings to Bellus, along with their ship crews, of course. Once settled on the Trinity worlds we expect a forty-day turnaround for the return voyage and prep for the next group. The transports have been retrofitted with LEAP reactors and there is more than enough room for livestock in the cryo hold. My expectation is that you'll be able to do the trip ten times a year. That's about three hundred thousand colonists per year moving to the Trinity worlds."

"At that pace it will take us more than a decade to complete the migrations from the Rim worlds." Clement looked down at his com pad. "By the latest census estimates the Rim population will decrease about six percent per year, but that's still not fast enough. We have to take into account that many people may want to migrate from Kemmerine, Virginis, even the Core worlds, just looking for new business opportunities and a change of pace. Let's request five more transports from Core Services; we need to speed things up."

"Of course, Admiral." Gracel looked down and made a note on her com pad.

"Oh, and keep in mind that my parents will be going on the first migration trip, so let's make sure all aspects of life on those transports is well tested."

"I have one hundred percent confidence, sir."

"Thank you, Amanda."

At that he turned to Colonel Gwyneth. "And how are our recruitment programs going, Colonel?"

Gwyneth cleared his throat and sat forward. Clement imagined he would have been quite the pompous officer back in his day, but he was very good at organization and thus quite useful to the admiral. "Ahem, we have more than enough specialized techs at the moment, so many, in fact, that we're starting to project them out to the future gunship crews coming on line. We also have a glut of senior staff being off-loaded from the Core and Virginis, many of them captains and commanders, almost all of them with long careers but little flying experience."

"Staff officers," said Clement, shaking his head. He looked up at Gwyneth again. "Get with Commander Yan and sort the wheat from the chaff."

He turned then to Yan. "Pick out the most experienced captains and senior officers for the ships we're taking to Trinity, only those with flying experience. We need sixteen staffs in two weeks for those cruisers and destroyers or we'll miss our mission-launch window, and no one wants this station full of a bunch of angry migrants waiting for their busses."

"If I may, sir, we actually need twenty-six full staffs. You forgot about the transports," said Samkange.

Clement threw up his hands in frustration. "Of course I did." He quickly recovered his bearings. "Minimum commander rank required to fly the transports, Yan. Everyone else needs to be captain rank, preferably with battle experience."

"Sir, there aren't that many left with battle experience; many of them retired after the War of the Five Suns," said Yan.

Clement nodded. "Just do your best, Captain."

"Aye, sir."

Gwyneth cleared his throat again.

"Colonel?"

"There is one more problem, sir."

"Of course," said Clement, frustrated. "I'm sure whatever it is has slipped my mind in the last week."

"It's the junior officer corps, sir. Hardly any experience among those with the ranks of lieutenant, ensign, etc. All the Core and Virginis are offering us are midshipmen out of their academies at the moment."

Clement rubbed at his chin. "They're giving us the newly wed and the nearly dead, eh, Karl? Clearing out the deadwood so they can promote their best and brightest. Well, we'll just have to promote some ourselves. Any junior officers with flight experience go up one step in rank upon accepting our offer of a commission. And throw in a bonus as well, see if that helps. And let's make sure we get the cream of the crop from the academies at the very least. Any cadet with flight experience, even if it's an internship, goes straight to first lieutenant."

"Aye, Admiral," replied Gwyneth.

Clement looked around the room one more time. "Anything else?" The staff was silent in response. "Good enough. We leave for Trinity in fifteen days, ladies and gentlemen. Let's stick to our schedules and make sure everyone gets to Bellus in one piece. Dismissed."

They all stood to leave but Clement remained seated. "Commander Samkange, if you would stay for a moment?" Samkange nodded as the others shuffled out. Yan hesitated at the door but Clement waved her off, indicating she could leave the conference room door open. When they were all out of hearing range he turned to Samkange, who had sat down next to him.

"Commander, there's something I need to talk to you about," he said, then hesitated.

"Is there something wrong with my report, sir?" asked the eager young man.

Clement shook his head. "No, nothing like that. In fact, just the opposite. You've done a fantastic job the last twelve months on the construction and refit program. So good, in fact, that I want to offer you a promotion."

"I'm flattered, sir," said Samkange.

Clement continued. "You should be. I want to put you in command of the light cruiser flotilla, all six ships. You'll be captain of the *Corvallis*, the flagship of the cruisers. In this role you'll answer to me, no one else in between us except Captain Yan on board *Agamemnon*. If I'm out of commission you'll take orders from her as if they were my own, understood?"

"I do, sir."

"Good. Just to let you know I consider the light cruisers to be critical on these missions as transport support and security. The cruiser flotilla will be the main line of defense on the migration journeys as well as providing primary security at Trinity. There will be a few of the destroyers available but quite frankly I don't want them on caravan duty. They're just not durable enough, even after the refits. I'll want to keep them for support in-system at Trinity."

A look of concern crossed Samkange's face. "Sir, if I may ask, all this focus on security, and military experience—are you expecting to go into battle?"

Clement leaned forward. "Let's not say concerned, Captain, let's say cautious. The three Trinity worlds are the most precious commodities in humanity's little universe. Admiral DeVore wanted them for her own purposes, and even the Earthmen sent out a military force on a fifty-year mission to try and take them. We need to be prepared just in case our name gets called."

Samkange nodded. "You realize I don't have any combat experience, sir?"

"I do. But I also noted that you got ninety-four percent on your combat school training, and that's even better than I got. No one in this fleet is going to have real experience in a battle situation, Harry, so we'll all be learning as we go. Now I suggest you brush up on your battle training just in case. Oh, and I'll need you to report to *Corvallis* by noon tomorrow. That will give you slightly more than twenty-four hours to complete the transition, if you accept, that is?"

"Of course. Yes, I accept, sir. And thank you, sir."

"You're welcome, now just one or two more items. You're not married, are you, or have a family?"

"No, sir, no time."

"I see. That's just as well as this position will keep you away for quite a bit of the time. It may even eventually lead to a permanent assignment in the Trinity system, if we ever get a station set up there."

"Understood, sir, no issues."

Clement nodded. "Then one last thing, who do you recommend as your replacement for the construction and refit program?"

"That's easy. Lieutenant Commander Tereza Ayo, sir. She's been my number one throughout this program and she knows the specifics of everything we do."

"Excellent. Tell her that she's got a promotion too, to full commander."

"I will, sir!"

At that they both stood and Clement shook Samkange's hand in congratulations. "Make sure you pop in to Captain Yan's office and have her handle the promotion paperwork. It will probably take a day or two to make its way to my desk but you can assume acting command on my personal authority immediately."

"Thank you, sir." Samkange headed out of the conference room with a large grin on his face. Clement sat back down and pulled up his com pad, checking for new alerts.

"Ah," he said out loud, "the enthusiasm of youth."

Clement waited ten minutes for Samkange to clear Yan's office, then he picked up his pad and headed there himself. He came in and plopped down on a particularly comfortable leather side chair, his favorite in the room.

"Feeling better, Cranky?" she teased without looking up from her monitor.

"Yes, Captain. And thank you for the coffee and croissant."

"I had to do something to fix your mood," she replied, then she poured him a fresh cup from her desktop pot and slid it over to him. He took it. "You really should eat something and have your coffee before you start work in the morning, especially after a leave."

"Now you're sounding like a wife."

She turned her head toward him. "We've had that discussion before, Admiral. Maybe someday. But in the mean time you do need someone to keep an eye on you. The Five Suns has put you in charge of two entire sectors and having your blood sugar affect your mood and attitude can be a serious challenge, especially if you have to make quick decisions."

"I don't need a babysitter." Clement took a sip of the coffee. It was Sumatran, no doubt shipped in from Yan's home world of Shenghai, and one of Clement's favorites. Being a Fleet Admiral did have its benefits, such as picking from the best of the goods passing through the station.

"And I don't have time to babysit you. I'm suggesting we pick one of the yeomen from the clerical pool to handle your dietary and scheduling needs on a regular basis. I, you see, am busy running a fleet for you, Admiral."

Clement considered her suggestion. "All right then, I'll let you arrange it. But I don't want anyone trailing me around the station with a calorie counter."

Yan smiled and pressed a button on her desk com. "Already done, sir. You should expect your first meal at lunch."

"Lovely," he replied sarcastically. "And well played, Captain."

She laughed.

"Now to more important things. This mission is about establishing the migration plan and settling our people on the new worlds, but I want us to remember that the natives will not have their rights or freedoms impaired in any way. That would be counter to everything I believe in."

"I'm not sure I understand that, Admiral, at least the part about rights and freedoms. We already have a mitigation plan and a statute's in place for that eventuality. You designed them."

At this Clement sat back in the chair and thought deeply for a moment.

"The thing is, Yan, the natives on Bellus are innocents. They don't have the depth of knowledge or experience that we have with possible hostiles. So it is therefore imperative that we be their protectors. That means protecting them from both external threats like the Earthmen and *internal* ones, from people that would exploit them for their own gain."

"I understand, sir."

He leaned forward again. "Do you? I fought in the war because the Five Suns was neglecting the Rim worlds, exploiting our people, my friends and neighbors. That's why this is so important to me. I want you to understand it comes from a very deep part of me."

"I do, sir. I've seen that in you, and I respect it."

He stood. "I just wanted you to understand where I was coming from, and what my concerns are based on."

She stood then.

"You have my understanding, and my loyalty in this regard, sir."

"Good. That's all."

Then he walked away from her, satisfied.

✶ **3** ✶

Two days later Clement took a break from all the planning and organizing, which was frankly bogging his mind down, and made an impromptu "inspection" of *Agamemnon* just after lunch, leaving Yan and everyone else back at the office.

He stopped on the observation deck to take a look at his new behemoth, and she was a beauty to behold. Thirty-three decks of exotic titanium alloy metal superstructure with a conductive ceramic and nanotech skin, fully teeming with activity. He watched as the exterior construction crews in EVA suits swarmed over her, checking every seam and seal for flaws, the occasional spark light from a coil weld flashing in his eyes. Her stout rear propulsion units had five nozzles, three for the non-FTL ion plasma impeller drive and two more for the conventional chemical maneuvering thrusters. She was a mighty beast, broad and fulsome in her design. He could only imagine what the tech crews inside were doing to test and validate her internal systems.

He exited the lifter and took the station rail car to *Agamemnon*'s dock, number 39A. The car came to a stop in front of an open cargo bay door and Clement got out. All the bustling workers in the area stopped and took notice of the station's Fleet Admiral in their midst, many of them saluting, even though that wasn't standard protocol. Clement returned some of their salutes and then wearied of the task and simply began waving the workers away as he made his way through the stop-start of the crowd.

He hurried from the officer's lift to *Agamemnon's* command and control deck. Unlike the traditional "bridge" that was perched on top of a Navy ship, the CAC was nearly in the center deck of the enormous battlecruiser. As the lifter doors opened he stepped onto the primary hub of his new command.

"Admiral on the deck!" yelled the officer of the deck, following Navy tradition. At that, several heads whipped around from the many stations set around the CAC in a circle and they all stood to attention.

"At ease," Clement said, and they all resumed their duties, though with an eye on their Fleet Admiral.

Clement stepped up onto the command platform and a female Marine officer immediately stepped up and saluted him. "Colonel Marina Lubrov, Admiral. I'm leader of the Marine contingent on *Agamemnon* and I currently have the con in the absence of Captain Yan. Will you take the con, Admiral?" she said. Lubrov was tall and thin, as Ukrainian descendants often were, with light brown hair which she was wearing down over her shoulders in a casual style. She had the high cheekbones and striking eyes common for her Slavic ancestry. From what Clement could tell she was probably under thirty years old, a young age for a Marine colonel, but such were the times in the Kemmerine sector that young officers with talent could advance quickly through the ranks. Clement remembered reading her file, but as far as he knew he had never met her. Those kinds of introductions were often better left to the ship's captain.

"Not necessary, Colonel," said Clement and returned the salute. Lubrov broke off her salute but still stayed at attention. "At ease, Colonel. I'm here to do an inspection. As you know we are less than two weeks away from our first migration mission to the Trinity system. I'd like a tour of the CAC and a basic breakdown of the ship's systems, if you have time?"

"Of course, sir." Lubrov assumed a more casual pose, hands behind her back, waiting.

Clement looked around the large room. It was bigger than any space on any Navy ship he had ever served on, fully three decks tall with multiple workstations arrayed in a nearly full circle. A huge multisided visual display projected above the deck, visible to all corners (and any station) at all times.

"I didn't expect you today, Admiral," said Lubrov. "Your schedule looked full. If we'd known you were coming, we could have prepared a more formal greeting."

"No need for that, Colonel, but thank you for the thought." Clement looked to the captain's station, a large, curved console lit up from below displaying a variety of ship systems, star charts, and visual displays at a fingertip's touch. There were also papers strewn about the console in a haphazard matter. When Lubrov saw where the admiral's attention had been drawn, she quickly gathered the papers up off of the console and stepped aside to the XO's position. Clement stepped up, taking in the console. It came up to just above his waist, about ninety centimeters tall. "Run me through the console, would you, Colonel?"

"Of course, sir. You have a variety of views possible from here, sir," started in Lubrov, by way of explanation. "On your left are ship's internal systems. You can bring up any one of them, or multiple views, by dragging and dropping them in the primary display area, where they will pop up in a 3D heads-up display for you to view. At the top of the console you have access to tactical maps, deep-space scans, weapons status, and a variety of other command functions. To the right are your science displays, including speed of the ship, course, distance from the nearest star, etc. The simple touch of your fingers on the display console will automatically configure the desktop to your personal preferences. You can save your configuration with a simple voice command."

"Thank you for the tutorial, Colonel," said Clement as he began reconfiguring the desktop, moving communications, propulsion, navigation, helm, weapons, gravity systems and science displays so that they were within an arm's-length reach at all times. On a whim he brought up the propulsion and weapons systems. The two systems displays floated in the air just at his eye level, and could be rotated or expanded at his will. Propulsion was dark, save for a thruster test set to run at 1600 hours. Weapons showed the ship was stocked to sixty percent capacity, with a large complement of missiles (over six hundred, including twenty nukes) that would eventually be available, though the nukes would be the last weapons loaded. The rest showed an inventory of rods (formerly called Hell Lances, the nomenclature changed by Yan to "Rods of God"), DEW weapons, and other kinetic weapons such as scatter mines. Clement waved the displays back down to the console and said, "Save configuration, Clement 1." The console computer gave him an affirmative beep.

He came around the console then and stood at the safety railing to look at the other stations, taking in the CAC. He'd seen it before in various stages of construction, but never this complete and functional. Lubrov joined him at the platform railing and Shepard took up a position just behind him.

The CAC was arranged with stations and duty officers for each of the ship's main functions spread equally around the room. Clement counted twelve stations with their own consoles. It had three entry points, the lifter station just to the left of the command platform, plus two large adjoining access corridors, one to each side of the room at about forty-five degrees to the command console.

"Any of these stations can be relocated at any time, depending on your preferences. Of course they are currently configured to mine, and no doubt your preferences will be different," she said.

"No doubt. There will be plenty of time for that later though, Colonel."

"Of course, sir."

Lubrov motioned for Clement to follow her, stepping down onto the deck and showing the admiral the main display screen. The large, circular plasma hovered over the center of the room, giving all stations access to the same view. They toured the different command stations, Clement stopping at each one to meet the duty officers and make small talk with the people manning them, asking about their lives, their enthusiasm for the mission, etc., all to make *them* more comfortable, not him.

Clement noted that almost all of the stations were manned by junior officers, not department heads. "That will have to change," he said to Lubrov, once they were together in the admiral's private office behind the command platform. He and Captain Yan had identical working offices side by side.

"That won't be popular, sir. Most of the department heads prefer to work at their primary station locations and just report up through the duty officers."

Clement smiled, but he was not happy. "I prefer to have my department heads on the deck when I am on duty, Colonel. I find if there are decisions to be made or arguments against a certain policy that they are best conducted in person. It's hard to read a person's intent over a com line or on a small portrait display."

"I understand, sir, but I think—"

"Please prepare a memo to the staff about my new preferences. They are to be implemented on Monday," Clement finished over the top of her. He had very little patience at the moment, and he wondered if it was because of the new low-calorie diet Yan had put him on. He made a mental note to get that changed as soon as possible.

Lubrov hesitated a second, then continued. "We do

most of the staff assignments on Tuesdays, sir. It might be better to—"

"Monday, please, Colonel. And read in Captain Yan on my changes. I want all of us on the same page. We'll have nearly a month of travel time to the Trinity system to get things down, but by the time we get there I expect us to be perfect." The two officers looked at each other across the desk. There was no doubt which one of them sat in the admiral's chair.

"Monday then, Admiral." Lubrov looked down and made a note on her personal com pad. "I'll have the duty list to you by Sunday evening. Will you be taking up your quarters onboard by then?"

Clement thought about that. "Not quite yet," he said. "I'm expecting some important migrants to arrive on the station soon. I think it would be best if I stayed on the station until they're on board."

"Of course, sir. Any special accommodations I can arrange for them?"

"No. I've already arranged a VIP guest cabin for them."

"Of course, sir. Anything else?"

"Yes, actually. Please inform Captain Yan that I expect her to move her personal quarters to *Agamemnon* by Sunday evening. As of Monday morning this ship is on operational status. Our mission begins then."

"Very well, sir," said Lubrov, then she stood to leave. "With your permission, Admiral?"

Clement looked up at her. "Just one more thing, Colonel," he said. "I prefer that my senior officers, my female senior officers anyway, wear their hair in a less casual way if they keep it long. I'm not saying you have to cut it, but it should be properly pulled back and... restrained in some way. And just so you know, I insist any male officers above cadet keep a clean-shaven face when on duty, and no neck beards or man buns. It's different with the tech ratings of course, but I want my senior staff to be an example of discipline."

Lubrov didn't flinch at the comment, and stayed rigid in light of what could be considered a criticism. "Understood, sir," she said evenly. "Permission to speak freely, sir?"

Clement leaned back in his chair. "Of course."

"With respect, sir, you yourself are currently sporting the five o'clock shadow look, and often do so for days at a time, I'm told. Isn't that technically a beard?"

Clement thought about that for a second, then shot back, "I'm the admiral of the fleet, Colonel." Lubrov waited for more, saying nothing, but her face was expectant. They stood there staring at each other for a few moments, Clement unwilling to give in on the point, but impressed by the challenge the colonel presented. He could tell she was a proud officer and not afraid to speak her mind, just as her personnel file had stated. He liked that in her.

"Anything else before I return to my duties, Admiral?" The question was asked respectfully enough, but Clement noted she was pointing out to him that she had better things to do than spar with the Fleet Admiral.

Eventually he replied, ignoring her challenge. "Tell me, Colonel, do you know the current location of Chief Engineer Hassan Nobli?"

Lubrov was nonplussed. "I believe he's in the reactor room, sir, as he is on most days. He doesn't mingle with the crew much, and he rarely reports in to me when I have the con."

"I see. I'll have to have a talk with him about being more social. Um, what deck is the reactor room on?"

"Decks 11, and 12 and 14," she said. "It's a big room. But the entrance is on deck 11, sir."

"Thank you. You're dismissed, Colonel," he said. At that Lubrov turned to finally leave. "Oh, and Colonel . . ." She stopped and turned back to him. He looked down at his desk console, pretending to read coms. "You're correct about my personal grooming. As Fleet Admiral I will endeavor to set the prime example."

"Of course, sir," Lubrov said with a nod, and then was on her way.

Clement twirled in his chair a bit after she was gone, looking around the room, marveling at the sheer scale of everything. It wasn't at all like the close comfort of his former command, the *Beauregard*. She was a ship that if he allowed himself to admit it, he was much more comfortable on than this monster. Still, *Agamemnon* was a necessity in case any new adversaries showed up in the Trinity system. He found that a disturbing thought, so he got up and went to the command platform again.

"You have the con, Colonel," he called to Lubrov. The colonel turned and snapped off another salute, which was unnecessary but appreciated.

"Acknowledge. I have the con, Admiral." With that Clement departed, heading for the reactor room and to have a quick chat with his favorite, if eccentric, chief engineer.

❖ ❖ ❖

When Clement stepped into the *Agamemnon*'s reactor room, it was empty. All the control consoles were dark except one. Clement stepped up to the lighted console and saw that it was a system's diagnostic, running quietly in the background of the primary propulsion computer. The room was huge, every bit as impressive as the CAC, only more so because this one contained not one, but two LEAP reactors. These models were huge compared to the boiler-sized chamber they'd had on the *Beauregard*. These were easily twice that size, maybe more, he estimated. He was about to call out to see if anyone was on duty, perhaps lost in the distant mist of the ship's power center, but just then he heard a familiar sound, banging, metal on metal. Someone was using a hammer, and Clement thought he knew who that someone might be.

He walked past the first reactor. The inner chamber door was sealed and all was quiet. After a brief pause, the hammering resumed, and Clement could see from his position that the second reactor chamber had its door open. As he walked toward the yellow-colored metal cast reactor he heard a second hammer distinctly pounding. If it was just Nobli, he was using both hands. If it wasn't, he had a companion, which was a surprise. Nobli almost exclusively worked alone.

He came up to the open chamber door and stuck his head in. "Nobli, are you in there?" he called. His voice echoed in the hollow metal sphere. Clement could see a small arc light at the far end of the chamber illuminating the wall of the reactor, but couldn't make out any silhouettes.

Presently there were footsteps and out of the darkness

came Nobli and a young woman, obviously his new tech. Nobli stuck his head out of the reactor door, his hair a mop of messy curls, his glasses cocked off to one side and his face covered in grime. In short, he looked happy. "Clement! What the fuck are you doing here? Can't you see I'm working?"

Clement threw up his arms in a helpless gesture. "Nobli, can't you at least *pretend* I'm an admiral for once?"

"Ah, shit, I guess so. What can I do for you, Admiral?" he said, leaning casually against the chamber door. It was as formal as Nobli ever got.

Clement pointed to the deck. "Down here," he said. Nobli let out a sigh and came down the three-step ladder to the deck. His tech stood at the door opening. "You too." She dropped her hammer and came down the steps as well.

"What's this all about, Admiral?" said Nobli.

"Inspection," replied Clement.

"Inspection? Cut the bullshit, Clement. I don't have time for this. We leave in less than a week and if I can't get the outflow tubes on this thing to work correctly, we'll be doing it swimming with one arm all the way to Trinity. It's got to be fixed."

Clement hesitated a second before responding, looking back and forth between Nobli and his tech. "With hammers?" he said, incredulously.

Nobli shrugged. "The nanotube goo they use in these reactor castings sometimes leaves some edge flashing. I've found that the best method for removing it is to pound it back into the hull of the reactor. Plus, this stuff is almost impossible to trim off. And this piece is partially blocking one of the outflow tubes, so . . ."

"I see." Clement turned his attention back to the tech. "And you are?"

"Technician Assistant Third Class Kim Reck, sir!" she said with enthusiasm.

"Well nice to meet you, Tech Reck. You can resume your duties. I have things to talk with Engineer Nobli about."

"Sir!" said Reck again, practically shouting it. Clement waved her off and she scrambled into the dark of the reactor chamber. Presently the distant pounding resumed.

Clement looked to Nobli. "I never expected you to get a sidekick. I've only ever seen you work alone."

"Well, you need to get used to it. That girl is the find of the century. She's a natural specialist in electromagnetic systems and she's smart enough to fix anything around here, and I mean *anything*. If I could clone her I'd make another hundred of her and we could run the whole damn fleet. She may be a little rough around the edges, but so was I once."

"Once?"

Nobli shrugged again. "Point taken, Admiral. Now what can I help you with? I'm a busy man."

"I can see that. I just want an update on the status of this ship, and of course the rest of the fleet."

Nobli nodded. "Let's do it in my office," he said. He stuck his head inside the reactor chamber again and yelled, "I'll be in the office, Kim. Carry on until I can get rid of the admiral here."

"Got it, Hass," came back the echoey response. Both

men started for Nobli's office, the engineer leading the way.

"Kim? Hass?" Clement commented. "Pretty familiar. Is there something going on here I should know about?"

"We're just friends and coworkers. She's way too young for me, and besides, I'm still seeing Maggie."

"Ah, I see."

Maggie was a bar maid at the Battered Hull, Clement's favorite Navy bar on the station. She and Nobli had hit it off after the first Trinity mission. He had assumed everything was good between them, but the interaction with Tech Reck had given him a different impression, now resolved.

Nobli's office was twice the size of the one he had on the *Beauregard*. They stepped inside, Nobli sitting behind his desk and Clement taking up a side chair.

"So what do you want to talk about?" pressed Nobli, obviously put out that he had to waste valuable engineering time talking to his commanding officer, even if they were friends.

"First, give me an update on my flagship."

Nobli nodded. "She's ready to go. All of her conventional propulsion systems are ready and tested, I've got a good crew, and morale is high. Even the new people seem motivated. I am thinking about releasing Lieutenant Tsu to other duties, though. Frankly, there were enough station techs with way more experience on these systems than him that were anxious to sign on for the mission. I've filled out the duty rosters pretty quickly. Tsu mainly acts as my gopher, but I don't think he's very happy down here."

"Sounds like a change is in order," said Clement, pulling out his com pad and quickly sending out a reassignment order for Tsu. The young man had been useful on the first Trinity mission, but it was important that he find a good, permanent home on the *Agamemnon*. "Done." Then he put the com down on Nobli's desk.

"As for the other systems?" asked Clement.

Nobli looked up at him from under his round wireframe spectacles with a skeptical look on his face. "I suppose by that you mean the MAD weapon?"

"I do." The MAD weapon, which stood for Matter Annihilation Device, a term Nobli had coined, had been ingeniously improvised by the engineer on the first Trinity mission. It had been a tricky fix, involving coating normal metal pipes with a carbon nanotube goo used in the LEAP drive pipes that could handle the tremendous release of matter/antimatter energy the reactor produced. Clement didn't pretend to know all the particulars, he just knew that it worked and that Nobli was at least a minor genius for figuring it out. That fix had allowed Clement the ability to access the LEAP reactor's energy plasma and project it as a weapon, using a systems app on his command console onboard the *Beauregard*. Ultimately, all Clement really knew about it was that it was the most powerful weapon any known civilization had ever developed. The *Beauregard*'s smaller reactor size had limited the weapon to mostly single-use scenarios. *Agamemnon*, though, would be a different proposition.

"I have the app already programmed into your command console. It will be activated when the ship starts the voyage to Trinity and we turn the LEAP reactors on.

So, you'll once again have the power to destroy the gods who created you."

Clement tried to smile, knowing this was a difficult subject for Nobli and not something he had agreed with installing on *Agamemnon*. "I doubt I'll use it for that purpose, Hassan, but we may need it someday, and having it active on this battlecruiser is the safest strategy I can think of," he finished.

Nobli stopped then and looked at his friend. "This kind of power, it can only be used if there is no alternative. You understand that, don't you, Jared?"

"I do. When I had to use it at Trinity the first time, it almost broke me. All those lives lost. But did we have another choice?"

Nobli shook his head, expressing sympathy for his friend. "No, we didn't. If we hadn't used it Elara DeVore would be building her little empire on the backs of native slaves and the resources of the Trinity worlds would be cut off forever, and that would have condemned the Five Suns to starvation and death on a massive scale. You probably saved billions of lives with that single act, Admiral. And you should be rightly proud of that."

Clement nodded in agreement, but still, almost two years later, the decision to destroy so many people at one time played on his conscience. The Five Suns fleet had probably lost almost six thousand souls to the MAD weapon, and untold thousands were lost on the Earth Ark ship he had destroyed. Yan had told him once that she estimated there were probably thirty thousand soldiers on the Ark. It was a statistic he found he didn't really want to know.

Clement looked down at the floor of the office, thinking. Knowledge about a weapon with that kind of power had to be severely restricted to a need-to-know basis. Clement had determined there were precious few people he trusted enough to share that information with. He looked back to Nobli.

"Are you satisfied that the MAD technology is still a secret?"

Nobli nodded. "It is among this fleet, I'm sure of that, but DeVore had many of her scientists working on weapons applications for the LEAP energy. They would have figured it out eventually."

"Fortunately, she took all of her top scientists with her to Trinity, and now they're probably spending their days spearfishing for their dinners." Clement paused then, reflecting on the pain of the betrayal DeVore had burdened him with, both as a ship captain and as his former lover. It was impossible for him to ignore, but as time went on he felt the personal pain less and less, and he still held out hope it would one day be completely gone. Today was not that day.

"What are you going to do with her, Jared?" said Nobli softly. They had all been friends once. She had even set Nobli up on a couple of disastrous dates with some of her girlfriends back in their Rim Confederation days.

Clement sighed. "Honestly, I don't know. My focus right now is on this mission. Elara DeVore is something, someone, I don't have time to consider right now. And for the moment, her exile on Alphus is the best thing for all of us."

Nobli leaned closer to his friend, sensing his internal

struggle. "If you don't mind, I have a suggestion, friend to friend, not engineer to admiral."

"Go ahead. I'm listening, as a friend."

"Good. Jared, you have to stop thinking of her as your friend, as the woman we fought with and flew with and that we all loved in some way, you, obviously, differently than the rest of us. She's clearly not that person anymore, not after fifteen years. You need to, as much as possible, just think of her as Admiral DeVore, traitor to two nations, the Rim Confederation and the Five Suns Alliance. If you can do that, and I know it will be hard, then perhaps by the time we get back to Trinity you can be clear, and make a decision on the fate of Admiral DeVore, rather than Elara DeVore."

Clement looked at his friend. "You're a very wise man, Nobli. How did you get this far in life without sharing this kind of wisdom before?"

Nobli spread his hands. "Who knew, right? I'm just your friend, Jared, as well as your engineer and a loyal crewmate. I've seen you suffer through this situation for a while now. This is how I've been coping with the memories, the good and the bad."

Clement took in a deep breath. "Sound advice. I'll meditate on that for a while."

"That should help. Now, if you don't mind, I have to get back to my hammering. I don't want Tech Reck to have all the fun."

Clement laughed out loud, the first time he'd done that in a while, then dismissed his engineer. As he headed to take the lifter to the deck housing the admiral's cabin, he was grinning from ear to ear for the first time in weeks.

✵ 4 ✵

With five days to go until the interstellar caravan was scheduled to depart for Trinity, Kemmerine Station was a bustle of activity. The technical teams were all on station and almost all of the thirty thousand migrants had started to arrive, so many in fact that almost half of them had to be housed on the surface of Kemmerine itself. Among those on the station was a certain couple from Ceta named the Clements, whose son just happened to be the Fleet Admiral.

Clement made his way through the thick crowds on the Galléria deck of the station, heading for dinner with his parents at the Battered Hull. Yan had promised to join them at 1900. As he sifted through the crowd in a stop-start manner, he got his share of head-turns from the many migrants who had been lucky enough to be called up to the station first. He also got his share of salutes from passing sailors mixed in with the bustling crowd, which he just passed off with a nod. If he stopped to salute every officer and tech he passed on this station he'd never get where he was going. He pulled out his com pad as he walked and made a voice note to issue a memo to restrict saluting to just the admiralty offices or the individual ships. All of this respect was getting tedious in light of the chaos around him.

Yan had mentioned that the station's five thousand tourist berths had been completely taken up by the migrants and their possessions. The first ten thousand arrivals from Ceta, Argyle, and Helios were already on the transports. Over the next few days even more would be transitioned from the surface of Kemmerine to their transport ships in a (hopefully) orderly manner. Yan had planned out the logistics months ago and Clement was thankful for that. He also hoped things would go according to her plan.

He finally emerged from the crowd to stand in front of the neon sign over the door of the Battered Hull. Two Navy corpsmen saluted him and he saluted back, vowing that would be the last time until the mission started. It was partly his fault, as he had restricted the Battered Hull to Navy personnel until the caravan left for Trinity. His people needed somewhere to hang their hats away from the civilian overflow.

He stepped up.

"We have your booth ready, Admiral. Your parents are already here," said the female corpsman, gesturing for him to follow her inside. He did so, and was promptly greeted by eighty Navy personnel jumping to their feet and saluting him. He stopped and whipped off a return salute, then spoke to the crowd in a loud voice.

"At ease, everyone. I want you to all to know that I will soon be issuing a memo suspending the need to salute in the commercial areas of the station. Kemmerine is way too busy for every sailor to stop and salute when a senior officer walks by, especially me. In all honesty, I'm more than a bit tired of it. We all have a lot of work to do; let's stick to protocol only in the military areas of the station, and the Battered Hull is hereby declared a nonmilitary area. Now get back to your meals and ale." There was a round of cheers and applause at that and Clement waved to the crowd and then proceeded to follow the corpsman. She directed him to the booth and he sat down across from his parents, a haggard look on his face. He hadn't even got out a hello when Yan showed up. He looked at his watch. 1900 on the dot. She was nothing if not prompt. She said hello to his parents and then pushed Clement further into the booth so she could sit on the old wooden bench next to him. His father held a half-drunk ale glass in his hand while his mother was nursing her usual tea.

Clement let out a big sigh. "I can't believe it just took me forty minutes to navigate from my office to get here," he said.

"I had the same problem," said Yan, smiling.

"Well, here we all are, finally," he said.

"You look tired, son," said his father.

"Yes," chimed in Abigail. "I think this job is getting to you."

"That's what he has me for," said Yan, smiling.

"Enough with all of you criticizing me. I'm fine. I just need a station ale, pronto." Promptly the frosty ale showed up at the table, one for him and one for Yan. Clement took a deep drink of the beer while Yan took her customary smaller sip.

"So, how is everything going?" asked his mother.

"As well as could be expected, I guess. We have half our complement of migrants staying on the station or on their transports, and they all seem to be out and about today. There's another fifteen thousand more down on Kemmerine right now waiting to come up. If Yan here has planned this right, five days from now we'll all be on our ships and on our way to Trinity."

Yan took another sip of her ale before chiming in. "Well, everything is going to plan so far, and if anything goes off the rails I'll just make sure to lay the blame at the feet of the admiral here."

"Why not?" said Clement. "Everybody else does." He took another long drink.

"Sure you should be drinking that so fast, son?" said Cletus, looking down at his own drinking glass. "From what I've been sampling this stuff is pretty powerful."

Clement smiled. "It has to be, Dad. Otherwise the sailors would be too angry to fly anything. The only thing worse than a drunken sailor is an angry one." There were some light chuckles around the table at that. Cletus took another drink and then frowned, looking down at his thick brown ale with a look of distaste on his face. An uncomfortable silence settled around the table then, the unsubtle din of the Five Suns sailors filling the background.

The silence went on for a few more seconds. "Have you two ordered food?" said Yan cheerily, trying to move the conversation away from her perpetually grumpy commanding officer.

"Abby ordered the clam chowder, and I really think she made a mistake. I ordered the steak," said Cletus.

"I'm sure it will be fine, Cletus. I hope you two don't mind that we ordered ahead. Our time clocks are all off from being at home on Ceta and we were both pretty hungry."

Clement nodded his head at his mother. "I don't mind at all. These next few days are going to be crazy. Eat when you can and when you feel like it. Once we get on board the transports all the meals will be coordinated so you'll have to eat on their schedule."

His mother piped up at that. "But aren't we the parents of the Fleet Admiral? Don't we get some kind of special dispensation?"

"If I did that, Mother, I'd have to do it for everyone going on this trip, including the crews. I'm not sure I want that kind of logistical problem on my hands," Clement said, cracking a small smile.

Presently he and Yan were greeted by Maggie the barmaid, who also happened to be Nobli's girlfriend. She asked them what they wanted to eat and he and Yan punched up the Battered Hull's menu on their com pads. Clement ordered the pulled pork sandwich with coleslaw and cornbread on the side. Yan ordered her usual standby soup and salad. Maggie smiled and said, "Coming right up," then departed. Yan turned to Clement.

"Is that sandwich on your diet, Admiral?" she asked more than a bit impishly, trying to lighten the mood. Clement gave her a stern look and then said, "It is as long as you don't report it to the medical staff."

"Well, he's in a mood," said Abby.

"Mother, if you were running this station day in and

day out, you'd be in a mood too. I was born to be a sailor, not a paper pusher."

"Administration is not his strong point," said Yan.

His parents' food arrived then and Clement told them not to wait for him and Yan as the service was always unreliable. They both politely started eating, obviously famished. After a few bites of food his mother started in on the conversation again.

"You know, it occurs to me that you two act like an old married couple," she said. "Finishing each other's sentences, complementing the other's strong points, taking unnecessary responsibility off of each other."

"Mother . . ."

"Are you sure it's against the rules for you two to, you know, get married and all that?"

Clement rubbed at his brow, shaking his head, unhappy with this turn in the conversation.

"That is not happening, Mother, for all the reasons I've already told you. And besides, if I married her then she'd have to transfer out of my command, and I couldn't have her as my chief assistant. And if that were to happen, this whole project would fall apart completely."

His father put his knife and fork down. "Which leads me to another question, son. I wasn't all for this move, you know that. It's hard to start over at our age. We left almost everything behind us on Ceta, including our farming equipment, hell, even our seeds for the wheat and barley crops."

"You'll have all the seeds you need on Bellus, Dad, and far better quality than the crops you left behind on poor old Ceta. I know it's a new start and not something you expected at your age, but the Trinity worlds are a blessing that we can't even comprehend yet. It's like a gift from the gods."

"But what about things like cows and chickens and fish? We can't just live on fruit, corn, and bread all the time. That's what we left behind on the Rim."

Clement leaned in toward his father, trying to allay his concerns. "The transports are full of thousands of frozen embryos of every kind of animal you can imagine. Scientists have come up with accelerated growing processes, so we should have full herds of everything we could possibly need within a couple of months. As for cross-pollination and things like that, the survey teams that have gone to Bellus have said that the native insects take care of all of it. Compared to life on Ceta living on Bellus will seem like a walk in the park."

"We had plenty of parkland on Ceta," said Cletus.

Clement paused before responding as their food arrived from the kitchen. Apparently being the admiral had its privileges. "The parkland on Ceta was nothing but dirt, dust, and tumbleweeds," he said. "I promise you, you won't believe how lucky you are once you've spent a few days on Bellus. It's a paradise."

This time Cletus leaned in toward his son, who was busily working on his sandwich. "There's just one more thing that bothers me, son," he said.

"And what's that, Dad?" replied Clement between bites.

"What about the natives? How much of their land will we be taking away from them?"

At that Clement stopped eating and sat back in the

booth, putting distance between himself and his parents. "We've already discussed this, but just to remind you, we've reserved thousands of square kilometers for the natives, Dad. Our colonies will not interfere with their lives at all. As time goes on if they want to join our settlements, they'll be more than welcome. Believe me, no one is more concerned about the effects of colonialism and what it might have on the Trinity natives than I am."

His father looked him straight in the eye. "So the natives will stay on their reservations, just like the American Indians did. And then one day what will happen to them? One hundred years from now when you're long gone all of your goodwill will be left in the hands of other men. Men that may not share your values, or your care for those people."

Clement felt his face start to warm up with frustration. "Are you worried that I'll sell them out? Is that what you think of me?"

His father shook his head. "No son, I don't think you're that kind of man. Your mother and I raised you too well for that. But when we're all gone, back to the earth as they say, how can you ensure but the natives will be safe and protected?"

"I can't," admitted Clement. "All I can do is set up as many laws and rules of governance as I can while I have the power to do so. And right now it looks like I'll have that power for a very long time to come. So I guess you'll just have to trust me and trust how you and Mom raised me."

At that he stood to leave. "The bill will be on my tab," he said. "Enjoy the rest of your meal, and enjoy your time with Yan here. I find I really have too much work to do. Now if you'll excuse me?"

And at that he walked away, as fast as he could go.

Clement stayed away from his office at the station and instead ended up walking off his anger and frustration on the *Agamemnon*. He found himself on deck 9, near the science labs. After drifting down the hallway and disrupting what was surely important work merely by his presence, Clement eventually found himself at a place he had intended to go for a while. He knocked on the open door of Lieutenant Commander Laura Pomeroy. She looked up from her small work desk in her confined, rectangular space and smiled and then stood.

"Admiral," she said, "what a pleasant surprise."

"Quit lying," replied Clement, "nobody's happy to see the admiral." Then he reached out and shook her hand. Pomeroy was a career officer in her mid to late thirties, the kind that was indispensable on any important mission, as she had been on the first Trinity mission. There she had functioned as both an engineering tech and a field medic, though it was the medic role that had been most critical.

"Regardless, I am happy to see you."

Clement shrugged. "I'm just doing my rounds, checking in with everybody. I thought I would see what the old *Beauregard* crew was up to." He looked around the small room. There were about a dozen plasma monitors floating around, showing all kinds of data and what appeared to be high-definition photographs, geological analyses, and infrared telemetry scans of the topography that had been taken on both Bellus and

Camus, the third world of the Trinity system, during their first mission.

"Is geology your thing now, Commander?"

Pomeroy glanced around her personal information den before answering. "Well, I have to say my mind has been on exploring the Hill Place on Bellus ever since we came back from the first mission. And of course I'm extremely curious about those pyramid-shaped mountains on Camus. If we can get access to them, I mean, if we can get inside and figure out how they were constructed, and maybe even find out who constructed them, we may be able to unlock a key to terraforming new worlds on a massive scale. That could be very beneficial to the Five Suns Alliance in the future."

Clement nodded agreement. "Absolutely. You're right, of course," he said, "and I'm anxious to take that trek up to the Hill Place with you. I want to discover what the real mysteries of Trinity are as much as anyone. I mean, just the existence of the natives, *human* natives no less, is a mystery for the ages. But the fact that these worlds appear to have been almost 'manufactured' for the natives' use and put in perfect environmental balance, that's another question altogether. And of course I have to consider whether we are going to throw that balance off by migrating our people there. I want those answers."

"Those are all good questions, sir, to which I don't think anyone has good answers to right now. As you said, we have to figure out the mysteries first to discover the right questions to ask, and then find the answers to those questions. I have to admit I've become a bit obsessive about it."

"I can see that," said Clement, his eyes roving around the room again at all the data on the screens. "What's the scale of the expedition plans that you have so far?"

Pomeroy sat back down at her desk. "I'd like to keep the initial expedition to a small group, maybe five or six of us; and also, if we can find that native woman named Mary again, she may be helpful. We can use a small VTOL to get us up there from our settlement camp in a lot quicker time than Middie Telco's old pontoon boat, that's for sure."

"Hey, that was very innovative by Telco," said Clement, defending the one-time cadet's reputation. "And Mr. Telco is not a middie anymore."

"No, sir, he's not. But I have a hard time *not* thinking of him that way. I do have him on my shortlist for the trip up there."

Clement smiled. "Now I'm curious as to the names on that list of yours."

Pomeroy tilted her head. "Well, usually high-ranking flag officers such as yourself wouldn't be included on this kind of expedition . . ." She let her voice trail off.

"But?"

"Does there have to be a 'but'?"

"There does," Clement said firmly.

"But, since you're the Fleet Admiral, and in command of this whole operation, and you have previous experience at the Hill Place, *and* you're the one who gave me a field promotion to Commander, I think it would be pretty much impossible for me to exclude you."

"Right answer," said Clement, his smile turning to a broad grin now.

Pomeroy continued. "Captain Yan would also be hard to exclude since she most closely understands the natives' language and was able to converse with the native woman, Mary."

"Of course. It would be wrong not to include her."

"I'd be handling the geology and the flying. Nobli recommended Kim Reck for our engineering tech, and I was thinking Telco and Tsu for the muscle. Sir."

"Seems about right, Commander," said Clement, then he hesitated for a second before asking the next question. "So, Laura, I wanted to ask you something."

"Oh it's Laura now, is it, Admiral? Is this off the record?"

Clement thought for a moment. "Yes, I guess it is."

"Good. Fire away."

"About Mr. Telco . . ." Pomeroy rolled her eyes.

"Yes, Admiral, I'm still seeing Rob on occasion. He's a good young man, and I think he's almost over his infatuation with me since our little aphrodisiac-inspired tryst at the pond on Bellus. I think he has his eyes on a redhead tech down in systems engineering. It's been two years, probably time for both of us to move on to more appropriate partners."

"So, no conflicts I should be worried about then?"

She shook her head. "None from my side, sir. I have a good working relationship with the lieutenant, sir. We had our little adventure and it was a bit of a distraction for both of us at the time, but there are no personal issues between us interfering with work."

"Well, that's good to know," said Clement. "Always a good idea to tie up any loose ends before you go into the field."

"Of course, sir. I can forward you all of my technical plans for the mission for your review before we get to Trinity, if you'd like?"

"That would be a welcome change from the routine, Commander. Frankly, I've been looking for things to keep myself busy, hence my trip to see you. Rank may have its privileges but it also has its limitations. You have no idea how badly I want to take the *Beauregard* out for a spin."

"Oh, believe me, I understand, sir. I've never worked on anything as big and powerful as *Agamemnon* before. It presents all kinds of opportunities, but it also has some drawbacks. The *Beau* was a breeze to work with compared to this behemoth."

"Well, I certainly agree with you on that. All right then, Laura, thank you. I'll look forward to that planning report. Don't wait too long to send it. I want to make sure I have time to get my comments back to you and still leave plenty of time for you to make changes."

"Yes, sir. I'm well aware of the need to make editing changes on the fly, sir." Pomeroy stood. "One more thing, sir," she said to him. "What do you think the story is of the natives at Trinity? I mean, do you think they were sent from Earth, or do you think they're native to the Trinity system, or do you think it was some . . . other kind of influence?"

"It's hard to know. I guess that's a big part of why we're going." With that he thanked her and then left her office, once again making his way down the hall, not really sure which way he was going next.

5

The next morning Yan was in his office at 0900 for their Wednesday one-on-one meeting. Clement made no mention of dinner the night before and fortunately Yan did not bring it up. She laid out the final charts and plans for the migration mission on the conference room table. With the flick of her finger she threw the plan up on the room's main plasma display.

"Everything is on schedule," she said. "The last of the migrants have arrived and been processed through Kemmerine and are here on the station. All but five thousand migrants have already boarded their transports and are getting used to their new living quarters for the next month. There aren't many comforts for them as these were obviously military transports before, but they are adequate."

"Well if we have any complaints we can just leave them behind on the dock," said Clement. Yan wasn't sure if he was joking or not.

"I don't think that's really an option, do you?" said Yan. Clement shrugged indifferently and Yan continued. "The final total is 29,741 migrants. The new settlements are all prepared on Bellus, the advance teams have seen to that. Once everyone is settled in we should be able to have all of our farms and ranches up and running quickly. In any case, there's so much food to eat there no one will starve, but we also have two months' worth of rations for each family as a backup in case something unforeseen arises."

Clement looked down at the plans. "I'm not so much concerned about the migrants *after* they get there. I'm more concerned about what kind of trouble they might cause on the trip out. Thirty-four days one way, even for a sailor, is a long time. There will likely be family disputes, lover's spats, and some general unruliness. I hope you've prepared our transport captains and crews for those potential eventualities?"

"Of course. Our social scientists have told us what to expect and the crews have all been trained in how to handle those types of domestic situations. There will be no weapons on board the transports for any of the migrants to get access to, so things shouldn't get out of hand. Even if they do, we have full contingents of Marines that could be on any of the transports in a flash."

"Yes, but we've never actually tried to transport a shuttle from ship to ship while we're inside a LEAP field, have we? I mean, Nobli says we can do it, but only within a single, closed bubble. Make sure the transports all have a squad of Marines aboard. That should cover any trouble."

"Any thoughts on final deployment of the fleet?"

Clement thought about that for a second. "I'm inclined to use *Agamemnon*'s LEAP field to cover the majority of ships, but I would prefer we have backup LEAP pods led by the cruiser commanders just in case something goes wrong."

"Double redundancy?" said Yan.

"That's the way the engineers always plan it," replied Clement. "In any case, I'm more concerned about fleet communications than I am about having to move Marines from ship to ship. I realize I should be more up on these things, these details, but I can't do everything. And besides, that's why I have you." He smiled.

Yan smiled back and nodded an acknowledgement. "As far as communications, Nobli has designed what he calls a 'quantum tether,' a kind of tight frequency wave particle, but I can't remember the name of it. At any rate, this 'tether' will keep all of the ships in a single LEAP field bubble connected. The *Agamemnon* can be tethered to a cruiser, and then the cruiser to a destroyer, and then from the destroyers to a transport or gunship. So any kind of trouble that starts at the transport level would have to be brought up the chain before it even gets to us."

"It sounds like we're going to have to give the individual ship commanders the ability to make decisions on the spot, especially involving any onboard disputes. Frankly, if I could just sedate all the migrants for the whole month I'd do it."

Yan looked at him sidelong, cocking her head slightly. "I doubt that would be very popular," she said.

Clement shrugged again, his hands open. "It was just a thought. What about communication between multiple LEAP bubbles? Will that be possible?"

"Nobli was less clear about that," admitted Yan. "I don't think he really knows yet, but he did mention some mumbo jumbo about actually using a low-power version of the MAD weapon as a means of communicating a light-wave signal to the lead ships of the other bubble groups. As I understand it he's still working on that part."

"Well I hope so. We certainly don't want to use the MAD energy if we don't have to. It's not the kind of thing I would want to use casually. So I guess bubble-to-bubble contact is out. We'll have to rely on our crews to do their jobs properly."

"Nobli told me that he thinks the MAD application has great potential for interstellar communications. He even showed me a diagram of a potential ansible-style network that could be implemented to keep communications between Trinity and the Five Suns open."

"I'm not even sure how the MAD energy could travel faster than the speed of light. Maybe he has some ingenious way of putting it in a LEAP bubble and sending it back and forth that way? It's something we can experiment with once we're at Trinity. For right now I think we're going to have to go with our thirty-four-day one-way trip communications method. Anything beyond that is a tremendous leap in technology, no pun intended. And all this is really a conversation for another day."

"Of course, sir. I'll make a note to have Nobli prepare a communications plan and get some techs working on it once we get to the Trinity system. That does bring up another question, though."

"I'm open to hear it, Captain."

"How long are you planning on keeping the fleet at Trinity?"

"I hadn't really thought about that. The mission plan

has no set timetable for return. We have to get everyone settled in and make plans for the next migrant group before we scatter on back home. We'll have to leave some ships to defend Trinity, just in case. My best guess is we'll send the transports back within a week with a cruiser and a couple of destroyers as escorts to begin the next migration cycle. I haven't been to Trinity in a year and a half. Quite frankly I wouldn't mind enjoying some time on the surface of Bellus, breathing in some warm, moist air, maybe taking a swim in a pond, doing a bit of hiking. And I want to take a full technical expedition up to the Hill Place, near where we met Mary and her people. I want to know who built those pyramids, and frankly try to find out what's inside them and who may have built them."

"There may be a mother lode of technology up there. I'd already anticipated you would want to explore, so I put together preliminary lists of geologists, scientists, technologists, etc. I planned it for the second week after the landing of the first migrants."

"Actually, I've got Laura Pomeroy working on a plan right now. You should forward your ideas to her. I've got better things for you to do."

Yan nodded, then hesitated. "I hope this expedition includes me?"

"As of now, you're included in the plan. That's subject to change, depending on circumstances. You *are* in command of the most powerful ship in the fleet, you know."

"I do, sir. My plan supposed that you would want to make sure your parents are well set up on your claim property before any side adventures."

"I don't think any of us will truly ever have a 'claim' on Bellus or any of the other Trinity worlds. We'll just be tenants on the land of the natives. As for my parents, I may want to avoid them for a while. In fact, I'd consider it a favor if you'd take the initiative to check in on them every couple of days."

"Of course, sir. I understand."

Clement shifted in his chair. "Look, Yan, I just want to apologize for my behavior last night at dinner. Sometimes family tensions can come out at the most inopportune times, especially when we're all under so much stress. I know I certainly am."

Yan shook her head. "No apology necessary, sir. As much as I love your parents and especially spending time with your mother, I understand how their constant harping on you to settle down and get married and have more Clements has probably worn down on you. And we're all under stress, sir. Until we get this mission off the station and the migrants on the ground we won't even know if this idea will work."

Clement looked at her, suddenly very serious. "It has to work, Yan. It's only humanity's future at stake."

"I understand. If there's nothing else, I think we should proceed to the Departure phase of the plan."

"I agree, Yan. Let's get this show on the road." At that Yan stood up to leave, gathering her papers and closing down the display screen.

They walked together back into Clement's massive office. He looked around the vast room. "It's time to shut things down here. As of 0900 tomorrow morning we will be running everything out of our posts on the

Agamemnon. Time to batten down the hatches and get ready to sail across the sea to our own New World."

"Absolutely, sir," she said. I'll see you at your station on the *Agamemnon* tomorrow morning."

With that Clement dismissed her and started the long walk back toward his desk.

He hoped it was the last time he'd have to make that lonely walk for a long, long time.

☆ 6 ☆

When Clement arrived on the command deck the day of the caravan's departure, there was a noticeable buzz of excitement in the air. The officer of the deck called out "Admiral on the bridge!" and everyone stopped what they were doing and stood to attention, saluting him. He returned the salute and then stepped up to the command platform and proceeded to greet Colonel Lubrov at the main console. He looked around the huge room, taking in the large spaces and the bustle of activity, noting each of the duty officers at their different stations.

"Exciting day, Admiral," said Lubrov.

"Indeed it is, Colonel. I'm looking forward to it. Um, do you happen to know where Captain Yan is right now?"

"I believe she's in her office, sir," said Lubrov.

Clement nodded. "Of course. I guess I should have checked there first."

"Yes, sir."

"Please send out notice to all department heads that we will be meeting in the conference room in fifteen minutes. This will be our final go/no go meeting and everyone has to be there, including you."

"Of course sir," she said. Clement noticed she had changed her look. She was now very prim and proper, with her hair trimmed and pinned back in a ponytail and out of the way. Clement thought that it was better to have her looking like she was now instead of distracting the crew by looking like a runway model. He also noted that she had heeded his advice on her grooming, which was the sign of a well-disciplined officer. He had also heeded her advice, and was now sporting a freshly clean-shaven face.

Clement gave her a nod and then preceded back to Yan's office, there to find her hunched over her plasma display. He knocked twice on her door. "Come in," she answered cheerily, without taking her attention away from her screen.

"Full staff meeting in fifteen minutes, Captain," he said to her.

"It *is* on the schedule, Admiral," she said, glancing up at him with a slight smile.

"Looking at you I'm just wondering if you'll be able to tear yourself away from your com reports long enough to attend."

At that Yan turned and smiled at him. "It's called multitasking, Admiral. And I just happen to know that the conference room is forty-two steps from here and will take me less than twenty seconds to traverse, if you're worried I'll be late."

"I just don't want you to miss all the fun."

"I won't," she said, then turned back to her screen.

Clement looked at his watch. "Fourteen minutes, Captain," he said, then left the room.

☼ ☼ ☼

At precisely 1000 hours, Admiral Clement sat down at the head of the table in the command deck conference room. Around him were all of his principal flag officers, as well as some lesser crew members that were still necessary to the go/no go conversation. On the main room display were the faces of the transport commanders and others who couldn't be in the room for the meeting.

"Ladies and gentlemen," began Clement with enthusiasm, "I've called this meeting as our final check before our go/no go decision on the interstellar convoy to the Trinity system. Each of you has the authority over your own ship or area of expertise, and each of you has the responsibility to declare with one hundred percent confidence that this mission is ready to proceed. If you do not have one hundred percent confidence, then you must state so and relay to this entire team your reasons for not having full confidence in the mission. Do you all understand your orders?"

There were nods all around the table and on the display screen, so Clement proceeded with the roll call. He turned to Captain Yan on his right. "Captain?"

"*Agamemnon* is a one hundred percent go, sir," she said.

Clement nodded. He looked across the table in the other direction to Marine Colonel Lubrov.

"Colonel?"

"Marines are go, Admiral," she said in her forceful Ukrainian accent.

Next he looked to Hassan Nobli. "Engineer?"

"Go, sir, no hesitation," said Nobli. Another nod in response.

"Captain Samkange of the *Corvallis*."

"*Corvallis* is a go, sir," replied Samkange. The call went on like that all around the table, and eventually on the screen, where Clement had to refer to his list of officers' names more than once. The ship captains and commanders all certified that they were ready to go, and Clement replied to each with a nod. When the roll was finished, he stood and addressed the command staff again.

"Ladies and gentlemen, we have now reached a monumental decision point, both in the history of the Five Suns Alliance and in the history of humanity. We are undertaking the first interstellar migration from Five Suns Alliance space to the Trinity system. Thank you all, captains and commanders. Please proceed to your ships and prepare to disembark from the docks at 1300 hours today. From there we will form up in our migration pods and proceed to the designated LEAP point. Good luck, and good sailing. Be well. Dismissed!" he finished with a flourish.

There were nods all around the table and more than a few congratulatory handshakes as the flag officers left the conference room and the visual display shut down. Clement did his share of glad-handing and then turned his attention back to his remaining officers, the primary senior crew of the *Agamemnon*. This group included Yan, his helm officer Mika Ori and her husband, navigator Ivan Massif, plus Nobli, Lubrov, and Lieutenant Commander Pomeroy, his primary technical and communications officer. They all re-sat themselves at the near end of the room, close to the admiral's chair.

Clement sat back down when the room had cleared

and the doors were shut again. He looked up. "It's all on us now, people," he said, "to get this convoy to Trinity. I'd like status reports from each of you, starting with Captain Yan."

"Thank you, sir," said Yan. "All systems and stations aboard *Agamemnon* confirm ready to depart at your order, sir. This ship is as good as we can make her, and I have full confidence in her systems and her crew."

Clement nodded and then looked to Colonel Lubrov, who reported without being prompted. "We have Marines dispersed around the fleet, with fifty stationed on each of the transports. That should be enough to handle any disputes among the migrants. We have a full company of two hundred Marines split into twenty platoons stationed here on the *Agamemnon*. The other five companies are dispersed around the fleet at the discretion of the LEAP bubble cruiser commanders, Captain Samkange of the *Corvallis* and Captain Son of the *Yangtze*. All will maintain their designated stations for the length of the interstellar traverse. We haven't yet determined whether Marine shuttles can be used to transport troops from ship to ship inside a LEAP bubble. That is quite obviously Engineer Nobli's department," she concluded.

"Hassan?" asked Clement, looking to his chief engineer, and frankly, the miracle worker of his entire fleet.

"I don't recommend transporting troops inside a LEAP bubble," said Nobli flatly. "Frankly, we don't really know that much about LEAP space yet."

"I thought we were in normal space inside a LEAP bubble," stated Clement.

Nobli shrugged, his seemingly favorite gesture. "Technically, it *is* normal space, but it has trillions of quantum particles passing through and around everything inside. We just don't know how that would effect an unshielded ship, like a shuttle, that's not protected by a LEAP reactor field. It would be an unnecessary risk, in my opinion."

"I agree," said Clement. He looked back to Lubrov. "I think we've done all that we can do to make sure we have enough Marines aboard each of the transports. I'm less concerned about the Navy ships for obvious reasons. We do have *some* discipline within this navy, maybe not as much as I would like, but I think it's an acceptable level."

"I agree, Admiral," said Lubrov.

"Noted. What about coms?" Clement said to Nobli.

"We've had success with communications between multiple ships that are static inside a single LEAP bubble in testing, but even though we perceive the LEAP bubbles being composed of normal space, we have all that quantum soup to deal with. Coms between ships were a bit sketchy even in the tests without forward motion. What will happen at superluminal speeds is anybody's guess. My best guess is that we should rely on the quantum tether technology at all times."

"Which will limit us during the interstellar traverse phase of the mission, correct Lieutenant Adebayor?"

"Correct, sir," said Adebayor. "Radio waves just don't travel in any sort of a straight line in the quantum LEAP field, sir. But as Engineer Nobli said, we can get in contact with other ships in our bubble by burning a tether through the 'soup,' and we can also link through a tether to the other bubble groups, though only to a single ship running the primary LEAP reactor."

"Theoretically," popped in Nobli. "There wasn't really time to test that part of the theory, but any quantum tether will likely seek out the nearest ship with a functioning LEAP reactor."

"How will it distinguish between one ship, or one signature, and another?"

"The tether is a closed loop between two vessels. If we send it out, likely it will search for the next open port to make a connection."

"But we don't know, one hundred percent?"

"As I said, it's still a theory until it's tested under actual flight conditions."

"Well, thirty-four days is ample time to conduct in-service tests. Each bubble group commander has orders on how to operate autonomously from the *Agamemnon* if there's no coms available. I'll want all this tested early on in the superluminal part of the mission, and a full report from you, Lieutenant. Once we establish a communications protocol that works, I'll want links established at routine times every day with both the ships in our bubble and the *Corvallis* and *Yangtze* flotillas. I expect a full report of the previous day's coms on my desktop every morning, at 0700 ship time. Understood?"

"Aye, sir," said Adebayor.

Clement then turned to his helm officer. "Mika, how do you find the helm system of the *Agamemnon*?" he asked.

"Well, it's not like the *Beauregard*, obviously. *Agamemnon* is not nimble in any way, but she's very powerful and she responds well to commands. This helm system is different than piloting a gunship, for sure, but I anticipate she will meet all the mission parameters that were set for her by her designers. Just don't ask me to skim her off any atmospheres or cut between any asteroids. Remember, she's built for power, not speed."

"Understood. Thank you, Mika." Clement then turned to his navigator. "Are we ready for this journey, Ivan?"

"I think we are, sir," said the tall Russian. "Plotting a course for a group of ships in a large LEAP bubble is different than doing the same thing for a small and nimble gunship. Having said that, interstellar travel is more about getting the general direction right then it is about landing on a precise point in space. Our survey missions have actually optimized our travel route through interstellar space to the point that we can now get there in thirty-three days, three hours. We'll come out of the LEAP bubble approximately six hundred AUs from the Trinity star, probably very close to our initial arrival point when we flew the *Beauregard* there. After that we should be able to proceed in on thrusters as a group, arriving at Bellus in about twelve hours through normal space, sir."

"Thank you, Ivan," said Clement. He looked then to Laura Pomeroy, his chief technical officer. "Do you want to tell us about your plans after we arrive on Bellus?"

Pomeroy nodded. "I've set up an expedition for five days after our landing to check out the pyramids, or the mountains, or whatever they are, up at the Hill Place near the original settlement where we met the native Mary and her group."

"It will be good to see her people again," chimed in

Yan. Clement gave her a look, knowing she and "Mary," as they had called the native girl, had spent some intimate time together on their previous mission. Yan showed no sign of anything other than innocent intent at that statement, though, so he let it pass without a word. Clement continued with Pomeroy.

"As you might expect, Commander, I will be taking a place on that mission. I'm just as curious as you are to find out what lies inside those artificial structures."

"It should be a great opportunity to gain knowledge, perhaps even discover some unknown technologies that we ourselves don't yet have," replied Pomeroy.

"That would be a boon to our mission, undoubtedly," said Clement, then he looked around the table one last time. "I guess that's going to have to be good enough for now." He stood and his officers stood with him. "All stations, prepare for launch at 1300 hours station time." There was a chorus of *yes sirs* around the table and then Clement dismissed his crew. Just one more step for his fleet to take. And they seemed as ready as they could be.

And that was good enough for Clement. It had to be.

At exactly 1300 hours Admiral Clement opened the intra-ship com, its claxon blaring three times to alert the crew of an incoming message.

"This is Admiral Jared Clement. All hands to launch stations. All passengers secure yourselves in your cabins as instructed by your quartermasters. This is not a drill. I repeat, this is not a drill. All hands to launch stations." He hung up the com then and looked out over his console from the con position to the helm station manned by Mika

Ori; then to the nav with Ivan Massif; Kayla Adebayor at Coms; and even Nobli at the engineering console. It was a tight and experienced crew that he had supreme confidence in.

Captain Yan was at his left in her standard second position and Colonel Lubrov was at his right. He turned to Yan. "Captain," he said, "you are master of this ship and I am merely the commander of this mission. The *Agamemnon* moves at your command. Please give the departure order."

"With pleasure, Admiral," said Yan. "Helm," she called out.

"Helm here, Captain," replied Mika Ori.

"Clear all moorings. Release all lines. Give me a green light on all doors and hatches."

"All moorings and lines show clear. All hatches and doors are green," said Ori. Yan, of course, already knew the moorings and lines had been released thirty minutes prior, but the command was part of Navy ritual and as such it had significant symbolic meaning to the crew.

"Thrusters at minimum. Take us away from the dock, Pilot," Yan ordered, using the archaic term that Clement favored for his helm officer. Yan turned to Lieutenant Adebayor at the communications station. "Lieutenant, send to all ships in the fleet that they are ordered to be free and clear of the docks and to follow the *Agamemnon* to our designated embarkment point."

"Aye, Captain," said Adebayor.

"Clear of the docks," reported Ori.

"Give her one ten-thousandth light toward the embarkment point, Pilot."

"Sir. One ten-thousandth light."

"Are we on the correct course, Navigator?" Yan asked of Massif.

"We are, Captain. Estimate three hours to the embarkment point."

"Very good. And the rest of the fleet?"

"Moving out as specified in their deployment orders, sir."

"Excellent."

At that Yan turned to Clement to report.

"Admiral, the fleet is under way to the designated embarkment point. All is well and we are on course."

"All is well. Thank you, Captain," replied Clement. At that everyone took a deep breath and the command deck broke out in spontaneous applause.

"Captain Yan," said Clement over the din of celebration.

"Sir."

"Captain, you have the con. I will be in my office until we reach the embarkation point. Please recall me fifteen minutes prior to that time."

"Aye, Admiral, I have the con."

"Thank you, Captain." Then he shook her hand, and the room broke out in applause again as he left the command platform and Yan assumed the commanding officer's station at the console.

Clement smiled as he walked away.

Two and a half hours later Clement was gently snoozing in his office chair when he got a knock on the door. It was the OOTD, Lieutenant Sean Shepherd.

"Per your orders, sir," said Shepherd, "the captain wishes to inform you that we are arriving at the Trinity embarkment point a bit early."

Clement roused himself and cleared this throat to address the young officer.

"How early?"

Shepard checked his wrist watch. "Eighteen minutes, sir."

"Well, thank the captain for her efficiency in getting *Agamemnon* to the point early. Tell her I will be on the command platform presently."

"Sir," said Shepherd, snapping to attention and then walking off.

Five minutes later Clement walked onto the command deck of the CAC and was announced again by OOTD Shepherd. Everyone snapped to attention as Clement gave a half-hearted wave salute to the crew so they could quickly return to their jobs. He was getting tired of all the protocol, but he was the one who had instituted it for disciplinary reasons and felt at least some obligation to follow through on his own orders.

He assumed the command position at the main control console with Yan yielding and moving to the other side. "Great job on getting us here early," he said to Yan.

"The ship did most of the work," replied the *Agamemnon's* captain cheerily.

Clement smiled and nodded his head, then looked down to his personal display, already set up on the console, Yan again anticipating his needs. Clement pulled up the navigation and propulsion displays so they were floating in the air above the console directly at his eye level. He looked at the relative positions of the three different pods in his fleet and was pleased with what he saw. All three groupings of ships were indeed at their embarkment coordinates and ready to make the leap to interstellar travel. "Well done, Captain," he said out loud so the crew could hear him praise her. "I don't think we could have asked for more efficiency than what you've managed to produce here. Send out orders to each of the pod commanders to organize their ships and prepare for the LEAP bubble transformation in ... twenty minutes, by my mark." He looked up at the ship's clock and waited till it hit 1410 hours. "Mark," he declared.

Yan used the intercraft com to call Captains Samkange of the *Corvallis* and Son of the *Yangtze* and gave them their final formation orders. She also sent out a batch com to each of the individual ship commanders in the *Agamemnon's* travel pod and ordered them to form up by 1630 hours.

Clement watched on the main CAC display as all of the ships swam toward their leaders like young fish to their mothers. When everything was satisfactory, Clement nodded to Yan.

"Order all ships to station-keeping," said Clement. "We fire up the LEAP drive in eight minutes."

Agamemnon's group was the largest of the three at eleven ships, with the battlecruiser itself, two light cruisers and four destroyers, trailed by four of the ten transport ships. The other two pod groups were at a distance of ten kilometers each, port and starboard from the *Agamemnon*, with two light cruisers, two destroyers and three transports each.

The next few minutes passed quietly and quickly, the ships all closely formed now to their primary leaders. At exactly 1630 hours Clement called down to Nobli in the main reactor room. "Are you ready to fire up my universe destroyer?" he asked.

"She's warm and ready, Admiral," replied Nobli. "Universal destruction to commence at your order."

"Thank you, Engineer," he replied, then cut off the line and turned to Yan again. "Send orders to the fleet, Captain. All ships prepare for LEAP transport within the *Agamemnon* bubble. Please return confirmations."

"Aye, sir," replied Yan in a professional manner. A few minutes later she reported all ships were in position and reported ready.

Clement stepped back from the command console. "Please give the order, Captain. All lead ships activate their LEAP drives. All ships to accelerate in pace with the *Agamemnon* or their lead ship."

Yan got on the fleet-wide com and gave the orders. Aboard the *Agamemnon* they felt the low rumble of the massive twin LEAP reactors as they came to life. There was a rush of static ionized air through the CAC. As he watched the navigation display Clement saw the *Agamemnon*'s LEAP bubble forming in front of them and expanding to envelope her pod of ships.

"All ships report LEAP bubbles are active. All ships safely inside the *Agamemnon* or lead ship bubble perimeters. All ships ready for superluminal acceleration," said Yan.

"Thank you, Captain, you may release the hounds."

Yan raised her arm and then pointed to the Propulsion

team at their station, and at that moment all ships within the three pods began moving, surfing on a quantum-fluid wave generated by their LEAP drives.

"One-tenth light," reported Yan, then paused. "One-fifth light," she reported seconds later. It was a longer stretch to her next report, but "one-half light, Admiral," eventually came. The ship quickly accelerated to more than ninety-nine percent light speed. Yan looked to Clement for confirmation.

"Go," he said.

Yan waited a few seconds and then finally reported in. "Superluminal speeds achieved, Admiral. All ships within our bubble are safe and sound. Acceleration will continue to increase until we reach maximum cruising speed."

"Well done," said Clement, and then he gave Yan a round of applause. He was quickly joined in by the rest of the command deck crew. A few whoops and cheers spontaneously broke out. Clement stopped clapping then and waved his hands down to get the crew to refocus on their jobs. He picked up the ship's com.

"All hands, we are now traveling at faster-than-light speed, a feat once thought scientifically impossible. Our next stop, in about thirty-three days, is the planet Bellus in the Trinity system. Congratulations to all of you!" he said enthusiastically. "And just so you know, all members of the crew will be receiving a silver star pin as a commemoration, indicating that you have officially joined the most exclusive club in the Five Suns Navy, the Superluminals!" There was quick applause at that, and Clement brought over OOTD Shepard to pass out the pins to the command deck crew. He personally gave the pins to both Yan and Lubrov, who put the pins on each other, and also pinned one on Shepard's chest. Yan returned the favor for him.

After that little ceremony was over it was back to business. He went to the communications station and Lieutenant Adebayor. "Please begin the process of validating the quantum tether connections with each of the ships in our pod, then see if we can raise the *Corvallis* and the *Yangtze* through the quantum tether."

"Aye, sir," she replied.

"And if there's any problems, don't be afraid to call Engineer Nobli over there."

"Sir."

He returned to the platform and went then to Colonel Lubrov. "Please place in the log the time and date that the ship first went superluminal, and add a note from the admiral. All is well," he said to Lubrov.

"Aye, Admiral, all is well," she said.

Clement turned his attention back to his console, a true smile on his face.

✳ 7 ✳

A week into the interstellar traverse from Kemmerine Station to the Trinity system, things aboard ship had settled down to a non-frantic pace. Yan and Lubrov had developed a working daytime routine of running the *Agamemnon* with quiet efficiency. The two of them were coordinating split shifts at the con, overseeing ship operations from the command console with a couple of hours each day of overlapping duty time. OOTD Shepard had the honor of holding the con during the graveyard shift, something the admiral had personally ordered to give the young man a bit of experience.

Clement noted the two women under his command (from two different military backgrounds, the Five Suns Navy and the Marines) got along well enough professionally even if that was not shared in a close personal relationship. Frankly, in Clement's eyes, they didn't have to be the best of friends to work well together, and he didn't expect them to take that relationship off-line. They served two different purposes in his mind, Yan being the well organized and efficient one, and Lubrov being the one that worked best at keeping the crew sharp and running them through their paces. They each had their pros and cons, but he felt completely comfortable having the two of them as his captain and her XO.

He didn't want Yan to know this, but he actually believed Lubrov would be the one he would consult in a crisis. He'd read her file again and saw her top-level rating from the Five Suns Naval War College on Atlas. Each command program candidate in the Navy had to do a full semester at the college, and Lubrov had excelled in the class of 2509. Yan had been less distinguished in the '11 class, but still well above the median, just not as shiny as Lubrov.

Captain Samkange of the *Corvallis* had also been in that '09 class with the colonel, and he'd finished just outside the top ten candidates, while Lubrov had finished in the top three. The first two finishers and many of the others in the class of twenty-five cadets from '09 had been with the Five Suns Navy at the Battle of Trinity. Clement had to assume they were either dead (by his own hand using the MAD weapon) or exiled on the inner habitable planet of Alphus. In any case, he felt he had three excellent subordinates following him in the chain of command.

He tried to stay off the command deck as much as he could and let the crew do their jobs. An admiral with all that rank bling on his uniform could be a big distraction on a working deck. He tried to tone it down as much as he could, not being one for putting on much of a show, but there was no denying he had an impact on the crew whenever he came to the CAC, even on those that had served with him in the Rim Confederation Navy, like Mika Ori or Nobli.

He assumed a more casual schedule, what with things

so locked down and the ship running with such efficiency. Dinner with his parents had become a semi-regular occurrence, mostly held in their finely appointed stateroom. They had both come around on the migration, and he'd even managed to convince his father that they weren't going to be stealing any land from the natives. Still, reluctance remained, which was common among the migrants. They were leaving the only homes they had ever known to take a long, unprecedented journey through interstellar space to a new promised land that they had never seen. It required a great deal of faith on all their parts.

After a pleasant but quick lunch with his parents Clement had taken to making his rounds to different stations around the ship, checking in on junior officers, getting personal anecdotes on the running of the ship that weren't in his daily reports, and generally just keeping himself busy. He found being an admiral had its drawbacks, and at times, he even found himself bored.

His first stop on this day was the weapons bay and control room, an area of the ship that dwarfed what he had ever experienced on his tiny gunship, the *Beauregard*, now safely tucked away in the *Agamemnon's* huge landing bay. He stepped into the control room unannounced, there to find the stations being manned by the young Lieutenants Telco and Tsu, who had come aboard on the first mission to Trinity as final semester cadet candidates. Clement had seen fit to promote them both twice since then.

"Gentlemen," he said as he stepped on the deck. Both Telco and Tsu turned and snapped to attention.

"Admiral! We didn't expect you today," said Telco, looking surprised, as if he'd just been caught doing something he shouldn't. Clement glanced at the station monitors behind each of the men.

"It wouldn't be a surprise inspection if I told you I was coming, now would it?" the admiral said with a smile.

"No, sir," replied Telco.

"Lieutenant Tsu," said Clement, acknowledging the other young man in the room with a nod. "At ease, both of you. I'm not here for any serious business, just to get your personal overview of what you think of the weapons systems here aboard *Agamemnon*." Both of the young lieutenants relaxed a bit then and Telco turned from his console and blanked it, speaking first as the senior weapons officer.

"She's quite a bit different than anything we had on board the *Beauregard*," said Telco nervously.

"That much should be obvious," replied Clement with a smirk, trying to get the young men to relax.

"She's just got so many systems compared to what we ran before on the *Beauregard*. We have scatter mines, we have kinetic rounds, we have the Rods of God, our conventional missiles, antimissile torpedoes, DEW weapons, nuclear warheads . . . that's a lot to keep track of, sir," rattled off Telco.

"I'm sure of that," said Clement, "but tell me how are you two working together? I mean, who handles what responsibilities?" He looked to Lieutenant Tsu for an answer this time.

"Well, sir," started Tsu, also clearly nervous. "Telco here handles all the electronic systems. He's responsible for charging the Directed Energy Weapons, coordinating missile release loads, arming of the mines, etc. I mostly focus on making sure that the physical maintenance is done. Things like making sure the torpedo tubes and missile launchers are properly maintained and loaded, that there are missiles ready to load and go at any time, and that we have the nuke case available whenever the control keys are released by the senior officers."

"Those would be Captain Yan and Colonel Lubrov on this trip," said Clement. "I won't be getting involved in any of that unless one of them isn't available. I guess you would call it admiral's privilege, but it's more like I'm excluded from all the fun." They all laughed at that. Clement quizzed further. "How many support techs do you two have working for you?"

"Seven," said Telco. "They're all cross-trained. Most can handle almost any procedure, be it loading or arming mines or charging the coil cannons. It's a good crew and when neither Tsu nor I are on duty we have no problem handing things over to them. We have a tight crew and everybody has everyone else's backs."

"That's great," said Clement. "I just wanted to make sure everything was running smoothly."

"Sir," spoke up Tsu, "do you think we'll be needing all this weaponry when we get to Trinity?"

Clement hesitated a second before answering. "Well, son, I hope not, but you never know. We know the Earth government sent one colonization ship with that first ark we faced down, and you never know, there could be another coming right behind it. But we're hopeful that's not the case, and none of our longwave scanning indicates anything heading our way. But, as I said, you never know."

"Will we be establishing a permanent military outpost at Trinity, sir?" asked Telco.

"Eventually," replied Clement. "I mean, that's the plan. I wouldn't be bringing almost all of the remaining Kemmerine fleet here if we didn't plan on establishing some naval presence. But we don't really have the facilities yet to establish a full-on space station over the Bellus colony, so we're likely going to have to do things by caravan for a while. The smaller ships like the gunships and perhaps even some of the destroyers could eventually make camp on the surface, but I would really like to avoid spoiling the natural beauty of the Trinity worlds with military maintenance bases. Right now the *Agamemnon* will function as the base for the Trinity system, to protect her, to protect her worlds, her native sons and daughters and the new settlers that we're bringing in from the Rim worlds." Clement crossed his arms then and leaned against a console, taking a casual stance and looking down on the vast weapons bay. "This is quite impressive," he said, "and I can't think of two better officers to be handling this part of the mission than you two."

Telco smiled. "Well, sir, when you need brawn and not brains you can come to us."

"The brains are already up there on the command deck," chimed in Tsu.

"I assume by that you mean Lieutenant Adebayor? Are you two still a couple, Mr. Tsu?"

"I guess that depends on who you ask and what day it is," replied Tsu. "We're both pretty young and clearly on different career paths right now," he said with a chuckle.

Clement nodded. "Understood. All I know is we couldn't have gotten through the ordeal we had on the first Trinity mission without all three of you. You two were both vital then and I consider you vital now. You're both fine young officers and quite frankly you would probably both make excellent candidates for the Marines, but if you want to go that route you'll have to bring it up with Colonel Lubrov."

"That has been mentioned to us as a possible career path," said Telco. "But I'm not sure I'm ready to make that decision yet, sir."

"Well, if either of you want to make your home base here in the Trinity worlds, there will likely be a lot more work for Marines on the ground than weapons officers in space. You both would probably get a lot more opportunity to advance a lot quicker under Colonel Lubrov's command than you would under Captain Yan, but that's a decision you can make in the coming months. I'm not putting any pressure on either of you to leave, just so you understand."

"Yes, sir," replied Telco.

"Thank you for the advice, Cap—I mean, uh, Admiral," said Tsu. "In the end, though, sir, we want you to know that when it comes to your conventional weapons, we have this ship locked down. Anything you need, whenever you need it, we'll get it to you."

"Thank you, gentlemen," finished Clement. Then he shook both their hands, patted them on the shoulders, and turned to head out. "Oh, just one more thing," he said before leaving. "You should knock off running dueling war game simulations on the tactical computers. We used to do the same thing when I was a young officer, but, you just never know when you might need those systems for a real combat situation in a pinch." Then he smiled and stepped out of the weapons bay, sure that he was leaving two embarrassed young men behind him.

☆ 8 ☆

Clement stood at the command console in the CAC, his personal displays floating above the board at eye level in 3D high definition, his foot tapping impatiently on the grilled metal floor. The ship's clock was steadily counting down, with just three minutes to go now until the *Agamemnon* and its pod of companion ships became the first group to drop out of LEAP space and into normal space at the Trinity system.

To his left Captain Yan called up the ship-wide com system and spoke into it, addressing the entire ship at one time. "Attention. This is Captain Yan. Three minutes to exit from LEAP space. I repeat, three minutes to exit from LEAP space. All personnel should be at their transition stations, all passengers should be in their cabins. Lockdown orders are in place. Stand by." She hung up the com system and looked to Clement. "Locked down for the transition, Admiral," she said with a nod.

"Thank you, Captain. Colonel Lubrov, status of the companion ships in the pod?"

"All confirm ready for the transition, Admiral," said Lubrov.

"Thank you," he said again, then turned his attention to Ivan Massif at Navigation. "Course report, Navigator?"

The tall Russian responded immediately. "Course is steady and confidence in our data is high, sir. We should come out within twenty-five hundred kilometers of our designated Trinity system entry point, sir."

Clement nodded. "And that's pretty accurate for an 11.5 light-year journey through warped space."

"Thank you, Admiral."

"You're welcome," he said with a smile, then turned his attention to his helm officer and Massif's wife, Mika Ori. "Status, Pilot?"

"Speed decreasing steadily to 1.0086 light, sir. On schedule to exit LEAP space on the clock, sir. All subsystems report green."

"Thank you, Commander." He looked over to the empty engineer's station, not surprised that Hassan Nobli had chosen to ride out the exit from faster-than-light travel in the reactor room. Clement clicked on his direct com line to the engineer. "Lieutenant Commander Nobli, final report on the reactor status?"

Nobli's voice came through the line and over the speakers so that all the CAC crew could hear his report. "Reactor at one hundred percent efficiency and winding down, sir. No issues at this time. The exit from LEAP quantum-fluid space should be smooth and orderly, sir."

"Excellent, Engineer. Stand by. I'll want a full report once we're in place."

"Aye, sir."

Clement looked at the clock, two minutes, ten seconds. "Helm?" he asked, looking for an update.

"Deceleration already underway, sir. Sub-light speeds are confirmed. We should exit LEAP space with no forward motion," said Ori.

They all watched then as the clock counted down. The telemetry on Clement's speed display showed the rapid deceleration of both the *Agamemnon* and the rest of the companion pod. This kind of deceleration wouldn't be possible in normal space, but the quantum fluid of the Liquid Energy Absorption Propulsion system literally bent and distorted space, allowing them to do things that weren't possible in the unaltered natural universe and keeping them from ending up as blood spatters on the ship's interior walls.

They watched in silence as the clock counted down. At thirty seconds, Yan began to count down. When she got to ten she unhooked the ship-wide com line again and counted down to the entire crew. "Seven . . . six . . . five . . . four . . . three . . . two . . . one . . ." They all felt the slight shift like a gentle bump, almost undetectable, but noticeable to an experienced spacer. At zero the ship exited the LEAP bubble and returned to normal space, completely stationary.

"Status?" called Clement.

"Ship is at station-keeping with no forward motion," reported Mika Ori.

"We are 239.4 kilometers from our exact targeted entry point," reported Navigator Massif. "About 10.021 AUs from the Trinity star, sir."

"Thank you, Ivan. Status of the rest of the ships in the pod?"

"All ships in the pod are reporting they are in normal

space with no transition incidents," reported Com Officer Adebayor.

"Nobli," said Clement into the com, "how is our miracle reactor?"

"They're both perfect, sir, off-line and cooling down. I'll have the standard thrusters ready for you in ten minutes."

"Thank you, Nobli." He turned then to Captain Yan. "Prepare the *Agamemnon* to head inward toward the planet Bellus. Mr. Massif will give you the course."

"Absolutely, sir," replied Yan.

Clement turned to the *Agamemnon's* XO. "Colonel Lubrov, once the captain has set our course and speed please be sure the other ships in the pod are given same information with orders to follow the *Agamemnon* into the inner Trinity system."

"Aye, sir."

"Captain," he said to Yan again, "how long until the second pod of ships arrives?"

Yan looked at her floating display and swiped right twice to find the panel she wanted. "Estimate another three minutes for pod two to arrive, 6.5 minutes for pod number three," she reported. Clement merely nodded at that report and then went quiet, letting his people do their jobs as they waited for the rest of the migration fleet to arrive. Clement kept his eyes on the ship's clock.

The panic, when it came, was tight, quiet, and nerve-racking.

The second pod, led by Captain Samkange of the *Corvallis*, did not appear on schedule. Yan reported they were overdue, but Clement stayed tight-lipped, aware that all eyes in the CAC were looking at him to evaluate how serious the situation was.

At seven minutes post-mark both the second pod and the third pod, commanded by Captain Son of the *Yangtze*, were both overdue. It was time for Clement to act.

"Captain Yan," he said in a commanding voice, "go to station red, repeat station red." At his call the CAC broke into a bustle of activity. Automatic alarms went off throughout the ship. Orders went out to increase the ship's state of readiness and passengers were told via the alert system to remain in or return to their cabins. Clement looked at Yan. A look of concern was etched on her face.

"What do you have for me, Captain?" he said anxiously.

Yan hesitated for only a second, but Clement knew her well enough to know that pause was cause for concern. "Unknown situation, sir," she finally replied. "Both accompanying pods are overdue."

"Can we go back into LEAP space and try to contact them?"

"We can, but that would leave the rest of our ships unprotected."

"That may be necessary."

She looked at him deadly seriously. "We should wait, Admiral. Those ships were with us every step of the way, and I find it highly unlikely they've simply vanished from the universe at our journey's end."

Clement looked to Lubrov. "Colonel? Any suggestions?"

Lubrov's face was blank and dispassionate. If she was worried, she didn't show any of it outwardly. "In my opinion, sir, we have to take the *Agamemnon* back into

LEAP space, try and backtrack and locate the other pods, and if possible, try to reestablish communication with them through the quantum tether."

"And leave the rest of the fleet alone and unprotected in a new star system that they don't know?" challenged Yan. Clement sensed the unmentioned tension between the two women finally coming out. Yan, always the cautious one, clearly hated Lubrov's suggestion.

"Do we have another option?" snapped back Lubrov. Yan was about to respond with an even stronger argument, based on the rising rose color of her face, but Clement inserted himself into the conversation before tensions could escalate.

"We have other ships in the fleet that have LEAP reactors. It seems clear we should send one of those ships out to look for the two missing pods, but I don't want to leave this group alone or undefended in this system."

"What do you suggest we do then, sir?" said Yan. Her tone wasn't challenging, but it wasn't subordinate either. Clement thought for a moment, aware that both of his junior command officers and the entire CAC crew were watching him. They were all aware that he was about to make a critical decision, even if they had their eyes and ears focused on their stations and their work.

He made his decision. "Call the junior helm, navigation, engineering, and communications officers to the CAC immediately, Captain."

"Aye, sir," she responded, and proceeded to call the juniors to the CAC over the com.

Clement waved Ori, Massif, and Adebayor over to the command platform. He opened a direct com down to

Nobli in Engineering so that he could listen in as well. When all were present and leaning against the railing, he gave his orders.

"Engineer Nobli, you will prepare the *Beauregard* for deployment. Get your techs down to the landing bay and warm up her reactor. We're going out to find our missing ships."

"Aye, sir, but that will take maybe forty minutes," said Nobli.

"You have twenty, Hassan."

"Understood, sir."

Clement looked to the rest of his command crew on the railing. "The *Beauregard* has the most time running a LEAP reactor and operating in quantum space in this fleet. I intend to take advantage of that experience, and of the experience of her crew, to conduct a search and rescue of the missing pods." At that point junior officers began arriving in the CAC to take over at the empty stations. Clement looked to his trusted crew, who had come through a massive crisis the last time they were in the Trinity system. "I hope you all fancy a fishing expedition. I don't mean to be lighthearted about this, but we have two missing pods of ships and I'm not willing to leave the ships that *are* here undefended."

He turned to Yan. "Captain, you will remain here aboard the *Agamemnon* and you will lead this fleet inwards toward their destination at the planet Bellus. Colonel Lubrov will accompany me along with Commanders Ori, Massif, Nobli, and Lieutenant Adebayor aboard the *Beauregard* to search for our missing companions. Colonel Lubrov, I suggest we bring Lieutenants Telco and Tsu and a pair of your Marines in case we need some muscle to assist the lost ships. Our mission will be search and rescue, so prep the ship for up to two days of searching."

"Yes, sir."

"Clearly something has gone terribly wrong here. I don't want to risk my flagship on a rescue attempt when it might be needed here, in the Trinity system. We have eighteen thousand migrants and fourteen ships out there somewhere, and we need to find them. Now go and do your prep, everyone. We will meet down in the landing bay on board the *Beauregard* in twenty minutes." Everyone nodded and there were grave looks all around, but also grim determination in their eyes. Clement had been proud of this crew many times in the past and he was sure he would be again.

With that he moved to Yan's position and activated the ship-wide com. "Attention. This is Admiral Clement. We will be attempting a search and rescue of the missing ships in the other two pods aboard the Five Suns Navy gunship *Beauregard*. All other vessels are to proceed with the *Agamemnon* under the command of Captain Yan to the planet Bellus, where we will begin an orderly transition to the settlements that have been prepared there. Please do not worry until we know there is something to worry about. Focus on your jobs, your families, and your loved ones. We will report as soon as we have any new information. Admiral Clement out."

"Sir," started Yan, "how will we communicate with you if we aren't in quantum space? We won't be able to use the tether."

"We'll have to use the longwave packet system,

Captain. It may not be as fast as the quantum tether but it will be enough to keep you updated as to our progress."

"Very well, sir."

And with that Clement handed the con to Yan and headed for his cabin, there to get out of his formal uniform and into his EVA flight suit.

He had to send a com to his parents telling them he was leaving the ship and what the circumstances were. He got a supportive reply from his mother, but nothing from his father. He called in to Yan again to please keep an eye on them in light of his absence.

When he got to the *Beauregard* Clement entered through her cargo bay door and went up the familiar metal gangway to her bridge. There he found Ori and Massif at their familiar nav and helm stations, Colonel Lubrov at the XO's position, and Kayla Adebayor at Communications, talking back and forth and prepping the ship. He paused for a minute to take in the full bridge of the one ship he could truly call his own in this fleet. After a moment to absorb his surroundings one more time, he sat down in his command couch and hit the com, calling down to Nobli in the reactor room.

"How long until we're ready, Hassan?" he said.

"Give me seven minutes, Captain; I'll have her warm and humming."

"Time is important here, Nobli."

"I'm aware of that, Cap . . . Admiral. We're doing the best we can. We need to be safe, sir."

Clement took in a deep breath. "We do, Engineer," he said, "but we also need to be fast."

"Understood."

Clement swung around his command couch and sat down in it for the first time in nearly two years. He had to admit it, this ship, this bridge, this crew, felt like home.

"Hassan, in your opinion, how did this happen?"

"I don't know, sir, but it's at least possible that there is some sort of time/space displacement scenario going on."

"Which means, what?"

"It means that the LEAP drive may be powerful enough to warp not only space but time as well. Those missing pods might just drop out of their LEAP bubbles at any time, none the wiser that they were ever off-mission. This scenario was a theory that was considered, but we believed it was a very low probability of it occurring. The fact is, this technology is still early in its development."

"Thanks for letting me know this could happen in advance of the mission."

"Admiral, if I told you about every possible scenario—"

"Not now, Nobli. I'll write you up later. For now, we have to improvise, and I expect your best performance. Understood?"

"Yes, Admiral."

Clement cut the line and swung around his command couch to the XO's station.

"Colonel Lubrov," he said, "get this ship in position on the landing deck. I want us to be spaceborne as soon as Nobli gives the all clear."

"Yes, sir," said Lubrov, then proceeded to call in orders to the *Agamemnon*'s landing bay staff.

"Incoming call from Captain Yan," reported Adebayor.

"I'll take it," said Clement. Adebayor punched the com

through to the captain's console and Clement pressed a button to open the com channel. "What do you have for me, Yan?" he asked.

"Good news, Admiral! One of the missing pods has appeared at the designated rendezvous point; it's Captain Son and the *Yangtze* pod, sir. All ships are fine and all the captains and commanders are reporting everything is normal. There is a discrepancy of thirty-three minutes between their shipboard clocks and our shipboard clock. We're investigating this anomaly but I have nothing to report as of yet."

Clement hesitated for a second. "I trust you to work this out, Yan. Send me the data that you have and I'll bring it up with Nobli once we're back in LEAP space."

"Sir, we could wait to see if the third pod shows up."

"Negative. We're going out after them," said Clement. "Follow your orders, Captain. I will check in with you as soon as we have any more information."

"Yes, sir."

Clement called down to Nobli again, anxious for an update. "Still need five minutes, Admiral. This reactor hasn't been run in a while, since her initial tests. And we don't want an accident, do we, sir?"

"No, we don't, Nobli. I don't care what you have to do to get her warm. Have Tech Reck throw a hammer at it if you have to." He turned to Lubrov. "Estimate until we're in position in the landing bay, Colonel?"

"Six minutes, Admiral," replied Lubrov.

"I just bought you an extra minute, Nobli. Don't disappointment me. These are going to be the longest six minutes of my life."

"Aye, sir," said Nobli, then signed off.

Clement sat back in his chair, and waited.

Impatiently.

When they finally got their clearance from the landing bay crew to depart the *Agamemnon*, Clement checked in with Nobli one last time and simply got a green light on his propulsion app board in reply.

"Commander Ori, thrusters please," he ordered.

"Aye, sir, thrusters are hot."

The *Beauregard* lifted off the landing deck and proceeded slowly through the length of *Agamemnon's* massive landing bay, then crossed the environmental static shield and out into open space. Clement activated the com. "You may proceed inward with the fleet to Bellus, Captain Yan," Clement said, "*Beauregard* will report once we've made contact with the *Corvallis* pod."

"Good hunting, Admiral. See you at Bellus."

"Best of luck, Captain." Then he closed the com.

"Mika, give us fifty thousand kilometers before we engage the LEAP drive. Ivan, take us back on the same course we came in on. Kayla," he said, using Adebayor's first name as a way of showing her he considered her as one of his senior crew now. "As soon as we're in LEAP space engage the quantum tether and try and raise Captain Samkange and the *Corvallis*."

"Understood, sir."

He hit the com again. "Nobli, LEAP power to the pilot as soon as you're ready."

"Will do, sir." Clement remained pensive while he waited. Finally Ori signaled she had LEAP power ready.

"Go, Pilot," he said, and the ship began generating her quantum bubble in front of her nose, accelerating toward light speed as they entered the fluid space.

"Superluminal speeds achieved, sir," reported Ori a few moments later. Clement, and he assumed the rest of the crew, felt the gentle tug of acceleration as the *Beauregard* slipped above the light-speed barrier. It was almost imperceptible, but to Clement it signaled a significant crossing of the bridge, a step toward mankind's future. He allowed himself the luxury of that moment, before turning his thoughts back to the task at hand.

"Navigator, take us back the same way we came in."

"Aye, sir," replied Massif.

"Communications officer, activate the quantum tether and try to raise the *Corvallis*."

"Already on it, Admiral," Adebayor replied.

Clement sat forward in his captain's couch, his console pushed to one side as he focused on the main panel display at the front of the bridge. It showed a rich mix of visual and tactical readouts, along with telemetry about the ship's course, speed, and overall functioning. They were already making 1.5 light speed, and he could tell Ori was pushing the LEAP drive as hard as she could. Clement was shifting uncomfortably in his couch, so much so that the XO stepped away from her station and went to his side.

"Your crew know their jobs, sir," Lubrov said quietly, so that only the two of them could hear.

Clement looked at the colonel. "I know. It's still hard for me to sit here and feel like I can't do anything about speeding up this search or finding those lost souls."

Lubrov nodded. "This is part of the frustration you feel about being an admiral, isn't it, sir?"

Clement thought the XO was being a bit forward, but he had to admit she was also being very insightful. This was their first time working this close together, so he wanted to give her some slack on her approach to being his second-in-command. He turned away from her and put his attention back on the main display, then sat back in his chair. "I've never really been comfortable with being an admiral. I've always been a ship captain, because I felt at that level I could make a difference. You could do things to affect the outcome of an incident or a crisis. Where I am now I can really only set policy, not carry it out. And frankly, Colonel, that does wear on me. For now, though, I'm just happy to be back on the bridge of this ship."

"You consider the *Beauregard* to be *your* ship, don't you?"

"As much as any other ship I've ever commanded, yes. She represents many things to me, and if I was being honest with myself I would admit that I never wanted anything more than to be captain on board this ship."

"Well," Lubrov said, "when this is all over and we find our missing ships, maybe you can demote yourself back to captain."

"It's a thought. But who would I put in charge of the fleet, exactly? There's not really anyone in the Kemmerine sector that I know well enough or trust enough to put in charge of the Trinity worlds."

"Not even Captain Yan?" That surprised Clement. He thought of the two women as rivals, but what Lubrov had just said was a high compliment toward Yan. It seemed that both women under his direct command were more complex than he gave them credit for.

"I need Yan to captain the *Agamemnon*."

"What about one of the older officers at Kemmerine Station? Some of them would make good administrators."

"You're probably right," said Clement. "Right now, though, what we need are captains, commanders, and flag officers with deep-space experience. We're far short of that experience right now, and only by doing these kinds of missions will we get that experience. No, Colonel, I'm afraid I'm going to be stuck at the top of the Five Suns Navy pyramid for a while longer yet, until promising senior officers like you and Yan, and Samkange and Son, are ready to move up to the bigger roles."

"Very good, sir," she said. "I'll go back to monitoring the telemetry and see if I can pick up a residual LEAP signature." Clement nodded at that and she went back to the XO's console.

Clement asked for updates from his reports but none of them had any positive data to report. Growing pensive again, Clement put his com implant into his ear canal and called down to Nobli in the reactor room.

"Yes, Admiral," came Nobli's familiar voice in the com.

"Hassan, I need to know something. How likely is it that we would be able to detect and locate the missing pods of ships while traveling in LEAP space ourselves?"

"Well, sir, it's far more likely than a needle-in-haystack-type scenario, but at the same time, it's not easy. Once we dropped out of LEAP space and broke the quantum tether, we essentially disconnected ourselves from the network. LEAP signatures are easy enough to identify once you locate them, but we really know very little about how the physics actually work in LEAP space. It could be a long shot in finding them. Having said that, if Captain Samkange has figured out that they're missing or off course, he could conceivably devise a way to let us know he's out here."

"And what way might that be?" asked Clement. Nobli grunted, the verbal equivalent of a shrug for him.

"Well, I know he didn't train on this, but we did discuss shutting down the reactor energy flow for microseconds at a time as a way of leaving trace particles of protons or electrons, sort of like the old Morse code. Those particles could then be scanned by a searching ship; even in the quantum fluid it would leave a trail. It's by no means exact and certainly not something that we trained for, but that or something like that could attract the kind of attention that would help us find them. And Samkange was briefed on these scenarios. I'm just not sure how seriously any of the captains or commanders took that part of the briefings."

Clement rubbed at his face with both hands for a few seconds, then put his ear com on mute, but kept the line to Nobli open. He turned to Colonel Lubrov again. "Colonel, start prioritizing scanning for trace groupings of protons and electrons along our path. It's a long shot, but it might give us a chance at finding the *Corvallis* group pod, if Captain Samkange was paying attention during his briefings."

"Aye, sir. I remember those briefings on communications in a potential crisis. Perhaps it made an impression on Captain Samkange or one of the other ship commanders as well."

"Perhaps it did," said Clement, feeling in his gut that it was a long shot. Clement paused then before saying the next possibility. "You should also look for any sort of mass discharge of antimatter, just in case one of the ships exploded while shutting down her reactor."

"Aye, sir," said Lubrov, grim faced at that prospect.

Clement tapped his ear com to resume his conversation with the *Beauregard*'s engineer.

"I want the truth, Hassan. How likely is it that we will find the *Corvallis* pod and the missing ships?"

"I would say we have a better than twenty percent chance of finding them, sir, if they're still out there. But you have to remember that Samkange wouldn't necessarily know he's overdue if our space-time warp scenario is happening."

Clement rubbed at his neck now, more out of nervous habit than anything else. "Nobli, what if they couldn't shut down their reactor? What if they couldn't drop out of LEAP space?"

"Then they would likely be heading on the same vector that the fleet was coming in on."

"Which means in backtracking we'd be going the wrong way."

"That's true, sir, but remember, the *Yangtze* pod lost thirty-three minutes somewhere in LEAP space, but to their clocks they came out at the rendezvous point right on time. As we've discussed, the LEAP drive probably has properties that can bend not only space, but time as well, which makes sense as space and time are essentially part of the single dimension that we live in. But if that's true, then Captain Samkange and the rest of the pod could think they are perfectly fine, and still think that they are on their way right on schedule to the rendezvous point. In which case us searching for them is a waste of our time and resources."

"I don't think searching for lost or injured comrades is ever a waste of time and resources, Nobli."

"I know, sir, and I feel the same way or I wouldn't be here. We just have to remember sometimes that we're in the very early stages of using this technology, and we don't really know its full potential to affect our lives, either positively or negatively."

"Thank you, Hassan," said Clement, a feeling of dread rising in his gut, then he cut the line.

Clement decided to stay quiet for a considerable time, letting his people do their jobs. After two fruitless hours of searching Clement stood up and called the bridge crew to his station and patched Nobli in through the main ship com. "I want opinions from each one of you. Is there something that we're doing in this search that we shouldn't be doing, and conversely is there something you think we *should* be doing that we're not?"

Mika Ori spoke up first. "We're making about twenty percent more speed than the migration fleet did, sir. We've already passed the point where we had the last quantum tether communication with the *Corvallis* pod. We know they came this far, so I think searching for them further back on the course we came in on is probably a waste of our time."

Clement looked to navigator Ivan Massif. "Do you agree, Ivan?"

"I do, sir," said the tall Russian. "At this point, I think we have to assume that they overshot the rendezvous point at Trinity either because they didn't know that they were at the exit point, or because they simply couldn't stop. I would recommend we reverse course and work past Trinity to see if they overshot the rendezvous point."

"But if they did overshoot the exit point, where could they be now?" asked Clement.

Massif looked down at his watch. "They're four hours overdue at this point, sir. With the speed they were making they likely aren't even one one-hundredth of a light-year beyond Trinity."

"Can you plot us that course, and do we have the speed to catch them?"

"I can plot it, sir, that's the easy part. But Mika and Nobli will have to tell you if we can catch them."

Clement looked to his pilot. She didn't hesitate. "We're already traveling twenty percent above their speed relative to us, sir. We can definitely catch them, but we have to stop and turn around first."

"So ordered. Ivan, lock in our course. Nobli, prepare to drop us back into normal space, and then resume superluminal speeds along the navigator's new course."

"Yes, sir," replied Nobli. "That maneuver will take about twenty-one minutes to execute, sir. We'll need to lean out the reactor output to slow us down, then once we drop back into normal space I'll have to reset the reactor. That takes about ten minutes. By then we should be able to resume on the new course."

"Then let's get to it." The bridge crew scrambled back to their stations. Clement put out a hand to hold back Lieutenant Adebayor. "Kayla, I want you to send a longwave communications packet back to Yan on the *Agamemnon* after we drop out of LEAP space."

"Yes, sir."

Clement nodded. "Give her a full update along with our position, as close as we can estimate it. Let them know where we are and what we're doing. Request an update on the status of the Trinity fleet." Adebayor nodded and then went to her station to prepare the packet. Clement looked to Lubrov. She made eye contact with him and then shook her head. Clement nodded, acknowledging his worst fears about the crisis. Then he sat back in his chair and sighed.

Things were not going well.

✤ 9 ✤

Thirty-six hours later and the mood aboard the *Beauregard* was black despair. There had been no sign of either the existence or the destruction of the missing ships from the *Corvallis* pod. Yan had reported in several times using the longwave packet system, each time with no positive word on the arrival of the missing ships. No signals had been sent; no telltale signs had been found. The quantum tether returned nothing but static. It was like the *Corvallis* and her sister ships had simply vanished from the universe.

Clement had started rotations for each of the duty stations, with either he or Lubrov sitting in, but none of the crew really wanted to take any time away from their search. Clement was forced to order two hours rest out of every eight or no one would have taken a break. For his part, the admiral had not even gone to his cabin. He had raided the infirmary for stimulants to keep him going, but that was a ticking time bomb, and even though he had allowed others to take them he could tell from his own fatigue that they were all reaching a breaking point.

The *Beauregard* should have caught the *Corvallis* pod at sixteen hours, fifty-three minutes time since they had turned and reversed course. There had been no sign of them, though, and even Clement was beginning to feel but there was little hope left. Colonel Lubrov signaled to Clement as he sat bleary eyed in his command couch.

"Can I have a word with you, Admiral?" she said.

"Yes, Colonel," he replied, motioning her over, his speech slow and slurry. She took a step away from her console then and toward his station. "In your cabin, if you please?"

Clement stared at her for a moment, feeling too fatigued to even get up. Finally, though, he struggled to his feet. His legs were sore and tired, and he had a pounding headache, most likely from the stims. He came around his command couch and walked unsteadily down the short metal steps to the captain's cabin for the first time on this mission, gripping the handrail all the way. Lubrov followed him in and then shut the cabin door behind her. They stood in the entryway of the cabin, Clement refusing to go in any further to keep from being tempted by the sight of his bed.

"Yes, Colonel," he said.

"Sir, I think you know that it's my job to report what I see to you."

"Of course it is."

She nodded. "Sir, what I'm seeing is an exhausted crew and a search that has turned up nothing to give us any indication that we are close to finding those missing ships. Our water supplies are low, our food supply is nearly tapped out—"

"We can survive on half rations," he snapped, interrupting her.

She bit at her lower lip in response, choosing her next words carefully. "I'm sure we can, sir. But I have to tell you that I think whatever solution there is to this mystery, those of us on this ship are not any closer to discovering what it is. My recommendation as XO is that we turn the *Beauregard* around again and return to the fleet in the Trinity system. We can then form another search and rescue mission, perhaps with multiple ships and larger crews."

"I'd like to give it a few—"

This time she interrupted him. "Immediately, sir."

Clement looked around the cabin and then took a few awkward steps and sat down in his cabin chair. "So you're saying that, in your opinion, we've lost them, then?"

"I don't know that, sir. But I believe that the search we are currently conducting will not yield an answer to this mystery. At this point, sir, you're the only one of the crew who has yet to take any rest, and I'm prepared to order you to take that rest under the Five Suns Navy fitness-for-command guidelines."

"I see. And once you do that?"

"Then I will go to the bridge and turn the *Beauregard* around, sir."

Clement looked at her, barely able to keep his eyes open as the softness of the thick leather chair began to warm around him. Defeat seemed inevitable now, and fatigue was demanding that he rest.

"So ordered, Colonel," he finally croaked out.

"Thank you, Admiral," she replied.

Then the room began to fade around him, and he couldn't fight back sleep any longer. His last thoughts were of the ships of the Corvallis pod, drifting aimlessly across the ocean of space.

Lost forever.

Four hours later Colonel Lubrov was gently shaking Clement awake. His sleep had been fitful, elusive, and unrefreshing.

Clement, tired and confused, looked up at her through weary eyes. "Colonel?" he said.

"Sir, we have a contact on the quantum tether."

Clement jumped to his feet, forcing himself awake. "The *Corvallis*?"

"It could be."

He rushed out of the room and quickly ran up the four steps to his bridge, Lubrov following him. He called to Adebayor the moment he stepped on the bridge. "Kayla? Is it the *Corvallis*?"

She turned from her console. "Uncertain at this time, sir. It's not a vocal communication; it appears to be a repeating beacon of some kind. It's coming from an area of space that's about half a light-year from Trinity, sir."

"How long until we get there?"

Mika Ori turned from the helm station to answer him. "One hour, six minutes, sir, from our present position and maintaining our current course and speed."

"Can we go faster?"

"That's a question for the engineer, sir," Ori said.

Clement tapped on his com button to call down to the reactor room. "Nobli, can we get any more speed out of the LEAP reactor?"

A female voice answered. "This is Tech Kim Reck, sir,"

she said. "Mr. Nobli has been sleeping for about an hour. Do you want me to wake him?"

"Damn straight I do, Tech Reck," said Clement. He waited anxiously for Nobli to come on the line. After about thirty seconds he heard the familiar scratchy voice of his chief engineer.

"Tech Reck tells me you have some sort of quantum communication incoming?" said Nobli.

"Lieutenant Adebayor tells me it's a beacon of some kind. Is that something a stranded ship might send out?"

"Well you've got me on that, Admiral. It's not something I would have ever thought of, but if it's in LEAP space and giving off a signal then it must be artificial."

"I agree. How much more speed can you give me on the reactor?"

"I can get you forty percent over standard cruising speed, but I'm not sure how long that can last." There was an unintelligible conversation coming through from Tech Reck in the background and then Nobli covered the com with his hand. Clement heard cursing going both ways before Nobli returned to the line.

"Tech Reck says she can get you thirty-eight minutes at that speed, sir, and if she says that I believe her. That will give you about a three-minute cushion before I'd have to shut the reactor down completely. I can't lean her out fast enough when she's running that hot."

Clement looked to Mika Ori. "Will that be enough time to reach the beacon?"

She nodded in reply. "It should be at that speed, sir. Maybe even with a minute or two to spare."

"Do it, Nobli," Clement ordered. "And tell your tech I'm going to give her a promotion."

"I think she'd rather just have a pay raise, sir," replied Nobli.

"Good enough. Signal the pilot when she can go to full max."

"Yes, Admiral," replied Nobli, then he cut the line. Clement swung around into the captain's couch, feeling both optimistic and a bit rested for the first time in two days.

Thirty-one minutes later and they were right on top of the beacon as they reduced speed to its location. What it was, though, was still a mystery. From their longwave scans it was about a meter long, shaped like a cylinder, and emitting a steady pulse of proton energy into the quantum aether.

"From what I'm reading, the thing is stationary in LEAP space," reported Lubrov. "I don't know how that's possible."

"Neither does Nobli, but it's clearly technology we don't currently have," said Clement. "I'm sure Nobli would love to get his hands on it." He turned to his pilot. "Mika, is there any way we can pick this thing up? Bring it on board?"

The *Beauregard*'s pilot turned from her station and looked at the admiral incredulously. "At superluminal speeds? And with what would I grab it? No, sir. It would have to be in normal space to retrieve such a device."

"Noted, Mika. If someone in the *Corvallis* pod

designed this thing, I'm going to give them a medal. What's your best estimate of what the beacon actually is?"

"It's got to be a marker, sir. Most probably left by someone in the *Corvallis* pod to indicate where they exited LEAP space. That's my best guess, anyway. I recommend we drop out of LEAP space at the marker location and start our search for our missing pod of ships in local space."

Clement looked to Lubrov, who nodded concurrence. "So ordered, Pilot. Estimated time to normal space?"

"Seven minutes, sir."

"Proceed." Clement motioned back to get Lubrov's attention again. "Tactical considerations, Colonel?"

Lubrov looked up from her station. "It would seem a stretch that this is our technology, sir. If it is then we have an unknown genius in the fleet, and I doubt that. I've read every crew bio for this mission and approved them myself. I'd know if we had a hidden genius like that."

Clement contemplated her statement. "So, do you think this might be from . . . someone else?"

"I can't know that, sir. But I think once we have affected our rescue that we should circle back and try to obtain it any way we can."

"I agree."

Lubrov looked seriously at him, the only look she seemed to carry on her face. "There is one other consideration, sir."

"And that is?"

"This could be a trap set by some other force, origin unknown."

"Noted, Colonel." Clement turned away then and

called down to Nobli again on his private com. "Hassan, I'm going to need you to keep the reactor warm after we drop out of LEAP space."

"Of course, sir. May I ask why?"

"We may have a bogey on our hands, an unknown. I don't want to take any chances, if you get my meaning."

"The MAD weapon?" replied Nobli.

Clement hesitated for a second. "I think it would be wise to be prepared, Hassan."

"Understood, sir. When we drop out of LEAP space I'll be sure she stays warm and that you have the weapon at your disposal. I sure hope you don't have to use it, Jared."

"I share your feelings," said Clement, then signed off.

The ship quickly decelerated, dropping out of LEAP space just a few thousand kilometers past the beacon's position.

"Lieutenant Adebayor," said Clement, getting her attention. "I'm going to need your radio telescope to be deployed. Let's use the forward-looking infrared scanner to look for heat signatures from the pod ships. Also, I want you to send out a longwave general contact signal, on repeat. Maybe we'll get lucky and they'll hear us before we see them."

"Aye, sir, engaging the FLIR," replied Adebayor as she set about her tasks. Clement knew the process could be tedious, given the size of even local space, but he had confidence in the young officer. She had proven herself aboard the *Beauregard* before. Still the wait was nearly interminable, and Clement found himself pacing the deck as he waited for some news, any news.

It took nearly half an hour before Adebayor got a hit.

"Picking up something now, sir," she called from her station. "Appears to be a residual heat signature, possibly from a thruster. It matches the type of output we would expect from one of our destroyers."

That got Clement's attention. "Relay the location to the pilot, Lieutenant," he said, retaking his captain's seat. As Adebayor did the relay Mika Ori started logging the coordinates into her tracking computer.

"Eleven minutes from here on full thrusters, Admiral," reported Ori.

"Go," Clement said.

As they traversed the distance to the thruster sign, Adebayor began detecting other heat signatures. "I'm counting ten thrusters in various stages of cooling down, sir," she reported. "It looks like they've been tracking back toward Trinity, but in normal space rather than using the LEAP drive."

Clement looked to Lubrov "That's concerning. Are they tracking back in normal space because the LEAP drives aren't working?"

"That's a possibility, sir. But at least we've found our missing pod."

"That we have, Colonel. Kayla, try and raise the *Corvallis*, please."

"Aye, sir." It took a couple of minutes sifting through the crackling static of normal space, but eventually Adebayor got in contact with Captain Samkange of the *Corvallis*. Adebayor put him on the ship-wide com so everyone could hear.

"Christ, am I glad to hear from you, Kayla!" said the relieved voice of Samkange over the com.

"Admiral Clement here now, Captain."

"Sir! It's good to hear from you too, sir! Our status is—"

"Hold on, Captain. Let me ask the questions for a minute."

"Sir."

"First, can you get your LEAP drives functioning?"

"I believe so, sir. When we dropped out of LEAP space and discovered we weren't at the designated rendezvous point, I ordered the drives to be shut down. We've preceded back toward Trinity on our sub-light thrusters. I figured going in the general direction was better than just sitting there trying to figure out what went wrong with our FTL, sir."

"Good. Next question: What time does your ship clock say?"

"Umm, 1620 hours, sir."

"What day?"

"2517.086, sir."

"Hold," said Clement and then muted the line. He turned to Lubrov. "How far off are they?" he asked.

Lubrov punched in some calculations on her console, then: "By our ship clock, thirty-six hours twenty-two minutes discrepancy, sir."

Clement nodded and turned on the com again. "Harry, please tell me how long it's been since you dropped out of LEAP space?"

"About six hours by my watch, sir," replied Samkange. "Is there something wrong?"

"Harry, I've got something to tell you, and you may not like it, I know I certainly don't. We've been searching for you for more than forty-two hours. It's been that long, and a little change that you've been missing. The *Yangtze* pod was thirty-plus minutes late coming out of LEAP space, but their clocks reported that they were on time and they were more or less on target for the rendezvous point. It appears your clocks are also not in line with ours, but by a much larger factor. That means we have a major discrepancy in time, apparently caused by the LEAP drive itself. It could bend both time and space, which is something we didn't anticipate."

"Holy shit," said Samkange, then quickly apologized for his language. "Sir, at this distance, it could take us four weeks through normal space to make it back to Trinity. We thought we just overshot the rendezvous point. We didn't think we lost time as well."

"That's the problem, Harry. As long as we don't understand the consequences of using the LEAP drive we have to be cautious. So far the *Beauregard* has been working fine, like she usually does. My concern is that if we start you back to Trinity using the LEAP drive we may end up losing you again."

"That would be my concern as well, sir. What are your orders?"

"Stay put. Let us come to you. My shuttle will dock with the *Corvallis* in . . ." He looked to Mika Ori. She held up seven fingers. "Seven minutes, Harry. I'll come aboard with Nobli and we'll see if we can figure this out."

"Aye, sir," replied Samkange. "We'll roll out the red carpet."

"That's not necessary, Captain, but I appreciate the thought." With that Clement signed off and signaled to Adebayor to keep the line open between the ships, all the way to their rendezvous. He called down to Engineering one more time, seeking Nobli.

"Hassan, get your slide rule ready. We're going to board the *Corvallis*, and we're going to need some serious math work from you." Nobli acknowledged his call, and Clement shut down the line, thankful they had found their missing comrades, but worried about how they would get them safely to their new home.

Regardless of his orders, Captain Samkange did roll out the red carpet for Clement and his party. He came aboard to a Five Suns Navy anthem and a tribute squad, fit for a Fleet Admiral, but Clement quickly shut them down and got down to business. "I'd like to introduce my engineer, Hassan Nobli, and our shuttle pilot here is Lieutenant Tsu."

"A pleasure," said Samkange as he shook each of their hands.

"Now, let's go to your conference room."

"Aye, sir."

The conference room was two decks up from the shuttle bay. Though this Five Suns destroyer was a veteran of the Rim Confederation War, she had been updated to the latest systems per Clement's orders. He was glad he'd issued those orders now.

Samkange brought up a display screen at the far end of the room that showed the formation of his pod of ships. He introduced his chief engineer, a woman named Tyla Brown. They all shook hands before sitting down at the table. Clement nodded Tsu to one of the many chairs circling the back wall of the room before he started in.

"So, we have a problem, ladies and gentlemen. The

LEAP drive, in a complication previously unknown to us, has both a space and *time* displacement ability. We've been lucky this time, but if the problem was more extreme, we could have lost all of you. We need to isolate the problem and come up with a working solution. If we can't, I'm prepared to have this pod proceed back to Trinity on thrusters all the way, even if it does take four weeks. We can't risk losing you, any of you, so for now we have to assume the LEAP drive is off the table until we can determine that it is one hundred percent safe for both the Navy ships and our migrants. Understood?"

There was a round of *yes sirs* and then Clement passed the meeting off to Nobli. He began with a series of questions for the *Corvallis'* engineer, and he seemed satisfied with the answers, at least initially. After a few minutes, though, Clement got impatient.

"I need to know the consensus, right now. Can this flotilla return to Trinity under the LEAP drive, with a certainty of safety?" He looked to Nobli for his answer.

"Nothing can be verified with certainty, Admiral, especially when dealing with a new faster-than-light technology. But I'm convinced we can solve this puzzle, at least for the moment, and guide this pod to the Trinity system."

"And how will we do that, Hassan?" asked Clement. Nobli looked to Engineer Brown, who cleared her throat before speaking.

"From our brief exchanges here, Admiral, I believe the answer lies somewhere in the reactor energy output. I noticed a larger than expected output of both proton and electron particles from the reactor, but there was no indication it would have any effect on our final destination, either in space or time. I believe Engineer Nobli and I can work back from the reactor telemetry, and perhaps find our culprit," said Brown.

Clement looked to Nobli.

"I concur, sir. I'm hopeful we can work out a reactor formula that will allow us to isolate and even resolve the problem."

"Good. Please do so, unless you have some objection, Captain?" said Clement to Samkange.

"None I can think of, sir."

"All right, I'm empowering the two of you to fix this. If there's anything you need, just ask."

"I'd like Tech Reck to come over from the *Beauregard*, sir," said Nobli immediately.

Clement sat back in his chair, uncomfortable with that request. "I'd like to keep at least one engineer, even a tech, on board my ship for the duration, Nobli. Can't you communicate via com?"

Nobli nodded. "We can, sir, but she's pretty handy with a hammer."

"I've seen that," commented Clement, smiling. "Tell you what, I'll let you borrow Mr. Tsu over there. Didn't he used to work with you on the reactor?"

Nobli looked at Tsu. "He did, sir, on our last mission. I guess you'll have to do, Lieutenant." Tsu nodded and then the meeting broke up, Clement setting his people to their task while he and Lubrov headed with Samkange and his XO to the officer's mess, there to wait out their miracle workers.

❁   ❁   ❁

The officer's mess cleared out pretty quickly when the captain and the admiral walked in. Not unexpected behavior, as no one wanted to be around if "volunteers" for dangerous work were required. Once they were alone, Samkange started in with a question.

"I'm curious about something, Admiral."

"Ask away," said Clement, taking a sip of his tea.

"You told Nobli he could have anything he needed, then you denied him his first request, I was wondering why?"

"Pretty much just as I stated. Under these circumstances I need at least one engineer on my ship, even a tech. Nobli has become increasingly reliant on this Tech Reck, who quite frankly is brilliant from what he tells me, but she's a bit of a wild card."

"You think he's been relying on her too much?"

Clement took another sip of his tea. "I wouldn't say that, but I'd like him to work with your chief engineer on this one. Nobli does some of his best theoretical work when he's left to himself, and I wanted to get him back to that kind of thinking by taking him out of his element and not relying on someone familiar as a crutch. Let's just say it's an exercise in personnel management."

"I'll keep that in mind," replied Samkange.

Clement liked the young captain, a lot, and he wanted to do what he could to mold him into the kind of officer that could one day ascend to a higher position in the fleet, maybe all the way to the top.

The two men made small talk for almost ninety minutes before Clement grew impatient and called down to Nobli. The two engineers hadn't worked out a solution yet, and apparently Tech Reck was a bit chapped at being left on board the *Beauregard*, but Clement couldn't take her feelings into consideration. He reiterated that everyone had their job assignments, and they should get to them and find a solution.

As the afternoon stretched on into evening, Samkange gave Clement a tour of the refitted destroyer. The *Corvallis* was almost state of the art, and had become more of a missile destroyer than an all-around ship-of-the-line. Clement was impressed with the retooling job, which he'd never really had a chance to review properly or in detail prior to their departure from Kemmerine.

They had just sat down to dinner when Nobli chimed in from the reactor room.

"I think we've got it, sir," he said.

"Please inform me, Mr. Nobli," replied Clement.

"Well, sir, we've detected a quantum time-distortion side effect, something that could have easily gone unnoticed in our previous tests of the LEAP drive. It was really engineer Brown who detected it, sir. She ran the calculations and figured out that it's a quantum energy flow problem. Basically, all of our ships have to be on the same reactor settings, the same energy output frequency if you will, if we want them all to stay on the same time scale. Now, from the simulations I've run based on her calculations, any ships in the pod will end up converting their reactor flow energy output to the same frequency as the ship expressing the primary LEAP bubble. So literally all the other ships were linked to the *Corvallis* by her reactor frequency, and it was the *Corvallis* whose energy output was off. So the *Corvallis* being off of her optimal frequency caused a cumulative effect that effectively distorted time, so they ended up overshooting our target rendezvous point, both in space and time."

"That all sounds great, Hassan," said Clement somewhat sarcastically. "I'm not sure what any of it means, but is it safe for me to assume you have a solution?"

"Aye, sir, we do. Basically we have to make sure all the ships in a single pod have their reactors turned off so that every ship is tuned to the same energy output of the ship providing the primary LEAP bubble. Everyone should then be synced to the same space-time clock."

"So the amount of energy that was being poured out by the *Corvallis* distorted not only space but time as well?" asked Clement.

"Exactly, sir. We have to keep all our reactor frequencies within a limited range to keep them all on the same time schedule, sir. I would suggest that we link all the reactors to the *Beauregard*'s frequency and that we provide the primary bubble for the trip back to Trinity."

"I'll take that recommendation, Hassan. I'll have you coordinate with Captain Samkange here on the *Corvallis*. How long until you estimate that we can get the fleet restarted on our journey?"

"I'll ask for a couple more hours, sir, until Engineer Brown and I can work out the exact calculations that we want to run."

"Very good, Engineer. I'll leave you two to it. Send Lieutenant Tsu on up. I'll be heading back to the *Beauregard* presently. We'll set a tentative schedule of four hours from my departure for the return trip to Trinity. Is that enough time?"

"It should be, sir."

"Thank you, Nobli."

"Just doing my job, sir."

"Of course." Clement closed the com and looked across the table to Samkange. "It looks like we've solved our problem."

"It does, Admiral. You'll be returning to the *Beauregard*?"

"No reason for me to be here any longer at this point, Captain. I appreciate your hospitality. before I go, though, there is one more question I'd like to ask you. We found the pod because someone put some sort of beacon into the quantum fluid. It acted as a 'postmark' of sorts for where the pod's location was. I just want to know if it was some genius in your fleet that came up with that idea."

Samkange shook his head. "I'm sure it wasn't anyone from the pod, sir. We were all busy just trying to figure out where we were and what had happened. If someone left a 'beacon,' as you call it, in the quantum fluid, then I'm sure I have no idea who it was."

"Thank you, Captain, I had to ask. I'll be taking *Beauregard* back out to try and retrieve the beacon so we can get a look at the technology. If you could watch over the pod for the next four hours I'd appreciate it."

"Of course, Admiral."

At that point Clement stood and shook Samkange's hand, then made for his shuttle, there to go back to his ship and set about retrieving the mysterious beacon.

Once he was back aboard the *Beauregard*, Clement sent the shuttle and Lieutenant Tsu back to the *Corvallis* to be ready when Nobli was done with his reactor tweaking. In the meantime, whoever had left that beacon in the LEAP space quantum fluid was still a mystery he wanted to solve. He ordered Lieutenant Adebayor to use the infrared telescope to look for the beacon's heat signature. When she was unable to locate it, which was concerning, he ordered Mika Ori to take the ship back into LEAP space on a direct course for the last known location of the beacon.

However, when they arrived at the designated coordinates they were in for an unpleasant surprise. The beacon was nowhere to be found.

"Any signs of who might have taken it?" Clement asked Lubrov, his concern over the beacon mystery growing. "I mean, this thing has just appeared and then disappeared without a trace. Please tell me you have something to report?"

Lubrov looked at her console readouts and checked out multiple telemetry returns before giving her answer. "Nothing more than a dispersed wave of protons, sir. The trail isn't thick enough to determine a general direction, or even the size of the vessel that might have retrieved it. The best I can guess from this data, or should I say lack of data, is that the thing must have been self-propelled in some way, quite possibly automated. Our passing near it could possibly have triggered its programming to return to its original point of origin, whatever that is."

"I think that's even a more disturbing prospect than finding it in the first place. This is clearly not technology anyone in our fleet possesses. So the question becomes, whose is it? And why did they help us find our missing people and ships?"

"Maybe they're just friendly neighbors," said Mika Ori from her helm station.

"Someone we haven't met yet?" contemplated Clement. "That seems implausible, but if that isn't the answer then I'm getting more concerned over who it might actually be."

"Earth-ship fleet?" asked Ori.

"My first thought was that it might be Admiral DeVore," said Lubrov.

Clement took in a deep breath at that notion. "That's a possibility I hadn't wanted to consider. I did my best to make sure when I left them on Alphus that she and her crews had very little technology to work with. But if I know her as well as I think I do, she always had a backup plan, not to mention a backup for the backup. I wouldn't put it past her to have set up safeguards in case her first invasion of Trinity failed. As to why she'd leave us a beacon to help us find our people, her enemies, I don't know why she'd do that. It's certainly a question that merits further investigation at this point." Clement turned to Adebayor. "Kayla, please activate the long wave and get me Captain Yan on the *Agamemnon*."

"Sir," responded Adebayor. Less than a minute later Yan was on the line. Clement shared the latest about recovering the missing pod of ships, then turned to the problem at hand.

"What's your status, Yan?"

"We're all comfortably in orbit around Bellus, sir, waiting on your orders to go down to the surface.

Everyone is anxious to be there and get started colonizing. I'll need your go-ahead to start that process, though, sir," replied Yan over the scratchy quantum com line.

"It's given. Please proceed as soon as you're ready, Captain. There is one other thing I need you to do for me."

"Of course, Admiral."

"Send one of the gunships to Alphus. I want them to do a survey on the status of the exiles and their camps and provide me with an update as soon as possible."

"Understood, sir. I can spare the *Antietam* without too much problem. It will probably take them the better part of a day to go there and back."

"That's fine, Captain. This is of the highest importance."

"Understood, sir," said Yan, then hesitated a second. "Um, should I put the Bellus fleet on high alert?"

"No. Alert status two, please. No need to scare the migrants. Just proceed as you normally would, but I want all military ships on standby alert. And have the *Antietam* report directly to me once they get to Alphus."

"Understood, sir. What's your ETA to Trinity?"

"Well, we seem to have solved our time/space displacement problem, at least for the moment. We will be heading back your way under LEAP power in a little more than three hours. That should put us back at the rendezvous point about nine hours from now."

"Acknowledged, sir. It will be good to have you back."

"I'm sure we'll all be happy to be back, Yan." At that point they said their pleasantries and Clement signed off, ordering the *Beauregard* back to return to the *Corvallis* pod.

☆ 10 ☆

Once they were inside Trinity space again, Clement called down to Nobli and congratulated him on resolving the time/space distortion problem. The *Beauregard* led the *Corvallis* pod back into Trinity space and then on toward Bellus on full thrusters, a trip that would take seven more hours because of the low maximum speed of the transport ships. Clement was relaxing in his cabin when he got a buzz at his door.

"Come in," he said casually, looking up from the book he was reading. Colonel Marina Lubrov came through the door.

"*Moby Dick*?" she asked, glancing at his book.

Clement shook his head. "One of the Sharpe's series from twentieth-century Earth by Bernard Cornwell. It's about a rifle company commander fighting wars for the British empire in Napoleonic era Europe. It's been adapted to digital dramas several times, but I prefer the books. I guess I like to get away inside my own mind, interpret things the way I see them, not what some video director decided it should look like."

"I guess that's why people still read," she said, "to get

away from the constant one-way information flow that's constantly being poured into our minds these days."

"Technology has its drawbacks. It makes our lives more convenient, but does it really stimulate our minds, or are we just receptors for the information that all of our technology puts out? That might be a reason people want to migrate to Trinity. A simpler life."

"Interesting question, but something likely we should contemplate on another day," she said, then took a step closer to Clement. "Sir, Lieutenant Adebayor has been getting a signal from the *Antietam* for the last ten minutes. She's been having trouble trying to lock down the link so that they can report. I thought you'd like to be part of that process and hear the report firsthand."

"Of course," said Clement, and promptly shut the book without leaving a bookmark or folding the page. He got up and set the book down on his table.

They both headed out of his cabin then up the four open metal stairs to the bridge of the *Beauregard*. Clement took his place in the command couch and swung his control console into place. "Report, Kayla," he said.

The young African woman responded quickly. "Trying to establish the link with the *Antietam* now, sir. I've been at this for about twelve minutes. It almost seems like communicating inside the Trinity system is more difficult than it is communicating across light-years with the quantum tether."

"Well, the first thing we'll have to do is ask the Five Suns government for a communications network upgrade. But I need that link, Kayla, as soon as possible."

"Aye, sir." She worked for a few more moments then

signaled to the admiral with a thumbs-up. "Putting you on with captain Kagereki of the *Antietam* now, sir."

"On the bridge com, please, Lieutenant." They all listened then as the scratchy voice of the *Antietam's* captain came over the line.

"Admiral, this is Captain James Kagereki of the *Antietam*. I wanted to report to you as soon as possible, sir."

"Understood, Captain. Please proceed."

"Sir," said Kagereki, "I don't know quite how to say this, sir." The man was a young captain, and Clement recalled meeting him once before the fleet's departure from Kemmerine Station.

"Just proceed with your report, Captain, no need to be nervous. We don't kill the messenger in this fleet." Clement couldn't help but feel apprehensive now.

"Yes, sir." Kagereki's voice was still hesitant. Clement heard him take a deep breath before continuing. "Sir, I have to report that there is no one on Alphus. I mean that . . . there are natives, sir, but none of the Five Suns crew loyal to Admiral DeVore that we left behind in the camps are on the planet, as far as I can determine."

This was not good news to Clement. "Back up a minute, Captain. Tell me what your scans have found."

Kagereki hesitated a second again. "As I said, Admiral, there are just natives on the planet. All of the camps that you established before you left Trinity have been abandoned. There's no one there, sir, and it looks like that's been the case for a while, perhaps as long as six months. We've run deep scans. We've looked in the hills, even scanned under the ground up to half a kilometer.

There's just no sign of them, sir." Kagereki was now obviously upset at having to report this sort of news. Clement tried to calm him down.

"Captain," said Clement evenly, "James, is that what your friends call you?"

"Most call me Jim, sir."

"Okay then, Jim. We left almost thirty-three hundred people on the surface of Alphus. Are you reporting to me that none of them are there anymore?"

"Yes, sir. That's what I'm reporting. We cannot locate or identify that any one of them is still on the planet."

"Have you looked to see if perhaps they've integrated themselves into the local native populations to avoid detection? They've had plenty of time to migrate if they wanted to." Clement was now regretting not sending more probes to check in on the prisoners left behind from the Five Suns defeated fleet.

"We considered that possibility, Admiral, but from what we can find they haven't mixed in with the natives. There's no evidence of them moving from the camps to the native settlements, as far as we can tell, sir. It's like someone just came in and scooped them up off the planet."

"I'd like to see this for myself, Captain, but I'm still several hours out from you. Please get your ship out of there as fast as possible and rendezvous with the rest of Captain Yan's fleet over Bellus. Is that understood?"

"Understood, sir," replied Kagereki. "We're getting underway now."

"Thank you, Captain." Clement cut the com line and then looked to Adebayor again. "Raise Captain Yan on the *Agamemnon* immediately," he said.

"Sir," replied Adebayor.

Clement looked to Lubrov, who raised an eyebrow in curiosity. "It seems as though we may have a military situation here, Admiral, as you suspected."

"I would be remiss in my duties if I hadn't planned for this possibility. One thing we do have for sure, Colonel, is a mystery. Thirty-three hundred missing enemy prisoners to be exact." He turned to his pilot. "Mika, can you get us in-system any faster?"

"Of course, sir. The *Beauregard* can go much faster than the transports. From here I can have you to Bellus in fifty-six minutes, sir."

"Do it, Mika," he said emphatically.

Adebayor presently got Captain Yan on the line, and Clement motioned for Lubrov to follow him to his cabin. Once there they sat down at his worktable and he activated the room's com system.

"We have a situation, Yan," said Clement. "It appears that DeVore and her entire crew have been 'rescued' from the surface of Alphus, though when or how we don't know."

"That is not good news, sir," said Yan formally.

"No, I agree with you, not at all. We have to assume that she and her loyalists remain hostile to us and our migrants, not to mention the natives. Put the fleet on high alert. Mika says she can have me back aboard *Agamemnon* in a little less than an hour. I'm ordering you to hold the line there, Captain. Disperse your fleet. Prepare for a military strike at any moment. I'll be taking command of the fleet as soon as I can get back on your bridge."

"Understood, sir. Any idea how she could have managed this?"

"None whatsoever, Captain, but I doubt she could have pulled it off without help," said Clement, all business. "There is the unsolved mystery of the quantum-fluid beacon. That's not a technology we have but I would venture to guess that whoever is behind that technology probably has something to do with the disappearance of Admiral DeVore and her crews."

"Shall I suspend the migrant landings, sir?"

"Yes, effective immediately, until I can get back there and get a handle on the tactical situation, if any. But do it without alarming anyone. Tell them you have a maintenance issue on the transports, for now. Get anything in the air carrying settlers on the ground and tell any ships coming up your way to go back down. Take no chances, Yan."

"Of course, sir. There's just one transport in transit to the surface at the moment. She should be on the ground in the next half hour."

"Good. Once she's down get the migrants out of the transport and into the modular home units on the surface. A transport ship would make a huge target, even from space." Yan acknowledged and then signed off. Clement looked across the table at Colonel Lubrov. "Inform Captain Samkange that he's now in charge of getting this pod into a safe orbit around Bellus. Best possible speed . . ."

"Understood, sir," said Lubrov, then she stood quickly and left for the bridge.

Clement sat staring at the tabletop, his fingers nervously drumming a beat on the wood.

❂　❂　❂

Clement took command of the entire fleet the moment he entered the CAC on board *Agamemnon*. Yan looked relieved to see him; less so to see Lubrov as she took her station. After receiving initial reports, Clement was satisfied that the situation was stable, at least for the moment. He started in.

"The problem is that we know they're out there somewhere, and they must know that we're here. And someone left that beacon for us to find our lost pod, and we have no idea who it was. That's obviously a concern. Bring the fleet back down from high alert to standby alert," he said to Yan. "Colonel Lubrov, it's time to activate your Marines. I want them deployed on every migrant ship that goes down to the surface and I want units on this ship and all of the cruisers in case this becomes a hand-to-hand battle."

"Is that what you're expecting, sir?" asked Lubrov.

"I expect nothing but plan for everything, Colonel. We have to prepare for the worst-case scenario, Colonel. Your Marines could make the difference, all twelve hundred of them."

"What kind of attack are you expecting?" asked Yan.

Clement shook his head. "I'm not sure, but that Earth Ark came here on the first Trinity mission to establish a military base. Fleet Admiral DeVore's plan was to let the Earth forces build that base and then take it away from them. I have to assume her basic plans haven't changed. She wanted to conquer this system and set up her own little empire. I would expect any attack to be something on the scale of the previous one, or larger. She knows we have the MAD weapon, and she has nothing that we know of that can counter that."

"Understood, sir."

Clement turned his attention to Lubrov. "Marina, I'm going to assume you have a plan for deploying your Marines?"

"I do, sir."

"Then get to it. There's no time to waste."

"Aye, sir," said Lubrov as she walked away from the command platform.

Clement and Yan got down to developing a tactical defense plan. Clement pulled down all the floating displays so that the console desktop was the only place they could interact. That way their plans were out of the vision of the rest of the crew and they couldn't see what the two flag officers were doing. That was how rumors got started, Clement knew, and rumors could be the downfall of any ship, any fleet, or any plan.

"We have nine settlements to defend, Admiral," stated Yan.

"That was our original plan," said Clement, "but I didn't expect we might be defending against another invasion force. Those nine settlements will be too spread out, requiring cover from both the sky and troops on the ground. That's a breakdown of only about one hundred thirty Marines for every settlement. I don't consider that to be an effective fighting force, especially if they invade with ground forces like last time. We have to consolidate the settlements to make them easier to defend, and I want to stay away from the natives as much as we can. Let's get these colonists off their transports and onto the surface, then get them dug in. I'm going to need you to consolidate our people into three camps. Try to use as much of the

natural topography to defend the camps as well as we can.
I want you to pick the three best defensive locations and
then get everybody off the ships and down there as
quickly as we can."

Yan looked at the map on the tabletop. "I can already
tell you one of the best places will be near the original
settlement where we encountered Mary and her friends
on our first trip. The other two should be fairly close by
so that they can provide reinforcement or support to any
of the other camps. Either way there aren't going to be
enough living modules to accommodate everybody. The
ones that we placed here over the last year were based on
the original nine-settlements plan."

"I understand that. People are going to have to double
up and maybe triple up. Families are going to have to share
spaces. Our first priority is going to be getting all of our
people on the ground and into some kind of shelter. After
that it's going to be up to the Marines to build any ground-
based defenses. As for the fleet, we're going to have to
keep active and cover a lot of space. Always remember that
the migrants' and the natives' safety is our number one
priority, and they are equal in my mind. The last thing I
want to do is to surrender our new colony to hostile forces
and have them turn all of our people into slaves."

They were interrupted in the next moment buy an
alarm from Kayla Adebayor's station.

"Report, Lieutenant," demanded Clement.

"Sir, I'm picking up a distress call from the *Antietam*.
She's halfway home from Alphus but she's reporting some
kind of unknown vessel actively pursuing her on an
intercept course," said Adebayor.

"How far away is she?"

Mika Ori responded from her station. "She's still about three million kilometers out, sir. Almost four hours at maximum thrusters."

"Four hours for the *Agamemnon* or four hours for the *Beauregard*?" said Clement.

"Obviously, sir, I was reporting on our best speed here on the *Agamemnon*. The *Beauregard* could make it in twenty minutes if we use the LEAP reactor on a low-yield setting, sir."

"Why a low-yield setting?" he asked.

"We would likely overshoot the battlefield by a considerable margin if we used the LEAP drive on full, sir."

"I see." Clement activated his com link to the reactor room. Hassan Nobli, who was now back on board, responded quickly. "How can I help you, Admiral?"

"Is the *Beauregard* still warm, Hassan?"

"She's hardly had time to cool down, Admiral. Why do you ask?"

"I need you to fire her back up, right now."

"Of course, sir. Why?"

"*Antietam* is under attack, Hassan. We're going to have to go and rescue her."

"I'll get down to the landing deck myself and fire her up right away, sir."

"No," said Clement, his voice clear and firm in resolve.

"I don't understand, sir," said Nobli.

"I'd love to have the luxury of taking you along on this one, Hassan, but the fact is I need you here to protect the fleet and work with Yan here on whatever preparations we need to make to defend Bellus and the whole Trinity system. If you can spare your Tech Reck and you trust her to run my reactor, then I'll have her instead. But she has to follow my orders to a T, with no back talk like she does with you. This could be a critical turning point, and I want you safe with the fleet while I'm the one taking the unfortunate but necessary risks."

"With apologies, sir," cut in Yan, "but you're not expendable. I am, or perhaps Captain Samkange, but not you."

"Neither of you have any experience commanding in battle, Captain, but I do. This is my call and my responsibility. I'm going. You've already proven that this fleet can survive without its main figurehead, but I'm not sure it can survive without battle-tested captains."

"Those captains can't ever get that experience if you fight every battle yourself, Admiral."

"Your objections are noted, Captain, but my orders stand," he snapped. He looked up from the console table and activated the CAC com system. "Commanders Ori and Massif, report to the *Beauregard* immediately. Pass off your stations to your seconds. Lieutenant Adebayor, I'll be needing your services again, and please call down to Lieutenants Telco and Tsu and have them report as well. Tell them to bring the heaviest small arms they can carry on board the *Beauregard*. That's an order. Admiral Clement out." With that he hung up the com and turned back to Yan. "Bring the fleet back to high alert. Get me enough techs to run my ship and get them down to the landing bay fast. I'd prefer fresh faces over the ones who just got off of the rescue mission. And raise one of the

destroyers and send them after the *Beauregard* on the
same course. We may need more firepower than we think
for this situation."

"More firepower than the MAD weapon?" said Yan
quietly.

Clement gave her an angry look. "Personally, Captain,
I hope we never have to use that thing again. But when it
comes to this fleet and this mission I will use every
weapon in my power if I have to. Just pick a destroyer to
follow us, I don't care which one. And get those colonists
reorganized into the three defensive camps."

"Aye, sir," replied Yan. At that Clement turned and
walked quickly away.

Once they were spaceborne again and pulling away
from both the fleet and Bellus on full thrusters, the
admiral once again addressed his crew over the ship-
wide com. "I know none of you planned to go back out
this quickly, but the situation demands it. Our sister ship
is being pursued by an unknown enemy, and we need to
help her in any way we can. I know you're all tired from
the rescue mission; I am too. But I'm asking you to reach
down inside and find me that something extra I know
you all possess. End of inspirational speech," he said,
then sat back down in the *Beauregard*'s command couch.
"Kayla," he said to Adebayor, "raise the *Antietam*. I need
to know what's going on with them. Mika, you'll be acting
as my XO on this mission as I can't spare Yan or Lubrov.
That means I need not only your best skills in the pilot
seat, but also your opinions about the actions that I take.
I know we've worked together for a long time, but please

put any personal feelings aside, and let me know what you think about the actions I'm proposing. Are we clear?"

"We are, sir," replied Ori. "You know I've never wanted anything more than to pilot a good ship, but I can do this for you on this mission."

"Thank you, Mika. Ivan, set our course for the last known coordinates of the *Antietam* and let's get there as fast as we can." With that the admiral gave a wave of the hand and sat back in his chair, letting his people do their work. He flipped on the com down to the reactor room. "Tech Reck, please report on my reactor."

"She's warm and ready as a school girl on a Saturday night, sir," said Reck in her rough, husky voice. "I'll have us moving as soon as the pilot gives me the go signal," she said. Clement looked to Ori, who gave him a thumbs-up.

"Fire the reactor please, Tech. Low yield."

"Low yield, aye, sir." With that the *Beauregard* slipped once again into the quantum fluid of LEAP space, on her way to rescue her sister ship. Clement shut down the direct com to the reactor room and inserted his private earpiece to have a private conversation with the tech.

"Tech Reck, I assume you're familiar with the MAD weapon and its specs?"

"I am, sir."

"Have it ready by the time we reach the *Antietam's* coordinates. I expect to see a green light on my app board long before we drop back into normal space. Understood?"

"Understood, sir," replied Reck.

And with that Clement cut the line and sat back in his couch, waiting impatiently to arrive at the battlefield.

When they dropped out of the LEAP quantum fluid and back into normal space again, the *Antietam* was in deep trouble. Adebayor had been unable to raise them during the LEAP transition, and, frankly, Clement was glad to see that the ship was still in one piece. She was being pursued, though, by not one, but two unidentified ships.

"Raise the *Antietam*, Kayla, now!" said Clement, rising from his couch and hitting his com to the weapons room. "Lieutenant Telco, are my missiles and torpedoes ready?"

"Yes, sir," replied Telco, "six conventional missiles at your disposal immediately. Mr. Tsu has antimissile torpedoes ready to be loaded into all six launch tubes, sir."

"Good job, Telco, but take two of the torpedoes out of the racks and replace them with ten kiloton warheads. I want my nukes ready if I need them."

"Sir!"

Clement shut off the com and turned to Adebayor. "Can you raise them, Lieutenant?"

She shook her head. "No, sir. It seems like their com links have been burned out. She appears to have taken a lot of fire."

He turned to Ori. "Tactical status, XO?"

"I detect two unknowns in pursuit of the *Antietam*, sir. She's outrunning them for now, but she's taken several DEW hits on her hull. She's steadily taking damage while they chase her. They're trying to wear her down from what I can tell."

"Like hyenas hunting a lioness. Time to tilt the

battlefield a bit more in her favor. Displacement of the unknowns, are they the same as the Earth Ark ships from the last battle?"

"Similar, sir. I'd say they were an evolutionary upgrade from the ships we fought the last time at Trinity."

"Manned?"

She shook her head. "No, sir. Hunter-killers by design, sir."

"Suicide machines. They can use one hundred percent of their energy to kill an opponent. The kind of weapon that should be outlawed." Clement sat back down in his chair. "Time until we're in missile range of the HuKs?"

"Seven minutes at one g sir."

"Authorizing 3.5 g burn, Commander."

"That will cut the time to firing range in half."

"Do it."

"Aye, sir." They were all pushed back in their chairs as Ori accelerated the ship for a one-minute, thirty-second burst. They were coming in hard now on the two HuKs, who were less than a kilometer from the *Antietam*.

"Do you think we could take them both out with a nuke?" Clement asked Ori.

"Not without damaging the *Antietam*, sir. She's too close."

"Conventional missiles then. We'll fire straight across the line of fire of those HuKs. We'll probably get one, but if we're lucky and they fire their DEWs we might get both with an accidental detonation." Clement checked his board. All of his weapons systems were green.

"Ready, sir," Ori said, her hand hovering over the firing icon.

Clement watched the tactical screen, his ship bearing down on the two enemies at a ninety-degree angle to their pursuit course. He waited on the timing, calculating their speed relative to the *Beauregard*. "From my mark... three... two... one... fire!" demanded Clement.

Ori fired. Clement watched as the tactical display showed his missiles tracking the HuKs. It was like trying to hit a bullet with a bullet. It wasn't impossible, but the odds of success were small. The missiles both flared to life as they reached optimum detonation range of the HuKs. They lit up with a flash of explosive force, but neither hit their targets.

"Both HuKs have had to change their courses, sir. We missed them, but we bought the *Antietam* some time," reported Ori.

"Good. Now if only Captain Kagereki can take advantage—"

"*Antietam* is diving back toward the gravity well of Alphus, sir."

"Excellent! Get us turned back toward the HuKs, Mika. I want to come at them head-on if we can."

Ori looked up at the tactical screen. "That will take some time, sir."

"How long? We just bought *Antietam* some time, right?"

"She has a nine-minute lead now, sir, but it will take us eleven to get back into position for the kind of attack run you want."

Clement looked down at his board and did some quick calculations, then hit the ship-wide com. "Seven-minute burn at five gs coming up. Secure your stations," was all he said, then he leaned heavily into his acceleration couch. "Five gs, Mika. Now."

"Aye, sir." She hit the plasma drive and then they were all pushed back into their couches, straining against the oppressive gravity of the burn.

It was agony.

The crew took all they could handle with a seven-minute burn. When they were finally out of it Clement had to catch his breath. Taking those kinds of gravity forces wasn't getting any easier for him, nor any of the rest of the crew he guessed.

"Distance, Navigator," he said.

"130,000 kilometers from the HuKs," reported Massif. "At the speed we're closing we'll be on them in two minutes."

"Mika, will we be able to get between the HuKs and the *Antietam*?"

"I believe so, sir, but at this speed I don't think missiles are an option."

"The forward coil cannon then? Kinetic rounds?"

"You could leave scattershot in our wake," she said, "but it's impossible to know if we'll be able to spread them wide enough to make contact with the HuKs. Plus, they likely have limited tactical AI, and can change course to avoid our trap."

"Not if we give them no time to react."

"At these speeds, releasing at anything less than three hundred kilometers distance would be a good bet at success. They likely couldn't change course that quickly. But that would require precision flying, keeping to our ecliptic plane, and keeping them to theirs to guarantee a hit. Plus, the timing of the release would have to be perfect."

"Hence why I hired you, Commander," deadpanned Clement. He called down to the weapons room and ordered Telco and Tsu to load up two missile tubes with the scattershot. When they signaled they were ready, Clement released the firing solution to Ori. He watched on the tactical display as the *Antietam* continued her run back toward the gravity well of Alphus, hoping to get a slingshot around the small planet and perhaps make her escape. Clement's job was to keep those HuKs occupied long enough for her to do so. *Antietam's* Captain Kagereki was impressing him with his tactics and his ability to improvise since the *Beauregard's* arrival on the battlefield. Without direct communication from the admiral, Kagereki was exhibiting a strong tactical bent. "We have to try and give the *Antietam* a chance to slingshot around Alphus and escape if I'm reading her captain's intent correctly. So ordered, Commander."

"Aye, sir," said Ori. With that he started the deceleration burn and the *Beauregard* began to come in line with the HuKs' path. They wouldn't cross their line at exactly ninety degrees, but it would be close enough if they could drop the scattershot, which consisted of four-inch stainless steel spheres usually used as kinetic material in scatter mines, along their path. It was a risky play at the speeds they were traveling, but with a little luck it might bear some fruit.

Ori counted down to the release of the scattershot. Clement ordered the release and the metal balls spread

out from the *Beauregard*'s missile tubes. They had precious
few seconds and were precious few kilometers in front of
the HuKs when they made the drop. The scattershot only
had fractions of a second to disperse into the HuKs' paths
before they crossed in pursuit of the *Antietam*. The lead
HuK lit up with small kinetic explosions on her dorsal
surface. It was enough to force her to change course, but
not widespread enough to destroy her. The second HuK
was trailing slightly further back and was able to avoid the
field of debris with a quick burst of her maneuvering
thrusters. The first HuK started to swing off course and
away from the *Antietam*. The second was able to quickly
regain its bearing on the Five Suns gunship and eagerly
continued its pursuit. The two suicide machines had now
changed their positions, leading and trailing.

Clement eyed his new tactical board. The *Antietam*
was continuing her dive toward the nightside of Alphus.
The damaged HuK was trying to decelerate and get back
on track toward the Five Suns gunship. The second, which
was now the leading threat to *Antietam*, was back on the
hunt and closing the gap once again. Both were essentially
ignoring the *Beauregard*, which was still decelerating
away from the battlefield and out of position to help her
sister ship.

"If we do one more deceleration loop, can we face
them head on?" asked Clement of Ori.

"It's a fifty-fifty chance I can make that maneuver from
our current course and speed," said Ori.

"Fifty-fifty or not I think we have to go for it."

"Aye, sir," said Ori. She fed the necessary actions into
her helm console. "Ready, sir."

Clement hit the com. "Three-g deceleration burn for fifty seconds incoming on my mark, three . . . two . . . one . . ." The sudden burn knocked the wind out of him and he struggled to breathe while his ship groaned against the stresses of such an extreme deceleration. At that moment, he regretted that he had never installed the Five Suns Navy's inertial-damping field technology on his ships. That now appeared to be a major mistake. He had seen the technology in use during the War of the Five Suns nearly two decades ago now, but most of that tech had been destroyed in the first battle of Trinity. It had always been an option to include in his refurbished fleet, but with the exception of *Agamemnon* these were all old vessels and retrofitting the tech had not been deemed worth the expense.

When the gravity forces from the burn finally relented, Clement took in a deep breath and exhaled. "Tactical situation, XO," he demanded.

"The leading HuK is pursuing *Antietam*, but it's now four minutes from firing range. We have that trailing HuK in our sights. I'll have a firing solution for you on that in two minutes, sir," she said.

Clement hit the com to the missile room. "Lieutenant Telco, load one of my two-kiloton nukes. I want it ready in ninety seconds."

"Sir!" replied Telco. Clement smiled slightly at the young man's enthusiasm. Things finally seemed to be going their way for once. They just had to take out the trailing HuK, then close on the leader . . .

"Sir," said Adebayor, a warning in her voice. "Infrared telescope has a new sighting, rising from the surface of

Alphus on an intercept course with *Antietam*. She'll be in firing range in six minutes, sir."

"From the dark side?"

"Yes, sir, coming from the dark side of Alphus. Same profile as the first two unknowns. It's another HuK, sir."

Clement got a sour feeling in the pit of his stomach, like he'd just swallowed a rock.

In a flash, the battlefield had tilted again.

"Do we break off pursuit of the trailing HuK, sir?" The question came from Mika Ori at the pilot's seat.

"Would another burn—"

"No, sir. We'd actually be in a worse position to aid the *Antietam* than if we just continued on our initial course."

Clement looked at his tactical display. They were now outmaneuvered and outflanked. The *Beauregard* could take out the trailing HuK, but the lead one would get into firing range on the *Antietam* before they could assist, and the third interceptor would likely be able to finish her off before the *Beauregard* could get to her.

"We need another option," declared Clement, to no one in particular. The bridge stayed silent. There were no other options, that was clear from the tactical display. The *Antietam* would have to fight for her life against two HuKs closing from opposite directions, and Clement would have to pray that he could get his ship into position to help her before she was destroyed. After half a minute of silence, Clement gave the only order he could. "Stay on course and plan, XO. Let's get that trailing HuK." He said it quietly and with resignation at the tactical situation in his voice.

"Sir," replied Ori.

Clement turned to Lieutenant Adebayor. "Kayla, send position and telemetry on that third HuK to the *Antietam*'s captain. Maybe they can at least receive our communications, even if they can't respond to us. We know that they know that we're here, but being deaf and blind is the most frustrating thing I can imagine." Adebayor sent the communication to *Antietam* but there was no response of any kind. Likely her captain was busy trying to figure out how to save his ship from destruction.

"We've got the trailing HuK in range, sir," reported Ori a few seconds later.

"Then let's do what we can, Commander. Ready on the missiles."

"Reminding the admiral that we currently have a nuke in the tube, sir."

"I remember," said Clement. "I want this thing completely destroyed."

"Understood, sir," replied Ori. The nuke seemed like overkill to her, but it would guarantee destruction of the HuK with minimal wasted energy. Her husband sent her the firing coordinates and she locked them in to her weapons console. "Ready to fire on your order, Admiral."

"Fire," ordered Clement with no hesitation.

The missile lanced out and closed quickly on the HuK. The suicide machine tried vainly to launch countermeasures, but once the nuclear-tipped missile got inside of its safe detonation range it exploded, the bright fire consuming both the missile and the HuK.

"Simple enough," said Clement out loud, "now comes

the hard part. Estimated time to be able to assist the *Antietam*, XO?"

"Eight minutes on maneuvering thrusters, Admiral."

"Time before the *Antietam* is within firing range of the enemy?"

"Seventy seconds for the lead HuK, two minutes fifty seconds on the interceptor."

"If we don't get our miracle soon . . ." Clement let his voice trail off.

"Admiral," came the excited voice of Lieutenant Adebayor. "Another ship just dropped out of LEAP space just ahead of us, sir."

"Ahead of us? Is it ours or theirs?"

"Unknown yet, sir, but by displacement it's at least a destroyer, maybe bigger. It's on an intercept course with the *Antietam*."

"Well if it's not ours, we're fucked," said Clement, no hint of humor in his voice. "Can we identify it?"

"Not yet, sir. It's on full thrusters and the heat signature is blinding our infrared telescope," said Adebayor.

"She's twenty seconds from the *Antietam*, sir," declared Ori.

"Navigator, plan us an escape path, and quick. If that unknown gets a bead on us . . ."

"Understood, sir," said Massif. And with that there was nothing to do for the crew of the *Beauregard* but to watch and wait. The MAD weapon was not an option as it would likely destroy everything on the battlefield, the good and the bad, as would any nukes. All they could do was watch and wait while the seconds ticked down.

As they all watched, the unknown began battering the

lead enemy HuK with their forward coil cannons, a barrage of orange energy weapons. The HuK disintegrated in seconds in a fury of yellow-gold fire. A second later and the tactical board picked up a volley of three missiles outward bound from the unknown and heading directly for the intercepting HuK rising from the dark side of Alphus. The missiles did their job quickly, dispatching the interceptor with three direct hits. At that, the unknown began to quickly decelerate, burning thrusters hard to escape tumbling into the gravity well of Alphus.

"I guess she's one of ours," declared Ori.

"Apparently," replied Clement.

"It's the *Corvallis*," reported Adebayor, more than a bit of excitement in her voice. Clement watched as the *Antietam* began putting on her breaks as well, pulling out of her deep dive toward Alphus.

"Send to all ships, rendezvous and form up with us. And send a well-done to Captain Samkange aboard *Corvallis*. Tell him the cavalry arrived just in time."

"Aye, sir!"

And with that Clement sat back in his couch, relieved.

☆ **11** ☆

Captain Samkange of the *Corvallis* was able to locate the automated HuK base on the dark-side surface of Alphus. Clement had briefly considered going down to the enemy base to see what they could acquire in terms of intelligence and technology, but decided against that tactic on the basis that the base could be booby-trapped. He ultimately ordered it destroyed with a nuke, and they made three more passes of the planet just to be sure it was clean of any other enemy installations.

They also took the time to scan Admiral DeVore's old encampments. They were indeed abandoned and dark, as Captain Kagereki of the *Antietam* had initially reported, and it looked like they had been that way for several months.

The return trip to Bellus was a good one for all concerned, taking nine hours using the ion plasma drive. Clement ordered his command crew to rest up while they could, using techs to run the *Beauregard*'s main systems while his principals rested. The admiral kept an eye on things remotely from his cabin, but still managed four and a half hours of sleep, which for him was a full sleep cycle.

When they arrived back with the fleet at Bellus, Clement honored Captains Samkange and Kagereki with Star of Valor awards for their actions at Alphus. Both ship captains had shown innovation and strategic initiative during the battle, which was something Clement hoped to promote within the fleet. After the awards ceremony aboard the *Agamemnon*, which was broadcast fleet-wide, it was time for a situational strategy meeting.

Yan reported that the consolidation of the settlements into the three main camps was eighty percent complete. They had been successful in moving many of the modular living units to the camps, which Yan had designated Camp Alpha, Camp Beta, and Camp Theta. Clement thought this might be confusing with the names of the other habitable Trinity worlds, but Yan convinced him that the familiarity would be helpful. Camp Alpha was the one closest to the original settlement that they had encountered on their first trip to Bellus, and it also happened to be the closest one to the "Hill Place" station, which was clearly artificial and beyond the skills of the natives to construct. Setting that discussion aside for the moment, Clement turned to Captain Samkange for an update on the fleet's strategic status.

"We are well positioned to protect the three camps from space," reported Samkange. "I have nearly equal forces of cruisers, destroyers, and the gunships protecting each camp. We are well stocked with munitions and supplies, our crews have been rotated, and we're ready for whatever might come next. All of the transports are on the ground, tucked away as much as we can from attacks from space. All of the migrants are now on the surface, as well as Colonel Lubrov's Marines."

"Thank you, Captain. Please keep the fleet on high alert. I think it's obvious by now that we can expect more trouble, probably sooner rather than later."

"Do you think it's possible the HuKs you fought at Alphus are remnants of DeVore's original fleet?" asked Yan.

"That seems unlikely," stated the admiral. "Those HuKs didn't resemble anything in the Five Suns fleet. In fact, they seemed much more like evolutionary variants of the HuKs we fought from the first Earth Ark in the last battle."

"*First* Earth Ark?" said Yan. "Are we expecting another?"

Clement let a grim look cross his face. "I would argue that the mere presence of those HuKs is all the proof we need that there are additional Earth forces in the Trinity system as we speak." There were concerned looks all around the table at that, and on the captains' faces that were piped into the meeting via visual telecom. "But just to reassure you all, I've got every ship in the fleet scanning the system. We should be able to detect anything bigger than a ground car heading our way. Hopefully, it won't come to it, but I have my doubts that we will get through this without more battles. That's why I'm so thankful that Captains Samkange and Kagereki were able to get some battle experience. I think we're all going to get the opportunity to engage in battle before this mission is up."

"That brings up the question of what our mission

actually is now, Admiral," said Yan. "Has this migration become a military mission?"

"I'm not sure I know what you mean, Captain," responded Clement, with some annoyance in his voice.

"I mean that our original mission was to come to Bellus, bringing thirty thousand migrants here and settle them safely on the planet. It doesn't seem like circumstances are going to allow that mission to be completed."

"We can't know the full scope of our mission until we know what the full circumstances are, Captain. Are we facing another invasion force? Is it another Earth Ark–generation ship? We just won't know until we get further into the mission. Enemy forces have attempted to take out one of our ships, a gunship, in fact. Someone programmed those HuKs. Someone gave them a seek-and-destroy mission over the planet Alphus, which implies that they knew we were likely to at least attempt to observe our exiles on that planet. Were they trying to protect an escape by Admiral DeVore and her crews? Or have they been destroyed and we're facing another, unknown, enemy? We just don't know those answers yet, so in the meantime, the mission continues as designed. We need to get on with settling our people in the three camps and make them as safe and secure as possible. And we have to hope that our fleet will be strong enough to protect us from whatever is out there."

"Have you considered that we should stop the original migration mission right now and reverse course?"

"You mean take thirty thousand migrants back to their hopeless lives on the Rim? I don't see that as a viable option," snapped Clement. The tension between the fleet's two top officers was now apparent to everyone else in the room and on the telecom link. Whatever was decided, it would have far-reaching implications for all of them.

"As your second-in-command, Admiral, it is my duty to inform you of all the viable options at your disposal. Going back home to Kemmerine Station is one of those options," Yan said.

"And leave the locals to fight off God knows who while we're gone? No, Yan, we're too far in. We have too many lives at risk. They're all safer on the ground on Bellus than they would be on those transports."

"Are they? We don't even know who or what we may be fighting against."

Clement swiveled his chair to face her. "Captain, we have committed the fleet to defending Trinity, both the natives and the migrants. We have the full force of our fleet here now. If we retreated back to Kemmerine we would have to split our forces in order to protect both groups of people. No, we're safer together, and that's my final word on it." Yan opened her mouth to say something else, but Clement had turned away from her and then asked Colonel Lubrov for a report on her Marines.

Lubrov cleared her throat and tried to speak as evenly as she could to reduce the tension in the room. "I've got four hundred troops deployed to each of the camps. The men are busy digging shelters and hardening the defenses around the migrants. My hope is that each of the camps can be protected either from an attack from the air or on the ground."

Clement nodded. "Have you been able to repurpose

any of our existing equipment to defend the camps?" he asked.

"As a matter of fact, yes. We pulled the DEW cannons off the transports and set up antiaircraft perimeters around the camps." Clement's eyebrows went up in surprise.

"That's an innovative idea," he said. He didn't voice how impressed he was with her initiative.

"Well, they weren't doing us any good stuck to those sitting-duck transports. I don't know how effective they'll be since we've had to jerry-rig the targeting equipment, but at least it will be a surprise if any unknown aircraft venture into our space," said Lubrov.

"That it would be, Colonel. If all else fails, I guess there's always line-of-sight targeting, like in the good old days."

"Sir," acknowledged Lubrov.

Captain Son of the *Yangtze* came in with a question then. He was an Asian native of Shenghai, the same home as Yan. "I take it, Admiral, that none of these camps will be able to survive a nuclear strike from the air or space?"

"I think that goes without saying, Captain. Our defenses simply aren't that sophisticated, and quite frankly we didn't anticipate this sort of situation, so it was never even a consideration in our planning."

"Not to mention it would be difficult to recruit colonists if we told them they were heading into a possible nuclear war zone," interjected Yan. Again, Clement did not appreciate the comment, but he couldn't argue with her reasoning.

"All right, I want to wrap this up," said Clement. "Everyone proceed as we have done to this point. Stay alert, report anything suspicious, even the smallest thing, up the chain of command at your first opportunity. Anything else?"

"Yes, Admiral." The voice came from down the table, from Commander Laura Pomeroy. "There is the issue of our planned expedition to the Hill Place. You said you wanted to be involved in that."

"I did, Commander, and I do. Let's give it another twenty-four hours. *If* everything stays calm and we continue to make progress on our defenses, then I can see my way clear to authorizing your expedition. We could gain valuable technology from the base."

"Will you be joining us, Admiral?"

Clement sat back and crossed his arms, considering that. "I would like to, Laura, but that depends on the circumstances. Save me a seat, but don't plan on me unless I show up in person in my hiking gear."

"Understood, Admiral." With that the meeting closed and the officers began shuffling out of the room. Yan went to Clement to confront him one more time before he could leave the conference room.

"Are you sure you should be considering undertaking this scientific fishing expedition right now? You are the leader of this whole endeavor," she said as quietly as she could so as not to alert others still in the room.

"As you said, Captain, we came here with a mission. I'd like to stick to that original plan as closely as we can. If things remain quiet, I think it's important that we show life going on as normal as much as possible. That includes me leading scientific expeditions to unravel some of the mysteries of the Trinity system." He wasn't happy with her and his tone showed that. Instead of challenging him, Yan merely conceded the point with a nod. "One more thing, Captain. Please don't challenge me in front of the command staff again. Bring your concerns to me privately. That's an order."

"Yes, sir," replied Yan.

Twenty-four hours later and everything had been quiet. Yan had arranged (and provided translation) for a meeting with the local natives on the surface. They told Clement that Mary, the native they had connected with on their first mission, had left their village nearly a year ago and no one had seen her. One of the elder women said she was "called" to the Hill Place, whatever that meant. This made Clement a bit sad as she was a charming, intelligent and beautiful young woman.

After introducing the natives to some of the more prominent migrants, Clement turned over the integration task to Yan and decided to gear up and join Pomeroy's expedition. An eight-seat VTOL aircraft was on the landing pad warming its engines via the auxiliary power unit as the admiral approached. He noted the large detachment of Marines digging trenches into the nearby hillside and pouring nano-reinforced concrete into the defensive bunker moldings already laid down. It was an impressive sight.

He hustled over to the waiting expeditionary group in his full gear, coil rifle, pistol, backpack slung over his shoulder. He walked up to Colonel Lubrov and she saluted him, which he returned. "Impressive work by your men on the bunkers, Colonel," he said.

"Thank you, sir. We should be able to house five hundred souls in there by midnight, and another five hundred tomorrow."

"That's welcome news. If only we could be so sure that our adversaries would hold off attacking us until we can complete our work."

"Obviously, we can't assure that, Admiral. But it is progress."

"It is that."

Laura Pomeroy came up then and saluted him.

"We're just waiting for your go order, Admiral," she said, nodding at the VTOL. "This vertical takeoff-and-landing craft will do nicely for our run up the mountain, sir, and getting back and forth from the camp if anything requires your immediate attention should not be a problem."

"Good to know, Commander. Let's get this show on the road." With that he started walking toward the VTOL. His com buzzing in made him stop while the others walked on.

"Captain Yan," he said into the com, acknowledging her unique ID chime.

"Admiral. Still no activity within the defense grid. Requesting permission to send out the gunships to surveil the outer parts of the solar system." Clement thought about that.

"Impatience can be our undoing, Captain. I'd prefer we maintain the full defensive net, so that nothing can get through."

"Sir, with all due respect, you're about to go on a field trip." Clement didn't like the tone of that. Relations between him and Yan had definitely become strained.

"A field trip with some very broad implications for this entire star system, Captain. This is not a holiday trail hike. Besides, I doubt it will take longer than a few hours to do the survey, but please, don't be afraid to call me if there's any change in our circumstances."

"You mean, like a full-scale invasion?"

"Well, yes, if I'm being honest that's exactly what I mean. We know the Hill Place leads to an underground facility inside that mountain, and if it's artificial, as we suspect, it could contain technology that would help us even things out in case of a greater conflict arising."

"You mean, 'even things out' more than the MAD weapon currently does?"

Clement sighed. She was giving him a lot of static for something that had already been decided. "Yes, possibly. But once again I'm leaving this mission in your capable hands, Yan. Hopefully we'll see you again by nightfall."

"But, sir—"

"Listen, Yan. I know you're upset by not being included on this mission, but frankly Colonel Lubrov is more suited to it than you are, and you're more suited to commanding the fleet. So let's both do our jobs and see what happens."

"But, sir, I'm the only one who speaks the natives' language," she said, a last-minute attempt to get on the mission.

Clement sighed. "Commander Pomeroy has been studying their language for eighteen months. I need you to do the job I've assigned you, Tanitha," he said, using her first name (as he rarely did) for emphasis and emotional impact. He wasn't just ordering her as her commanding officer, he was requesting her agreement as his friend. She finally seemed to get it.

"Of course, Admiral. I'll see you when you return, hopefully with good news."

"Thank you, Captain. Clement out," he finished, then turned his attention back to the expedition team. They were all busy loading equipment onto the VTOL. Beside himself, Pomeroy, and Lubrov, the team consisted of Lieutenants Telco and Tsu, Tech Kim Reck, and a pair of healthy-looking Marines.

"Time is a factor, Commander," he said to Pomeroy. "Let's get this little safari off the ground."

"Aye, sir," Pomeroy said, then turned and yelled at the crew, telling them to expedite loading up and to get in to the VTOL transport bay. Lubrov nodded to Clement as she jumped in the back with her Marines, while the admiral sat down next to Pomeroy in the pilot's nest. At his nod she fired up the VTOL engines and they were off the ground in less than five minutes.

As they flew, Clement asked Pomeroy for an update. "How is your Imperial Korean study going?"

She shook her head. "Frankly, sir, I'm not good enough with their language to negotiate any treaties, despite my studying. Maybe you should have brought Captain Yan."

"She has other duties, and I know learning archaic Imperial Korean couldn't have been easy for you."

"No, sir," she replied, then they flew on. The trip to the

Hill Place took another ten minutes. From the air it did look like a mountain, but the ground-penetrating radar scans showed that the "mountain" was in fact artificial, shaped like an almost perfect four-sided pyramid. They landed just a few hundred feet from the Hill Place shelter that they had first investigated nearly two years ago. The crew deplaned and started loading up their scientific equipment and their weapons. They'd found nothing there in the Hill Place bunker the first time they had investigated it, but there was no point in taking any risks. They already knew there was a hidden stairwell behind one of the walls and Clement wanted to know where that stairwell led. As everyone loaded their equipment and packs, the admiral reconsidered. They were carrying a lot of stuff.

"Everyone leave their coil rifles, except the two Marines. We don't need to be burdened with too much equipment in case we have to make a quick retreat back to Camp Alpha. You Marines just bring your weapons and field rations. Everyone else stow their rifles and ammo magazines back on the VTOL, but keep your cobra pistols." Lubrov insisted on carrying her rifle, but Clement's decision considerably lightened the load for the rest of the expeditionary team. It did leave them more vulnerable to whatever they might find inside the mountain, assuming it was hostile.

After a few minutes' walk to the concrete bunker the natives called the Hill Place, the group went inside and quickly found the door location, hidden behind a wall of concrete blocks. Tech Reck did the first probe of the wall blocking the stairway entrance. "This is simple concrete, sir. Old, crappy, concrete actually. I'll have this open in a hot minute."

"You're authorized to do so, Tech Reck."

She set about placing five incendiary charges around the perimeter of the poorly constructed portal, setting timers on each one of them, then taking about ten paces back, holding a remote detonation device in her hand.

"Ready when you are, Admiral," she said. Reck seemed to have an almost childlike exuberance at the prospect of blowing things up. He guessed that's why most crew members spelled out her name as "Wreck" on their reports rather than the more accurate spelling.

Clement and the crew took shelter behind concrete pillars, then the admiral yelled out "Proceed, Tech Reck." They all took another step back then, even further behind her, just to be safe.

She pressed the remote, then scrambled back behind a pillar. Rather than an explosive charge, the incendiaries lit up as bright as a welding torch, slowly making their way around the perimeter she had set up. Two minutes later and the charges had burned out, leaving melted concrete in a small, gooey pile on the floor. Clement walked up and peered down the stairwell. It was dark and more than a bit foreboding.

"Laura, can we check for oxygen levels? I don't want to lead us down there and then find out we can't breathe. This has been here a long time."

"Aye, sir," Pomeroy stepped up and over the quickly hardening concrete threshold to start her scans. After a moment, she looked up at Clement. "Oxygen levels are rather rich, sir. I mean, some obviously came in from us breaking the seal, but if I'm reading this right then the O2 levels are actually higher the further down I probe. It seems as though the oxygen supply is coming *up* from whatever lies below."

"Implying that rather than a coal mine situation, we might be heading into some...underground oasis?"

Pomeroy nodded. "I'm detecting a warmer climate as well. It's only nineteen Celsius up here, but I'm reading twenty-three Celsius the lower down we go."

"Very odd," replied Clement. "How far down does this stairway go?"

"I'm guessing about five hundred steps, sir. Then there is a larger landing area. Beyond that, I can't say."

Lubrov came up. "Sir, this stairway is only wide enough for us to go single file. I recommend one of my Marines up front, one in the back, and you somewhere in the middle."

"Where will you be, Colonel?"

"Behind the first Marine, sir."

"Then I'll follow you. Pomeroy, you're behind me. I want steady reports. Telco and Tsu, you keep your eyes on the commander."

"Aye, sir," they both acknowledged. Lubrov signaled one of her Marine privates to lead the group, and the other to follow last.

And with that, they began their descent into the unknown.

"What do you think we'll find down here?" Clement asked of Pomeroy as they began their slow but steady descent.

"I don't know what I think, but hopefully we'll find

some evidence of the technology that was used to terraform the Trinity worlds. And hopefully, some of it is still working," she replied.

"So, do you think it was alien technology?"

"I don't know what to think, sir, except that I expect to be surprised."

They proceeded down the stairwell in orderly manner, the lights from their helmets illuminating the way in front of them. The stairs were dusty but otherwise showed very little sign of wear. They could've been abandoned for a decade, or a thousand years. After a few minutes of descending the first Marine and Colonel Lubrov reached the landing area. It was very dark and the room was shaped like a hexagon. On one wall there were double metal doors and what appeared to be some kind of control box. The box had no obvious sign of power of any kind, but there was a raised crystalline object in the middle of the box.

"What do you think, Commander," Clement asked Pomeroy.

"I'd say we're looking at an elevator, likely one that will take us down considerably further from where we are now."

Clement turned to Lubrov. "What's your recommendation, Colonel? Do we go on? How safe do you think we are?"

"I would say we're currently safe, Admiral. The question is, do we take another risk to try to find answers to our questions? It seems to me the only way to discover the mysteries of this place is to try and activate that elevator and go down further."

"Should we leave someone up here as a safety measure?"

Lubrov shrugged. "If you like, sir. Quite frankly, I thought this expedition was to find answers to the evidence of artificial construction that we've seen. I don't think we'll find those answers if we stay up here."

"Good point, Colonel. Nonetheless, I think caution is always a good idea, especially when you're facing the unknown, and this is about as unknown as it gets." He turned to his team. "Lieutenants Telco and Tsu, you'll remain here as our safety net. Stay in com link with Colonel Lubrov at all times. Sorry that you don't get to come down and discover Wonderland with the rest of us, but if there's trouble I think the Marines will be of the most use. If anyone besides one of us comes up this elevator, or you get an order to bug out, or you do so. Understood?" He got a pair of *yes sir*s in response, then turned to Commander Pomeroy.

"If you can't get these doors open, this is going to be a very short expedition."

"Understood, sir. I'll take a crack at it."

At that Tech Reck stepped up. "Admiral, let me do it. I don't think you have anyone else on this team as good with mechanical devices as I am," said Reck.

Clement looked to Pomeroy, who shrugged.

"I don't think we have anything to lose, sir," she said.

Clement nodded his assent. "Proceed, Tech Reck," he ordered. The diminutive woman stepped forward, pulling a pair of electronic devices out of her hip pack. She waved the first one over the lock mechanism, and then placed the second one in touch with the crystal on the lock itself. After a couple of seconds of lights blinking in sequence, the doors magically split open.

"Simple magnetic lock, Admiral. If this is the best security they have, we're going to have an easy time of it," she said confidently.

Clement couldn't help but smile. "Thank you, Tech Reck. Please remind me to include you in all of my future field trips, and to change out the locks on my cabin door."

"Sir," Reck said, smiling, and then stepped aside. The six remaining members of the expedition stepped on to the elevator. It was large enough to bring twice that many, at least. Inside, on the door panel, there was another control box.

Clement looked to the two young lieutenants he was leaving behind. "Take no chances, gentlemen. Wait thirty minutes, no more. If we haven't answered in that time, bug out back to the VTOL and get ahold of Captain Yan."

"We will, sir," replied Telco.

Clement nodded in return, then turned to Tech Reck. "Whenever you're ready, Tech." Reck used the same two devices to activate the crystal, which began to glow with a white pulsing light. The doors to the elevator slowly closed, and the team was quickly ushered down into the unknown.

The descent seemed swift, and at one point Clement was worried that they were in fact in free fall. But in the end there was the sensation of slowing, and then a gentle touching to the ground.

"Thirty-three seconds of descent, Admiral," said Pomeroy, "but without knowing what our speed was it's impossible to say how far down we've actually gone."

"Kilometers, I'd say. But that's just a guess." Clement turned to Lubrov. "Can you raise Lieutenant Telco?"

Lubrov shook her head. "I'm getting nothing down here," she said. "No com signals at all, and no uplinked telemetry from the fleet either. We are in the dark."

"So we are. Let's be hopeful that our two lieutenants are good enough sailors to follow their orders. Keep a watch on the clock, please, Colonel. Tech Reck, um, can you please open the doors?"

"Aye, sir." The tech did her magic again, and when the doors opened, Clement felt like they were indeed about to enter Wonderland.

Clement stepped out into a room that was cavernous, literally. Looking up, he guessed it was at least three hundred meters to the top of the cavern. There were dozens of natural-looking columns scattered throughout the cavern, and each of the columns emitted light from what appeared to be a purple-white bioluminescence, much like the type they had discovered at the pond on their original mission. But this light seemed to emanate from the columns themselves, and as they scattered through the open area they illuminated the whole cavern, far off into the distance. As the six souls stepped out onto a landing platform, they all stared in stunned silence.

The bioluminescent columns extended into what could only be described as an underground valley. "How far..." started Lubrov.

"Kilometers, I'm guessing," said Clement. There were buildings and structures far off into the distance. A gentle mist filled the cavern, and gave the air a warm, almost tropical humidity. The air smelled of flowers and blooms, and indeed there were many types of flora, different and lusher even than what was on the surface, scattered throughout the cavern. It was darker where they were standing than it was near the distant city, which was bathed in a gold-yellow light from above, almost as if there was a tiny sun illuminating the cavern. From where Clement stood, it looked like it could be raining over the city. He had to tear himself away from the sight before him and pay closer attention to what was directly ahead. Down a gentle, inclined slope, there was a large open platform, one side of which contained an entire wall of four uneven rocklike towers that were at least four meters high. The devices contained within those columns hummed and pulsated with light in a fluid, organic way. These devices, whatever they were, were clearly actively working at some kind of tasks. Clement took a couple of steps down the smooth ramp, looking closer at a central raised platform. There was a circle of command consoles, which looked designed to be accessed by something similar to the human form.

"Do we proceed, Admiral?" asked Pomeroy. Clement turned to look at the commander and then to Colonel Lubrov, who was silent.

"Colonel, are we safe?"

"That's impossible to say, Admiral, but we did come here to explore so . . ." She trailed off.

"We proceed then. I will lead us from here."

"Sir," said Lubrov. The two Marines fell in to line closely behind Clement, followed by Lubrov, her rifle drawn, then Pomeroy and Reck. As they descended down the long sloping ramp they could hear their boots clicking on the floor, as if it were a hard surface. Clement stopped and bent down to touch the dark purple material. It felt like an impossibly smooth stone, almost like slate, polished to an incredible fineness. The slope was low and easy, but it still took some time for them to walk down it with the heavy equipment they had in their backpacks. There was a strange sensation about their progress, almost as if the slope was getting smaller as they descended.

"This floor, it seems to be rising up to meet us as we walk," said Pomeroy.

"I felt the same thing," replied Clement. "What could it be?"

"Some sort of nanomaterial, maybe, employing both the principles of a solid and a fluid at the same time."

Clement held his hand up to stop the troop. "Tech Reck, see if you can get a sample of this floor material."

"Aye, Admiral," she replied, then turned and tracked back up the slope. She bent down on one knee and started hammering on the floor material with a small pickax she pulled from her backpack. The material just seemed to "flow" away from the chisel strikes and then return to its original form when she stopped pounding. It made no sound when she struck it.

"Try a different method," said Clement.

"Like what?" replied Reck, as if she were annoyed by the suggestion. "Sorry, like what method, Admiral?"

"I'm not sure. Maybe try something a little less, um, aggressive."

"Try scooping some of the nanomaterial a few

centimeters behind where we last walked," said Pomeroy, then handed her a glass vial.

Reck tried that, and after a few failures, the material finally gave way and slowly oozed its way into the vial, the "scooped" material being immediately replaced by more material. Reck sealed the vial and handed it back to Pomeroy.

"Almost like it *allowed* us to take a sample," she said to Clement.

"Will you get to analyze this or will I get a crack at it?" asked Reck.

"We can work on it together when we get it back to camp," replied Pomeroy. That brought a smile to Reck's face. Then Pomeroy nodded to Clement that they could continue.

The troop started up their descent again, the platform with the console on it drawing ever closer. As they closed in, he could feel the low vibration of equipment running, energy flowing, the towers of "rock" humming with power as they did their incomprehensible work. Everything on the columns lit up from moment to moment, displaying a vibrant array of colors that ran smoothly up and down. There were no visible controls of any kind, just a fascinating kaleidoscope of colors, shapes, and movements. It was like watching a stained-glass window in constant motion, changing form. It was mesmerizing, and Clement had no idea what it meant, or what the control columns were doing.

They reached the platform and Clement sent Pomeroy and Reck to investigate the towers closer while he, Lubrov, and the Marines went to the center control platform. The raised consoles were made of the same material as the floor, and though they were inclined for what appeared to be easy access for a pair of standard humanoid hands, they were completely featureless. Lubrov ordered her Marines to set up a perimeter looking down on the "valley" below just in case their arrival had triggered any unwanted visitors.

"What do you make of this?" he said to Lubrov, running his hand over the blank, smooth console.

"I'd say someone is missing some equipment. It seems logical that this console controls those stacks somehow, but without any input panels, it's impossible to guess how they might interact." Clement called Pomeroy over while Tech Reck continued to scan the towers.

"What's your report, Commander?"

"I'd say we're dealing with a vast computing system that might make up this whole complex, possibly controlled from these consoles."

"There's only one problem with that theory: these consoles don't appear to have any type of human interface."

Pomeroy looked at the console, then ran her hand over it. "It seems to be made of the same material as the walkway, and this platform for that matter. The towers and columns are made of a different material but where they intersect with the platform, it's a completely seamless join, like they're both part of the same mechanism or material but serve different functions. My best guess would be that you have to have some sort of key to unlock these consoles, and if you have that key likely all the interface mechanisms you need would simply emerge from the console itself. I could be wrong but that would be my working theory. Tech Reck seems to think that this entire cavern is part of one huge, singular mechanism. Although, based on the magnetic and electrical-pulse outputs we've been recording, this entire complex could also be organic, or maybe some combination of organic and mechanical materials. That's what I expect I'll find when I analyze this nano-goo," she said, holding up the glass vial to the light.

"That's a level of technology far beyond what we possess," said Lubrov to Clement. "As your security chief, that worries me. Contact with a higher technology, or a more advanced civilization, usually ends up badly for the less advanced civilization."

"Noted, Colonel," said Clement. "At this point, though, we're still in the information-gathering phase of this expedition." He turned to Pomeroy. "Continue with your investigation, Commander. I want as much information as we can get."

"Are we going to explore further into this cavern?" asked Lubrov.

"Unless the circumstances change, I think not. I gave us a three-hour window to complete this mission. We still have potential enemies and thirty thousand vulnerable migrant settlers on the surface above us. We'll do what we can, Colonel, but if it will ease your mind, I'll let you know that I have no intention of going further than we have to in order to start our analysis of this place."

One of the Marines called to Lubrov. "Colonel, we have movement in the valley." The two Marines were quickly on high alert, their rifles drawn. Lubrov went running to the edge of the platform with Clement close behind.

When Clement got to the edge of the platform he saw what all the commotion was about. About a hundred meters away there was a dull gray cylinder rising out of the pathway. It "grew" up to about the size of a standard human, and then stopped. A door then slid aside, revealing a dark interior.

The Marines, including Lubrov, raised their rifles, as they were trained. Clement stayed one step behind them, his pistol still sheathed in its holster. Then he motioned the Marines to one side and stepped around them.

"Admiral," protested Lubrov.

"Hold your position, Colonel," snapped Clement. They all watched as a dark-suited figure emerged from the cylinder. It stood in front of the opening for a few seconds, long enough for Clement to recognize the amber-colored skin and platinum blonde hair that was typical of the Trinity natives. As the figure began moving toward them up the pathway there was no question in his mind that it was both human, and female. Her hair hung down past her shoulders, and it was braided at the ends in an attractive style. As she approached them, Clement was impressed with both the femininity of her figure and the beauty of her face. And, to his great surprise, it was a face he recognized.

She stood directly below them now, and Clement signaled for the Marines to lower their weapons.

"Hello, Captain Clement," said the woman in perfect standard English. "I suppose you are as surprised to see me as I am to see you?"

Clement stood speechless for a moment, then took a few steps down off the platform to meet her at her level.

"Hello, Mary," he said. "How nice to see you again."

"Thank you, Captain. I wish I could say the same to you in return."

12

"It's admiral now, madam," said Lubrov by way of correction, defending her commanding officer's honor and stepping in between them to protect his person.

"Well, I see congratulations are in order then. A promotion is a nice thing, as I understand it, in less developed civil structures," Mary said, without a hint of emotion. She looked around at the group of people he had brought with him. "I see the woman Yan is not with you. It would be pleasurable to see her again, as it is pleasurable to see you," she said with a slight smile.

"She is invaluable to me in another assignment. I couldn't spare her for this expedition," he replied by way of explanation. Perhaps Yan had been right, and her presence would have been helpful.

"It is unfortunate that we meet under these circumstances, Admiral. A reunion with Yan and yourself would have been very desirable." Again there was just the hint of a smile, and Clement was unsure whether he should be embarrassed at her suggestion or not.

This was definitely not the simple, carefree young woman he had met on the previous mission to Bellus. Her eyes were clear and focused, her face relatively emotionless. He wasn't really sure what to say to her, but he had to start somewhere. He motioned Lubrov to the side and stepped up to his visitor.

"Forgive me for asking this, Mary, but how is it you are here, in this vast complex? The person I knew before was a simple and happy young native woman, living in the villages," Clement said.

Her lips turned up in what was almost a smile. "That is who I was, Admiral, but never who I was supposed to be."

"I don't think I understand that."

She looked pensive now, turning her face away and thinking, seemingly about how to answer.

Clement stepped in. "If there are things you're not supposed to tell me, I understand that," he said.

She refocused on him. "It's not that, Admiral. It's more about how to put things in context for you. The presence of you and your people was never something the Makers prepared us for."

"The 'Makers'?"

She looked around the vast cavern and lifted her arms up. "The ones who made . . . all of *this*."

"So, this wasn't made by your people?"

She laughed. "Heavens, no! We are at our core very simple people; we live the way the Makers intended us to live."

At this, Lubrov stepped in again, always the defender. "But who are these 'Makers'? They obviously have a very high level of technology, much higher than ours."

"I cannot really tell you that because I don't know. We are merely the"—she seemed to search for the right word

again—"the ... caretakers of this world; we are not the
owners. We who are here, inside this complex, are few,
less than one thousand by your count. We run this planet
according to our given skills and abilities."

"But ... how have you transformed from the simple
woman I knew before into who you are now?" asked
Clement, genuinely curious. To his surprise, Mary
reached out and took his hand, then guided it up under
her hair, to touch her scalp behind her left ear. He felt a
clear bump behind the ear, a couple of centimeters long.
She held his hand there for a few moments.

"An implant?" he asked. She nodded as she let go of
his hand and it fell down from her scalp.

"Most children here are born naturally, but some of us,
perhaps one in a thousand, are born here, in the caverns.
Once we are old enough we are released into the general
community, where we conduct our lives as the Makers
intended. But when the time comes, or when we are
needed, the Makers send us a ... calling, and we come to
this place, where we are enlightened, and given our role
of service to the planet and to the people."

Clement then asked the next question. "Did our arrival
here, two years ago, result in you being 'called' away from
your former life?"

Again, the shrug. "I do not know that, Admiral. But it
is likely my interaction with you was part of my calling.
I've been taught your language so that I can communicate
better with you, and now I am here, and you have
returned. But, there are very important matters to attend
to, and I suggest we set about those tasks," she said,
pointing toward the empty consoles.

"Of course," said Clement, then followed her up the platform steps to the waiting consoles. As they walked the few meters to the console, Clement commented, "It may be easier if you call me Jared, since I call you Mary. Things can get confusing with all the ranks floating around down here."

"I understand. Jared," she replied, trying out the name but not breaking her stride. They arrived at the console, and the lifeless purple-black material began to vibrate. It was as if her mere proximity to the console had given it life and power. Pomeroy and Reck gathered near the console as Clement signaled the Marines to guard the perimeter.

Mary passed her hands over the console and multicolored controls began to emerge from the previously blank surface. Colored lights flashed into her eyes, rapidly winking at her, but her eyes did not blink nor waver in any kind of response. She merely seemed to absorb the information being transmitted. Clement wasn't sure if it was coded or if she was receiving communication through her implant.

"You need to make contact with your men near the surface," she stated. "You are allowed to do this now." Clement signaled to Lubrov, who walked away and immediately connected her com with Lieutenants Telco and Tsu. As Lubrov told them to stay ready, Mary continued to commune with the console. This went on for several more minutes, her eyes never blinking. They all watched as the large columns began lighting up, colors furiously whirling through them, conducting unknown tasks.

Finally she pulled back from the console and looked to Clement. "You must go back to your camp, and to your ships. There is a fleet of vessels incoming. You have made a grave mistake in bringing your people here, Jared. These worlds were never intended for you."

"What fleet?" demanded Lubrov. "Who are they?"

"Who they are does not concern us. They are your problem. If they, or you, put our people in danger, the Makers will protect us."

Clement looked to Lubrov. "Some sort of planetary defense system, likely run from this complex, or one like it," he said. Lubrov nodded agreement. He turned back to Mary, who had assumed a rigid posture. "We will defend this world, and all of its people on the surface, if we can. That is our pledge to you. But the Makers cannot attack my ships. They would be destroying their greatest ally."

"The Makers need no allies to defend us, Jared. They will act when it is necessary."

"And if we just happen to be in the way?" said Lubrov.

"I do not make those decisions, Colonel."

Clement held Lubrov back with his arm as she was about to press her point. "Mary, I'm asking you, please call off the Makers. Keep them from attacking my ships. We aren't here to harm your people."

Mary stared at him for a second, as if downloading a response. "Your people's history is riddled with stories of those who came to help others, but ended up exterminating them in the end. The Makers will not allow that."

Clement decided to try a different tack. "Our people

on the surface, they are as vulnerable as your people are. Maybe we made a mistake in coming here, not knowing that we would anger the Makers. But our intent was never to harm you and your people. We are simply trying to save *our* people from starvation on our own worlds. Can't you see that?"

"I can understand that, Jared, but the Makers see things differently. They know only of the good of their children, the 'natives' as you call them. I cannot call them off, nor control their decisions. The protectors of this planet that you call Bellus will make decisions that are in the best interests of this world, and her children."

"So, your world is run by an overarching artificial intelligence that you cannot override or argue with, even if you disagree with them. And the Makers who made that AI are long gone from this world, and their children. Is that in your best interest?"

"Again, I cannot make those decisions, Jared. But I warn you that you have only five hours before that fleet arrives over this world. You must go *now*, if you are going to defend your people."

"You could bring them all in here, you could protect my people and yours inside this complex."

"There is room, yes. But your people are not part of the Makers' plans. I cannot override their decisions," she said yet again.

Giving up, Clement ordered his team to form up, but he had one last parting shot for the Makers. "Then consider this, Mary. You and I, my people and yours, are made of the same stuff. We are all human, all brothers and sisters, all worthy of protection, by you, or the

Makers." With that he ordered his team to fall out back to the elevator.

Mary called to him just as he stepped off the cavern floor and onto the elevator. "I will . . . consult . . . about your proposal for protection, Jared, only because I trust you. But I can promise you nothing."

"Thank you, Mary," said Clement, then he signaled to Reck to activate the elevator, heading for the surface.

The VTOL ride back to Camp Alpha was rough and fast. There was no room for the comfort of his people now. When they landed, Clement was out of the vehicle and making for his shuttle as fast as he could, sending orders to Yan via the com to detect the incoming fleet and deploy her defenses. He also filled her in on the surprise of seeing Mary again, and the implications she had made about the mysterious Makers. He left Lubrov and the Marines behind on the surface to work on the colonists' ground defenses.

Another twenty minutes and he was aboard *Agamemnon* and in the CAC, at the command and control console, surveying the looming battlefield. "Situation report, Captain," he demanded of Yan.

"We've detected the attack fleet, Admiral. More than fifty ships of various classes inbound from the orbit of T6. They used the gas planet's gravity to accelerate inwards toward us, and Bellus."

"Is there a capital ship?" asked Clement.

"There is a vessel that matches *Agamemnon* for size and displacement. Our estimates are that it's the lead battlecruiser of the attack fleet. But they also have twenty heavy cruisers, eighteen destroyers, and most worryingly, fifteen automated hunter-killers."

Clement studied the potential battlefield. There weren't many options. He had only eight destroyers and six light cruisers plus *Agamemnon* and the five small gunships she carried like children in her belly. It was far too weak a force to face what was incoming at them.

"Do we split our forces, sir?" asked Yan.

Clement shook his head. Likely splitting his forces would merely lead to their quicker destruction. "We'd get torn apart. We'll have to form a defensive wedge behind the *Agamemnon*. Like it or not, this ship is really the only modern warship we have in the fleet. Everything else we have is either outdated or upgraded to barely functional levels." He stopped then, and contemplated the board one more time before oming to a decision. "Deploy the fleet per formation Delta Seven-One." Delta Seven-One would put the *Agamemnon* at the point of a wedge, supported above and below by three light cruisers each, and further back by the eight destroyers in a spread formation. Beyond that, he only had the five former Rim Confederation gunships. It wasn't much, but Clement didn't have many options. At least the formation would put their most modern and powerful ship at the forefront of the battle. Likely the enemy fleet commander would do just the opposite, stay behind her forces and let her heavy cruisers, destroyers and HuKs do most of the damage.

Her.

He realized he was planning his defense as if the other attack force was being led by his former lover and great betrayer, former Fleet Admiral Elara DeVore. He wasn't sure if that bias was good or bad under the circumstances. He pushed those thoughts out of his mind for the present. "Lieutenant Adebayor, do your scope scans give us any indication of where these ships are based at? A fleet this big must have some sort of supply vessel or support ships elsewhere in the system."

"Negative on that, Admiral," replied Adebayor. "But our scope of the system is not complete yet."

"Then I suggest you rush your scans, Lieutenant. You have forty minutes," he said, then turned his attention back to his tactical board.

"Aye, sir," said Adebayor, urgently motioning over an assistant scopeman to help her at her station.

Clement turned his attention back to Yan. "Our biggest problem is going to be those hunter-killers. We know they're just suicide machines and they'll be willing to expend all of them in this battle. Planning this engagement would be easier if I knew who was in command of the attack fleet."

"Since she's missing, can we assume that it's Elara DeVore?"

Clement flexed his neck, as if trying to eradicate a kink. "I've already taken that into consideration. But, until I see more in the way of tactics, I can't be sure and I don't want to make any assumptions that might be fatal to our defense."

"Sir, all ships are signaling that they are in formation Delta Seven-One and ready to move out on your order," called Mika Ori from her station.

"We'll hold here for now, Pilot. All ships must stand ready."

"Aye, sir."

Clement returned to his console. "They're coming in way too fast for conventional propulsion. I think we have to assume that they have inertial dampening technology, and that means only a few of our ships can match them for maneuverability."

"We have four hours and seven minutes until we make contact with that fleet. Even with inertial dampening technology they're going to have to start slowing at some point," replied Yan.

"Agreed. But we don't know how good their ID technology is. If we're measuring it by our level of tech, then they'll have to start decelerating thirty minutes from the battlefield. If it's better than ours, then they might be able to drop in right on top of us, in which case we'll all be dead."

"It's safe then to assume that inside of thirty minutes we have to admit their technology is better than ours. And we still don't have a plan to deal with those HuKs."

"Leave the HuKs to me, Captain. I want you to focus on strategies for the main ships in the fleet. If we get caught in an attrition battle they will cut us to pieces simply with their superior numbers. But . . . if we can use tactics to tilt the battlefield in our direction, then we at least have a sharpshooter's chance at a Hail Mary."

"First rule in battle school: if the battlefield isn't to your advantage, then move the battlefield," said Yan. She pointed to the L2 Lagrange point between Bellus and the third world in the Trinity system, Camus. "If we were to wait until they were decelerating toward us, we could move the fleet to this position, and force them to turn and pursue us, burning fuel and slowing them even more."

Clement leaned forward on the console table. "And if we left a surprise behind for them here, something that could deliver a gut punch, maybe we'd make them think twice about pursuing us."

"That would buy the *fleet* time, but what about the colonists?"

"We'd be abandoning them in favor of a better strategic position for our ships, but then we'd have to be the attackers, we'd have to take away the high ground we freely ceded back from them. Right now, though, moving the fleet is just about the only advantage that we have."

"If we go, who will defend Bellus? We'll be leaving thirty thousand colonists and all the natives at their mercy, and we've already seen what they think about the native population."

"From what Mary told me, the Makers have left planetary defenses that can deal with any attackers. If that's true, we may find that we have them in a pinch instead of us being in theirs."

Yan shifted her feet. "A question, though. If these planetary defenses Mary talked about really exist, then why didn't they use them the last time we were in this system?"

Clement thought hard about that. "I don't know, and I don't have time to chat with Mary about that right now. We have to assume they will not intervene, based on our previous mission here. We need to rely on what we have, and we need to find something that can help us, and quick."

"You said we needed a gut punch. Would the MAD weapon constitute a 'gut punch'?" asked Yan quietly.

"It could," replied the admiral. "But that might be our only chance to use it. I would imagine they would be coming onto the battlefield with their weapons hot. Even if we could get off a decisive shot with the MAD weapon, say at their main battlecruiser, it would be fifty-fifty whether we survived the encounter long enough to fire it a second time, and I doubt we'd be able to take out their entire fleet with that one shot. No, I think our best chance is to change the battlefield and hope they pursue us. If they get spread out, we might have a better chance."

"Well, just maybe, these 'Makers' of Mary's will grant us a reprieve."

"Based on what your *friend* Mary said, I think that's highly unlikely." Yan winced at Clement's comment. She and Mary had had a more than just cordial relationship on their first, brief visit to Bellus. Clement was either too deeply involved in his battle planning or he was simply too callous about her feelings to notice her response. The relationship was embarrassing to her now. She had let her guard down that day, and that may have vast consequences for them now, and in the future.

Clement continued without further comment on Mary. "I think it will have to be scatter mines," he said. "I just don't see any other alternative."

"I agree with you," said Yan, regaining her composure. "Scatter mines will take out a few of their ships, or at least damage some of them enough to slow them down."

"Again, it's those trailing HuKs that have me the most worried. They will cut our destroyers to ribbons if we don't take them out in the first wave of the attack. Then their heavy cruisers will be able to mop up our light cruisers with ease."

"For all we know their destroyers may be as powerful as our light cruisers. If we lose all of our support ships then *Agamemnon* would surely be done for."

Clement swiped at his panels, looking for something. When he found it, he popped it up so Yan could see it. "Look at their energy curve. It's twice what ours is. Even if we took out all of their HuKs we'd still be overmatched by two thirds. I don't think we have any alternative, Yan; we have to try our Hail Mary. If we leave the *Beauregard* there, behind the wall of mines, it likely won't survive the initial attack wave, MAD weapon or not. Our gut punch will have to be the MAD weapon, and we'll have to pray that it's enough."

"And I suppose you think you're going to be in command of the *Beauregard*? The one staying behind to fight to the death? Last man going down with this ship, all those clichés. You may be a great ship captain, Jared, but you're a lousy Fleet Admiral. We need you here leading this fleet."

"I'm afraid that's a luxury we can't afford, Yan. I'm sending you and the rest of the fleet to the L2 Lagrange point as soon as we know they're decelerating. The *Beauregard* is the most powerful ship in this fleet, in either fleet, we both know that. And we both know who her best commander is. It's up to me to lay the trap, just like the Five Suns Navy did for me at the Battle of Argyle Station."

"But we're not fighting the Five Suns Navy this time, Admiral," argued Yan.

"Aren't we?" snapped Clement. "If I was commanding their attack fleet I'd set it up exactly the way they are. I'd play on my strengths and keep those HuKs in reserve for the kill shot. I'd base everything on the idea that we would stay in our position and defend Bellus. No, I think we are facing an enemy navy that's commanded by someone trained in the same tactics as I did. I believe this fleet is commanded by none other than Elara DeVore."

"So you've decided you're going to fight this battle personally, to get your revenge on someone who hurt you very deeply," said Yan.

Clement brushed her off. "I'm just trying to give us the best chance to win, Yan. My orders stand. *Beauregard* will stay behind the scatter-mine field. After the initial confusion wears off, I'll be able to get off a kill shot on their HuKs."

"And then?" asked Yan. "How will you escape the rest of the fleet?"

Clement look back down at his console. "We'll have to try a short-range LEAP jump to the L2 Lagrange point. We've done it before."

"And you almost broke the LEAP reactor and stranded us in this system."

"Yes, *almost*, but we didn't. We succeeded. I'm going to hope our luck runs out sometime *after* this next battle."

"So say you pull this off, then what? We'll still be outgunned by two thirds against their remaining forces. By my count it will be thirty-nine of their ships against fifteen of ours. And my guess is except for *Agamemnon*, every one of our ships is inferior to the same class of theirs."

"Once we regroup at the L2 Lagrange point, we'll have to determine a new strategy. There's no other way."

"And what about the colonists on the surface? Not to mention the natives?"

"We'll just have to hope that Mary and her friends truly have the favor of the Makers, and that the planetary defense systems will keep this attacking fleet at bay."

"And if she doesn't? If the Makers choose not to act, like the last time we were here?"

"Then we have no hope," said Clement.

At that moment Kayla Adebayor called for Clement's attention. "Admiral, I think we've located this fleet's base of operations. There appears to be an Ark ship orbiting the T6 gas planet, sir."

"Do we have any telemetry on the Ark ship, Lieutenant?"

"Very similar in size and displacement to the Earth Ark ship we destroyed on our last mission here two years ago, sir."

Clement looked down to his board, which was growing darker and more desperate every second.

"So," he said, "now we have another problem." Then he wiped clean the displays on his console in frustration.

✡ 13 ✡

Two hours later and Clement was boarding his personal command, the *Beauregard*. Captain Yan had been left in charge of the fleet, with orders to retreat to the L2 Lagrange point if they detected any form of deceleration coming from the enemy attack fleet.

Clement led all five of his gunships out of the belly of *Agamemnon*, there to get to the task of deploying the scatter mines in what he hoped would be an effective pattern. The scatter mines were programmed to accelerate toward and explode near any vessel in their range, which was about ten kilometers. They had very little time, and had to make their best guess as to where the decelerating attack fleet would impact the battlefield. It was imperative that they got to the enemy fleet while they were still moving and vulnerable to the pre-stationed mines.

After an hour of planning and laying mines, he ordered the other gunships to return to *Agamemnon*. He was willing to sacrifice his own ship, but not any of the rest of his fleet. He gave his final orders to Yan and the other commanders to make for the L2 point on his command.

There was nothing more to do now than to watch the incoming attack fleet as they approached Bellus at frightening speed.

Clement looked around his bridge. He had an experienced crew, the best in the business as far as he was concerned. Mika Ori was at the helm, her husband, Ivan Massif at Navigation, Kayla Adebayor was his communications and longscope officer, and Nobli and his assistant, Tech Reck, were down in Engineering. He told himself he didn't need anyone else for this mission and that's the way he wanted it. There was no point in putting inexperienced technicians in charge of stations and systems that they wouldn't understand anyway. He had the staff that he wanted, and the ship had been updated and automated enough that he really had all the crew he needed. He glanced at the empty executive officer's station, where Yan had been on the previous Trinity mission. There was a hole there, no doubt, and he would miss both her tactical and practical advice, but he was determined it wouldn't stop them from completing their mission.

He turned back to his console and brought up the tactical breakdown of the battlefield. The large group of enemy ships were still coming at his tiny fleet at breakneck speed. He surmised their inertial dampening systems must be highly advanced, with some sort of gravity wave distortion field that could minimize the effects of a sudden stop. It wasn't hard to figure out that his Five Suns fleet, a flotilla really, had little to no chance against an enemy this advanced and in such numbers. He stared at the field again, looking for some sort of advantage, any advantage, or even some idea he simply hadn't thought of yet.

"Eleven minutes until their fleet arrives here, Admiral. That is, if they don't start decelerating," reported Massif from the navigation station.

"I don't expect them to do that, Commander. They must have some sort of advanced inertial dampening tech that allows them to stop on a dime right in front of us, otherwise they'd be mashed potatoes on their inner hull." At that point he stood, looking at the *Beauregard*'s main visual display. "There's no more time to waste. Raise Captain Yan aboard the *Agamemnon*," he said to Adebayor. She did as instructed, and a second later Clement was on the com with his fleet captain. "This is Clement," he started. "I'm ordering you to make for the L2 Lagrange point without delay, Captain."

"Orders received and acknowledged sir," replied Yan, "but, I must protest your current course of action. Staying behind the rest of the fleet with a single ship will not have any material impact on the outcome of this battle. As your second-in-command, I insist that you return the *Beauregard* to the *Agamemnon*'s landing deck."

"Your recommendation is noted, Captain, but we will maintain our tactical status. Get my fleet to that Lagrange point. I will carry out whatever rearguard action I can, and then I will join you there. I have no intention of sacrificing my ship or my crew," he said. There was a long silence on the com line.

"A rearguard action with one gunship against an entire fleet? That sounds like suicide, Admiral."

"You can note that in your log as well if you wish,

Captain, but my orders stand. Now get your asses away from this planet. Acknowledge receipt of order," Clement responded.

"Orders received, Admiral. Good luck to you."

"And to you, Captain." With that she cut the com line from her end, seemingly angered by his actions, which she no doubt regarded as reckless. He watched as his flotilla began to accelerate away from Bellus and the incoming enemy fleet. In many ways the conversation they had just showed how far the two of them had drifted apart since the first Trinity mission. He didn't have her as his advisor on board *Beauregard* anymore, and he was more than able to make the important decisions on his own, but, deep down, he admitted to himself that she was an asset to him, one that he wouldn't have in this particular battle.

"Enemy fleet is not reacting to the *Agamemnon* flotilla's acceleration burn," reported Massif again from Navigation.

"They probably can't react at the speed they're making," said Clement. "Their stopping point is likely predetermined by their navigation AI program. Their big advantage is that they can approach the battlefield at virtually any speed, but it's very difficult to correct your course if you have sudden movement on the battlefield in front of you. They will have to come to a complete stop and recalibrate their position relative to our ships. That's the moment, probably the only moment, where we'll have a possible advantage."

Mika Ori swiveled in her couch toward him. "What's your idea, sir? I mean, we all assume you have some brilliant but dangerous idea," she said without a trace of humor or sarcasm.

He tapped his lips pensively with his forefinger, then pointed it at the tactical display. "The scatter mines will pick up anything inside of ten kilometers, correct?"

"Correct, sir. Any ship with engines displaying a heat signature will be a target for the scatter mines."

"But if I was their commander, I would let our mines bounce off their forward destroyers and heavy cruisers. If they have the inertial dampening tech they appear to have, then it's likely they can generate gravimetric shielding that would probably result in minimal damage to those size of ships."

"Aye, sir, that would be the likely strategy."

"And I need to take out their fifteen hunter-killers, but they're protected by the other ships in the fleet so that they can use them to take out *our* destroyers and light cruisers." He thought again for a second, then: "How fast can a scatter mine go in pursuit of a target, Mika?"

"Just under ten thousand kilometers per hour, sir."

"And an HuK?"

"Approximately fifteen thousand kilometers per hour. If the scatter mines aren't close enough to pick up the HuK engine signatures before they get warm, they could never catch them."

"From a *standing* position, correct, Commander?"

"Well, yes, sir, if neither group were in motion. What other situation would we be engaged in?"

All three of the bridge crew turned to look at Clement now, sensing something was about to happen that might affect their futures, and their lives. "If the scatter mines were already in motion, at full thrust, ten thousand kph, how long would it take for the enemy HuKs to fire their engines and begin to retreat?"

"Well, we can only guess, but based on our standard of technology, I would say at least three minutes to reach a full burn and begin to pull away. Remember, the scatter mines only have a small range of effectiveness."

"I remember that, Mika."

She frowned at him, looking very serious. "What do you have in mind?"

He waved her off, then turned to her husband. "Ivan, can you estimate where that fleet will come to a stop?"

"Already calculated, sir. I figured you would ask. Approximately twenty-eight hundred kilometers out from our current position, sir."

"Time?" Clement asked again.

Massif looked to his console. "Eight minutes, seven seconds," he replied.

Clement looked down and made notes again on his tactical board.

Then he stood up. "Range to our scatter mines?"

"Just outside of fifty kilometers from us, sir."

Clement turned to Ori again. "Mika, take us back to the scatter mines. When we hit ten kilometers' distance, arm and activate them."

"But, sir, they'll pick up our engine heat signature. Then *we'll* become their target."

Clement nodded. "We will, Pilot. That's why I expect you to be able to keep us ahead of them, all the way."

"All the way to where?"

"All the way to those HuKs, Commander," he said, then sat back down in his chair.

After the startled looks had gone off of Ori's and Massif's faces (Adebayor was too disciplined to let out an expression of shock at her commander's orders), Clement sat back down in his acceleration couch as Ori fired up the ion plasma thrusters and began moving the *Beauregard* toward the scatter mines. He clicked on the com link and brought Nobli in on his private line.

"And what miracle would you be wanting today, Admiral?" said Nobli, expecting the worst.

"I know you won't like this," Clement started.

"You're going to try and break my ship again, aren't you, Clement?" cut in Nobli.

"Um, well, yes, I guess . . ."

"Just get to the bad part."

"I'm going to need one of your in-system LEAP drive jumps," said Clement, cutting to the chase.

"That almost broke the LEAP reactor last time we tried it," snapped Nobli.

"I know, but—"

"But it's our only hope. I get it. Just tell me when you need it."

"Ivan will give you the jump coordinates. The when will need to be available on my console, at my command."

"As an app, I expect? You're a hard man, Admiral. You enjoy breaking things too much," Nobli said.

"An app on my console would be preferred, yes," said Clement, ignoring the last comment.

"How long do I have?"

Clement looked up at the main tactical display. "Seven minutes," he said.

"Good thing I had it ready," replied Nobli, then cut the line. About ten seconds later a square white icon appeared on Clement's console, with the blue letters LJ on it, which Clement assumed meant "LEAP Jump," or something similar. It would do.

"Time to the scatter mines, Pilot?" he asked of Ori.

"One minute, thirty seconds," she replied. He keyed in a parabolic course and sent it to her.

"Use this flight pattern, please," he said.

"Aye, sir."

"Do you have coordinates for the L2 Lagrange point, Navigator?"

"I do, sir," replied Massif.

"Please bring the LEAP reactor to hot, Commander Massif. I will have jump control at my console."

"Yes, sir."

"Is that flight plan set, Pilot?"

"It is, sir. We're going to drag the scatter mines with us, aren't we, sir?" said Ori.

Clement stood once more. "We are, Pilot. It's our only hope of a 'Hail Mary' in my opinion. Like it or not, it's our best chance."

"Better than the MAD weapon?"

"Better? No. But not as destructive, and possibly achieving the same goals with less loss of life."

"A surgical strike rather than indiscriminate firing?"

"Affirmative," Clement replied. He didn't feel like he had to explain his feelings on killing other human beings with a terrible weapon of destruction. Then his eyes went to the ship's clock. Two minutes, thirty seconds until the enemy fleet arrived. He hit the main ship com.

"All hands, stand ready," he said, then shut down the line.

The clock continued counting down.

The *Beauregard* was already in motion, dragging the mass of scatter mines in her wake when the enemy fleet came to a full stop over Bellus, bursting on to the scene like a hundred tiny suns being birthed at the same moment. Clement wasn't sure how the gravity-wave dampening tech worked, but it was certainly impressive in practice. In an instant, almost as if they had appeared from nowhere, the entire enemy fleet was suddenly looming over both the *Beauregard* and the planet Bellus. It was a frightening sight in both its scope and scale.

The *Beauregard* was making three-quarter thrust on her engines, enough to keep the scatter mines on her tail but not so fast that they would pull out ahead of their preprogrammed attack range. Massif's estimations had proven to be accurate as the current group of scatter mines trailing the tiny gunship had nearly cleared the enemy fleet's formations of destroyers and cruisers. Clement was making an end run "under" the main formation, speeding rapidly toward the enemy HuKs. Those unmanned ships were likely programmed to attack any enemy within their range of defense, which for a typical design was likely a thousand kilometers. With luck, the HuKs might actually help them achieve their goal by seeing the scatter mines as an approaching enemy. Their AI would automatically default to self-preservation, and with luck, both groups of pilotless vessels would attack each other, with no human casualties.

Ori had gotten the *Beauregard* close enough to the positions of the scatter mines to attract almost all of them, which numbered close to two hundred. He had left about forty of them behind, and those forty were now going active and making for the enemy formation's frontline destroyers. The crew of the *Beauregard* watched nervously as the scatter mines went into action, charging down and then exploding near the destroyers. To Clement's surprise, the destroyers were taking heavier damage than he expected, with orange-yellow fireballs bouncing off the hulls of several enemy ships.

"Mika, what are we seeing here?" he asked.

"I'm not sure, sir, but it looks like the destroyers weren't able to get their defensive fields up fast enough. The scatter mines are exploding directly against their hulls, sir."

"That's a surprise! It could be that their gravity-dampening technology takes too much power away from their generators, so they can't activate their defensive fields until the generators get fully rebooted."

"That would be one explanation, sir. Either way our little group of leftover mines is doing more damage than we hoped."

They watched together as the scatter mines did their work, blowing holes in the side of the enemy destroyer's hulls. There were only six ships affected by the attack, just a third of their total number of destroyers, but enough to do more than just skin their knees. One of the destroyers lost its directional capability and it started listing heavily to starboard and toward a second destroyer that was already burning profusely. They watched as the listing destroyer, which had already fired up its engines to pivot toward the Five Suns fleet, accelerated quickly into its sister ship, causing a large and dramatic explosion.

"Well, that's two more of those than I expected to take out with this attack," said Clement, nodding his acknowledgement, then turning to Ivan Massif. "Position of the main fleet, Navigator?"

"Pivoting now, sir. But it looks from here as if they are trying to regroup and send their ships after our flotilla, toward the L2 Lagrange point. They don't seem to have any interest in us."

"That's because they didn't expect us to be here, Mr. Massif. And my bet is that none of their current maneuvering is taking us into account. Are there any ships in position to take us out?"

"Not currently, Admiral. The only ship that might have a shot at us at this range would be their battlecruiser, but she would have to do some quick thinking and adjusting to catch us now."

"Time to targets, Pilot?"

"We'll be in range of those HuKs in nineteen seconds," reported Ori.

Clement watched as the enemy HuKs began to react to their automated programming and turn into self-preservation mode. The HuKs accelerated, firing their engines to engage the approaching gunship and its trailing mass of scatter mines.

"Do we slow our approach, sir?" asked Ori.

"Negative, Pilot. Maintain speed." On the tactical

board hanging above them the group of HuKs was now fully engaged, diving planetward in their attempt to destroy both the *Beauregard* and the group of mines trailing in its wake. Clement's hand hovered over the LEAP jump control icon, watching as his single ship streaked toward the swirling group of hunter-killers. Their formation had become fluid, constantly changing as its tactical AIs adjusted their course and intent according to their preprogrammed mission. They were literally acting on instinct now, as if instinct could be programmed into a machine. That was certainly the designer's original intent, although it appeared to be working against their basic design principles right at this particular moment.

"Slow to two-thirds speed," said Clement. Ori turned to him in surprise.

"Are you serious? That would put the scatter mines within ten seconds of hitting us at their top speed."

"I'm aware of the situation, Pilot. Please follow my orders." Ori did, but not without serious reservations.

"Two-thirds speed, sir."

"Ivan, do we have a clear path to the L2 Lagrange point?"

"Course is open and available, sir."

"Pilot, give me a countdown to when we're vulnerable to the firing range of the HuKs."

"Twenty seconds, sir. Fifteen … ten … five … four … three … two … one …"

Clement hit the LEAP jump icon, and the *Beauregard* shifted in both time and space.

A kaleidoscope of colors filled his senses for the briefest fractions of a second, then in the same instant returned to normal. He quickly shifted the tactical display to show the battlefield over Bellus that they had just left behind. It showed more than a dozen of the hunter-killers burning from multiple impacts from the web of scatter mines the *Beauregard* had thrown at them. Three of the HuKs had been nimble enough, and their AIs smart enough, to escape the battlefield, although at least one of the three had taken a hit from a scatter mine. The rest were now burning streaks of light heading for the upper atmosphere of the planet, where they would undoubtedly be extinguished. It made for a brilliant fireworks display.

Mika Ori retched at her station, but managed to keep from vomiting on the bridge.

Short-range jumps through quantum-fluid space could have that effect. Clement himself fought off the urge as well. After some deep breathing by the bridge crew, they all regained their composure. Clement pulled up the Five Suns fleet position from the long-range tactical display.

"The fleet is seventy-three minutes from the L2 Lagrange point, sir," reported Massif.

"Our position?"

"Nearly spot on, sir. We're within thirty-three hundred kilometers of dead center on the L2 point, sir. Not bad for jumping through an alternate space-time dimension."

"Not bad at all, Ivan."

"Should we move to the exact position, sir?" asked Ori.

"No, Commander. Station-keeping, please. Let our fleet come to us. How long until the enemy fleet regroups and adjusts for our location?"

Ori responded first. "I'd guess at least two hours until they would be able to engage us, sir."

"I concur, Admiral. We've dealt them a tactical blow," agreed Massif.

"Yes, but not a decisive one. We've bought more time, that's all," replied Clement.

"But that's better than nothing."

Thirty seconds later, Nobli gave his admiral the bad news.

"You've broken the reactor with your little antics, Admiral."

"How bad?" asked Clement.

"What do you mean how *bad*? It's *broken*, Admiral. There's a crack thirty nanometers wide in her casing. I don't have the material to fix it. If we try to use this reactor again, we'll blow a hole in space-time several hundred AUs wide."

"Several thousand!" yelled Tech Reck in the background of the com. Either way, it was bad news.

"What are my options?" demanded Clement.

"You don't have any, Jared. Barring a full replacement of the reactor at the Kemmerine Shipyards, the *Beauregard* is done. The MAD weapon is done. I'm sorry, Admiral, but the only way this ship is going home again is in the belly of the *Agamemnon*."

Clement absorbed that for a moment, then cut off the com line to his engineer. "Maintain status," he said to the bridge crew. "Give me updates on the arrival of our flotilla and the location of the enemy fleet. Let me know when either one of them changes their status. I will be in my cabin," he said, then quickly jumped up from his console and made for the place he had spent more time in than any other on board the ship.

He had a bottle of Argyle scotch out on the table two minutes later, and poured himself a sizeable shot into a glass. He stared at the glass of whiskey, a reminder of so many times in the past when he had sought solace inside a bottle, and how long it had been since he had needed to go there. He contemplated the whiskey as he thought over his predicament.

Losing the LEAP drive, and more importantly, the MAD weapon, his one true advantage, left him at a loss as to what their next move could be. He pulled up the tactical screen on his tabletop plasma display and watched as the enemy fleet regrouped, trying to compensate for their newfound lack of hunter-killers. They still had twenty undamaged heavy cruisers and sixteen functional destroyers in addition to a full-sized battlecruiser. If their commander was smart, and Clement believed he or she was, they would restack their formation, putting the remaining hunter-killers out in front of the destroyers to exact maximum damage from their next attack. The logical thing would be to mix in a handful of cruisers with their destroyers and hold back the rest for an all-out assault on the *Agamemnon*. He watched as the enemy fleet organized itself in just that way. That was all he needed to know about who the commander of this fleet was. She was organizing her forces just as a Five Suns–trained fleet commander would; just as Elara DeVore would. Clement poured himself another drink, then screwed the cap back on the bottle. He knew his limits, but if there was anyone who could have driven him to drink in a crisis, it was her.

He had hoped to avoid ever seeing her again, let alone

facing her again in battle. But she had always been a chameleon, changing her stripes as the situation flowed, always planning for the worst contingencies, always staying a step ahead. She was a long-term thinker, and Clement, well, he had to face the fact that he was at his best when he was on the battlefield. He was a situational thinker, a seat-of-the-pants battle commander, not a long-term planner or a scheming politician. His forte was his thinking in a crisis. Perhaps that's why peace had eluded him so much in this life. He took the scotch in his glass down in one shot, then put the bottle back in its cabinet, from where he hoped he would never have to take it again. He straightened himself up in his cabin mirror, tugging gently at his duty uniform, preparing to make his return to the bridge, where his friends and crew would be expecting him to come up with yet another miracle. Only this time, he wasn't sure he had one.

Forty minutes later and his flotilla had reassembled at the L2 Lagrange point. Despite Captain Yan's insistence, he refused to take the *Beauregard* back to the landing deck of the *Agamemnon*. In fact, he ordered the other four Five Suns Navy gunships back out into space. He coached their captains that their new assignment will be to take out the remaining hunter-killers in the forward formation of the enemy fleet. It wasn't an easy job, but the four gunships had at least a fifty-fifty chance to eliminate the remaining suicide weapons in the enemy fleet.

As for his flotilla's formation, it was going to have to be much different than what their enemy showed. That fleet had left three destroyers and two cruisers behind at

Bellus, undoubtedly to begin landing operations and to establish a beachhead on the planet itself. There had been no reaction of any kind from the planetary defense system, so Clement had to assume that either Mary had been wrong about the Makers' abilities, or that they simply didn't care enough about what was going on above their world to bother to react to it. He wished he could get in contact with Colonel Lubrov and her Marines on the surface, but that was impossible, both because of the distance involved and because of radio interference by the enemy fleet. There was nothing Clement could do about that situation except hope that his people were well-trained enough and dug in well enough to survive the coming onslaught.

The primary enemy fleet was now well underway toward the Lagrange point, and his flotilla. They had the luxury of eighteen undamaged heavy cruisers that could no doubt dispatch his eight destroyers and six light cruisers with ease. His only real chance was to put *Agamemnon* at the front of his formation in order to protect his lighter armored ships. *Agamemnon* was so much bigger than even the heavy cruisers that the enemy had that taking her on full force would be a tough ask for the enemy. Clement could chip away at the destroyers and cruisers in the enemy fleet with his forces, but not in any decisive way. He could prolong the battle, but without the *Beauregard* and its MAD weapon he had no knockout punch. Eventually, the enemy commander would bring in their battlecruiser, which, combined with their superiority in heavy cruisers and shear number of destroyers, would bring the battle to an end. *Agamemnon*, perhaps, could fight off the enemy cruisers for a while, but she would take a beating in doing so, and eventually lose the battle to the enemy's flagship. Clement felt he had to at least consider surrender for the sake of his crew and his fleet, and the many lives they represented. But the first blow had already been struck, and he doubted that they would back off now.

No, his crew were trained, and trained well, to fight when the situation called for it, and protecting the thirty thousand migrants on the ground, not to mention the natives, was a cause worth fighting for. They would have to fight, even if the odds were long, and pray for help from, if not the outright intervention of, the gods. In this case, those gods were called the Makers, and Clement wondered what he would have to do to raise them from their slumber. In the end he put the *Agamemnon* out front, at the point of the spear. It was the only option he really had. He inverted the protective halo around her, however, placing his heavier armed cruisers on her wide flanks and the lighter armed destroyers in close support above and below her. The gunships would stay in the shadow of *Agamemnon*, and act only if the enemy hunter-killers were brought into battle.

He sat at his bridge station, surveying the incoming enemy fleet and his own tactical formation. There were no miracles on this board, no Hail Marys. He had what he had, and that was it.

"I have Captain Yan of the *Agamemnon* on the com, sir," said Adebayor from her station.

"In my ear," replied Clement, referring to his personal com implant. A second later and she came on the line.

"Got your next miracle planned out?" came Yan's voice, part with sympathy, part mocking in tone.

"No," he replied, then he stepped out of his command couch and headed down the steps to the rear of the cabin sub-deck, and *Beauregard's* small galley. He sat down, his display pad in front of him. "I was hoping you had something for me."

"Other than being the battering ram of this formation?" replied Yan. "I'm fresh out of ideas, Admiral. I suppose the MAD weapon is now off the table?"

"It would take days to replace, even at Kemmerine Shipyards; Nobli says he can't repair it."

"I guess we're screwed then."

Clement sighed. "I guess we are. Aren't you supposed to give me alternatives as my second-in-command?"

"I wasn't sure that was still part of my job, since you seem to ignore my every recommendation."

"It is still part of your job. Have you heard anything from the surface?" Clement said, changing the subject.

"Colonel Lubrov's last report was six hours ago. They are dug in and as ready as they can be, but I think they're going to be severely outgunned. Just like us."

"Any word from your friend Mary?" he asked, probing.

"Nothing, and no response to my direct calls, either. I don't think she likes me anymore."

"She liked you well enough on the first trip," said Clement, then instantly regretted it. He rubbed at his eyes. Stress, fatigue, and stupidity had made him say it. There was silence on the other end of the line. "I'm sorry, Yan. I shouldn't have said that."

"Apology accepted, Admiral. Now, on to the situation at hand. Any tactical orders you'd like to pass along?"

"Yes. Tell Samkange and Son I expect them to protect your flanks at all costs, and those destroyer captains have to protect the cruisers. The gunships know their orders: take out the remaining hunter-killers. As for you . . ." He trailed off.

"As for me?"

"Unleash holy hell on them, Yan. Take out their heavy cruisers. Hold off that battlecruiser as long as possible. Other than that, pray for a miracle."

"Aye, aye, Admiral. *Agamemnon* will not let you down."

"I expect not, Captain. Good luck."

"Sir." Then Yan cut the line from her end.

Clement sighed.

With forty-five minutes until contact with the enemy fleet, Clement headed down to his engine room to see his friend, Hassan Nobli. To his surprise, both Nobli and Tech Kim Reck were crawling all over the bright yellow LEAP reactor casing.

He cleared his throat. "Well, what do have we here? I thought I broke your reactor," he said.

Nobli, standing on top of a ladder, whipped his head around. "You damn well did, Admiral, but that doesn't mean *we* give up on her." Clement watched as Tech Reck poured a liquid gray goo onto the surface of the round LEAP reactor casing.

"What's that stuff?" he said.

Reck snapped off a reply. "A combination of carbon nanotubes and liquid helium-3 from the ion thrusters. It's just a hunch, but it could provide enough of a seal to let you use the reactor once more, *if* you're so inclined."

"You're using helium-3 fuel on the reactor casing?" said Clement, incredulous.

Reck looked up at her commanding officer. "You got a better idea?"

Clement had nothing to say to that, so he motioned Nobli into the engineer's office. "We need to send her to finishing school," he said once the door was closed. Nobli shrugged, then leaned back on his desk.

"She'll never be a prim and proper officer, but I still believe she can fix almost anything."

"Can she fix my reactor?"

"*Your* reactor? Like I said, Admiral, it's unfixable. But her chemistry is solid and this could provide you with an option."

"The MAD weapon?"

Nobli nodded. "Maybe one more shot, Jared, or maybe we blow up a large portion of this solar system. Either way, it would stop the invasion."

"That it would, and end all of our lives."

"I don't see that we have much choice."

Clement shook his head. "I don't either, Hassan. But destroying almost every living being in this system isn't an option, either. We have three options that I can see: Fight, and lose. Fight, and win through some miracle I haven't thought of yet. Or surrender."

"Surrender? To Elara DeVore? She'll skin you alive and hang you upside down if she gets her hands on you."

"Will she? I wonder." Clement paced the small office. "In any case, if I can negotiate for your lives, I will. She'll need a good engineer, especially the one who built the MAD weapon. Mika and Ivan and Kayla would be valuable as well."

"You're forgetting about Yan. If DeVore gets ahold of her she'll be killed too, almost immediately. I know you don't want that on your conscience."

Clement nodded, grim-faced. "I don't. So . . . we'll fight, for as long as we can and as hard as we can, and maybe hope for a stalemate, or a noble surrender."

"In either case, Jared, you can't let this ship fall into her hands. Not with the MAD technology. She could destroy the Five Suns with it."

Clement straightened. "The *Beauregard* will not fall into enemy hands. Not now, not ever. You have my word on that."

Nobli looked up at his old friend over the top of his wire-rimmed glasses. "I know I do. Good luck, Admiral."

And with that, Clement was gone, back to his bridge.

The enemy fleet was just ten minutes away from the L2 Lagrange point, and they had arranged themselves in the formation Clement had predicted with only a few exceptions, small differences in his eyes. Clement had his flotilla lined up exactly as he wanted it, with *Agamemnon* on the point, his six light cruisers in close tactical support to his battlecruiser, and his eight destroyers protecting the light cruisers. The cruisers would carry a fair punch, and they likely could handle any of the enemy's destroyers. They were overmatched, though, against the enemy heavy cruisers, so those would have to be taken out by his battlecruiser. Undoubtedly the enemy fleet commander would unleash his (or her) heavy cruisers on *Agamemnon* first, trying to take her out of the battle. But that wouldn't be easy. She was built as good as Five Suns Navy technology could make her, Clement had seen to that.

From their position on the battlefield, Clement decided that he needed to move his forces, if only to create some variability to the enemy's apparent plan of attack. Doing so wouldn't necessarily give his flotilla a tactical advantage, but it would buy them a bit more time. He ordered the flotilla to advance 0.06 degrees "south" to the plane of the ecliptic of the Trinity system, at one-quarter thruster power. This would require the approaching fleet, which was coming in much slower than their previous advance from the outer gas planet, to modify their course with a tactical burn. Clement's calculations were that it would give the flotilla approximately ten extra minutes before having to engage the enemy. Though the L2 Lagrange point was gravitationally unstable, there was little use Clement could think of to gain an advantage from that condition. This was going to be fought purely on battle tactics, and the enemy was in a far superior position.

"Lieutenant Adebayor, has the enemy responded to our movement yet?" Clement asked after three minutes of thruster burn.

"Negative, sir. Longscope scans indicate the enemy fleet is maintaining the same approach vector," the young African officer reported.

"Which means either they haven't seen our movement yet, or they believe they have such a tactical advantage over us that they don't care what we do."

"Either way, sir, I for one am getting tired of just sitting around and waiting," piped in Mika Ori.

"I agree with you, XO, but I'm not sure I can spend many of our resources just to give them trouble. We'll need everything we have for the battle."

Just then Adebayor reported that the enemy fleet was now moving toward their new position.

"Less than a hundred thousand kilometers now, sir," she reported. Clement looked up at his tactical screen and saw that the enemy had moved their three remaining hunter-killers to the forefront of their formation.

"Time to the battlefield, Pilot?"

Ori responded. "I make it eight minutes and eleven seconds, Admiral."

"How far away are those hunter-killers from the main formation?"

Ivan Massif responded. "About ten thousand kilometers out front of them, sir. Just outside of their destroyer's energy weapons range, but just *inside* their accurate missile range, or should I say our best guess at their missile range."

"So . . . they're trying get those hunter-killers in position to hit *Agamemnon* early in the battle. If I'm right, I'm guessing those HuKs will start accelerating any second now. Miss Adebayor, what do your longscope scans show?"

"No additional acceleration at this time, Admiral." Clement contemplated that. Despite their superior numbers, the enemy fleet commander appeared reticent to lose any more of her resources. They were playing things very conservatively. But then again, they had the luxury of numbers.

"Kayla, raise the gunship *Antietam*, please."

Adebayor swept her hands over her console for a few seconds, then said, "Captain Kagereki on the line, sir."

Clement activated his com. "Jim, I'm going to need you to do something dangerous."

"Yes, sir, I understand, Admiral. What do you need from us?"

"I need you and the other gunship captains to accelerate toward the enemy HuKs. I need you to get close enough to engage their automated AI defense systems. If we can't get them to move further away from the rest of the fleet you could come under fire from the enemy destroyers. We need you to get those hunter-killers out into open space where we can pick them off. The *Antietam* and the rest of the gunships will have to be the bait. Do you understand what I'm asking you, Jim?"

"I do, sir. We stand ready and able to carry out your orders."

"Stand by, Captain. My longscope officer will send you a ping when I need you to go. Good luck, Captain."

"Thank you, sir."

With that Clement cut the line and turned to Adebayor. "Current position of the hunter-killers, Kayla?"

"They are now about eleven thousand kilometers in front of the main enemy battle group, sir. It looks like they've begun accelerating in preparation for an attack."

"As I hoped they would. Lieutenant, send the *Antietam* our ping."

"Sir," she said. They all watched on the tactical display as the four Five Suns gunships began accelerating toward

the hunter-killer formation. There were three of the
suicide devices left, and he hoped his four remaining
gunships could handle them, but it was by no means
certain. The *Beauregard* remained behind, still
undergoing repairs to her LEAP reactor, and now at the
location of the tactical center of the fleet. Clement fought
an urge to join the battle. He did have conventional
weapons after all, missiles and torpedoes, even some
nukes, but no coil cannons. Those ports had been taken
over for use by the currently off-line MAD weapon.

"We should be out there," said Ori.

"We have to command the battle from somewhere,
XO."

"Understood, sir. They are making a very conservative
approach, though. Do you think they fear that we still
have the MAD weapon to use on them?"

"I think that's exactly what they fear. They don't know
that it's knocked out, and, they're probably hoping that
I don't have the guts to use it again." Clement went
silent then and watched the four gunships quickly
bearing down on the hunter-killer formation. From
their current angle and approach speed, the gunships
could strafe the hunter-killers and escape fire from the
rest of the enemy fleet before turning back on the HuKs
once again.

"Time . . ."

"Ten seconds," said Ori.

The gunship formation, led by captain Kagereki and
the *Antietam* in a standard attacking diamond, swept
across the paths of the three hunter-killers. They blasted
the enemy vessels with their forward coil cannons, and

then swung out into open space, there to quickly decelerate and turn back on their opponents. The energy weapons fire ricocheted off of the hulls of all three hunter-killers, but the initial attacks weren't decisive. The HuKs responded according to their programming and began pursuit of the gunships. They were all now watching the opening skirmish in what would eventually become a much larger battle.

The enemy HuKs quickly pulled away from the rest of their fleet, which was beginning to decelerate toward the main battlefield. The enemy made no move to protect their HuKs with any additional firepower. The HuKs were now too far distant from the main fleet to be supported by destroyer fire or missiles. The hunter-killers were obviously expendable to the enemy commander, but leaving them untended would pose a higher risk to Clement's flotilla. He had to take them out, but she didn't have to defend them.

She, he thought to himself. It was a big assumption, but probably an accurate one.

The gunships completed their turn and closed again on the HuKs, decelerating to enable their full range of weaponry. When they got within firing range, *Antietam*, the lead ship in the diamond, let go a volley of six missiles, all conventional, two aimed at each of the three hunter-killers. At the sight of the missiles, two of the hunter-killers broke from their formation, heading directly for the outer gunship in the diamond formation, the *Danville*. The third HuK accelerated toward the *Antietam* and its incoming volley of missiles. It began firing energy from its central coil cannon, trying to take out the missiles. It got two, but three of them hit their target, destroying the HuK, while the last missile missed badly and flew off into empty space.

The *Danville* meanwhile had begun evasive maneuvers, spilling out chaff and defensive flack in an attempt to distract the two hunter-killers on an intercept course. Because of the formation, the other two gunships were not in a position to help the *Danville*. It would be a do-or-die situation for her. The *Danville* turned and twisted, trying to escape from the two suicide machines closing in on her. She fired defensive torpedoes, a few of which hit the incoming HuKs, but they had little effect against the heavily armored weapons. Clement watched, helpless, as the two hunter-killers pounded the *Danville*'s hull with their energy weapons. Suddenly, the *Danville* erupted with orange-yellow explosions as her inner hall was breached and life-supporting oxygen escaped into space from the wounds in her side. The HuKs kept coming, even as the three remaining gunships tried to turn and help defend their wounded friend.

But it was too late.

Both hunter-killers impacted against the *Danville* in a tremendous explosion of ice crystals and fire from burning oxygen. There were secondary explosions as her cache of weapons were detonated by the impacts. What remained of the ship were only bits and pieces of broken metal and burned hull.

Clement spoke low and slowly. "Lieutenant Adebayor, recall the gunships. Tell them they have five minutes to look for survivors of the *Danville*, then they are ordered to return to the main fleet. I want them in the back, away from the battle. They will conduct search and rescue operations only for the duration of this engagement."

"Yes, sir," replied Adebayor in a subdued voice, then carried out the recall.

Clement sat back in his couch. One gunship and twenty crew possibly lost. Three HuKs taken out. It was not a good trade.

Not at all.

✦ **14** ✦

The enemy fleet was right on top of Clement's flotilla, which was now only three minutes from missile and energy weapons range of the forward forces in the attack group. Clement had Adebayor raise Captain Yan aboard the *Agamemnon*. It took seconds to get her on the line.

"It looks like the situation hasn't changed, Captain. The enemy is still leading with their heavy cruisers and using their destroyers to plug holes in the formation. They will be coming at you with everything they have in about two minutes. What's your plan?"

"I was about to ask you for recommendations, Admiral," she said, "but just in case, I had my own ideas ready."

"I'd be interested to hear those."

"I'm thinking we'll open with the Rods of God. I have two hundred of them, but I think forty should suffice for an initial volley."

"Nothing like some kinetic energy weapons to get a battle off to a vigorous start. Might even catch some of their missile volleys."

"My thoughts exactly. We've raised the gravimetric

defense fields; that should help in pushing any incoming ordnance away from our main hull."

Clement nodded, even though she couldn't see him over the voice-only com. It was a solid opening plan. "I wish I'd taken the time to put that technology in all of our ships. But I didn't plan on us coming here and fighting a war."

"It would have been advantageous," agreed Yan, "but there was no way for us to know we would be in this much trouble on our first settlement mission."

"I'd almost forgotten why we came here in the first place. Carry on, Captain. I will communicate any advice I have through the tactical system."

"Good luck to you, Admiral."

"And to you, Captain." With that Clement closed the line and called down to his weapons bay, where Lieutenants Telco and Tsu were on duty. Telco answered the line.

"Weapons bay here, Admiral."

"Mr. Telco, I need you to load my nukes." The *Beauregard* still had five of the small-yield nuclear missiles on board. Clement hadn't thought he would need them on this mission, so his was the only gunship that carried this heavy ordnance. They were ten kilotons each, enough to take out an unshielded destroyer, but likely not effective against the heavy cruisers or a battlecruiser.

"All five of them, sir?" asked Telco.

"No, just four. I want to keep one in reserve. Load the other two launchers with conventional warheads."

"Yes, sir. That leftover nuke isn't for self-destruction, I hope," said Telco in his usual cheery way. But this wasn't the time for humor.

"I will let you know when I need them, and what I need them for," snapped Clement. "Right now I need you to do your duty without question. This isn't a lark, Lieutenant. Good men and women on both sides of this battle are going to die in a few minutes." He cut the line abruptly, unwilling to listen to the young lieutenant's likely apologies. He simply had no time for it.

"Time, Mika," he asked.

"Thirty-nine seconds until their forward cruisers are in range of the *Agamemnon*, sir." Clement didn't respond, but watched the clock count down to the beginning of a battle he may have already lost.

The two fleets came together in a slow ballet of steam and fire. The fire came from the Directed Energy Weapons of both fleets; the steam came from the trails of incoming missiles. The enemy had led with ten cruisers, all of which fired eight missiles each from their forward launch bays. Yan had countered with the Rods of God, fifteen meters of solid titanium shot out of her forward rail gun launchers. The kinetic force of those forty "telephone poles," as Clement had referred to them once, could be devastating. They were hard to "aim" in any conventional sense, but there was no defensive field, gravimetric or otherwise, that could really stop them. Only the largest of war vessels, the battlecruisers, could even carry weapons this large and massive. They were usually used for close infighting, ship-to-ship combat between capital ships. In this case, Yan had led with them from a longer distance, and that was undoubtedly a surprise for the enemy's forward heavy cruiser captains.

A few of the rods were damaged by missile hits, which pushed them off in odd directions. In some cases they could be more destructive spinning crazily through space, trying to shed their kinetic energy, than they would be if they were fired directly at an enemy. Most of the incoming missiles missed the rods, which had no propulsive heat signature, and corrected course toward the *Agamemnon*. Yan countered this development with a barrage of defensive torpedoes and DEWs from her forward launch tubes and coil cannons. They were joined in this chorus by the supporting light cruisers of the Five Suns fleet, which also used a substantial number of torpedoes to blunt the first attack. The torpedoes were lighter and smaller than conventional missiles, with smaller warheads, but also much more accurate. Yan's counter was an effective one, with a flurry of torpedo/missile impacts in the middle of the battlefield. A handful of missiles got through, but they were easily dispatched by Yan's DEW weapons and her gravimetric shielding. *Agamemnon* had survived the first enemy volley.

The enemy cruisers, though, had a different set of problems. The Rods of God were still spinning their way directly into the heavy cruiser group's path. They would only have seconds to correct their courses or take serious damage. A few of their captains acted quickly and got their ships out of the way. The heavy cruisers, though, weren't nimble like a destroyer or even a light cruiser would be. They were slower to react, harder to turn, and thus, much more vulnerable to an unexpected type of attack, like the Rods of God.

The rods slammed into three of the forward heavy

cruisers. Those ships exploded with multiple impacts, taking heavy damage, and although they were substantially built, they couldn't take the level of kinetic pounding that they were receiving. They were at a minimum knocked out of the battle for now. At best, they would have to be evacuated and abandoned. At worst, they would go down with all hands lost.

Two of the other cruisers suffered glancing blows from the rods, and as a result they had some heavy tears in their hulls, but they were still operational.

Clement looked at the tactical board, and made a decision.

"Take us in, Pilot, full burn. Navigator, set a course for those two damaged heavy cruisers. Let me know when we're within missile range."

Ori got the *Beauregard* moving fast. Both of the enemy cruisers were clearly damaged and struggling to stay in contact with their healthy siblings. Clement saw Yan moving *Agamemnon* into a position to attack the cruisers with a missile volley, but that would leave her starboard flank vulnerable. Clement got on the com and told Yan to hold her ship back. "We've got this, Captain," he said.

"Are you sure?"

"Yes. Maintain your current posture and continue to attack the center of their lines."

"Glory hog," he heard her say before she signed off. He smiled.

The minute it took for the *Beauregard* to get within nuclear missile firing range seemed like an eternity to Clement, and probably everyone else on board too. But when they reached the firing threshold, the admiral didn't hesitate.

"Mika, target and fire our full complement of missiles at those cruisers."

"Aye, sir!" replied Ori, but she didn't really need to. Her commanding officer knew she would do her job.

The enemy captains must not have anticipated this kind of rogue move from Clement, attacking cruisers with a single gunship, but they were wounded birds. They didn't react to the incoming missiles, two nuclear and one conventional targeted at each of them, until it was far too late. The missiles locked on and exploded directly onto the hulls of both retreating ships. The results were devastating. Those cruisers, likely with crews of close to two hundred people, were completely disintegrated in the nuclear fire. That made five enemy heavy cruisers destroyed. They had given the enemy a serious bloody nose in the first real fight they had been in. Both sides took the opportunity to put some distance between their fleets before taking any additional action. They had succeeded in taking out one quarter of the enemy's heavy cruiser complement. It wasn't decisive, but it was a start.

"Round one to us," said Clement. "Fourteen more to go." The reference was to old-style championship boxing, which lasted fifteen rounds.

Mika Ori had already executed an escape burn before Clement could even order it. As the *Beauregard* streaked back to a position of relative safety, Kayla Adebayor called from her workstation.

"Incoming communication, sir," she said.

"From Captain Yan?"

"No, sir. I make it as coming from the enemy battlecruiser, sir."

Clement sat down deep in his captain's couch. "Put it through, Lieutenant," he said, knowing full well whose voice he expected to hear.

"Well done, Clement," said the husky female voice on the other end of the line. "But you're going to have to do better than that to take out my entire fleet."

Clement sat back in his chair, contemplating a response. The voice was undoubtedly that of former Five Suns Navy Fleet Admiral Elara DeVore.

"Cut out the bridge com," ordered Clement. "I'll take this in my quarters." He stood up brusquely and left the bridge, and his crewmates, behind. Once inside his cabin he sat down at his worktable and brought up his tactical desk plasma, then tapped his ear to activate his personal com link.

"What do you want, Elara? I'm trying to fight a war here."

"Maybe you don't need to, Clement. You do have other options."

"Such as?"

"Surrender now, before things get serious. Unnecessary killing isn't your style."

"I've considered that already, if you must know. But I've rejected that option based on what I know of my enemy. And besides, I just won the first battle."

"The odds are still weighed heavily against you; you know that from one look at the tactical screen."

"True, but that fact isn't enough for me to trust you with my life, and the life of my crew."

"You don't trust me that I would give you favorable surrender terms?"

"Not in the slightest. Also, there are certain things that are worth fighting for, Elara, like the freedom from slavery, freedom to choose your own life and not have it imposed on you, things you wouldn't understand. Those things are worth defending. To the death, if necessary."

"And if it's not necessary? What then?"

"Then you'd have to convince me that your version of reality is true. At this point, I don't believe a word you say. And besides that, who *exactly* would I be surrendering to?"

There was a pause then, before DeVore spoke again. "I represent a government called the Solar League. It encompasses Earth and the other Sol system colonies: Luna, Mars, Ceres, Titan, and the rest. It is a unified government and it's a just one."

"They sent a military Ark to enslave the natives of Trinity," Clement said flatly.

There was a heavy sigh, then a reply from DeVore. "That's not correct. The Earth Ark that was sent here was launched almost eight decades ago, Earth time, by another, more corrupt government. A remnant of the old Pan-Korean empire on Earth. Their intent was conquest and colonization, but the Solar League's is not."

Clement held his response for a second, contemplating her answer. He wasn't satisfied she was telling the truth. "Let's suppose I believe what you say, for the sake of argument. Just how much contact have you had with this so-called Solar League? And how much can you trust a government that's more than forty light-years away?"

"I've met with their government leaders, at the highest level. I trust them because I've looked them in the eye and spoken to them in their language, and ours. The Solar League is primarily run by descendants of the people who colonized Helios, from the old Earth country of Brazil. They are very dedicated to spreading peace and prosperity throughout the stars, and to new colonies. But they are determined to colonize the Trinity system," she said.

"That's something they may have to bring up with the natives. And another question, how did you make this contact? It's a long journey to Sol. I'm guessing you gave them the LEAP drive."

"Of course I did. What else did I have to bargain with? I went to Earth a full year before your mission to Trinity, and I gave them the LEAP technology in exchange for an alliance. In return, they warned me about the sleeper Ark that had been sent by the Pan-Korean empire remnant, and how soon it would be arriving in-system. That's why I needed you, Clement, as a scout, to measure their strength. I never thought you'd end up in an all-out war with them. That was my fleet's job."

"So, *you* gave this Solar League LEAP technology? Do you realize how dangerous that could be? You never thought I would develop a super weapon like the MAD based on that technology. What if they develop it?"

"That was something we hadn't planned on. Our engineers, and theirs, never saw an application like what your man Nobli came up with. If I'd known how smart he was I'd never have let you take him with you."

Clement was frustrated at the conversation, bordering on exasperation, and he became verbally short with her. "All of this is quite interesting, Elara, but the fact remains that you have a better fleet, but I have the ultimate weapon in this star system."

"True, your MAD weapon is a risk, I've seen what it can do, but I can also read your energy signatures, and your ship is not running a warm LEAP reactor, so I'm guessing maybe your super weapon is off-line."

"Guessing is a big risk. I have other ships with LEAP reactors, and by deduction, they could all have MAD weapons," he lied.

"They could, but I suspect that's a technology you'd want to keep secret for as long as possible. It's far too dangerous a weapon to be used haphazardly, or to be trusted to inexperienced junior ship captains."

Clement had reached the end of his patience with the verbal sparring between them, so he decided to change the subject. "So, I take it that it was this Solar League that rescued you and your crews from the surface of Alphus?"

"They had a mission planned soon after I gave them the LEAP engine. I knew they would come, and probably before you came back to Trinity. The Ark you detected in this system is theirs. They only arrived a few weeks ago, but we were able to signal them and get rescued. Per my agreement with them, or rather our alliance, I was given command of the overall Trinity mission. What you don't know, Clement, is that there are three more Earth Arks on their way to Trinity soon. I'm not sure of their exact arrival time; it could be next week or next year, but they will be coming, and their mission is to pacify this system and prepare it for colonization from Earth."

"Interesting. That's a bit like what I'm trying to do here right now, Elara, but without the conquering part. I brought thirty thousand peaceful migrants to Bellus, and they're on the surface of the planet right now. The forces you have over that world threaten those migrants. If you were to withdraw your forces from over the planet, I would be willing to give your proposal some further consideration."

"Let's be realistic, Clement. You know I'm not going to withdraw my forces from Bellus, and I know that you aren't going to give up the planet without a fight. My job here is to prepare this system and all three habitable planets for those colony ships that are coming from the Earth system. If that means I can get your surrender, then great. But, if it means that I have to fight you then I'm prepared to do that as well. You're not in a position to dictate any terms to me, and I'm not in any position to grant you what you would be asking for. I'm here to deliver Trinity to the Solar League, and that's the end of the conversation. Now will you stand down and surrender, and allow our troops to board and occupy your ships?"

Clement thought about that long and hard. DeVore knew him, and knew this was how he was, and she gave him the time he needed, keeping the line open but saying nothing. Eventually, he replied. "You know I can't do that, Elara. Despite your guarantees, which are questionable at best, I know nothing of this Solar League and nothing of the kind of people who comprise it. When I accepted command as Fleet Admiral of the Five Suns Navy, your old job, I took an oath to defend the Five Suns and all the people that live there, whether they're core dwellers, or Rim rats, or even natives on an alien planet."

DeVore didn't respond immediately. Clement quickly looked down at his tactical display to make sure she wasn't launching an attack while they talked. The display thankfully showed both fleets at station-keeping, staying in their respective positions. No one, it seemed, was anxious for this battle.

Finally DeVore responded. "I've already sent you a gesture of my goodwill, Clement. The beacon that you found in LEAP space? My people left it there for you to find, otherwise you might never have found the missing ships from your fleet. They could have been lost forever. I'm not asking you to trust me personally in this matter, but I am asking you to trust what I say about the Solar League. That gesture, the LEAP beacon, that's part of the value system that they espouse. The natives will be taken care of. They will live productive lives, lives that will be enriched by the presence and the protection of the Solar League. Can you say the same about the Five Suns? Under our rule, the Trinity system will be developed for the benefit of all humankind. My hope is that eventually the Five Suns, Trinity, and the Solar League will all agree to merge into one."

"Yes, one entity ruled by you and your people."

"I admit that my governing of the Trinity system was part of my alliance with them. I believe it will be best for Earth, Trinity, the Rim, and the Five Suns. Now I urge you to accept my offer of surrender and amnesty for all the people in your fleet and the migrants on the surface of Bellus below. This is the last time I'm going to offer this compromise."

Clement thought hard once again; the future of many thousands of people, perhaps even millions one day, was in the balance. He wanted his friends to survive this battle. He wanted them not to have to fight it at all, but there were other issues to consider besides his own personal feelings. The bottom line was he just didn't trust Elara DeVore anymore. At all.

As he looked down at his tactical plasma display again, he saw her destroyers firing up their engines and beginning to maneuver into position for an attack on *Agamemnon*. Six of her heavy cruisers quickly did the same. She wasn't waiting for his final answer, she was sending him a warning of what would happen if he didn't give in to her demands. He kept his silence watching as the approaching fleet bored down hard on his flagship. It was a classic power move.

"You have very little time left to make a decision, Clement," DeVore said. As he watched her cruisers and destroyers bear down on his fleet, he made the only decision he could.

He cut the com line, and headed back to his bridge.

✵ 15 ✵

By the time he sat down in his command couch his ships were already engaged in battle. He looked up at the tactical view on the main plasma display to weigh the situation. The flotilla of Solar League destroyers were swarming his Five Suns light cruisers and destroyers, battering them with DEW weapons fire and short-range, low-yield missiles. These weapons weren't really designed to take out an enemy vessel in one volley, but rather continuously weaken their defenses. This indicated a strategy of trying to knock his ships out of the battle by attrition, and that indicated that Elara DeVore wanted to board his ships and capture his crews.

Six Solar League heavy cruisers were coming in behind the destroyer line and pounding the *Agamemnon* with higher yield conventional missiles and DEW fire. *Agamemnon* was for the most part fending off the enemy using her gravimetric shielding to push the missiles off course and dissipate the Directed Energy Weapons fire. But it wasn't a perfect defense. At the range they were engaging, mere kilometers or even at times hundreds of meters apart, not all the incoming fire could be deflected away from his flagship's hull. She was taking strafing hits from the energy weapons, and the missiles were exploding in close enough proximity to cause hull damage and exposing sections of the ship to space. Undoubtedly, there were bodies and material being lost into space that couldn't be seen on the tactical screen.

Meanwhile the enemy destroyers were continuing to pound at his light cruisers and destroyers. One of his destroyers was overwhelmed by three attacking enemies and began spewing out escape pods before exploding. Captains Son and Samkange were doing their best with their remaining cruiser group to fend off the incoming destroyers, but the problem was that in that defensive mode they could not assist *Agamemnon*.

Clement switched his focus. Yan was doing her best to fend off the Solar League ships, but the fact was that the enemy cruisers had gotten too close to his battlecruiser, and her offensive missile systems simply weren't much help. They were designed to be used at a greater distance than *Agamemnon* was currently fighting at. If she fired her high-yield missiles here, she could damage herself more than the enemy. The coil cannon were her most effective weapons at this range, but the fact was that she was fighting the battle from a diminishing position, one that she would eventually lose.

As the second group of enemy heavy cruisers broke ranks and made for *Agamemnon*, Clement felt a large rock forming in the pit of his stomach. Yan responded with missile fire, but at the distance the cruisers were at they would have ample time to raise their defenses or fire torpedoes to take out the incoming conventional missiles, and the two battle groups were too close to each other to use nukes.

Clement stood up from his command couch. "Lieutenant Adebayor, raise Captain Yan on the *Agamemnon*." The lieutenant acknowledged receipt of his order and then pointed at him when the com line was open.

"I don't know how much time I'll have to chat, Admiral. I hope this isn't a pep talk," she said through a cracking and popping com line.

"Nothing of the kind, Yan, all tactics. You've got to get those cruisers and destroyers off of your hull or they're going to peel you like an onion."

"Tell me something I don't know!" she snapped at him. "They are too close to us now for conventional missiles, let alone a nuke, and coil cannon just aren't powerful enough. The heavy cruisers have a primitive form of gravimetric shielding. It's pushing everything I fire at them away from the ship's hulls, minimizing our effectiveness."

"That's what I've observed. I wish our remaining cruisers and destroyers could help you, but they're fighting for their own lives right now."

"Orders, Admiral?"

"None, except don't lose my flagship. At this point, Captain, my only recommendation is that you think outside the box, otherwise this battle will come to an end sooner than we think."

"Outside the box"—the line crackled and broke up— "... us luck, Admiral ..." At that the com went down and Clement looked to Adebayor, who shook her head no. The signal had been lost, likely for the duration of the battle. Clement sat back down.

He switched focus onto his gunships, which were conducting search and rescue operations. The enemy was at least courteous enough to allow them to conduct that action as long as they weren't firing any missiles, which would likely have minimal effect on the outcome of the battle. The gunships were picking up as many escape pods as they could. Clement noted the numbers weren't enough; they had already lost too many sailors.

He looked at the overall board. Five of his eight destroyers were either gone or hopelessly crippled and spewing escape pods. His six light cruisers were now down to an operational three, but thankfully both *Corvallis* and *Yangtze* were still in the battle. He ordered them to break off with the enemy destroyers and move into close support of the *Agamemnon*.

The Solar League fleet were losing far fewer ships. He'd given them a bloody nose with his first maneuvers, but now they were holding his fleet down on the ground and pounding their faces. The tactical board was as grim as he'd ever seen it, including in the Rim rebellion. He decided to give his fleet five more minutes before he would call in his surrender to Admiral Elara DeVore.

In desperation, he called down to Nobli in the reactor room. "Any chance of using the MAD weapon?" He had to wait a few seconds for his engineer to reply.

"Tech Reck says no, Admiral. The goo she put in the cracks hasn't solidified yet, so unless you're planning on blowing up this entire star system . . ."

"Will she hold together for one more short LEAP

jump?" He heard arguing and yelling in the background before Nobli came back on the line.

"Tech Reck says no, but that won't stop you from trying, will it?"

"It won't," admitted Clement. "Tell Tech Reck thank you for her efforts."

Again there was off-line conversation, more subdued this time. "She says to wait as long as you can before you try the jump. Every second the nano-goo has to form up is a second it might take to make her patch work."

"Good enough, Nobli. Transfer control to my console." Clement shut down the com line and then looked at the tactical display again. Captain Samkange and the *Corvallis* were in trouble, while Captain Son had managed to maneuver the *Yangtze* and the remaining destroyers into a position to at least support *Agamemnon*. The situation was grim, and his only chance was another Hail Mary that might just result in the destruction of all life in the Trinity system. He made his decision.

"Lieutenant Adebayor, raise the enemy battlecruiser."

"Aye, sir," said Adebayor, then she turned to her com board to send out a ship-to-ship com.

At that moment things changed.

The *Agamemnon* was spewing out dozens of defensive torpedoes, aiming for the heavy cruisers and destroyers which were swarming all over her like circling wasps. She carried almost five hundred of the torpedoes, and it looked like she was firing them from every missile launcher, of which she had forty. The torpedoes' main function was intercepting incoming missiles, but Yan was using them as close-range attacking weapons to surprising effect. The Solar League destroyers had no kind of gravimetric shielding and were being pounded by them. It may not have been enough to destroy the enemy ships but it was certainly enough to damage them and even take some of them out of the battle for repairs.

"Hold that call, Lieutenant!" said Clement, just as the com line cracked open. Adebayor shut it down instantly. Clement returned his attention to the tactical screen. The enemy destroyers were retreating, trying to gain distance between themselves and *Agamemnon*. That was sound strategy, but perhaps not the wisest of moves under the current conditions. The heavy cruisers had ceased their pounding of the flagship, and were now busy fighting off the swarm of incoming torpedoes. In both cases *Agamemnon* was gaining something she had precious little of in this battle—space; breathing room between herself and her attacking enemies. That distance was quickly becoming enough that she could fire her heavy missiles without risking damage to her own hull. It was a brilliant strategy, a long shot for sure, but he reminded himself to decorate Yan for her ingenuity, for thinking "outside the box."

Once *Agamemnon* had the distance she required, Yan let loose with a volley of twenty conventional missiles from one of her port missile launchers. She had pushed the enemy back with her torpedo swarms until she could get a safe range to fire her missiles. The missiles hunted down the enemy ships, still scrambling from the torpedo fire, and locked onto them with deadly precision. Missiles impacted many of the enemy ships, and at least six enemy destroyers exploded. Clement was able to identify two cruisers that were obliterated and three more that took serious damage. There was material blowback, metal shrapnel, from the explosions onto the *Agamemnon*, but thankfully her gravimetric shielding minimized the damage. Yan then repeated the missile launch from her starboard launchers. The result was effective, but not quite as much so as the launch from the port side, which had caught the enemy completely by surprise. The enemy attackers quickly began a disorderly retreat. Clement ordered his support ships not to pursue the enemy and regroup around the limping *Agamemnon*.

The incoming reserve heavy cruiser fleet fired a volley of missiles at *Agamemnon*, but though they were in range, their position was not optimal. *Agamemnon* was able to fire off another volley of torpedoes from her forward missile bays, and this had the effect of taking out most of the incoming conventional warheads. The ones that did get through were picked off by her forward DEW cannons, or deflected away by her gravimetric shielding. A minute later, as the enemy retreated and regrouped, things changed again.

The Solar League battlecruiser began moving on an intercept course for the *Agamemnon*. For Elara DeVore to commit her capital ship to the battle was an indication that she was not happy with the proceedings and was prepared to take things into her own hands.

Now, Clement thought, *it's time to take the battle to you*.

As the battlefield descended into chaos, Clement saw his chance, and it was Yan who had given him the opportunity.

"Pilot, lock down the ship. Navigator, plot us a course that will put us right under the belly of the enemy flagship." Both Ori and Massif turned and looked at him like he was crazy.

"Are you sure, sir?" Ori asked.

"There's no way we can get through their entire fleet, even at maximum burn. They'll pick us off long before we can reach the battlecruiser," stated Massif.

Clement hesitated only a second. "My orders stand," he said. They both acknowledged as the bridge crew all strapped in to their acceleration couches and Ori broadcast a general order for the rest of the small crew to do the same. Clement switched to his personal com line and spoke quietly over the hum of the bridge. "Nobli, are we any closer to having an operational LEAP reactor?" Again he heard arguing and shouting in the background.

Finally Nobli got on the line. "Tech Reck thinks you're insane, but she says we might just hold together."

"I'll take that answer," said Clement, "and tell the tech if this works I owe her one."

"She says she knows that, sir."

"Activate the LEAP application, on my console only, Engineer."

There was a longer pause, only seconds, before Nobli responded. "May the gods of space shine on you one more time, Admiral."

Clement allowed himself a small smile before shifting the line to the weapons bay.

"Mr. Telco, I need you to take out the missiles and load as many torpedoes into the racks as you can. I'm going to need you and Mr. Tsu to load those torpedoes quickly, even if that means disregarding safety protocols. We're only likely going to get one chance at this."

"Sir," replied Telco, concern in his voice, "don't you mean load missiles, not torpedoes?"

"Negative, mister. I mean torpedoes. Fill the racks before we make our move and keep them coming. And I want you to load a nuclear warhead into one of the torpedoes, but you have to hold that back until I tell you to put it in the launcher. Are we clear?"

"We are, sir. I'll get Mr. Tsu to load the nuke while I rack the launch tubes. You'll have every torpedo we have at your disposal whenever you need it, sir."

"Thank you, Lieutenant. Um, how many torpedoes is that, by the way?"

"You have thirty-two torpedoes. Good luck, sir."

"Good luck to us all, Mr. Telco." He gave them two minutes to complete racking the torpedoes before he got a green light from Telco. At that moment he sank into his couch and called to his pilot.

"Prepare for LEAP jump, Pilot," he said. "Match course and speed with the enemy flagship. When we come out of the jump, I'm going to need you to react quickly to the situation."

"To keep us from ramming the battlecruiser, sir?" she asked.

"Exactly," he said, his hand hovering over the LEAP app. Clement sank into his safety couch, feeling like someone had just put a fully loaded lead safe on his chest. He reached out a finger toward the activation icon . . .

✦ ✦ ✦

By the time the jump ended, which was microseconds, Clement felt like he couldn't breathe. He took in a deep, gasping breath, then looked up at his tactical screen.

The enemy battlecruiser was looming over the tiny *Beauregard*, and they were accelerating toward it at a frightening speed. But they were still in existence. "Mika . . ." he croaked out, but she was already acting.

The ship lurched as it decelerated, pulling all the air out of his lungs again. Slowly the deceleration burn abated, and everyone on the bridge started to breathe, fitfully, again. By the end of the burn, they had matched course and speed with the battlecruiser. Clement looked up at his tactical board, and brought it front and center of the main bridge display.

The *Beauregard* had indeed taken advantage of the confusion on the battlefield as both the Solar League fleet and his own scrambled to take up new positions. The enemy was getting out of the way, making a hole for their main flagship. Elara DeVore's battlecruiser was coming through at high speed, and there was no question what her target was: *Agamemnon*. She was now prepared to slug it out with Yan and her ship, using the big guns. He estimated they had five minutes until the ships were in mutual firing range. But *Agamemnon* had already taken a pounding. DeVore would undoubtedly have the advantage in any one-on-one matchup, and her support ships were far bigger and stronger than what Yan had left.

Clement admitted to himself that his plan had little chance of success, but in his mind there was no other choice.

He called down to Nobli. "Did she hold together?"

"Well," said Nobli, "we're still here, aren't we?"

"I guess we are, but it's not as simple as that. What's the status of the reactor?"

"Kim's scanning the casing for micro-fissures now, but it looks like against all odds the damn thing held together."

"Does that mean I can use it again?"

"Well, there's no way I trust this thing if you're thinking of using the MAD weapon. But you might get away with one more short-range jump."

"That's what I needed to know, Engineer. Clement out."

"Wait a minute, Jared. There's something else you need to know. If you're gonna make another short-range jump it's quite possible that when the reactor cracks at least some of the energy generated by the LEAP drive system will escape into space."

"Meaning what?"

"Meaning don't expect to use this thing again in a dangerous way without suffering casualties. And I don't expect those casualties to be limited to our local area."

Clement said nothing to that for a few seconds before responding. "I will keep all of that in mind, Engineer. Thank you, and good luck."

"And to you, Admiral."

He couldn't escape the warning from his engineer; the next time they used the *Beauregard*'s LEAP reactor would be the last, and it would cost lives, likely all of the crew and possibly more.

Clement turned this attention back to something he could control and called down to the missile room again.

"Lieutenant Telco, please tell me you have my short-range torpedoes loaded."

"I do, sir, and I've put one of the nuke warheads on a missile, but I'm holding that one back, as you ordered, sir."

"Good work, Lieutenant." Clement closed the line again and turned to his pilot. "Where are we, Mika?"

"About three hundred meters beneath the enemy flagship, sir. We're too close for them to use missiles or even torpedoes against us because of the high yield all their ordnance carries. But our torpedoes are designed to be used at these short ranges, sir. They have smaller yields, so we shouldn't have to worry about blowback from our own weaponry."

"What about their DEW weapons?"

"Their Directed Energy Weapons are not designed to be used at this distance either, sir, and there's one other factor in our favor."

"Which is?"

"I don't think they know we're here."

He smiled just slightly at that.

Clement looked down to his command console and fed in a course to his helm officer. "I want you to follow this course, Mika. Repeat it as many times as necessary, and until you hear orders from me to do otherwise."

She looked at the course he fed her curiously, then said, "Understood, sir."

Clement turned to the *Beauregard*'s navigator. "I need one more local LEAP jump calculation from you, Ivan."

"Sir."

"Plot us a path back toward Bellus, and get us as close

to Admiral DeVore's task force hovering over the planet as you can."

"Aye, sir," said Massif, then turned back to his board to make the calculations.

"Kayla, your task will be to monitor enemy communications during this entire maneuver. I want to know when and if they start sending in smaller ships to do the cleanup work on us. They never planned on being vulnerable to a ship this small, but they're about to find out just how much power we can throw at them. When they do discover us I expect they're going to be pissed off. And one more thing, I want you to monitor for any special locator beacons coming from any ejected escape pods."

"Sir?"

"Let's just say that I'm expecting a high-value person to attempt escape if my plan works as well as I think it can." With that they all had their orders, and it was time to act.

Clement looked down at this console one more time and then addressed his bridge crew while tapping in Nobli and Telco. "All weapons control and the use of the LEAP drive will be at my command and mine only." There were nods from his three crew on the bridge and beeps of acknowledgement from the engine and missile rooms.

"One minute from battlefield range, sir," said Mika.

"Begin your preselected course, Pilot," he ordered. She did as instructed as the *Beauregard* began a slow orbiting pattern underneath the enemy battlecruiser. The pattern was similar in shape to a paper clip or an elongated oval. With luck, the battlecruiser-scanning officers would think the *Beauregard* was a large piece of another vessel, stuck in the different wells and waves of her gravity shielding.

As Clement watched, the two capital ships locked horns, like enormous metal rams, smashing each other's skulls. Lances of orange DEW weaponry fired out from both ships. At the distance they were currently at the weapons could only weaken energetic shielding, but eventually as one or both of them wore down in power, those lances would begin to take their toll.

Agamemnon fired, using a barrage of conventional missiles directly at the Solar League flagship's bow. The bow, plus her midships, would likely be the most heavily defended areas of the ship, and that was the least likely to be heavily damaged in an initial attack. What was surprising, though, was Captain Yan's use of the Rods of God immediately after her missile barrage. Even the slightest of weakening in the flagship's bow defenses could allow a large number of the rods to get through her shielding. The first volley of about twenty missiles exploded against her energetic shielding or were pushed away by the gravity-wave deflector. The missiles carried on their deflected courses, and one struck an enemy destroyer head-on. Only seconds later the kinetic metal rods smashed into the flagship's bow. The resulting sparks of energy made for a pretty display, but they were not to any great effect; their kinetic energy dispersed as they were pushed away from the main hull of the Solar League flagship.

For her part Elara DeVore responded with a barrage of about thirty conventional missiles. None of them bore the signature tag of an atomic warhead, which would be suicide at the distance the two behemoths were apart. Swiftly, two groups of three enemy heavy cruisers swept past *Agamemnon* on either side, strafing her broadsides with conventional missiles and DEW energy. The remaining defending Five Suns cruisers and destroyers were too slow to provide cover. Yan responded with energy weapons fire, but the cruisers were too fast and took minimal damage.

Next, DeVore sent in a group of five destroyers, who attempted to repeat the same maneuver, but using lighter weapons. They were not as fast as the cruisers nor as effective. Captains Samkange and Son were able to use their light cruisers and remaining destroyers to counter their attack. Without energetic or gravimetric shielding the destroyers were much more vulnerable. The two cruiser captains picked off one destroyer each with their missiles, and the *Yangtze* damaged the propulsion engines of a second one. The two captains quickly repositioned themselves on the *Agamemnon*'s flank, preparing for the next wave of attacks.

Yan's frontal assault on the Solar League flagship continued for several more minutes, but to little effect. Likewise, DeVore's flagship wasn't making much progress in wearing down *Agamemnon*'s frontal defenses either, but with their superior numbers and firepower the support ships were steadily wearing down *Agamemnon*'s ability to defend itself from DeVore and her ship.

Captain Son lost a support destroyer in a fireball explosion that left little possibility that any of the crew survived. His second destroyer limped away, being left behind for the other enemy forces to take out.

Samkange fared slightly better. Both his destroyers were still active but based on Clement's reading of their tactical telemetry, both were at severely depleted capacity. At this point their greatest value to the defense of *Agamemnon* was simply as targets for enemy weaponry.

The battlefield was now littered with debris from destroyed and damaged ships as well as expended ordnance from both sides. They had reached the point where the fog of war would be thickest.

It was time to act.

Clement looked down to his control console. He brought up the torpedo-firing controls and hit the launch icon. Six of his antimissile torpedoes launched upward from their launch tubes and quickly impacted against the hull of the Solar League flagship. The damage was minimal, similar to poking pencil holes in a large lump of clay, but still they left a mark.

"Reload," ordered Clement to his missile techs. They did so quickly and Clement launched a second volley. He repeated the pattern three more times while circling underneath the belly of Elara DeVore's flagship before they reacted. As he sought to repeat the pattern and increase her hull damage, the enemy flagship started pushing out gravity-wave deflectors. The result was that although they were close enough that their torpedoes still hit the ship, they couldn't repeat the pattern by hitting them in the same spot, and increasing the size of the holes in her armored hull.

"I think they see us, sir," said Ori.

"Indeed they do, Pilot. Continue to repeat the pattern." They continued the barrage and the torpedoes continued to do their damage, chipping away at the battlecruiser's hull but not achieving any decisive edge.

A quick glance at the main battlefield showed the two behemoths passing each other and firing in the broadside, once again not decisively, but *Agamemnon* was clearly taking more damage than DeVore's ship.

As both ships maneuvered for a second pass at each other, the former Fleet Admiral of the Five Suns Navy changed her tactics, focusing on the buzzing bee stinging her belly. She began pushing gravity waves directly out from her hull toward the *Beauregard*.

"Admiral," warned Ori.

"I see it. Keep us as close to our original flight pattern as possible."

"That's not going to be easy against these waves. Their technology seems much more advanced than ours."

"That may be, Pilot, but I'm counting on you to keep us close to her. She's trying to push us out away from her ship so she can fire her missiles or her DEW weapons at us. We can't let her do that. Right now she's just realized we're inside her effective weapon's range, and she hates that." The *Beauregard* bucked and rumbled as she was hit by wave after wave of gravity from the giant battlecruiser. DeVore was succeeding in pushing the *Beauregard* off her chosen course, but she wasn't successful in getting her out to a range where she could be hit by the enemy's heavy weapons. Clement continued to fire his torpedoes at as close a range as he could risk.

When they were finally out of torpedoes, Clement had a choice to make.

The two flagships had reengaged and once again

Agamemnon was taking the worst of the pounding. Clement briefly considered ordering Captain Yan to abandon ship, but he knew she wouldn't stand for that.

Lieutenant Telco called up from the missile room. "All we have left are the heavy missiles, sir. The torpedoes are all gone, except for the one with the nuclear warhead. Sir."

Clement didn't hesitate. "Load that torpedo into the launch tube, Lieutenant," he ordered. "Then you and Tsu get yourselves to escape pods."

Clement got a green light on his panel once the nuclear-tipped torpedo was loaded. He called down to Engineering, "I'm about to fire a nuke into DeVore's flagship. You and Tech Reck have two minutes to get to your escape pods."

"That won't go down well here," said Nobli.

"Who's in charge down there, Nobli? It's not a request, it's an order. As soon as we finish this last LEAP jump, I want everyone off the ship. Is that clear?"

"It is, sir," said Nobli. "Good luck."

Clement addressed his bridge crew. "That goes for everyone here as well. Once we make the final LEAP, and we're over Bellus again, I want you all off my bridge. In fact, I want you to do so now."

"But who will fly the ship?" protested Ori.

"I will, from the command console. Ivan, I assume you have the course back to Bellus already programmed in?"

"I do, sir."

Clement nodded. "Kayla, hold a spot for me on the last escape pod," he said. "The rest of you are ordered to vacate your stations immediately and eject your escape pods the moment our LEAP jump is complete."

"That's a thirty-meter run from here and down two flights of stairs, sir. You'll never make it, especially not after the disorientation of a LEAP jump," said Ori, acting now in her role as his XO.

"That's my problem, XO, and besides, someone has to be here to launch the nuke."

"Sir—"

"My orders are final, crew. Get to your escape pods. Now."

Finally, giving up the argument, Ori stood and secured her station. Her husband did the same, followed by Adebayor.

"Good luck, sir," said Ori. Clement merely nodded as his three bridge crewmates passed him, quickly heading for the escape pods. He swiveled in his command couch, watching Ori and Massif break to starboard while Adebayor broke for the port-side pod. He hoped he would have time to join her.

He returned his attention one last time to the tactical display. DeVore had sent two destroyers from her fleet attacking the *Agamemnon* on an intercept vector with the *Beauregard*. He estimated he had ninety seconds before they could take him out. Rapidly, he scanned through his telemetry screens looking for something that might give him an edge. There was one area of the enemy flagship that was emanating massive amounts of subatomic particles. He wasn't sure, but his best guess was that this was the area where the flagship's LEAP reactor might be. He hit the thrusters, pushing the *Beauregard* to that point. When he had his ship positioned directly under the holes in the hull that his torpedoes had made, he sighted in as carefully as he could from his weapons display. There was one hole in the area that was larger than the others, thus allowing the lone remaining torpedo a greater chance of getting deep inside the enemy ship.

His finger hovered over the firing icon for the briefest of moments, and then he fired the torpedo.

At the same moment he began an escape burn trying to get his ship as far away from the Solar League battlecruiser as he could. The enemy destroyers were bearing down on him now, and the g-forces from his escape burn made him feel sluggish and heavy. He took one last look at the tactical display that showed the enemy flagship engulfed in a nuclear blast, her hull splitting apart as she bled off escape pods and the other ships in the Solar League fleet scrambled to get away from her. The two destroyers sent to take out his ship, however, were still coming.

He looked down at the LEAP control and set it for a fifteen-second delay.

He hit the icon to activate the countdown.

Clement scrambled from his command couch and made it down the four-step metal stairs to the cabin deck with the heavy help of the stair railing. Once on the open metal floor, though, the going was tough. Gravity from the acceleration was holding him back, but he wouldn't quit.

Down the second flight of four stairs, he turned to port, grabbing the railing and moving as fast as he could to make it to the escape pod. He wasn't counting and he didn't know whether he would make it before the LEAP drive kicked in or not. If he did, he had a small chance of survival, if he didn't, the reactor casing would likely crack for the last time and he would find himself being disintegrated by the expulsion of the LEAP energy plasma.

The door was in sight, if not within reach. Kayla Adebayor was already locked into her side of the pod. His door was still open, but for how many more seconds he couldn't guess. He simply *had* to get there.

A moment later and he was inside the pod and slamming the door shut behind him with no time to strap in safely.

The *Beauregard* made her final LEAP.

In microseconds the ship reappeared in normal space over the planet Bellus. The escape pods were automatically ejected and Clement felt himself pressed facedown against what was supposed to be his safety couch. Again, feeling the pressure of gravity, he tried to turn around and see out of the pod window, but he didn't have the strength, and he didn't really need to.

There was an intense flash of light over his shoulder and Kayla let out a gasp that was nearly a scream.

"It's gone," she said. "The *Beauregard* is gone!"

Then Clement stopped struggling, and put his head down on the safety couch. There was nothing more for him to see. His ship was gone, his command over.

Then the escape pod was hit by a severe percussion wave from the *Beauregard*'s explosion. He closed his eyes, and let the blackness take him.

✲ 16 ✲

When Clement woke up, he was in the infirmary aboard the *Corvallis* with several IVs and monitoring wires attached to him. He'd been out for nearly sixteen hours, so the doctors and nurses told him, he was sure more than once.

He asked the main doctor to get him Captain Samkange, and after about twenty minutes of casual chatter with his crewmates, Samkange showed up to spoil the party. Clement was still foggy from the effects of the LEAP jump, as well as from the g-forces in the escape pod and the medication they had been giving him. He asked Samkange for a situation report as his friends scattered. The cruiser captain pulled up a chair and sat down next to Clement's cot.

"Well, first and foremost, Admiral, you succeeded in planting a nuke right inside the enemy flagship's reactor room. I don't know if it was luck or great planning, but you literally split her in two. There must have been a thousand escape pods pushed out while she burned. At that point the enemy fleet panicked and scrambled away while the rest of us made our way back at full burn to get to Bellus. When you completed your jump, your LEAP reactor overloaded and the resulting stream of released energy vaporized the enemy flotilla over Bellus."

"But no harm to the planet or to any of our ships?"

Samkange shook his head. "No, sir. Your navigator placed you in a perfect position to take out the enemy ships, and your man Nobli said he set the reactor to the absolute minimum setting to accomplish the jump."

"Well, at least we didn't destroy the entire Trinity system and several million people."

"Yes, sir. You and Lieutenant Adebayor were picked up by the *Antietam* shortly after the event, and I had you transferred here because we have more experienced doctors and a much better infirmary."

"Where's the Solar League fleet now?" said Clement, noting the croaking sound in his own voice. He'd been out a long time.

"The sight of their flagship being split in half spooked the hell out of them, sir. They managed to regroup. I have no idea who was in charge of that operation, and they eventually vacated Bellus space and headed back out toward their Ark ship parked out near Trinity-6, sir."

"The icy gas planet. Better them than us."

"Yes, sir."

Clement cleared his throat. "What about *Agamemnon*?"

Samkange took in a deep breath. "We pulled her home. She was badly damaged in the battle, sir. Captain Yan says she doesn't think that the ship is salvageable. She expended every weapon she had in the fight, sir. Right now she's in a decaying orbit, slowly being pulled into the planet's gravity field. Her engines are so badly damaged that it seems unlikely she can be saved from burning up in the atmosphere."

Clement took that hard. *Agamemnon* had been their most modern ship, and now he was going to lose her. "What else do we have left?"

Samkange looked down at the floor and then back up to the admiral. "Not very much, sir. *Corvallis*, the *Yangtze*, both of which have sustained considerable damage, and one destroyer, the *Benfold*."

"You said the *Antietam* picked me up—"

"Yes, sir. Three of the gunships survived, they've been on nearly nonstop search and rescue since the battle broke up, sir."

"You said I've been out for sixteen hours?"

"More or less, sir."

"Those escape pods only have enough environment to survive twelve. Call the *Antietam* and find out when the last time was they pulled in an escape pod with anyone alive in it. If it's been more than two hours, recall the gunships immediately."

"We're suspending search and rescue operations?"

Clement nodded. "There's likely no one out there to rescue anymore, Captain. And it sounds like we're going to have to evacuate the *Agamemnon* before she goes down."

"I'll see to it immediately, Admiral." Samkange stood and started to go, then came back. "Admiral, when you're good enough to get out of that bed—"

"I'm good enough now," said Clement, pulling off his sheets and sitting upright in the bed while unplugging himself from several of the monitoring wires. He wobbled for a few moments, then closed his eyes and quickly opened them again, blinking, hoping to steady himself.

"Yes, sir. What I meant was, when the doctor's cleared you . . ."

"Spit it out, man," said Clement, growing impatient.

"There was some more bad news, sir." The look on Samkange's face was grave. He looked down to the deck, sighed deeply, then, "Kayla Adebayor, sir. She didn't make it."

Clement looked away. "She was in the escape pod with me. How . . ."

"When we opened your pod she wasn't breathing. She . . . the doctor thinks she fractured her skull when the *Beauregard* disintegrated. We tried everything to save her, sir . . ."

"I'm sure you did." Clement fought back tears; sitting on the edge of the bed, he put his feet on the deck, then covered his face with his hands for a few moments.

"How . . . how did I survive? I wasn't even in the safety couch," he asked.

"Blind luck, the doctor thinks. There was a shockwave after the *Beauregard* exploded. Somehow you survived, but she didn't."

An overwhelming sense of sadness came over him. Healthy twenty-three-year-old women weren't supposed to die, even in space.

Even in battle.

"Schedule a memorial service for her. All honors. And preserve the body. Her family deserves to get their daughter back."

"Yes, sir. There are still some pressing matters before—"

"Obviously I meant we'll have the service when this crisis is over, Captain," snapped Clement. His rising grief was bubbling over as misdirected anger.

"Of course, sir. I do need to tell you that we've picked up quite a few enemy escape pods. There is one prisoner, sir, down in our brig, that I think you might want to talk to personally."

"That will have to wait, Captain. Right now I have to figure out what this fleet has left to fight with, if anything." Clement started looking around the room for his uniform. "Now get that goddamn doctor in here," he said, "and find me my fucking clothes!"

Once he was dressed he left the infirmary with a nurse trailing behind him at the doctor's insistence. He made his way to the bridge of *Corvallis*, and once there he went to the communications console and asked the com ensign to raise Captain Yan aboard *Agamemnon*.

"What's your status, Captain?" he asked when the line was open.

"Admiral, it's good to hear your voice," replied Yan. "I just want to say that I'm sorry about Kayla. We all loved her."

"We did, but there's no time to talk about her now, Captain. I'd like a situation report," he said, testy at being reminded of his grief.

"Of course, sir. We took quite a battering from their heavy cruisers and their flagship. I can quite easily say that without your maneuvers and your nuke, we would not be here at this moment. Currently our engines are doing everything they can to keep us in orbit over Bellus, but we're being inevitably pulled in. We took so much damage and this ship is so big we simply don't have the power left to push away from the planet and keep ourselves afloat."

"How long until we lose the ship?"

"Best estimates are seventeen hours, Admiral. I've got my entire engineering team and every tech I can spare working on getting the engines repaired, but it's a big ask."

"Tell me about the condition of your LEAP reactor."

"It's completely trashed, sir. The enemy clearly knew where it was located on the ship."

"They did have the advantage of advance knowledge of the design," replied Clement, staying very businesslike, but it was yet another betrayal by Elara DeVore. He tried to shake that feeling off. "Status of your weaponry?"

"All of our kinetic weapons have been expended. We have a couple of dozen torpedoes left and about thirty heavy missiles, including six nukes."

"Get those weapons organized and down to the loading dock. I'm going to be sending over the gunships to pick up all that weaponry. Prioritize off-loading the nukes. Do you have small armaments left?"

"Quite a bit, Admiral; in fact, that's almost all we have left. Are you planning to shoot at the enemy ships from EVA suits floating in space?"

"No, Captain, and I wish you would stay on subject," he snapped. His head was starting to hurt. "Make sure those weapons are also off-loaded onto the gunships and taken down to the surface. We may need them there."

"Permission to comment, sir?"

"I can't seem to stop you anyway, can I, Yan? Go ahead."

"Are we planning on fighting this out on the ground?"

"Once *Agamemnon* goes down there's really no point in trying to fight a space battle. We still have thirty thousand settlers to protect on the ground and that's what we're going to do, protect them. If that means hand-to-hand fighting in close proximity with energy weapons and stun grenades, then that's what we'll have to do."

"Understood, sir."

"Last bit of business, Captain. I want your crews to stop working on trying to repair the engines. All of your efforts need to be turned toward getting the weapons and food supplies off of your ship and down to the surface. That's where we'll have to make our last stand. I'm sorry *Agamemnon* won't be there for the fight, but I don't know what else we can do."

"I'll give the orders right away, Admiral. Now if you'll excuse me, I have a ship to disassemble."

"One more thing before you go, Yan. Start organizing your crew into vital and non-vital personnel. Start moving the non-vital crew off the ship as fast as you can. I don't want people staying onboard simply because it's their assignment."

"Of course, sir," she replied, and the conversation was over.

Clement turned to Captain Samkange.

"I may be the senior officer, Captain, but this is still your ship, and I trust you. Right now everything has to be focused on getting personnel and equipment down to the surface. And send orders that I want the other camps to break up, and all the settlers and any natives you can find need to go to Camp Alpha. That's where we'll concentrate our defenses."

"Aye, sir."

Clement sighed. "Now, as to that prisoner in the brig. I'm betting I know who it is, and I'm not happy about having to have this conversation. At all. And I want you to know I blame you."

Samkange nodded, uncertain how to respond to that. Clement then gave him a slap on the shoulder. "You've done an excellent job, Harry. Now let's finish it."

And with that he was off for the *Corvallis'* brig.

He found the brig two decks down, near the conference room he had been in when he first came aboard. He ordered the guard to unlock the heavy metal door, which he promptly did. Inside there were three metal-barred cells, no fancy monitoring equipment of any kind and no amenities. The third cell down, furthest from the door, had a single person in it. A woman with dark hair and a very familiar face. He took six short steps down to her cell and then sat on a metal bench facing her. She sat on a metal pallet for a bed, and there was a small sink and a toilet. Otherwise the cell was dull and gray.

Elara DeVore just stared back at him from the pallet, her face smudged with grease on one cheek. Her uniform was a stark crimson and black, with several rank ornaments on it. The uniform jacket she wore was torn in several places and it was clear she'd been through a very rough time. She was noticeably thinner than the last time he had seen her, in exile on the planet Alphus. Her eyes, though, were as they always were: clear, dark, and compelling.

"Are you here to gloat, Clement?" she finally said.

He shook his head. "Not in the slightest, Admiral. What happened today didn't have to happen, and too many good people lost their lives because of you."

"Because of me?" She stood up, angry. "What about you? How many of my people did you kill today? Do you think I'm the only one responsible here? And I agree with you, this didn't have to happen, but you made it impossible. Your bullheadedness, your inability to see beyond the simple fog of the battlefield makes it impossible for you to see any bigger picture. You're a soldier, Clement, and nothing more. I should've just taken you out at the first opportunity, but I thought I could reason with you. That was my mistake. Ultimately, you're just not that kind of man."

"You forced my hand, Elara," he snapped back at her. "You knew I could never give in to a 'peace' that would end up with the Trinity natives subjugated, and we both know that's what would have happened."

She started pacing her tiny cell, not looking at him. "You blew up my flagship," she said softly, almost like he'd hurt her personally.

"I'm sorry about that, but it had to be done. And it's not like it didn't cost me anything dear."

She stopped to look at him over one shoulder. "That was quite a trick you pulled. I never learned that one in battle school."

"I'm a student of history, you know that. I got the idea from a little personal reading I did, many years ago. You should read up on a man named Thomas Cochrane and the H.M.S. *Speedy*, in the Napoleonic wars, when you get a chance."

"Well, I have plenty of time, but we appear to be short of reading material in here."

"I'm sorry our accommodations aren't everything a Fleet Admiral would expect."

She turned away then, unwilling to continue the banter, and sat back down on her "bed."

"I will get you a mattress, though," he said.

"That's very thoughtful, but we still have important issues to discuss."

"Then let's do that, Admiral. I'm all ears."

She sat forward, eyes down, clearly thinking about what he was going to say. As she started talking, she chose her words carefully. "As I told you before, you're wrong about the Solar League. They are honest and virtuous people, they want humanity to unite, and the LEAP drive gives them the opportunity to do that, for all humans, the ones in the Sol system, the Five Suns, the Rim, and Trinity."

"I'm not sure that being under their leadership would be a good thing, and the fact is I don't know anything about them except what you've told me. That's not a lot to go on given our recent track record of cooperation."

She shuffled her feet, unwilling to look up and meet his gaze. "I know you don't trust me, Clement, and frankly I don't blame you for that. I did have ambitions for Trinity, but you stopped that. Eighteen months on the surface of Alphus gave me plenty of time to think. Foraging for your own food and water to stay alive once your rations run out will do that to you. In my thinking, I kept coming back to the ambitions of the Solar League. Higher ambitions than mine had been. You taught me a harsh lesson, Clement, one I'm not likely to forget anytime soon."

"It's lovely to hear how you fared on your holiday, Elara, but I can honestly say I'm not sure where you're going with all of this."

She stood now and came up to the bars, grasping the cold rolled metal as she looked down at him from a few feet away. "Come with me out to Trinity-6, to the Ark ship. Meet the commanders there, the men and women that serve in the Solar League Navy with honor and dignity. I think you'll be impressed with them, and I believe once you've talked to them we can reach an agreement, an agreement that brings a lasting peace to the Trinity system and ends the conflict over these beautiful worlds once and for all."

Clement thought about her words, spoken softly and (he thought) sincerely. She had deceived him before, and even if his heart wanted to believe her now, his head told him not to trust her. "I have thousands of settlers, and perhaps millions of natives on the planet below, on Bellus, that I am responsible for. I can't abandon them and leave them leaderless when you still have an active fleet and a ship out there powerful enough to destroy everyone in this system."

"But that's the point! If you go to them under a flag of truce, with me at your side, I'm certain they will receive you, and not as an enemy. We can begin peace negotiations then and can bring this all to an end with no more bloodshed."

"And if I don't?"

"Then they have standing orders in my absence to come to the inner system and take control of Bellus. We knew you would come back, but we didn't know you'd be coming with thousands of civilians. I moved the Ark ship out of the way so that your fleet could make its way here. Hell, I even dropped that buoy in LEAP space to help you find your missing people. Haven't I proven I'm worth taking a risk on? Especially a risk that could save everyone, every human, in this star system?"

Clement stood to leave then, staring at a woman that he used to love just a few feet away from him. "I'm sorry, Elara, but I just can't trust you, at least not now. If your people would agree to leave representatives in this system, without weapons, then I would be willing to negotiate with them. But that Ark has to leave this system."

"But I just told you, Clement, they have standing orders and without a signal from me they will carry them out."

Clement looked at her, trying to make a judgment about her real intentions. It was something he had mistaken many times before. "Then I have to prepare for your force's arrival, and defend the people I'm sworn to protect. Any negotiations like what you propose will have to wait until I've secured my people."

"Then they will come," she said, "likely soon. And you no longer have your ace in the hole, your MAD weapon. It, and the *Beauregard*, are gone."

That hurt. She knew how important the ship they had both served on was to him. Clement eyed her. She seemed sincere, but then she always seemed that way to him. "I understand the situation, Elara. But, for now, I have a lot of work I have to do." With that he took the few short steps toward the brig door and tapped on it to signal the guard to let him out.

"Clement, don't do this," she said in a calm voice. "Don't give up on a chance for real peace."

"You'll have my answer shortly," he said, then the door opened, and Clement stepped through without another word.

Two hours later and Clement sat across from Elara DeVore at a small eating table in the tiny galley of the Five Suns gunship *Antietam*. Clement watched her as they shared coffee together.

"This isn't bad for military rations," she said. "Of course, it's not as good as what we grow on Helios."

"I'll bet it's been a long time since you've had a cup of Sumatra Gold," he replied, referencing what he knew was her favorite coffee blend.

"True enough," she said, then she set the cup down and looked across the table at her former lover and current adversary. "I appreciate all of this, Clement, but why am I on this ship and where are we going?"

Clement kept his gaze on her steady, giving away nothing of what he was thinking or feeling inside. "The simplest explanation would be that I took your advice, and that we're on our way out to Trinity-6 to meet with your Solar League representatives." The *Antietam* was two hours from Bellus, where Clement had left Yan, Harry Samkange, and Marina Lubrov in charge of preparing the Five Suns defenses, as much as they could prepare for an impending invasion that they couldn't stop.

"That would be the simplest explanation but I doubt it's the complete one, knowing you as I do," said DeVore. "First I'm in your brig, then you ignore me and my pleadings for peace, and then suddenly I'm here, and it appears that you're taking my advice, which I highly doubt is your true intent. Tell me, Admiral, does this gunship come with your MAD weapon too, like the *Beauregard*? Did you bring me along to watch the annihilation of my fleet, and the only people that can help you achieve peace in this star system?"

"If I told you that I would be giving information to the enemy, and that would mean I'd have execute myself for treason."

She smiled. "Not likely, I agree. So what then?"

"You'll know soon enough, Elara," he replied cryptically. "Now enjoy your coffee. We do have some MREs here if you are hungry."

"I've lost my appetite, frankly. And the coffee is just fine for me." Then they sat in awkward silence, each of them taking the occasional drink. This went on for several minutes, neither of them willing to break the deadlock. Eventually, though, DeVore had to ask the unasked question.

"If there was peace in the Trinity system, there might actually be some hope for you and I."

"As a couple?" Clement scoffed at that. "I'm not sure that would be good for peace in this system."

DeVore eyed him from across the table. "You can't deny there's always been something between us, something that went beyond just the normal casual or convenient relationship. Serving under you was the hardest decision I've ever had to make because it meant giving up our love affair. I think in many ways, that decision is what led me down the path I took after the war."

"You betrayed me, and the ship," he reminded her.

"And which one of those hurt you more?"

Clement shook his head at her. "Ending our relationship was something that had to happen for us to continue serving together. Betraying the ship, that was your choice."

"And so you've answered my question without really answering it."

"I think I've been fairly clear with you, Elara. I don't see that we have a future of any kind, under any circumstances."

"We could have taken a different road. We could have found each other again, been together, perhaps even have a family."

He shook his head, arms crossed, looking down at the tabletop, unwilling to look her in the eyes. "All I can see when I look back on that time is pain, and no sane person would want to go back to that pain again." She looked away then and he raised his eyes to study her face. Even after so many years between them he still found her to be an unparalleled beauty. But it was what he knew of her heart, and of her betrayal, that made it impossible for him to feel love for her again.

"When this is over, if you survive, you'll have to end up somewhere. I could make your life satisfying if you chose to serve in the Solar League," she said.

"And what about happiness, Elara? Is there any room for that in your fantasies?"

"Always, Clement. And no matter how hard I've tried, I've never felt anything close to what I felt with you. Circumstances got in the way of our being together. I made choices, I know I'm responsible for them. But I had to do what I did, if not for myself then for the greater good of humanity. Now we're at a tipping point, and whatever happens in the next few hours or days will determine whether mankind goes forward, or takes a massive step back, one we might never recover from. Please come with me and make peace. I'll guarantee that you will have your place in this sun, a home, even love and a family if that's what you want. And, if not with me, then with someone else of your choosing."

"Sweet words, Elara, but it really changes nothing. Neither of us knows how this is going to end; we've both escaped death more than once. I don't believe we have nine lives, so whatever we choose to do next will ultimately decide our fate." At that the ship-wide com rang in.

The voice belonged to the *Antietam*'s Captain Jim Kagereki. "We've reached the designated coordinates, Admiral."

Clement clicked on the com panel to respond. "Prepare the shuttle as ordered, Captain. I'll be down in the landing bay in five minutes." He shut off the com and faced DeVore again.

"I'm afraid this is our exit, Admiral."

"Are you going to take the shuttle out to the Ark ship? Are you going to take my advice and negotiate peace?"

Clement set down his coffee and stood to leave. He gestured toward the gantry way. "After you," he said. He followed her out as they made their way down the metal ramp to the *Antietam*'s landing deck. Her only shuttle was warm and prepped, just waiting to be rolled into the airlock to make her exit. DeVore stood beside Clement, looking at the ship.

"I take it you can pilot this thing?"

"I can," he said as a half dozen technicians scrambled around the shuttle, making their final adjustments. "But I'm not going to. The shuttle will run on autopilot, a preprogrammed course to take you back to your fleet."

DeVore looked startled. "So you're not coming with me? Is this some kind of a stunt?"

"No, Elara, it's tactics. I'm sending you back as a gesture of peace. If these people you speak so highly of understand the gesture, then they will take their Ark and their remaining forces, and they will leave Trinity space. My terms, which you are to convey, is that they may send one ship, unarmed, to Bellus where we will open up negotiations. You, however, are not allowed to stay in this system. You'll have to go back to Earth with the rest of the fleet. If these people are as sincere as you say they are, then perhaps we can work something out. That's the only thing I'm offering you."

She looked at him, disappointed. "I should've known you'd never be willingly kind to me. If I agree to your offer then I live in permanent exile on Earth. If I don't take your offer, then once again I've proved myself to be the villain. It's perfect for you. It eliminates any guilt from your own mind about me. But you said this was tactics, and I don't see how—"

"I've just bought myself and my forces at least six hours to better prepare our defenses. Two hours out to this point, another four in the shuttle for you, and then you'll have to discuss what your next move is with your compatriots face to face, because I cut off your long-range com."

"I see," she said, in a quiet voice. "Naturally I'm disappointed. It appears this is all we have left, Clement. Using each other for our own ends."

"And that is something you taught me, Elara. Now goodbye," he said, motioning over a pair of guards to put her on the shuttle.

Then he walked away, not turning to look back.

✦ 17 ✦

Three hours later and Clement was on the ground at Camp Alpha, meeting with Colonel Lubrov and going over the camp's ground defenses one last time. He followed her into her command tent where she had maps, charts, and electronic displays strewn out on several flat tables.

"What's our best-case scenario?" he asked of her.

She pulled at her regulation ponytail with her left hand and then swept it behind her shoulder. "Even with the rapid-cure concrete bunkers we've installed, I can't protect more than about half of the migrant population, especially now that you've combined all three camps into one. That's just the reality of it. We have minimal antiaircraft batteries and just the small arms that we came with. We have three shuttles we can get off the ground, one from each of the transports, but nothing heavier than that. If the fleet can't provide us with cover from above, we're not going to last very long down here on the ground against an enemy that would likely have air power, ground troops, plus armor and artillery. It would be a slaughter."

Clement looked out the open tent door as hundreds of

exhausted-looking settlers straggled through the camp; the looks on their faces were forlorn. He had to decide if risking their lives, and the natives', was worth it. *Perhaps*, he thought, *taking Elara up on her offer of peace negotiations had been a missed opportunity.*

"At this point, Colonel, the attacking fleet from the L2 Lagrange point has dispersed and is rendezvousing out near T6 with the main Ark ship. I've sent Elara DeVore out to their fleet, mostly as a diversion, but if they decide to come back in and take this planet there is really nothing we can do about it, at least from a naval perspective. And fighting here on the ground just doesn't seem like an option."

"We do have nuclear weapons as an option," said Lubrov.

"Yes, six small-yield warheads. I don't fancy myself using nukes in the Garden of Eden," he responded. "I'd rather not go down as Trinity's serpent in the garden. We're loading the nukes from the *Agamemnon* onto the remaining cruisers and our destroyer. *If* they are used it will be in space, not on this planet."

She stiffened. "Understood, Admiral."

Clement paced across the tent, back and forth. There were no real good options for him to defend the planet or any of its inhabitants. He didn't trust DeVore, or the so-called Solar League, enough to accept her offer of peace, which simply could be an elaborate trap. He mused on this as he paced, Lubrov allowing him all the time he needed by staying silent. Finally, he addressed the Colonel again.

"Carry on with getting the settlers into the camp, and

get them as close to the mountain where the Hill Place is located as you can. Keep everyone that is already in a bunker protected, but your orders are not to fight unless you are fired upon first. If you encounter ground troops and they demand your surrender, you are hereby ordered to stand down."

Lubrov bowed her head and then looked back up, swallowing hard at her unpleasant orders. "Understood, Admiral, but I wish to convey that I'm not happy about it."

"And I understand your position, Colonel. If I was in your place I'd say exactly the same thing. But we have to prevent a slaughter, and the only way to do that, it appears, is not to fight, at least not on the ground." Clement ended his pacing and sat down heavily in a metal folding chair and sighed.

"You're tired, aren't you, sir?"

"Yes, Colonel, very. You'd think sixteen hours out like a light would make me feel more refreshed."

"Losing the *Beauregard* and Lieutenant Adebayor was a trauma, sir. The g-forces you endured, even while unconscious, take a big toll on your body. You should think about resting some more."

Clement rubbed at his face. "There's no time for that, Marina," he said, surprising her by using her first name.

"Perhaps, sir, there is one other option that we could explore before we give up. Maybe you're just too tired to think of it right now."

"I'm open to any suggestions at this point."

Lubrov came around the table to stand in front of him. "You could go back to the Hill Place, back to that woman

Mary and the natives. I'm just guessing, but they may have the technology to stop this thing. It's our job to try and convince them to come in on our side."

"I feel like we've tried that already, Colonel," he said, then he bowed his head. "They had an opportunity to intervene when those Solar League ships took orbit right above them, but they didn't, so I have to assume they won't get involved this time."

"Isn't it worth another chance? To at least ask them?"

Clement looked up at her, thinking. "You're right, Colonel, it is worth a chance." Then he stood. "I'll take Commander Pomeroy with me back up to the Hill Place. Maybe I can convince them that we are worth intervening for."

With that he was out through the tent opening and into the dusky sunlight of Bellus.

As he made his way through the crowds of anxious settlers toward the VTOL, the crowd parted and he found himself face to face with his parents. He stopped, then approached them.

"Hello, son," said his mother, giving him a big hug, which he instinctively returned. His father stood back a step and merely nodded to acknowledge his son. "You look terrible," Abby said.

He laughed. What could he say to that? "I'm sorry, Mother, but I lost my ship, a young crewmate, and a battle today. Not the best of times."

"I'm sorry for all that, son. Please know that we love you."

"I do, and I love you too." He looked to his father. "I'm

so sorry for getting you both involved in this. I should have left well enough alone and let you stay on the farm on Ceta."

Abby shook her head. "You did the right thing, son. Your father here won't tell you, but we wouldn't have survived on the farm for another year. We came for the right reasons, and you didn't make a mistake in bringing us here."

"Well, I've made plenty since we got here."

"It's all right, son. We're going to be okay," said his father.

"I . . . I have to go," Clement said, looking in the direction of the VTOL.

"Do what you have to do, son. We're well taken care of," said Abby. With that he got another hug from his mother and then a handshake from his father. He walked off then, purpose in his pace.

Clement rounded up Laura Pomeroy and fifteen minutes later they were taking the VTOL back up to the Hill Place. The ten-minute ride up the mountainside allowed him to clear his mind a bit by closing his eyes and meditating. He was still foggy from his unintended sleep.

"You look like you could use some more rest," said Pomeroy.

"Does every woman on this mission feel the need to look after me?"

"I'm sorry?" quizzed Pomeroy over the hum of the VTOL turbines.

Clement sighed. "It started back on Kemmerine Station. Yan tried to put me on a diet which made me irritable. DeVore tried to get me to surrender and run off with her to Earth or somewhere. Lubrov told me I needed more rest just now in the command tent, and now you're at me. I just don't have time to rest right now, Laura. When this is over—"

"This might never be over," she said.

Clement didn't respond for a few moments, then said, "I've lost wars before."

"One with this high of stakes?"

He nodded. "In the War of the Five Suns I was defending over seven million people on three planets. Those were pretty high stakes."

"Yes, but it was only the Navy that was truly threatened. The Rim planets themselves were never actually attacked."

"True enough," he said. "That would have added insult to injury. The Rim planets had no way to defend themselves. It would have been a slaughter." Then he leaned back in his couch and resumed his meditation. With his eyes closed, he said, "Laura, I'm going to need you to take over communications for the rest of the mission. We lost Kayla . . ."

"I heard, sir. I'll just add it to the rest of my duties. Not a problem, sir."

"I need someone I can trust there."

"I understand, sir."

They flew in silence for a few more minutes until they touched down outside the hollow concrete bunker the natives had called the Hill Place. Clement opened his eyes and the two of them exited the VTOL, taking minimal equipment with them. It just didn't seem to Clement that weapons would be needed as they were only there again to plead for mercy.

As they walked toward the bunker Clement went to the hill's edge and stopped, looking over the ridge and down on the lush green valley below. Even without field glasses the activity was obvious. The native encampments dotted the countryside, their gentle firelights burning against the tepid ruby "night" skies of Bellus. The bustle of Camp Alpha was there, what with thirty thousand migrants making their way to the base of the mountain. The sounds of the bunker construction machines echoed up to them as the Marines worked furiously to provide protection to the populace, both settlers and natives, from the coming attack. Clement was keenly aware that the settlers had come here on his promises, and how much he had let them down and led them into peril.

"That's what we're trying to protect," he said to Pomeroy.

She stayed quiet for a second. "It's a worthy cause, Admiral. It's not your fault that things haven't worked out as expected."

"It may not be my fault, Laura, but it is my responsibility." With that he turned away from the ridge and they headed inside the bunker.

This time the elevator door was open and waiting for them, humming with energy. They made their way inside and the doors closed without an action from either one of them.

"It looks like we're expected," said Pomeroy.

"I just wish I knew if that was a good sign or a bad one," replied Clement.

"Well, they do appear to be inviting us down."

"True enough."

The elevator doors opened on the vast and beautiful underground cavern once again. As they stepped out Clement noted that the native woman, Mary, was already at the console, manipulating floating 3D displays at her whim. The two Five Suns Navy officers walked down the ramp and quickly up to the control console.

"I suppose you know why we're here," said Clement without hesitating. Mary seemed to ignore him for a few seconds, her hands swishing across and through various colorful three-dimensional displays.

"It's agreeable to see you again, Admiral," she said without looking up from her work. "But if you'll give me just a moment, I can pay greater attention to our conversation." With that her hands continued to whip through the displays, moving some, combining others, and reaching "inside" still more to pluck what he could only assume were components being moved from one system to another. It was a fascinating kaleidoscope of color, sound, and motion. Clement looked away while she was at her task and examined the rest of the cavern again. He could see many more of the amber-skinned natives than he had ever seen before moving about the cavern, undoubtedly tending to important tasks and activities. In the distant "village" beyond this maintenance area, basking in the amber-gold "daylight" of the cavern, he could also see people and vehicles moving about.

He turned to Pomeroy. "Looks as though they're preparing for something," he said quietly, so as not to interrupt Mary's tasks.

Mary picked up on their conversation. "If you will just give me a few more moments to complete my tasks ..." she said. Both Clement and Pomeroy took that as a hint for them to shut up. Mary continued her work for a few more seconds before clearing the displays and looking up at the two of them.

"I know why you're here, Admiral, and as you've already guessed we *are* preparing for something, something we did not expect."

Clement didn't bother to waste any time with niceties. "We're here to ask you to intervene on our behalf against the invading force forming up at the planet we call Trinity-6."

In response Mary pulled up a visual display and "tossed" it into the air above the three of them. "The enemy fleet has already formed, Admiral. Our monitoring equipment allows us to see things in real time throughout our star system, as opposed to your equipment, which has, of course, a temporal delay due to its inferior quality."

"We understand our technology is limited compared to yours," said Pomeroy, "that's why we're here, to see if you have anything that might help us defend the planet," she finished.

Clement watched as the Earth Ark and its fleet of surrounding ships was already in motion and on a direct course for Bellus.

"I'm curious, you told us the planetary defense systems would work automatically, but when the Solar League ships took orbit above Bellus, the defense system didn't react in any way."

"And that goes to what we did not expect, Admiral. The

planetary defense systems appear to be off-line. In all of our diagnostic examinations the system is always shown as operating and ready. However, when the threat came above our skies, the system did not react. Upon further examination we discovered that system has been disabled, perhaps a long time ago."

"Disabled? By whom, or by what?"

"We don't know the answer to that. It may have been that the system was designed by the Makers to go off-line at a prespecified time if no threats were detected, or it could be that the system simply failed. That would be a surprise, though, as almost every other system is working perfectly. In any case, at the moment why it has happened is irrelevant. We're focusing now on how to get the system back up and running, and we're clearly in a situation that threatens both the people and this planet."

"So, you're saying you have no way to help us?" asked Pomeroy.

Clement held up a hand to quiet her. "What will have to be done to get the system back online?"

"We are trying a variety of automated techniques at the moment. If they do not work then one of us will have to interface with the system directly."

That was concerning to both Clement and Pomeroy. "What do you mean by 'interface directly'?"

She gave him an odd look, tilting her head slightly to one side. "I mean what I said, Admiral: interface directly with the system through a physiological connection."

Pomeroy could not contain herself. "You mean you're going to *merge* with a machine? Has that ever been done before?"

"Not to my knowledge," replied Mary, "but we do have that capability in case some portion of the planetary artificial intelligence were to breakdown, as it appears to have happened in this case."

Clement felt a shot of dread go through him. "Mary, are you implying . . . I mean, what happens to *you* if you do this? Your personality? And can it be reversed?"

"I don't know that, Jared. I can't know, for I haven't experienced this process before."

Clement hated that answer. "When will you know if you have to do this interface?" he asked.

She looked at him blankly. "The enemy fleet will be here in nine hours. The interface and repair will require at least two, so we have roughly seven hours to try to get the system back up and running before I must make that decision."

"Mary, we came here to ask you for your help in defending us, but I'm also here for humanitarian reasons. The people outside, at the foot of this mountain, my people, are innocent. They are merely pawns in a much larger game that they never should have been involved in. I cannot help them, and we're no longer strong enough to defend them. I'm asking for your mercy. I'm asking you to let me bring as many of my people down here, inside this cavern, as I can before that fleet gets here. I don't know if you have the capacity—"

"We do, Jared, and your request will be granted. Your people are welcome inside the cavern, but understand that without the planetary defense system working I cannot guarantee their safety."

"I understand that, Mary, and I thank you for granting

our request. I will try to start moving our people up here as quickly as we can, but I'm worried we won't have enough time to get everyone up the mountainside and down here through the elevator. It may end up being only a handful of people that we can protect."

"It's not necessary for your people to come here the same way that you did. We can open the cavern up for your people to enter directly."

"How?" asked Pomeroy.

"We have bunker doors that are at ground level. Your people can enter there without the need to come up the mountain. They can shelter in the village, and there is plenty of room for them to set up their own shelters once the village is filled up. There are abundant natural water sources, and food can be provided by the Maker machines. Our people will see to your people's needs. I will also call many of our nearby people to join us here. But even with all of this, please understand that I cannot guarantee we will be safe from an all-out attack."

"Understood," said Clement, "and thank you. I will get my people moving as soon as I can get topside to send the order."

"Very well. And I will see that the bunker doors are opened thirty minutes from now."

"Excellent." He looked to Pomeroy. "We'd better get moving."

"Aye, sir."

Clement turned to go but Mary's voice called him back. When he looked again she was already back to manipulating virtual displays.

"Keep in mind, I may not be here to speak with you by

the time you return. Every minute that passes without the planetary defense system coming back online on its own brings me a minute closer to having to undertake the Ascension."

Clement and Pomeroy exchanged confused glances. "What is the Ascension?" he asked.

"My interface with the Machine. Once it occurs I will be responsible for running all the systems on all the Trinity worlds. This is a process from which I, as an individual, may never return."

"You mean you'll be permanently linked to the Machine?"

She paused from her work to look at Clement.

"No, not linked. I may literally become part of it, inseparable for the rest of my days."

And with that she went silent and returned to her work.

Clement and Pomeroy made their way out of the cavern and back toward the elevator. Once the doors were closed, Clement turned to her. "We have to do everything we can to keep her from undergoing this Ascension. It could cost her soul."

"It could at that," agreed Pomeroy.

�ֵ **18** ✶

Forty minutes later Clement was stepping back onto the deck of the *Corvallis* with Pomeroy in tow. Below him on the planet's surface, Colonel Lubrov was already getting her settlers out of the bunkers and into the mountain cavern as fast as she could. The base of the hillside had literally opened up, and the opening was so large that they could fit virtually any of their equipment that was mobile inside. It was a movement of tremendous scale; people rushing for shelter, carrying anything they could on their backs. It reminded Clement of a story he had once read as a child about the people of Israel rushing across a sea of water that threatened to envelope them at any moment.

The transports, though, had no real way of taking shelter inside, so Clement ordered their crews back aboard and into space, sending them deeper into the star system and down to the ground on the planet Alphus. If they had any hope of ever getting the settlers safely out of the Trinity system they would have to have those transports.

What was left of his battle fleet was still in orbit over Bellus. It consisted of his two flagship light cruisers, the *Corvallis* and *Yangtze*, the lone destroyer *Titus*, and the three remaining gunships, *Antietam*, *Choctaw*, and the *Knoxville*. His battlecruiser, *Agamemnon*, was struggling with every orbit to stay afloat. Localized fires had been breaking out more frequently than anticipated and Captain Yan had been forced to evacuate her crew more quickly then she had hoped. It had left them shorthanded, but Clement didn't know the depth of the crisis until he talked to the *Agamemnon's* captain.

"Raise Captain Yan," he ordered. Pomeroy responded with an affirmative. When he had come aboard Clement had named *Corvallis* his new flagship, and had regretfully relieved Captain Samkange from his duty as her commanding officer. Samkange would now be serving as his XO, and Clement had brought his own crew from the *Beauregard* to take the main bridge positions. It wasn't anything against the *Corvallis'* original bridge crew, it was just his own preference to have people he was familiar with in key positions. He also sent Nobli and Tech Reck down to take over the engine room.

When Yan came on the crackly com line, her voice sounded both weary and stressed.

"Admiral," she said, "I am quite literally fighting fires over here. So if you called for a pep talk . . ."

"I didn't, Captain. Situation report, please."

There was a pause and he could hear Yan yelling orders in the background to fire relief crews. Then she came back online. "I've got a fire two decks down, Admiral, and it is quite literally out of control. Our situation is critical. Batteries are quickly depleting, and will go under twenty percent power in the next thirty minutes. We've managed to get about thirty-five percent of our weapons and ammunition off of the ship, including all the nukes, but the rest is not in my opinion safe anymore. If you bring ships in to dock with us they are as likely to get blown up by our own weapons exploding in the fires as they are by any enemy they may face in the coming hours."

"I'm sorry to hear that, Captain." Clement took in a deep breath before giving his next orders. "I believe we have done all we can do without risking more lives. Therefore, Captain Yan, I am ordering you to abandon your ship with all possible speed. How many crew do you have left on board?"

"By my best count about one hundred twenty, including the fire crews."

"Do you have enough escape pods left for all of those sailors?"

"Yes, sir. Most of the crew were able to get off via shuttle transport or are already on board other ships. We're just down to the bare minimum now."

"Get your fire crews off right now. Ask your engineers to hold off until the last possible minute. We need to keep those engines running while we collect your crew. I'm also ordering you to take the captain's shuttle and transport yourself over to the *Corvallis* with immediate effect."

"With all due respect, sir, I request permission to stay aboard—"

"Denied."

"Sir—"

"Denied, Captain. You're the most important person on that ship. I want you off as soon as we break communication, then I want you on board the *Corvallis* in ten minutes."

"Admiral—"

"Yan, we may have to nuke the *Agamemnon*."

"Sir . . ." she said, hesitating at that news.

"She'll be coming around to the light side of the planet in thirty-four minutes. At that time she'll represent a danger to the planet, and the natives, below. We have multiple nuclear reactors aboard her, and we can't risk her going down in populated areas. We'll have to take her out while she's still on the dark side of the planet, which means we have about nineteen minutes to collect your people and make sure she goes to ground in a safe place. Do you understand your orders, Captain?"

She didn't respond for a moment, then, "I will see you in ten minutes, Admiral."

"Good luck, Captain."

She was good to her word and was on the bridge of the *Corvallis* nine minutes later. He greeted her with a hug of condolence. "I'm sorry, Yan. I know this isn't how you wanted your first command to end."

"No, it isn't, but we gave them hell, all we had, and we took plenty of them out before they got us." He pulled back and he looked at her. Her face had smoke stains and smudges on it, her hair was tousled about her head, and her uniform was covered in grease and tiny tears. It was clear she'd been fighting some of the fires herself. Absently, he thought she had never looked more beautiful, but that wasn't a thought he had time to dwell on. Captain Samkange offered to relinquish the XO's position to her, but she declined and took an empty chair near the environmental station. She'd be there if they needed her, or if Clement asked for her.

When the clock reached seventeen minutes to the light side of the planet, Clement had the rescue of the escape pods suspended. There was no more time, and all of the escape pods seemed to have been accounted for. Clement asked Samkange to get a count of the crew recovered, then turned his attention to the sagging battlecruiser. *Agamemnon* was deorbiting much more rapidly than before. There was no engine crew to fight fires and man the propulsion. She was sinking like a broken old sea liner going down below the ocean waters of Earth. The projections showed her crash into the planet at a good one hundred thirty kilometers into the light side of Bellus, which they could not allow. There was a very good chance her nuclear materials would spread upon impact and poison both the land and the people below. He had to act now.

"Helmsman," he said to Mika Ori formally, "lock missiles onto the *Agamemnon*."

"Aye, sir," she said, with more than a bit of sadness in her voice. Clement called down to the missile room, making sure they had loaded two nuclear-tipped missiles into the launch tubes. It might have been overkill considering the condition of *Agamemnon*, but he couldn't really take the chance she would go down in a populated area. He ordered firing control locked in to his console.

"Stand to orders," he said, and all the crew on the bridge rose to attention. The main view display showed the *Agamemnon* listing and burning. She was dying, and Clement had to help her on her way. "Present arms!" The bridge crew raised their hands in salute.

Clement's hand reached down to the firing icon. "Fire," he said, while depressing the icon.

The two missiles launched out of the port and starboard launch tubes of the *Corvallis*. It took them a good ten seconds to reach their target, which was agonizing to watch. The crew all held their salutes to the end. When it came, there was a blinding flash of orange and white light as *Agamemnon* disintegrated in the nuclear heat of the exploding warheads.

The fire remained for only a few seconds before small pieces of the once great battlecruiser fell, streaking into the atmosphere, burning up as they went.

"All hands, return to stations."

Then he sat down in his command chair, and sighed heavily.

By this time the tactical screens had shown the Solar League fleet in motion, diving in toward Bellus at a high angle of inclination. This attack pattern indicated that they would sweep down on the planet at rapid speed, scattering any remaining ships in their path. Clement had no intention of leaving any of his ships over Bellus, and he had already ordered Captain Son in the *Yangtze* and the sole remaining destroyer *Titus*, plus the ten grounded transports to the orbit of the inner habitable planet of Alphus. There they were to maintain orbit until they were either confronted by the enemy or their surrender was demanded. In the latter case, he had left orders that they were to surrender unconditionally, with no loss of life risked. Clement himself had stayed aboard *Corvallis* in a last stand defense over the planet below. They still had four nuclear warheads and he intended to use them if he had to, even if that wouldn't change the ultimate outcome at all. All he could do was to hope the nukes could slow the incoming enemy down and give Mary and the Trinity natives time to reactivate the planetary defense grid.

What was clear, though, was that the enemy fleet had rallied without its ostensible commander, Elara DeVore. Her shuttle was still alone along its preset course to the gas planet Trinity-6, where a small contingent of support craft had been left behind by the attacking fleet. The main formation of the fleet had, in fact, already passed DeVore's position, and by now they had surely shared communications. The answer to Clement's overture to the Solar League was evident in their actions. They were planning to take Bellus by force, and whatever influence DeVore had over the fleet was now clearly gone. The Ark ship was in the midst of the fleet, protected on all sides by her heavy cruisers. When they arrived over Bellus he expected a demand for their immediate surrender, and Clement would give it to them if only to save lives. But the fact was they would probably end up becoming slaves of the Solar League, no longer having the choice of free will over their own lives.

The only chance Clement could see for a positive outcome was if Mary was able to get the planetary defense system back online. It was barely three hours now until forward units of the enemy fleet arrived, and an hour before that Mary would have to make her life-altering decision of merging with the planetary artificial intelligence in order to activate the defense grid. And even if she was able to do that, there was no guarantee she could complete the repairs in time to stop the Solar

League takeover of Trinity and the enslavement of all of her children, native and migrant alike.

Clement gathered his command crew in the *Corvallis'* conference room for one last strategy session. When everyone was seated Clement started in immediately. "Ladies and gentlemen, we have four nuclear warheads left and only this ship to protect Bellus and its people. I can think of only one strategy, and admittedly that is no winning strategy, it's only a rearguard action while we get our transports safely to Alphus. I want your opinions, and none of you are allowed to keep those to yourself. If you have any ideas, any thoughts at all, I want to hear them and that is an order," he said.

He shifted his weight in his chair, trying to get comfortable, but nothing could make that happen under the conditions they faced. He started in again. "My current plan is to take *Corvallis* out toward the enemy fleet and unload our four nukes at them, then retreat as swiftly as we can. I've identified what appear to be three heavy cruisers that by configuration look like they would be command and control ships. If that is, in fact, the case it's possible we could knock out enough of their communications to confuse them for a while."

Yan spoke first. "How long is 'a while,' Admiral?"

"My estimate is twenty to thirty minutes."

"And what would that time buy us?"

"Time to retreat back to Bellus, disembark our command staff on the last shuttle, and for *Corvallis* to then retreat and join the remaining ships in orbit around Alphus."

"With all due respect, sir, *Corvallis* wants to stay in

orbit here, defending the camp," cut in Captain Samkange.

"I appreciate that, Captain, but my orders are for you to join the other ships. We need to protect those transports, as it's possible the enemy may allow the migrant settlers to leave at some point in the future. We'll need those ships and at least one of your cruisers with a LEAP drive to make that trip home."

"But what if they attack Bellus with full forces? Should we quietly surrender to them then?"

"In that case, Captain, if you see Bellus being attacked, your orders will be to take your remaining ships, including the transports, exit the Trinity system and return home to Kemmerine at best possible speed."

Samkange was uncomfortable with this strategy, and it showed in his posture as he turned to face Clement more directly. "Sir, I have to protest this course of action. Those settlers came here because they couldn't survive in the Five Suns anymore. They have no other home."

"If we take the transports away—" started Mika Ori.

Clement cut in. "The simple fact is that we don't have time to get them off the planet or I would send them all back now. The choice between returning home or being slaves of the Solar League here at Trinity doesn't seem to be much of a choice."

At that Hassan Nobli spoke up from the far end of the table. "There is one more possibility, Admiral, but it's not a pleasant one."

Clement shifted in his chair. "I'm open to hear it, Hassan."

Nobli started in, very slowly and deliberately. "This ship

has a functioning LEAP reactor. As far as we know an active LEAP reactor is the most powerful potential weapon in the universe."

Clement cut him off right there. "This ship is not equipped to use a LEAP reactor in that way. The *Beauregard* was the only ship in the fleet equipped with the MAD capability."

"You're right, Jared, but I wasn't thinking of using the reactor the same way as we used it on the *Beauregard*."

Clement hesitated a moment before answering. "Then spill it, Engineer," he said.

"We know from the *Beauregard*'s destruction that releasing LEAP energy into normal space can create a massively destructive reaction. If we were to use the *Corvallis* for this purpose, it's quite possible her reactor explosion could be large enough to destroy the entire enemy fleet."

"And likely half the planet," said Yan sharply.

Nobli eyed her over the top of his glasses. "From the *Beauregard*'s explosion we can determine that the blast range of a cracked reactor is about 0.0025 AUs. Now, that's not very much in terms of the space between the Trinity planets, which as we know are packed in tight together. In fact, if we get far enough away from Bellus we'll have plenty of room to make sure the planets stay safe, but it would certainly be a big enough explosion to completely destroy their fleet in the current configuration they are in. The rub, however, is we would have to get moving now in order to meet the enemy fleet and execute this maneuver out in 'safe' space."

"So we'd be committing suicide," said Yan. Nobli

merely nodded his head in response. She turned to Clement. "Admiral, you can't possibly be considering this course of action."

Clement looked around the room at each of their faces. Young or old, he could tell by looking into their eyes that they were all committed, and that they would follow his orders, even to their deaths. That was not a path he was willing to take.

"I've been in wars before. I've seen many people die, most of them at my command. I'm not prepared to ask this crew or these settlers to take any such risk. We've already lost one of our most precious young souls in Kayla Adebayor. I'm not willing to sacrifice any more. This idea is rejected. I'd like any additional thoughts on my initial proposal of action."

Ivan Massif cleared his throat before speaking up. "Sir, have you considered that your rearguard action might actually make things worse? Possibly angering the Solar League people to the point that they seek retribution from among our settlers, our ships, or even the natives?"

"That's a possibility we would have to weigh against what we would gain by delaying them."

Yan spoke up again. "I'm just not sure why exactly we're trying to gain a little bit of time in exchange for possibly angering the enemy to the point that they take it out on us or our people. And by our people I mean all of us, including the natives."

Clement looked down at his wristwatch. "In another forty-five minutes the native woman Mary will have reached a point where she has determined that the planetary defense systems cannot be repaired by 'external' means. I'm trying to buy her as much time as I can, and maybe a little extra, before she's forced to take her next steps."

"Which are?" All the faces at the table turned toward Clement then.

"Merging her body, and her consciousness, with the planetary AI in order to conduct the repairs. Based on her timeline, she would need about two hours from the beginning of that process to reboot the planetary defense system and put it into operation."

"If she has to do it, then she has to do it, right?"

Clement looked directly at Yan. "I don't think you understand, Captain. If she does this it can never be reversed. She will become one with the Machine, and she will lose her consciousness, her very being, forever. For however long she lives, she will cease to be herself, and be only the Machine."

Yan and Clement locked eyes.

"Then let me be the first to propose that we abandon the rearguard attack plan based on the possibility that it will anger our opponents, who have an overwhelming military advantage over us," she said. "And let Mary make her own decision about defending her planet. After all, it is hers much more than it is ours."

"True enough." Clement looked around the table one last time. "Are there any of you who disagree with Captain Yan's proposal to abandon the nuclear rearguard action?" Again, looking from face to face he could find no hint of disagreement among them. It was clear; they all wanted to minimize bloodshed and protect as many of the civilians as they could.

"I'll take that as consensus," stated Clement, "and although I am the commander of this mission and have full authority to act on my own, I acknowledge your experience and your wisdom in this matter. We will stand down and hope that the planetary defense grid can be reactivated by the native Mary. In lieu of that happening, I will send out a longwave communication toward the enemy fleet, indicating our surrender and asking them to give quarter to all our ships at the planet Alphus."

He stood up and they joined him. "It has been an honor serving with each and every one of you. I now turn command of this vessel back over to its captain, Harry Samkange. I and the rest of my crew from both the *Beauregard* and the *Agamemnon* will return to the planet's surface on the shuttle to lend whatever assistance we can to the transition. Thank you all, and may God bless you," he said.

Fifteen minutes later and Clement had finished conveying the unconditional surrender of the Five Suns fleet to the Solar League ships. Even with the four-minute delay taken into account, he didn't wait for a response, and none came. He, Yan, and Mika were the last to board the shuttle, which Ori quickly detached from the *Corvallis* on its way down to the surface of Bellus. In the back the rest of his crew sat quiet and unhappy, but he could do nothing to cheer their spirits.

Captain Samkange moved his ship off toward Alphus as quickly as he could go. As the transport shuttle fell from the sky, Clement wondered if he should have sent the Navy ships at Alphus back home immediately to warn

Kemmerine that an invading force from Earth had taken the Trinity system. It would likely make little difference if the Solar League decided to attack, as he had essentially left Kemmerine Station undefended with his expedition. Any attempt to take the station by the Solar League fleet would be unstoppable.

As he stared out a porthole in the pilot's nest, Yan, still dressed in her tattered uniform, unbuckled her safety belt and pulled herself across the cabin (in zero-*g*) to eventually sit next to him and buckle herself in again. She sat with him silently for a few moments as he continued to stare out the window, hand to his chin.

"There really wasn't much else you could do," she said quietly. When he didn't respond, she continued. "This was an unwinnable situation from the beginning. Perhaps we never should have fought in the first place."

Clement finally turned to her. "Oh, I'm convinced fighting was the right thing to do. This Solar League, whatever that actually is, is coming at an unarmed planet at a high rate of speed with the full power of its force bearing down on us. They've had my surrender message for thirty minutes now, well beyond the normal time delay, and they've said nothing nor made any move to stand down from their attack. It seems to me more and more likely they are determined to sweep our forces and our influence over Trinity completely away from the face of this system. That could mean the harshest possible outcome for our people. We were the only ones that have the technology and the weapons to resist them, unless by some miracle Mary can get the defense grid working again."

"What do you think the odds are of that happening?"

He looked down at his watch again. "I would say very low. The natives have been at this themselves for the better part of the day with no progress reported. My guess is that the system failed some time ago, and that the Makers either never bothered to return to fix it or they simply don't exist anymore. They could have been wiped from the galaxy a long time ago, we just don't know it yet. But pinning the defense of an entire star system on one young girl seems unlikely to give us the positive outcome we want."

A look of concern came across Yan's face. "Our people are protected by the Hill Place pyramid now. Do you think we'll be able to fight them off on the ground?"

Clement shook his head. "I just don't know. Twelve hundred trained Marines against thousands of heavily armed soldiers with total air superiority, nuclear weapons, and advanced ground-based vehicles would say otherwise. But while we have time there is always some glimmer of hope." He leaned back in his couch, closing his eyes then and letting out a large sigh. Whether it was in relief or despair, Yan couldn't tell. She took his hand in hers and gripped it tightly, then she laid back as well, closing her eyes as the transport rocked and rolled its way to the ground.

☼ 19 ☼

The transport shuttle pilot landed right inside the Hill Place mountain cavern. Clement was quickly out of the ship and sought out Colonel Lubrov, passing several thousand settlers who had pitched makeshift shelters inside the cavern. It was rough going for them, but he got no anger directed toward him for the situation, at least not to his face.

"Situation report, Colonel," he said curtly once he had found Lubrov inside her command shelter. He may have been beaten, but he was still in command.

"All of the settlers are now inside the cavern, sir. Some of them have taken up residence inside the native structures in the village. Others, as you can see, have set up camp themselves."

"Have you done a head count?"

She nodded. "Twenty-nine thousand four hundred seventy heads accounted for, sir, including every one of my twelve hundred Marines. I still have them stationed in the bunkers and on our defensive fortifications. They still have fight in them, sir."

"Very good, Colonel, but the fact is that they're sitting

ducks out there. I have no idea if these walls will protect us from the kind of attack we'll be facing, and I don't want to sacrifice any of your Marines just for the sake of giving the Solar League a good fight before we all die. Recall all your troops and station them around the cavern, and do so immediately." Again he glanced down at his watch. "We have a little over two hours before that fleet is in striking range of us. Get them all in here and let's get set up defensively as best we can."

"Yes, sir," said Lubrov, but it was obvious again from her stern face that she didn't agree with Clement's decision not to fight. Clement noticed this and stopped to make one more comment.

"Colonel, I know this isn't what you want, and as soldiers our instinct is to fight. But this is a situation where the best we can do now is defend the innocent. I hope you can understand that."

She stiffened at what seemed to her to be a rebuke. "I do understand, sir, but I don't have to like it."

Clement smiled wryly at that, and at her resolve. "No, Colonel, you're right you don't have to like it. Carry on, Colonel Lubrov," he said, and saluted her. She snapped off a salute back at him.

Just then, Yan came into the tent. "Clement, I think you'd better come see this," she said, a grim look on her face. "It seems your friend Mary has jumped the gun."

Clement was startled. "What do you mean?"

"I mean she's already started the merging process with the AI, and from all indications, it's not going well."

Clement just nodded at Lubrov as he and Yan swiftly left the tent together. He turned to her as they walked.

"Call Laura Pomeroy. I want a medically trained observer to see this."

"Of course," said Yan, switching on her com and contacting Pomeroy with her orders. They ran double-time from the village toward the command platform, a good half a kilometer away. Neither of them knew how to access the subterranean transport system, so that wasn't an option. They quickly made their way through the village and up to the command platform and its wall of machines. Before they got close to the platform, Clement could see what was happening.

Mary was standing at the console, wires extending from the mechanism into her head and hands. Her hands were working frantically at lightning speeds over the holographic controls. Occasionally circuit displays would pop up and she would modify the components, shifting their composition and arrangement, like revising a schematic, and then just as quickly drop the circuits back into the console with a downward sweep of her hand.

Laura Pomeroy arrived then and took up a position to one side of Clement, with Yan on the other. A half dozen native technicians were attending to her, running scanners over her and reading outputs, then making changes to handheld equipment or using the devices that were attaching themselves to her body.

Clement sought out one of the natives to explain to him what was going on. A man named Letine was willing to speak with him. He had the look of the "awakened" natives, human in every way with the exception of his light amber skin color and white hair, which was cut short as Mary's was.

"I was told she wouldn't try this for another thirty minutes. When did this happen?"

Letine looked at him strangely, as if he was trying to understand his words. Finally he spoke. "I am . . . not that familiar with your language . . ." Then he hesitated, as if he was receiving a download of some kind. "She . . . could not wait. It was apparent that we would not be able to repair the defense system. The AI that the Makers left behind . . . did not seem to . . . remember . . . how to activate the system. Direct intervention was then required, and she chose to begin the process of Ascension," he said, his use of the language getting better with each exchange.

"Ascension?" asked Yan.

Clement turned to her. "The merging of human and machine," he said.

"She chose this path," said Letine.

"I understand the process is not going well," said Clement.

"There have been many complications. None of us has experience with this type of . . . transfiguration. The Machine is not yet accepting her."

"Will it?"

"That is uncertain."

"Is she conscious?"

Again Letine looked as if he was having trouble understanding Clement, then after a few moments a look of clarity came over his face. "She does not speak," he said. "If the Ascension works, then she will speak."

Clement wanted to explain that what he really wanted to know was if she felt any pain from the process, but he doubted Letine would understand. All they could do was stand by and watch her as the Machine took more and more control over her body.

Letine gave out orders in the natives' language and the workers scrambled to complete their ordered tasks. Suddenly, Mary started twitching violently, pulling at the tubing and straining the connections the wires had into her body.

"She's having a seizure," said Pomeroy. She pulled out her medical kit and reached out to Mary as she fell away from the console, catching her before she fell to the floor. Pomeroy quickly scanned her body with her monitoring equipment, then reported. "Her body temperature is running very high. This process is proving very difficult for her. It is as likely as not that we may lose her."

Letine and his people began to scramble, injecting her body with yet more fluids and other unknown technologies, most likely nanobots. When her body seemed to calm, Clement grabbed Letine by the elbow to ask him more questions.

"What just happened?" he demanded.

"The Machine is rejecting her. We must disconnect her before the rejection kills her."

"Then do it, man!" demanded Clement. The technicians sprang into action, pulling wires from her body, sealing wounds as they disconnected her from the Machine. Pomeroy cradled Mary's head in her lap.

"Laura?" asked Clement. She just shook her head in reply, uncertain if Mary would die.

"If we lose her, we lose our last chance of defending ourselves," said Yan.

"Then we can't lose her," said Clement forcefully. Letine seemed to get the message and nodded as his people began working even more frantically on the young girl's body. Pomeroy continued to pull out micro-fine fibers from her head, obviously connected to interface with her brain. Small beads of blood emerged as the wires were removed.

"Her body will not give up its life," stated Letine. "If she does not surrender to the Machine soon, the Ascension will fail, and she will die."

"If she dies, then we're lost, completely lost," said Clement. He went down on his haunches next to Mary and took her free hand in his.

Yan reached out to him, putting a supporting hand on his shoulder, trying to comfort him. "You couldn't have known how this would play out. None of us could," she said gently.

Clement released Mary and placed his hand over Yan's and pulled it off of him as he stood again, but he would not meet her eyes. "I should've known. I'm the one who bears the responsibility. This mission, all these people, this is all on me. All the death, all the destruction . . ." He trailed off into silence.

"If you're responsible then we're all responsible."

"Really?" he snapped. "*I'm* the one who convinced these people to come here, hell, even my own parents! *I'm* the one who put them in danger. *I'm* the one who asked for that girl's help, and now she's dying, and nothing you or anyone else can say will change that." He looked down at the young woman who had probably sacrificed her life for them, her head cradled in

Pomeroy's arms, her breathing harsh and shallow. Slowly the technicians backed away from her, waiting for the inevitable.

Clement made a decision.

"Letine, can you bring up a display that shows us where the Solar League fleet is right now?" The man nodded and went to the nearest raised console where he waved his hands, trying to bring up displays as Mary had done. Only a handful of the circuits came up, and they were bland and mostly colorless.

"This looks worse than the system was before," stated Yan. "More systems dark, less available. Even if we could influence it, it doesn't seem like there's enough left of this machine to help us."

Clement could only nod. It seemed as if Mary's attempt at the Ascension had damaged more systems within the Machine. After several tense moments Letine managed to bring up a real-time display over the planet.

The Solar League fleet was decelerating, but still on an attack vector. Undoubtedly their target was now the caverns and the abandoned Camp Alpha. "How long until they get here?" Clement asked. The native swept a hand over the display and indecipherable characters suddenly changed to minutes and seconds.

Just twenty-two minutes to go.

Clement turned to Yan. "Get the shuttle ready."

"Why?"

"Because I'm going up there to surrender, personally. They can blow me out of the sky if they want. This may be a completely futile gesture on my part, but I'd rather die up there, trying to save a few lives of the people I love than die down here if they use their nukes to turn this mountain into melted rock."

Yan knew she couldn't stop him. She also didn't want to disobey what could be his last order to her. She used her com to call down to Colonel Lubrov and have her prep their single remaining military shuttle. "Five minutes," she said to him when she got off the com.

Clement turned to Letine. "Once I leave you'd better get those cavern doors shut and get your people away from them. I don't know if this place is hardened for atomic attacks or not, but even if it is you need to take as many precautions as you can."

"I do not know what we can do. Only Mary, or the Maker machine, would know. Defense is not my function."

"Well, my friend, it is now," he said, and slapped him on the shoulder as he started to walk away.

"Clement!" called Yan from behind him, excited.

Clement turned around. Yan pointed at the floor, where Pomeroy still cradled Mary's head in her hands. The was a purple light swirling on the floor, surrounding the outline of Mary's body. Pomeroy gently laid her head down on the floor and backed away.

"What is that?" Yan asked.

Clement looked to Pomeroy, who shrugged. "I'm sure I have no idea, sir," she said. Letine also shrugged, imitating her gesture.

The light now surrounded Mary's prone form on the floor, and began to slowly pulsate, growing faster with each second. The deep purple nano-material oozed from the floor onto her body, and into the wounds where the wires had been. Her body began twitching again, but much less violently this time. They watched as the purple material covered her face and body completely, sparkling with gentle power and warmth. Then Clement had another sensation. *This material is feeding her life*, he thought. Seconds went by, and just as quickly as it had come, the lifegiving fluid receded back into its perfectly formed "floor."

They all watched in astonishment as Mary's eyes fluttered, and then opened.

She stared blankly forward without any hint of emotion or recognition of her surroundings. After a few seconds had passed, she rolled onto her side and slowly got to her feet. She moved off the platform spot where she had been reborn and took a few hesitant steps toward Clement. It was like watching a child learning to walk for the first time. After taking a few steps she stopped and looked down at her hand, flexing the fingers as if she was trying to determine how they worked. She looked up at Clement with ice blue eyes and attempted to speak.

"Admiral . . ." she said in a voice that was more mechanical than organic. She repeated the word twice more, and by the third time her voice approximated that of Mary's. "You must take me with you on your shuttle," she said.

Clement looked back and forth with Yan, then addressed Mary. "I was planning on going into space to surrender, or sacrifice myself in trying. Are you sure you want to go with me?"

She looked at him oddly for a second as if she was trying to analyze what he had just said. "I know what I am requesting, Admiral. We have very little time to quibble. Please come with me and I will try to explain the situation as we go."

Clement nodded to her and then looked to Yan again. "You heard the lady. The two of us are going into space. I'm putting you in charge of everything down here. Don't get killed," he said.

"I won't," she replied, standing firm, "as long as you promise me that you won't get killed either."

"I have to go," he said to her. And then, without really thinking about it, leaned in and kissed her on the lips, lingering for only a second. Yan was surprised at that.

Clement turned and they both watched as "Mary" started walking haltingly toward the subterranean transport station. Clement took off running after her, as her stride was growing stronger and more confident with each step. He caught up to her as they entered the station.

Once inside the tram, it quickly took off, humming along toward the village. Clement attempted to engage Mary in conversation. "Why are you coming into space with me? I only have a small shuttle and we'll be facing off against an entire battle fleet, including that Earth Ark ship."

"That will best be explained once we are on the shuttle. For now, I will try to explain to you about myself. As you may have guessed the Ascension process failed. I was unable to activate the planetary defense grid as it appears to be broken at the source."

"Where is the source?" he asked.

"The third habitable planet, the one you call Camus.

We must go there so that I can attempt the Ascension again."

Clement looked at her incredulously. "Mary, the ship we have available cannot get to Camus. It has no LEAP drive or anything of that nature. To get past the Solar League fleet we'll have to have a LEAP-capable ship, and none of the crews onboard the ships I have at Alphus have ever attempted a LEAP jump inside a solar system before. It could easily go wrong."

"Your ship's crew has made several in-system LEAP jumps, haven't they?"

"Well, yes . . ."

"Then they must join us on the shuttle, there's no time to waste."

Clement jumped on his com then and got hold of Yan, telling her to round up the bridge crew of the late *Beauregard* and meet them at the shuttle. She acknowledged and cut the line. "This will take more time to round up my crew."

"If what you say is true, then we must have them."

With that, the small tram car arrived at the village, and they both hustled out and down to the waiting shuttle. He was having difficulty keeping up with Mary, who was running at a surprising pace while dancing through the crowd of civilians with effortless dexterity. Her control of her body seemed to be increasing with every passing second. Colonel Lubrov was waiting for him at the shuttle and saluted as he approached.

"No time to chat, Colonel. Once we're out of the cavern get with the native man Letine and get the blast doors shut, and get our people as far inside the mountain as you can. If they hit this mountain with a nuke anything could happen. We don't know how good the ground defenses are or even if they'll be operating. Take every precaution you can."

"And what about you, sir?" she protested.

"There's nothing about me, Colonel. If I come back you'll know we had a positive outcome. If I don't then you'll know the results of that as well. Captain Yan is in command until and unless I return. Understood?"

"Clearly, sir."

With that he was gone, running into the shuttle.

It took another six minutes until the full *Beauregard* bridge crew (plus Nobli and Tech Reck) were aboard and strapped in. Yan waved at Clement from the ground as the shuttle rolled away toward an unknown fate.

Four minutes at maximum thrust and they were outside the atmosphere of Bellus and accelerating toward the incoming Solar League fleet. The shuttle's onboard chronometer showed they had eleven minutes until the fleet reached targeting range on the camp. Any long-range attack would likely come with missiles, either conventional or nuclear. A more direct tactic would be to send landing craft, attack ships, and troops to the surface, unless, of course, their intent was simply to wipe out the Five Suns presence on Bellus. They would know very shortly.

Once the shuttle was on course for the rendezvous point, Clement went back to his crew and explained their first task. "You'll have to call up the *Antietam* and walk their crew through the process of making a short-range

LEAP jump. Once we rendezvous with them, we can transfer to the con and run the second jump on our own."

"Are you insane?" said Nobli. "Two LEAP jumps in-system, one by an untrained crew?"

"Yeah!" chimed in Tech Reck.

"They won't be untrained. They'll have all of you to rely on. So start making plans, tie in your coms to the shuttle system and prepare to give detailed instructions to your counterparts. There's absolutely no room for error on this." There was general grumbling at the assignment, but no further objections.

Clement returned to the pilot's nest, and Mary. "They have their assignments, but no understanding of how they will communicate. Because of the distances involved there will be a four-minute delay in the instructions being transmitted."

"I will explain. We have technology to make this possible. The Ascension may have failed, but I have gained a great deal of . . . functionality . . . even through the temporary merging with the Machine. For now, you must reduce your speed and bring the shuttle to a full stop in space within thirty-one seconds, Admiral."

"Well, nothing like a bit of lead time." Clement brought the shuttle to a full stop five hundred kilometers above the camp, right on time.

Mary extended her hand and spread her fingers as a three-dimensional holographic display popped up inside the pilot's nest. She spun the display with the index finger of her left hand, moving it around to see the formation of the enemy fleet and their current position. A mixed group of six Solar League cruisers and destroyers (three each) were moving away from the main body of the attacking fleet and headed on a different course.

"Where are those ships going?" Clement asked.

"They're heading for the planet you call Alphus," said Mary. "I assume to take out the remaining ships that you have stationed there."

"Those ships have orders to bug out for Kemmerine Station as soon as they detect that movement, which will likely be in about three minutes."

"I suggest you cancel those orders, Admiral."

"This shuttle doesn't have a com system that strong. They'll see those Solar League ships coming before I could countermand their existing orders."

She said nothing to that, instead using her left hand to pull out a circuit display and place it in front of his face. "This system can communicate your orders in what you call 'real time.' It is already matched up to your fleet frequency."

Clement looked at the transparent floating icon, which he supposed vaguely resembled a communications device, or at least a microphone. "How do I—"

She reached over again and tapped on the hologram with her finger. "It is now active, Admiral."

He leaned slightly forward and spoke into the "microphone." "This is Admiral Clement. I hereby countermand my previous orders to bug out and return to Kemmerine Station. Put as much distance between yourselves and the incoming enemy flotilla as you can. Keep the planet between you if you have to, but maintain your distance and stand by. Please acknowledge receipt of new orders."

"They will not be able to acknowledge you, Admiral. Your ship's communications systems are not strong enough to respond to your communication in time. I suggest you complete your orders and trust that you have trained those crews well enough that they will follow your commands."

Clement looked at her as she continued spinning her display, moving circuits around, in and out, combining some components and splitting others apart. He "tapped" on the communications hologram again. "Belay acknowledgement of last orders. Proceed as instructed and stand by for further communications on this frequency." He turned to Mary. "I have to contact the *Antietam* separately and let them know what's coming."

"I will link you directly with your vessel," she said. Her hands played in the air for a few more seconds, and then she nodded at him. He tapped the microphone icon again and called the *Antietam's* Captain Kagereki to explain the situation. Once completed, Mary linked in the *Beauregard's* bridge crew with their counterparts and the process began.

Clement looked up at the chronometer. "Six minutes," he said.

"We are in position for the rendezvous," she said, continuing her manipulations.

He was uncomfortable just waiting for things to get done, and being passive, so he stuck his head into the crew cabin where Mika Ori, Massif, Pomeroy, Nobli and Tech Reck were all busy communicating with the crew of the *Antietam*. He felt like this was the longest of long shots.

He came back to his pilot's couch and sat down with a

sigh. Then, turning to Mary he said, "You told me you'd explain about the condition of the defense grid when we got up here. Well, now might be a good time for that explanation."

She didn't stop her manipulations of the circuit displays for a second while she responded to him. "I am still attempting to activate the planetary defense grid. I have not had time to analyze *why* the system-wide defense grid failed on the world you call Camus, but it did fail. If I am successful in the next"—she looked up at the clock—"five minutes, then perhaps we can avoid any losses to our people on the ground."

"Our people?"

"Yours and mine, Admiral, or rather, yours and the Makers' children."

"I understand, Mary," said Clement. "And you may call me Jared from now on. I find 'admiral' to be a bit too formal."

"Agreed, Jared."

"Am I distracting you from your task by asking you these questions?"

She actually shook her head, a very human gesture, while answering "No. I am fully capable of multitasking to complete this process."

"What will happen if you get the local planetary defense grid activated?"

"The system will automatically evaluate any threats to the inner planets or to the people and will act accordingly. It should project a temporary defensive shield to protect the planet from attack, at least for a while. I am hoping that time will allow us to make the jump to Camus and fix the entire system from there. That system is located on the islands of the planet, but it is not operating correctly at this point. I must be able to repair it."

"Will you attempt to undergo the Ascension again?" he asked, concerned.

"I must. Only this time I must not fail. Undergoing the ordeal once already has shown me where I have failed."

"But if you've already failed once, how can it work a second time?"

"I did not allow the system to completely immerse me. My human instinct for survival was too strong. I am a young woman, Jared, with all the drives and urges any woman my age would have on your worlds. Love, sex, family. I now know that I must completely obliterate those feelings and impulses if I am to be one with the Machine."

"That doesn't sound like an easy task. Are you sure it's what you want?"

She did not immediately answer. Then: "No other outcome is possible to protect Trinity's children. You have very little faith in the Makers, Jared. And in me."

"I'm a man who prefers certainty, Mary. I have thirty thousand people down on Bellus that are my responsibility, and I worry for them."

She looked away from her work for a few seconds. "I have chosen with my free will to take responsibility for you and your people. I will protect them as if they were the Makers' own. There are things I do not have time to explain using human language, but once we are past this current crisis, hopefully there will be time for you and me to discuss both the future of your people and of the Makers' children, but now is not that time."

He acknowledged the point with a nod. "How will we be able to discuss these things if you will become part of the Machine?"

"You are confused, Jared. I will not merely be part of the Machine; I will *be* the Machine. The artificial intelligence that operated autonomously before will operate in union with me. What I know, the Machine will know, and vice versa. This is the beauty and perfection of the Makers' design."

Clement took in a deep breath at the depth of the sacrifice she was contemplating. "Well then, blessed be the Makers."

"Blessed be the Makers," she replied.

☆ 20 ☆

Their time expired with the jump of *Antietam* still incomplete. Mary, for her part, was still working hard on at least raising a defensive field over Bellus, but was otherwise silent. Clement checked in with his crew, and they reported progress, perhaps ten minutes until *Antietam* could attempt the jump. "This *is* rocket science, you know," quipped an irritated Nobli. Clement could only wait. If this jump didn't work, they were doomed.

Clement fired the shuttle's thrusters to attempt to put some distance between them and the incoming fleet, which was decelerating heavily now onto the battlefield. They had to get out of range of the Solar League ships, which were in range and preparing to attack, but stay close enough to Mary's "rendezvous point" to be in range of the *Antietam* when she jumped in.

He felt helpless as he watched a group of twelve destroyers break away from the main fleet. The destroyer pack (broken into two groups of six) took up positions over the Hill Place mountain camp where all of his people no doubt sat huddled in fear, five hundred kilometers below. They had good reason for their fear.

Dave Bara

The leading group of six launched missiles from their forward launch tubes. The missiles descended on the mountain and Camp Alpha. If they were conventional, they would cause a great deal of damage. If they were nuclear, he didn't see how anyone on the surface could survive. He swallowed hard. His parents were down there. His heart started racing in fear.

In mere seconds the missiles impacted the ground. He let out a deep breath of relief when he saw the signature of the missile explosions; they were conventional and not nuclear. As the second group of destroyers took up position to launch their volleys, he switched to a visual display of the damage below. Thankfully just Camp Alpha and not the mountain had been targeted first. The bunkers that they had so rapidly and robustly built had been reduced to a smoking ruin. If his people had been outside the cavern during the attack, it would have been a bloodbath. He had no idea if the Solar League ship commanders knew that the bunkers were empty or occupied, but their intent would become clear in the next few minutes.

The second volley of conventional missiles struck the camp again, with one exception: a single missile targeted the Hill Place complex on the side of the mountain/pyramid and completely destroyed it. By this time his tactical board showed a single heavy cruiser had joined the grouping. According to his telemetry, the ship moved into a position that placed it directly over the mountain where all of his people were hunkered down. There was little doubt in Clement as to its intent. It was preparing to launch a nuke.

Desperate to stop it, Clement looked anxiously for the shuttle's manifest to see if it had taken any weaponry on board from either *Agamemnon* or one of the other ships. As he expected, the shuttle had only small arms aboard, but it did have one other thing that could be used as a weapon—a nuclear engine.

An engine with a nuclear reactor was not designed to be detonated, but it could be used as a "dirty bomb" to try and stop an attacking vessel. What Clement was contemplating was suicide, and the death of both Mary and his friends. Had he been alone in the shuttle, his choice might have been different. He looked over to Mary, whose hand motions in the hologram displays were a whirlwind, and then up to the tactical display. The enemy destroyers were now backing away as the cruiser took its time setting up the missile launch.

"If you can get this done, now would be the time," he said to her. "Otherwise . . ."

Without moving her attention from her work, she replied, "Two minutes," which was at least encouraging.

It took Mary less than the two minutes promised to come through. She activated Bellus' defense grid with the pop of a yellow holographic button, and an orange latticework of energy engulfed the entirety of the planet. Ironically, the defense field over Bellus looked markedly similar to an electronic shield that had taken out the *Beauregard* in its first life as a Rim Confederation gunship. This field, however, appeared to be much more powerful.

The cruiser was now stuck above the shield (while the shuttle was below it), but she must have been too deep in her countdown or too slow to react to the new tactical situation. She fired her missile.

She was only a dozen kilometers behind the shield when the missile launched. It hit the energy field almost immediately and exploded on contact. The field seemed to absorb some of the explosive energy, but at the short range the detonation could not be fully stopped from rebounding against the cruiser.

She was completely engulfed by the explosion, disappearing into the white-hot light of the nuclear flame. He had to look away from the shuttle windows as the light from the explosion penetrated the pilot's nest. When he opened his eyes again, the tactical display showed only a fragment of the vessel remained intact. He switched to his visual display and saw the cruiser burning for a few seconds, until all the oxygen and combustible fuel was exhausted. Then the hulk of the cruiser was dark.

"A ship of that size probably carried five hundred sailors, or more," said Clement.

"They should not have been attacking my people. As you can surmise, I was able to initiate the defensive field over Bellus, but I was not able to activate the system-wide defensive weapons. The planet is safe for now, but the damage to the defensive systems has required me to initiate a complete 'reboot,' as you would call it, of the Machine. All of Trinity is still vulnerable to attack until I can make my way to Camus and integrate with the Machine there."

"And what of my people?"

"I do not know how long the shield over Bellus will hold. Even Maker technology has its limits, and with the damage done to the system, repair time, or even if the system can be repaired, is still a question I cannot answer until we get to Camus."

"I'll check on my people and see if they're ready yet for *Antietam* to jump back to us. But I have a question: Will the gunship be able to jump back through the shield?"

"The shield will know a friendly ship from an enemy."

"How?"

"Remember, Jared, I am now part of the Machine. What I know, it knows."

He nodded at that cryptic answer, then went back to check on his bridge crew.

"What do you have for me, Nobli?" he demanded.

"Well if you're done blowing things up with nukes up there, we're getting close. I'd like to do one more test run, though, before we start the two-minute clock."

"Start the clock now," ordered Clement. "There's no time to waste. Bellus and the camp are protected by a shield at the moment, but the system is damaged and Mary can't make us any promises about how long the defense systems will last."

"That's pushing it pretty fine, Admiral," said Mika Ori. "The *Antietam*'s crew has no experience with this process."

"Understood, Pilot, but we don't have the luxury of time. Start the clock," he repeated. She did so and that was followed by a flurry of communications from each of his officers to their counterparts aboard the gunship. Clement took up a position behind Nobli to monitor the process as it was carried out.

Mika counted the clock down to zero and suddenly the

gunship appeared to their starboard, about six kilometers away. Within seconds they got acknowledgement that *Antietam* had arrived safe and sound, even if their stomachs were a little unstable.

"Take the controls, Pilot," Clement ordered, "and get us docked as fast as you can." With that Mika disappeared into the pilot's nest and the ship started moving, for once in this long mission it seemed, in the right direction.

After the shuttle was stored in *Antietam*'s cargo bay, Clement sent Nobli and Reck to the engineering room and motioned for the rest of his crew (plus Mary) to follow him to the bridge. Once there he relieved Captain Kagereki with his thanks and settled his own people into their familiar positions: Mika at Helm, and Ivan at Navigation. Mary sat in the empty XO's chair, looking anxious for this part of the mission to be over. The XO position itself was empty, and he felt a twinge at Yan's absence; but he decided for this mission, he could live without an XO, and he preferred not to have Kagereki in that slot as a captain's advice about his own ship would surely come into conflict with an admiral's opinions.

After taking the captain's console he called down to the engine room and got ahold of Tech Reck. She insisted Nobli was too busy inspecting the reactor to come to the line, but after arguing with her for a few seconds he ordered her to put Nobli on.

"Dealing with that young lady is like wrestling with a wolverine," Clement commented once his engineer was on the line.

"Damn smart wolverine if you ask me," replied Nobli.

Clement smiled. "What's the condition of our LEAP reactor?"

"She's in good enough shape for what you're going to ask of her. Some microfractures of the casing, but that's to be expected now that we know what kind of strain we put on her with these in-system jumps. At least I don't have you pressuring me to give you a new MAD weapon."

"Believe me, in these circumstances, I would if I could." Nobli laughed uncomfortably, and to Clement's surprise Mary approached this console then.

"Perhaps I can help you, Jared. I understand the technical issues of creating this weapon. Are there other reasons why we cannot use the ship's power to give you this advantage?"

"Well, for one," said Nobli through the com line, "if we let the LEAP energy out of the reactor through our normal Directed Energy Weapons piping, we'd probably disintegrate everything in this system."

"Is this the only problem?"

"Well, technically, yes," said the engineer. "Our admiral here had all of our ships retrofitted to possibly accommodate a MAD weapon in the future."

"That's true," Clement said. "Can you help us, Mary?"

"Where is your reactor located?"

"Three decks down and to the rear of the fuselage."

"I will go there." And with that she left the bridge.

"Looks like you're going to have company, Hassan."

"Great," he replied sarcastically.

"Give her some leeway. She's smarter than either of us, that's for sure. Oh, and be sure to keep her and Tech Reck separated."

"Always wise advice, Admiral. I'll let you know what she recommends."

"I'm sure you will, Engineer. How long until we're able to make the jump to Camus?"

"Well, Reck is sealing microfractures now. To be safe give us fifteen minutes."

"Will do, but no more. And do everything you can to get that MAD weapon operational."

"Yes, sir."

With that Clement sat back in the captain's couch. "All stations, full diagnostic check in preparation for LEAP jump. I'm setting the ship's clock for fifteen minutes," he said, then watched as his people went about their business.

With five minutes to go Nobli called up to complain. "Your native girl has gone a little crazy down here, Admiral."

"In what way?"

"Well, right at the moment she's pouring some sort of purple goo out of her veins and in to my MAD weapon piping."

"I'll be right down," said Clement, cutting off the com. "Bridge crew, hold the clock at five minutes."

"Five minutes, aye, sir," replied Mika.

With that Clement jumped up from his couch and ran down to the engineering room. When he came through the door he wasn't ready for the sight that he saw.

Mary was on one knee on the floor, draining the purple nano-goo from her open wrist into the piping system and holding Tech Reck off of her feet by her coveralls with the other hand. Reck, for her part, was cussing and swiping at Mary's arm to get free. Nobli was merely standing to one side, staying out of the fray.

It would have been amusing if the situation wasn't so serious. He elected to address Mary first.

"Um, Mary, what's going on?"

"I am attempting to introduce the nanobiology in my system into your energy weapon's piping in order to coat it at a sufficient enough strength to handle the output of energy from your reactor that you use for the weapon. This woman was interfering with my process."

"Goddamn it!" said Reck. "Get this robot freak off of me!"

Clement was growing concerned. "Um, Mary, won't you eventually run out of the . . . nano-material? Won't that kill you?"

She looked up and shook her head no. "My body can produce whatever I need. I have the seeds of the material inside my body."

"Do you mean like stem cells?"

"Something like that, Jared, but the biomechanics are much more complicated."

"I see," he said. Reck continued to struggle and curse, to no avail. "Mary, could you put my crewman down please?"

"Of course," she said, and promptly dropped the tech unceremoniously on to the reactor room floor. Reck scrambled to her feet and rolled up her coverall sleeves.

"You goddamn—"

"Tech Reck, stand down," ordered Clement. Reck looked at him and then backed off.

"Aye, sir," she said, still fuming.

Clement turned his attention back to Mary. "How much longer will this process take?" he asked.

"Just a few more seconds," she replied. The goo continued to pour out of her arm at an alarming rate, but just when he thought she couldn't give anymore she abruptly stopped, snapping her wrist back into place seamlessly. She stood and addressed him. "You should now have all you need to fire your weapon, if that's what you wish. I will have much more powerful weapons at my disposal once we get to Camus."

More powerful than the MAD weapon? he thought. *That would take some doing.* "My hope would have been that we wouldn't have to use any advanced weapons to resolve this situation, but that's a faint hope at this point."

"I understand, Jared," she said.

"Um, how did you manage that feat that you just did?"

"As I've stated my failed union with the Machine gave me certain physical enhancements, but not the link that I need to activate the full defense grid. The nanotechnology comes from the material you found all over the cavern. While it hasn't replaced my human blood, it has enhanced it and given me the ability to reproduce it on a large scale. I am biomechanical now, a hybrid of machine technology and human physiology," she finished.

"Plus, there's that whole superstrength thing you've got going on."

"That is another byproduct of the merging."

"Well, uh, good then. Thank you for the help, but if you're finished here I'd like you back on the bridge."

"Of course, Jared," she said, and promptly walked out of the room. When she was gone Clement turned to face his crewmen.

"Tech Reck, return to your duties. Immediately." She trundled off back to the reactor, her pride hurt as much as her ego. "As for you, Mr. Nobli, please analyze that material and make sure that it's up to the task of holding onto the MAD weapon energy."

"From what I've seen there isn't much it can't do. I'd love to get a look at it back on Kemmerine in my engineering lab."

"That will have to wait for now. We have an entire star system and millions of inhabitants to save first."

"Understood, Admiral. I'll have your stress test for you in a few minutes."

"Better hurry," said Clement as he left the lab. "I'm starting the jump clock again as soon as I get on the bridge."

Then he exited the reactor room, anxious to get back to his bridge.

Once on the bridge Clement swung into the command couch and restarted the LEAP clock. As time ticked down he scanned his bridge, looking for any situation to be concerned about, but found none. Finally he turned to Mary, who was once again at the XO's station, but seemed to be in a state of meditation.

"Mary," he said, as her eyes opened in response to him. "The jump is almost here."

"I know, Jared."

"I was wondering, when you were in the reactor room,

did you have a chance to repair the reactor casing as well as coat the energy weapon's pipes?"

She shook her head, still a very human gesture. "I did not. The biomechanical material is very versatile, but in its virgin state it could not fuse to the reactor while it is functioning. It would have to be introduced when the reactor was shut down and in a cold state. I am sorry if that's inconvenient for you."

"Don't be, not at all. We've worked through these problems before, we can do it again."

"You have a very reliable crew."

"Thank you for saying so." Absently he thought about the term she had just used, "virgin state." She was giving up a lot, making sacrifices: sex, love, family. He remembered how she had been on their first mission to Trinity, a carefree young girl who pursued the pleasure of human contact at every opportunity. He wondered if *that* girl would give all of those things up had she had a say in the current course of events: first enhancement by the Machine from which she could never go back, and then the partial merging with the Machine which had made her something even more now. He felt sorry for her, a victim of circumstance. She could never have known the Machine would call her, and take away all the possibilities of a normal, human life.

"One minute," called out Mika Ori, then she updated every ten seconds thereafter. At the count of twenty Clement ordered all ship's personnel to prepare for the LEAP jump. At ten seconds Mika started the countdown to zero.

The universe shifted as it normally did during short-range jumps, and Clement and the bridge crew fought off the momentary nausea brought on by the jump. As his head and his stomach both settled, he imagined the regular crew of *Antietam* were faring much worse than their more experienced counterparts. "Let's give the ship's crew two minutes before we start ordering them around, shall we? The first few jumps are always the hardest."

Pomeroy flashed him a knowing smile from her station and the others nodded their agreement. Mary, however, popped up from her couch and was more than ready to go.

"We must get to the surface as fast as we can. I estimate that the shield over Bellus can only stay up for another few minutes. Those Earth ships are weakening it even now. If that shield goes down, the planet will once again be open for attack."

Clement couldn't argue with the need for urgency. "Very well then. Commander Ori, you have the con."

She jumped up from her couch. "I should be going with you. I'm the best pilot you have, even better than you, sir. You know that."

Clement was about to argue when Mary stepped in. "If she can get us down there faster, you should take her. Time is of the essence."

Clement made his decision. "All right, Mika, you're in. Ivan, please allow me to borrow your wife for a while?"

"As if I could stop her, sir," the navigator said.

Clement turned to Pomeroy at the com console. "Call Captain Kagereki and his XO to the bridge, Commander. He has the con until we return."

"Yes, sir," she replied, and made the call.

Clement turned to his colleagues. "Let's get to the shuttle," he said, and they were off the bridge in seconds.

21

The shuttle hurtled downwards to the blue-gold surface of Camus. The planet had a great deal more open water than the other Trinity worlds, basically being an "eyeball" planet with a central ocean and significant dry land only around the rim. In the center of the ocean there was a string of nine large islands, the middle one of which was their destination, according to Mary. It contained the largest "mountain" in the entire Trinity system, a four-sided artificial pyramid, undoubtedly constructed by the Makers many thousands of years ago. It also served as a maintenance station and central terraforming device for the entire planet, helping to create a pleasant tropical climate from pole to pole. The far side of Camus, like the other tidally locked worlds of the Trinity system, was an icy, frozen waste. Looking down on the central island as Mika Ori took them in at the fastest speed possible, it was a lush and beautiful place, somewhere Clement would have liked to visit in a more peaceful time.

For now, though, as they endured the bumpy ride down to the surface, Camus and the island were still places of mystery that contained many more questions than answers. If this was the controlling complex for the entire star system—the environment, maintenance, caring for the natives on each of the Trinity worlds—it had somehow fallen into disrepair. Why was unknown. *If* it could be repaired was unknown, and thus, their ultimate fate was also unknown.

He looked to the young woman at the center of all of this. Mary still carried the appearance of a girl in her late teens or early twenties. Her failed merging with the Machine on Bellus had led to her being "enhanced," but in many ways he felt she had lost some of her humanity. If she had her way and completed the Ascension process on Camus, she would become not just part of the Machine, but its central and controlling force, and the fate of all the people of Trinity would be in her hands.

"I can have you on the ground in three minutes," said Ori to Mary. "Is there some place of preference you'd like me to set down?"

"I do not know much of this planet, only of my home world. Can you use your observational skills to find a likely landing location where I can quickly gain entry?"

Clement shared a glance with Ori. That wasn't the answer they were looking for. "Get us down to one thousand meters above the island; we'll circle the mountain, take reconnaissance."

"Sir," Ori responded, then did as instructed.

As she spun them down closer to the ground, the island appeared covered in greenery, mainly jungle-type trees, roots and vines. The vegetation was heavy, and it didn't look as though the island was inhabited by any of the natives as there were no open areas where settlements would have been. Clement pondered this.

"We're at one thousand meters, sir," said Ori.

"Take us down to five hundred, then start a slow circumnavigation back up the mountain, raising our altitude a hundred meters on every pass."

Ori took them down ever closer to the tree canopy where Clement used the shuttle's instruments to look for signs of any access point or points into the pyramid. For several minutes they circled slowly, rising with each pass as they looked for an opening.

Clement turned to Mary, seated between him and the pilot. "Are you sure you don't have any idea where this entrance might be? The mountain looks like it goes straight into the ground and down for several hundred more meters, but there's no opening at ground level, or higher, so far."

"All I know is that this facility was meant to run autonomously. It is even possible that unlike the Hill Place pyramid on Bellus it was never intended for this mountain to need any human interactions."

"You mean, there could be no way in?" asked Ori, frustrated.

"That is possible, but not probable. More likely any entrance to the facility would be hidden by some sort of stealth technology."

"That's not what I wanted to hear. How long until the shield protecting Bellus collapses?"

"Unknown, but in your terms, I would say 'soon.' The energy reserve for the Bellus defense grid is shrinking quickly."

Ori eyed him from the pilot's chair. "Continue our search," he said.

They were nearly at the five-thousand-meter height when they found something.

"Do you see it, sir?" said Ori, excitedly.

"I do. A large opening fifty meters wide and almost perfectly round on the north side of the mountain. It's covered in overgrown foliage; that's why we missed it on our initial pass. Can you take us in closer, Mika?"

"I can sir, but . . ."

"But what?"

"This shuttle has limited VTOL capabilities in the atmosphere. Flying into a small space when we don't know what's inside and then presumably landing vertically on a pad of some kind, even for me that's some tough flying," she said.

"That's why I brought you, Pilot. You're the only one I know of that could pull this off."

"Thank you, sir," said Ori with more than a bit of sarcasm.

"Take us in at the slowest speed you can without stalling us," ordered Clement, then turned his attention to Mary.

"What can you tell us, Mary?" She had been busily moving her hands and fingers as if she were once again manipulating the holographic systems, but there was no visual display that either he or Ori could see. She went on for a few more seconds as the shuttle slowly approached the ominous dark opening in the side of the pyramid.

"There is nothing, Jared. I can't sense the Machine's higher functions at all. There are several basic and rudimentary systems running, but everything else is dark."

Clement gave that a moment to set in, then: "We came here for a reason. Take us in, Pilot."

She did as instructed.

The shuttle crossed the threshold of the opening as Clement took readings of the mountain's material. It took several seconds to pass through the opening, but once inside, they were in an open but very dark cavern similar to the one on Bellus, but larger by a factor of ten.

"Lights," ordered Clement. The shuttle's forward search lights and lower landing lights came on. As they illuminated the interior walls of the pyramid, something became apparent: there was severe erosion inside the mountain; water dripped through the opening and fell a great distance toward the floor, like a waterfall; large sections of latticework metal had partially detached or fallen thousands of meters to the floor below. As they descended it could be seen that the interior walls of the pyramid held massive facilities for what looked like residences, laboratories, or work facilities of unknown function.

"Thousands could have lived and worked in here," commented Clement.

"Highly possible," replied Mary.

"Was it your people?"

"No, Jared. This was the handiwork of the Makers. We could not have constructed or maintained a facility of this scope. It would be impossible."

"Sir, I'm detecting a platform below. There appears to be room to land. The base of this thing must be dozens of square kilometers across."

"More than that," said Mary confidently.

"I'm detecting a considerable amount of debris on that

platform. It looks like destroyed landing craft or some kind of military gear. Pick your best spot, and then set us down, Pilot, but be careful. It's clear a battle of some kind was fought here. Probably long ago. And no need to remind you that time is of the essence."

"Sir," she replied. Ori took them down at a faster pace and started looking for a safe landing space. Two minutes into her accelerated descent she had it. "There, sir. Some sort of holding facility, a warehouse or something. If it will hold, I can land on the roof."

"That seems risky," commented Clement, then he was overridden by Mary.

"No, this place will not do. Continue to the west approximately 1.5 kilometers."

Ori looked at Clement.

"Are you sure? Are you in contact with the Machine?" Clement asked.

"No," she said honestly, "but I can feel its energy, what remains of it. It's there," she said, then quickly punched in coordinates to the nav system.

"Go," said Clement to Ori. "We really have no other option at this point."

The shuttle set down gently on a floor very similar to what had been in the cavern on Camus. Once they stepped outside, however, the comparison ended.

There were columns like in the original cavern, but none of them were illuminated. The floor was dark, hard and brittle. There was what appeared to be a central control platform, and Mary ran quickly to the console and managed to raise several dim projections over it, but nothing compared to what she had previously rendered on Bellus. He and Ori approached the platform.

"The system is at a critical low function," she said. "It is only running the most basic residual programs. I'm not sure if it can be fixed. Please give me time to investigate."

Clement looked at his watch, concerned. "How much time do you need?"

"That much is uncertain," she replied, then focused her full attention on what her meager displays were able to show her.

Clement signaled Ori away from the platform, leaving Mary to her work. They used their lights to illuminate their immediate surroundings. Whereas the cavern on Bellus had columns of tall walls which contained their version of the Machine, this facility dwarfed it by comparison. The components of this machine were like skyscrapers, hundreds of meters tall and broad as a city block at the base. And there were dozens of them. There was also heavy debris, what looked like military equipment, strewn about the cavern.

"I guess this is what you would expect from a facility that controlled the environment of an entire star system," said Ori.

"You would, but there's more to it. This complex didn't just fall into disrepair, nor was it abandoned. It was evacuated, and in a hurry. There was a huge battle here. Perhaps this was the control center for the entire star system, and two different factions were fighting for control of it."

"So one side won, the other lost, and then the winners just . . . left?"

"There's evidence of it all around. Facilities hastily abandoned, equipment strewn about the floor, and the most damning evidence of all."

Ori looked confused. "What do you mean?"

"That 'hole' we came through. Almost completely round. Made of melted carbon fiber and exotic alloys I couldn't define, and, perfectly smooth. A meteor or some kind of natural disaster didn't make that hole. It was an unknown high-yield Directed Energy Weapon. This station was definitely attacked from the outside."

"By whom?"

Clement shrugged. "It appears that several thousand years ago, the Makers had enemies."

"Jared!" called Mary suddenly from the platform. He went running to her.

"What is it?"

"My interaction with the systems here has caused a ripple effect throughout the system. It is coming back online in a limited capacity. There may be a danger—"

At that moment an orange DEW blast swept over Clement's left shoulder and burned a large hole in the ground. Clement grabbed Ori and threw her to the ground, looking for cover. He took her by the hand and dragged her behind a melted vehicle, likely thousands of years old.

"What the fuck!" said Ori.

"An internal defense grid! It was likely activated by Mary's tinkering with the system."

Another blast and then another and another rained down on their position and they had to scramble to another position behind a small bunker-type building. The next DEW blast disintegrated the vehicle they had been hiding behind.

Clement looked up at Mary, who was now furiously working at the platform controls.

"Can she stop this?" asked Ori. Another DEW blast hit the bunker, destroying almost half of the building.

"Christ, I hope so!" He pointed to another smashed vehicle, but more together than the first one. "There!" he said, pointing the way to the vehicle, about twenty meters. They both scrambled out from behind the bunker.

The next shot disintegrated the vehicle when they were halfway there. They were now exposed, in the open. Clement leaned back toward the bunker but before he could even move it was destroyed by the DEW fire from high above their position. He put his arms around Ori, to protect her, then yelled out.

"Mary!"

The next shot hit about five meters away and they were both knocked to the floor. Clement was sure that they were finished.

Then the firing abruptly stopped.

"I have shut off the defense system," shouted Mary from the platform.

"Thank fucking god," said Mika. They picked themselves up off the floor and dusted themselves off before approaching the platform again.

"That was close," stated Clement to Mary.

"I am sorry, Jared. I was trying to access the defense systems and I may have inadvertently activated the internal security systems."

"May have?" said Ori.

"Yes. By activating the systems in this sequence I have managed to get a reading on the Solar League fleet over Bellus. The defensive shield has collapsed. They have broken through."

"Broken through to do what?"

"I detect multiple landing craft, materiel carriers, ground equipment, and the like. In short, it looks like they are preparing a full-scale invasion. They have also sent three destroyers to intercept us here."

Clement glared at Mary, his anger rising. "You promised me that you could defend our people if we brought you here to Camus, now we're here and you're telling me this is a lost hope? I'm prepared to return to Bellus with the *Antietam* and bring the MAD weapon to bear on their fleet if they start killing my people."

"You must give me more time. I need to raise more systems up to functional levels if I'm to activate the Machine."

"Damn the Machine! We have to go, now. There's no more time, and we're out of options. It's the MAD weapon or nothing."

She pivoted swiftly toward him. "If you must go, then go. I must stay behind here and perform the Ascension, or my people will become slaves of your enemies. That is my choice, and my will."

Clement looked to Ori, who nodded in agreement. It was time to go.

"Mary—" started Clement before she interrupted him.

"Jared," she said softly. "This is the last time I will be what you call 'human,' one of the people, one of Trinity's children. I am frightened by what awaits me. Would you please stay with me for these last moments?" The plea was heartfelt and emotional, and left Clement in a quandary as to what to do.

"Every second we stay could cost lives on the ground," said Ori.

Clement turned to her. "If I was facing the end of my life, I would welcome some human contact, of any kind," he said, then turned back to Mary. "Of course we will stay with you, Mary," he said. "It would be wrong to deny you your last request of me."

They both stepped up to the platform. Clement saw a tear run down Mary's face and she wiped it off, annoyed. When she was done with her settings, she turned to them both, the console at her back.

"Jared, in another life . . ."

"In another life, Mary," he replied softly.

The floor began to vibrate, subtly at first, then growing stronger. Behind Mary, the console began to glow white, pulsating at a steady rate, like the heartbeat of a living being. As the light enveloped her, wires and tubing began to interact with her, making their way out of the floor and entering her body and boring into every part of her, including her head. She whimpered softly, in pain. Clement presumed that the Machine would give her something to numb the pain, but for now, she was clearly suffering.

The tubing, like viscous, translucent flesh, wrapped and enveloped her. She spread her arms wide, and all he could see of her skin was turning from its normal light amber to a dark matte purple, the same color as the biomechanical nanomaterial he had seen come out of her before. The material of her clothing was absorbed by the spreading purple nano-goo, and for a moment she was naked from the waist up as the tubes and wires continued to snake over her entire body.

Her eyes had lost most of their color, and the irises were gone, replaced by a blank, white stare. The scene reminded him of a religious necklace he had seen once on Ceta, called a crucifix. From what he knew of the story behind that necklace the analogy was appropriate.

It was a horrific sight.

The roiling confluence of wires and tubing enveloped her at a rapid rate.

"The merging of human and machine," he said to Ori, repulsed by the sight. This type of technology was something the Five Suns had rejected on purely moral grounds decades ago.

Ori nodded, watching helplessly. "Is this our only choice?"

"No. But she chose this path," said Clement, "and it was *her* only path."

"Do you think she's in pain?"

"I hope not."

All they could do was stand by and watch her as the Machine took more and more control over her body. Her skin vanished underneath translucent tubing and wires as she became less and less recognizably human with every moment. Ori reached out a hand to Clement and he took it. It was small comfort over what they were watching, but even the simplest human contact was somehow reassuring as they watched her transfiguration into . . . something.

"She was so beautiful," whispered Ori. Mary's face,

the last human part of her, grimaced in pain and she let out an audible moan as they watched her struggling to survive, to preserve the last remnants of her humanity. The rumbling throughout the complex began to rise again; the floor beneath them was shaking, building to a crescendo.

Suddenly a burst of light came from Mary, spreading out and roiling across the platform, up the consoles, and into the stack of machines. The purple lightning of the burst seemed to be picking up energy from everything it touched: the consoles, the walls, even the floor itself. The stacked buildings in the complex began to crack with energy and light.

When Clement turned back to look at Mary, her face was engulfed by the biomechanical material. She was now nothing more than a mass of purple tubing and wires in the vague shape of a human being.

The energy continued to swirl around and through her body, then in an instant the mass of material pulled in upon itself and collapsed into the platform floor.

Everything stopped.

"What in God's name?" said Ori.

"She's gone," said Clement in the now dead silent cavern. "It's time for us to go." He led her back to the shuttle, where she took the pilot's seat and fired up the engines.

"Do you think it worked?" Ori asked.

Clement looked around the dark mountain cavern as the shuttle rose vertically off the platform. "I don't know, but we're on our own now. I hope she lives on in some form, but when this is over, I will mourn her loss."

"So will I," replied Ori.

They made the rest of the trip back to *Antietam* in complete silence.

✲ **22** ✲

Back on *Antietam*, Clement and Ori took their places again and Clement asked Captain Kagereki to stay on at the XO console. He started in immediately with status reports from his officers. Clement called down to Hassan Nobli in the reactor room.

"Do you have everything you need, Hassan?" he asked.

"That depends on what you're going to ask of me, Admiral," Nobli replied.

"Fair enough, Engineer. I need a fifteen-minute countdown for one last in-system LEAP jump. Can you be ready?"

"Aye, sir, we can, but once again the reactor might not hold together with this many jumps in such a short time. We saw that with the *Beauregard*, God rest her soul."

"Yes, God rest her soul. I need that reactor to stay together, Hassan. After the jump I'll need the MAD weapon as soon as possible or we're doomed."

"So the mission to Camus was a failure?"

"We don't know that, but we have to plan accordingly."

"Of course, sir. Please understand, I can't guarantee the ship will survive that kind of energy expulsion, especially in such close proximity to the jump."

"What about the nanomaterial Mary put into the pipes? Will that hold?"

"Not with a cracked reactor, but you might get a chance at one shot. From the tests I've run the goo should hold. It's stronger than Tech Reck's stuff, but it's still an untested alien technology."

"I'll take that as a yes. Start the clock, Hassan."

"Yes, Admiral."

Clement looked to Ori, who put the countdown clock up on the main display and made the ship-wide announcement of the impending jump.

Next he went to Pomeroy. "Lieutenant, send a longwave com to our ships at Alphus and order them to start back to Bellus. If we're going to get our people off the surface we'll need those transports. If we fail in forcing an armistice or at least a cease-fire, their orders are to surrender to the Solar League forces. And tell them to stay ahead of that flotilla chasing them."

"Aye, sir," she said, and started the com.

Next was the navigator. "Ivan, as usual I'll need a miracle. Get us as close as you can to the Solar League fleet, especially that ark ship, but far enough away from the rest of their forces to ensure we don't end up on top of one of their cruisers."

"Of course, sir, the usual," he said, smirking at his captain. "No problem."

He didn't have to tell Mika her orders; she knew her job.

Last up was Captain Kagereki at the XO station. "I'll need you to be my weapons officer through this battle, Jim. I want you to know I'll do everything I can to protect your ship, but I can't guarantee we won't be blown to bits in a few minutes."

"I'd prefer that didn't happen, Admiral, but I understand the circumstances. My people know what we're up against. They'll be ready," he said.

"Thank you, Captain."

Then Clement sat back and looked up at the clock.

Thirteen minutes to their destiny.

Clement found himself remarkably calm as the countdown slipped to under a minute to the jump. He was resigned to fate now. Either everything would work out or they would be destroyed, but either way his biggest hope was that they could deal such a huge loss to the Solar League that they would withdraw from Trinity. That was a slim hope, but it was something.

At thirty seconds to jump he got on the ship-wide com. "All hands, this is Admiral Clement. In the next few seconds *Antietam* will be undergoing her third and final jump inside the Trinity system. By now you've all experienced what short LEAP jumps are like. I ask you, now of all times, to recover from the jump effects as quickly as you can and attend to your stations. Reaction time will be critical to our survival in the next few minutes. I know you will all give me your best. I believe in all of you. Admiral Clement, out." With that Mika Ori took over the com and completed the countdown. The universe blurred around them all.

As fate would have it, *Antietam* reappeared in normal space just a few thousand meters off of the massive, cylindrical Solar League ark. The only advantage they had was that even their navigator was surprised at how close he came to their target.

"Ivan! For Christ's sake, we're right on top of them!"

"Sorry, Admiral! I can't help being over-accurate."

"Mika, full reverse on the plasma thrusters, get us out of here!"

"Aye, sir!" She did as instructed, powering up the plasma thrusters, but when she looked up at the tactical display the tiny Five Suns gunship was right in the middle of the Solar League fleet, surrounded by enemies on all sides. "Where to, sir?" she asked frantically.

"Anywhere! Just get some distance between us and that ark!" With the thrusters warm she put the ship in motion and they began accelerating away from the ark ship.

"We're backing right into a group of cruisers and destroyers!" warned Kagereki from the XO's station. "Fortunately they're all facing toward the planet and not us."

"Noted, Captain," replied Clement. "It will take them time to get turned and attack us, but we'll have to worry about the clusters of ships that we're in the line of attack with."

Almost on cue a destroyer volleyed a compliment of six missiles at *Antietam*, while others in the line of sight opened up with DEW fire. "Antimissile torpedoes!" ordered Clement, and Kagereki responded quickly.

"Torpedoes away, flak and chaff countermeasures active," he said. "Static shields engaged against incoming Directed Energy Weapons fire."

As the missiles streaked in toward *Antietam* Clement called down to Nobli. The MAD weapon icon on his command console was still dark. "Nobli, what's your status?"

The line was silent.

"Nobli, report!" After a tense few moments the engineer responded, but it was not good news. "Admiral, Tech Reck and I barely made it out of the reactor room before the hull cracked wide open and exposed her to space."

"Is the reactor still on line?" He prayed the answer would be yes.

"Well, yes, but I can't operate her from out in the hallway."

"Then get on an EVA suit and get back in there! I need a green light on my board for the MAD weapon in thirty seconds or we're all dead." The com line stayed open and Clement could hear Nobli arguing with Tech Reck again, but couldn't make out what they were saying. "Nobli!" he demanded.

"Reck's on her way in now, sir! While I was jabbing with you she was slipping in to her environmental suit. She's opening the airlock now..." The line popped and crackled, but he got no further communication from Nobli. Any hit that was powerful enough to open a hole in the reactor room hull would likely have damaged communication as well.

Clement looked down to his board; the MAD weapon icon was still dark. Then he looked at the tactical display. It was bleak. The ship shook from multiple near misses and DEW hits on their shields. "Tactical report, Captain."

"More missiles coming in, thankfully none of them nuclear, sir," said Kagereki.

"We're too close to the ark ship for them to use their nukes. That's some small blessing."

Ori turned from her console to face her commander. "About that, Admiral. We're close to a kilometer off of the ark now, sir. We're under the effective range for their weapons. If we go much further, we could subject ourselves to the ark's forward coil cannon, sir."

"That would be a negative development I hadn't thought of. Reverse our course. Keep us under the belly of the whale."

"Admiral"—it was Kagereki again—"cruisers are backing off. They're forming up into a tactical team with their destroyers, sir."

"Going after us with their smallest ships. More pinpoint accuracy. My guess is they will batter us with DEW until our shields fail and we crack open like fresh-cooked crab legs."

"What do we do, sir?" asked Ori.

"Maintain course. Get us as close to that ark as you can, Mika." Clement looked down at his tactical board. The MAD weapon was still off-line. He smacked the com button again. "Nobli, we're running out of time!" There was no response. "Nobli, can you hear me?"

Everything was silent on the bridge for a second. Then the MAD weapon icon lit up green. "Everybody grab onto something. I've got a green light on the MAD weapon. Will commence firing in ten seconds." Everyone on the bridge braced themselves as Clement's finger hung over the MAD weapon icon. He tried to aim as best he could . . .

"Three . . . two . . . one . . . fire!"

The bright white MAD energy shot out of the *Antietam*'s DEW cannon ports and went straight up to the belly of the ark. The beam began splitting her from stem to stern, cutting a tight line, much more refined than the wild and uncontrollable energy from the first time they had used the weapon on board the *Beauregard*. Debris, metal, regolith, equipment and people were ejected into space as the ark was cut clean in half. Secondary explosions filled space with bright flares of red, orange, and gold as the ship broke apart, colliding with many nearby support vessels, including auxiliaries, cruisers, and destroyers. It was a devastating blow.

No one on the bridge cheered. They had just participated in the killing of thousands of their fellow human beings, something they had come to Trinity to avoid at all costs.

Clement looked down at his console. The MAD weapon icon was dark again. Likely the reactor was gone as well. They had nothing to fight with now, and when the Solar League fleet recovered its senses, they would be pursued and destroyed.

And with that went their last hope. Clement sat silently as the incoming missiles (and more to follow) were taken out by their torpedoes or misdirected by their countermeasures, but they would eventually run out of defenses.

Clement ordered a rescue team down to extract Nobli and Tech Reck from the reactor room, if they were still alive. He turned to his oldest-serving crewmate, Mika Ori. "Take us out of here, Pilot. Best guess as to which course we should take," Clement said, subdued. This fight had cost him nearly everything he held dear; he hoped it wouldn't cost him his friends and the crew of the *Antietam* as well.

Ori looked to him, a mixture of grief and sadness on her face. "Aye, sir," she said as the ship rocked from nearby missile explosions and DEW-fire impacts. By destroying the ark they had lost their cover and the enemy fleet was attacking with renewed vigor now. They had regrouped and were closing in on them, and Clement doubted it would be with any mercy in their hearts.

Ori reached down for the thruster controls and pressed the activation button.

Nothing happened.

"Pilot?"

"There's no power to the thrusters, sir; or rather, there's power but no forward motion indicated."

"What? Why?" Clement started out of his couch.

"Sir, the visual display!" The excited voice belonged to Laura Pomeroy. Clement reached down and switched the primary display to visual views. On the left view of the screen it showed the atmosphere over Bellus. The orange-beaded blanket was up once again, covering the large area over the Hill Place pyramid and the former Camp Alpha. A Solar League transport vessel struck the shield and disintegrated. The second display showed ships where the ark flagship had been. They were quickly being surrounded by small metal probes, as were many other ships in the Solar League fleet. The small probes were flowing and moving at frantic speeds, enveloping the ships and then engaging an orange-colored energy blanket around them, trapping them inside. The third monitor showed the exterior of the *Antietam*, also now enveloped in the protective field.

All the fire toward *Antietam* had now stopped and the battlefield was eerily silent.

Ori stood and looked at her commander. "Mary?" she said.

Clement looked to Pomeroy. "Use the longwave, try and raise . . . someone . . . in the direction of the planet Camus." Before she could respond, a voice came over their ship-wide com, loud and clear.

"Admiral, no need for you to do anything more. I have the situation under control. Please stand down from your weapons."

Clement hesitated. The voice was mechanical, if slightly feminine. "Mary?" he asked. The system hummed and buzzed for a few seconds, then responded.

"If that is what you wish to call me, I will try to respond as that persona if it eases communication between us." The voice was now more feminine, and recognizable. "I am pleased to hear your voice again, Jared."

"Mary, are you alive, or . . ." He spread his arms wide, looking for the source of the mysterious voice.

"Both, and neither. I am the protector of the people now, but I retain this personality, her thoughts and experiences, within me. I have communicated terms of surrender to the invading forces, and they have agreed to withdraw, but I will see to their retreat myself."

With that the tactical display showed the Solar League ships being carried away toward the remnant of their fleet, out near the sixth planet, secured in their orange safety blankets. It was power that the Five Suns could never equal.

Antietam was soon alone over Bellus, and after a few hours, the defensive shield came down and the last remaining Solar League ships evacuated the surface of Bellus, trying desperately to catch up with their quickly retreating fleet. Mary had gone silent, and would not respond to their calls.

The last Battle of Trinity was over.

✷ **EPILOGUE** ✷

Clement returned command of the *Antietam* to Captain Kagereki before taking his personal crew on one last shuttle ride down to the surface of Bellus. Nobli and Reck had been recovered safe and sound and Kagereki was already patching the hull hole to his now useless reactor room. She would have to catch a ride home to Kemmerine in the LEAP bubble of one of the remaining cruisers with an operable reactor.

Once they were back on the surface of Bellus, they were greeted like heroes by both the settlers and the natives alike, but Clement didn't feel like one. He avoided the celebrations that followed their "victory" and received frequent reports from Letine that the "Protector Mary" was busy fixing systems throughout the whole Trinity star system, and would be contacting him "shortly." Clement was fine with that.

The Solar League fleet departed without another contact, no doubt with its tail between its legs. He thought about Elara DeVore one last time, thinking about his regrets before putting them away. She had made her choices, and he was certain he would never know her fate, good or bad.

He found a small bungalow inside the village, far away from the bustle of the people, and slept away the better part of two days. He reflected during that time on what had been lost fighting for Trinity: too many young men and women (including Kayla Adebayor, who he felt a special responsibility for), too many ships, and one beautiful young native girl that was denied that most human of things, a chance to have her own life, free of the obligations that her society placed on her.

For the most part no one bothered him, except for the occasional native bringing him meals or Lubrov stopping by for instructions on what to do next. "Wait," he told her. Wait until Mary contacted him again, as their fates were in her hands.

On the third morning of his rest he got a visit from Yan.

"So this is where you've been hiding out. It's nice," she said, reaching into a bowl of fruit and grabbing something similar in taste and texture to a yellow apple and taking a bite. "God, these are delicious. I wouldn't mind eating these all year round, which I guess you can on this planet." She sat down on the edge of his modest bed while he sat in a side chair, drinking tea, and put down the book he had been reading. "What do you have there?"

"*The Guns of August.* It's about the prelude to a great war on Earth five hundred years ago. It's from my father's collection. I read it once as a student, but not in the last thirty years or so."

"Gods, Clement, you avoided one catastrophic war and now you relax by reading about another."

He took a sip of his tea. "I am what I am," he replied, then set the tea down. "Would you like some?" he asked her.

"No, thank you, this apple-thing will likely keep me hydrated for days." Clement smiled at that. "So," she said between bites, "what happens now?"

"Nobody knows what's going to happen tomorrow, Yan," he said. She looked annoyed at his answer, and then changed the subject.

"You know, I think I'd like you to stop calling me that. It seems kind of distant for all we've been through. I want you to use my given name from now on, in casual conversation, anyway."

"Tanitha?"

"No," she put the apple-thing down on the bed table. "My real given name, Xiu Mei."

"All right, Xiu Mei then." She looked up at the ceiling, thinking about that for a minute. "Say it again." He repeated her name three more times before she waved him off. "Let's just go with Mei."

"Mei it is. And no more 'Clement' please. I rather liked Mary calling me 'Jared.'"

Yan shifted on the bed. "You had affection for her, didn't you?"

Clement nodded. "She was special in every way. I admired her, her strength, her will, to make that choice..." He trailed off.

"Jared, I'm leaving the Navy," Mei said abruptly.

He nodded. "I've considered the same thing," he replied. "This has been a wearying experience."

"Time to go home and start having little Clements?"

"I don't really have a home anymore, Mei. Ceta is a failing colony, the Rim as a whole holds nothing for me. If they allow it, I might just choose to stay here."

She stood to go. "Certain things are only possible without the responsibility the Navy places on us. I just came here to communicate that to you." Then she grabbed the apple again and leaned over the chair to kiss him on the cheek.

"Make the right choice for you, Jared. You deserve it."

He watched her go, having no idea what that right choice might be for him.

The next day he was called to the platform by Letine, who promptly informed him the "Protector" would be contacting him shortly. He didn't have long to wait.

Less than a minute later the floor of the platform began to take form, growing into a physical reflection of Mary. "Hello, Jared," she said, as if her "appearance" was an everyday occurrence.

"Hello, Mary," he replied, "if that is the proper way to address you?"

"I am now part of the Machine and the Machine is part of me. Where the one ends and the other begins, I could not tell you, Jared. I have all the feelings and emotions and share all the experiences of the woman you call Mary, but I am now also bound to this world, this entire star system, in a way that I could not comprehend before. When you met me on your first trip to Trinity, I was a simple village girl. When you encountered me for the first time here in these caverns, I was augmented, enhanced to my full potential, but I was merely a servant of the Makers. Now, I am the hand of the Makers, the protector of the people of Trinity. I now understand their purpose in creating these worlds, and I understand the great responsibility that has been given to me."

"I'm sensing that a final decision about my people's fate has been reached?"

She nodded. "As protector of the people I must think of them first. The destruction of the complex on the world you call Camus was from an enemy of the Makers, and it happened nearly four thousand of your years ago, when the Makers were still living here in this system. Since then the people have been happy, but stagnant. That will now change under my guidance, but because of this decision, I'm afraid it's not possible for your people to stay here. The people of Trinity must make their own way, free of the influence of colonial forces, friendly or not."

"Mary, we came here because our worlds cannot support the people we have now. Sending these people back to the Rim worlds will be sending them to their deaths, and will be condemning the entire Five Suns Alliance to the same fate within decades."

She smiled at him, a very human gesture. "Perhaps not." She motioned with her right arm and three shapes began to emerge from the nanomaterial on the floor of the platform. They grew in size and shape into four-sided pyramids less than a meter across.

"What are these?" he asked.

"Hope, for your future. A gift from the Makers. These 'pyramids,' as you call them, will terraform your Rim worlds. They will make them as beautiful and lush as any of the Trinity planets. These devices are my thanks for all you have done for Trinity. Take them back to your worlds, and make them into the paradise you want them to be."

She formed a small device out of her hand, the size of a small data storage unit, and gave it to him. "This will explain all you need to know about their function. You will find that as your worlds grow, these devices will replicate themselves until the entire planet is rich and green. This is my gift to you."

"Thank you, Mary," he said.

"Thank you, Jared." Then she hugged him, but she was cold and hard, almost mechanical to the touch. He pulled back, took the storage device and wished her and her people well. Then she was gone, and he made his way back to camp, there to tell his people to prepare to depart Trinity forever.

Two Years Later

Jared Clement stood on the back deck of his parents'
home on their family farm, munching on a piece of toast
made from fresh-baked grain bread and topped with his
mother's strawberry preserves. He watched her from the
deck as she tended the orchards herself. It wasn't work to
her; it was an act of love, connecting with the soil of their
adopted family home. On the "far forty" acres of the farm
his father was running the harvester through the wheat
fields, kicking up dust. Clement thought his father had
been as happy as he had ever seen him these last few
months.

The sky above them was ever bluer, and the
surrounding hills, once barren and dead, were full of
greenery, and getting greener. In the distance he could
see his father's reborn fishing pond, recently stocked
again. Above it all was the looming artificial pyramid
mountain near Ceta City, spewing out its life-giving water
vapor, organic material and seedlings. The city was now
twice the size it had been before as new homesteaders
made their way out to the Rim and the great opportunities
it represented.

"Are you going to stand there all morning?" came the
voice of his wife from behind him. He turned, putting the

last of the toast in his mouth and crunching it down, then walked to her. She was sitting on the white country swing while she gently fed their son from her breast. He bent down and kissed her, then sat next to her, admiring what they had created.

"I might go fishing later," he said. "Maybe take little Cletus here. He needs to learn the basic skills."

"He's four months old."

Clement sighed. "You never know what he might pick up."

"Like fishing and catching rabbits and shooting birds?"

He shook his head. "No, no shooting. And no more violence in our lives. If you ask me, we've had quite enough."

"That we have." The baby squirmed then in his mother's arms. "Ow! Cletus Graham Clement, you're as bad as your father."

"What happened?"

"He bit me. Damned teeth. I wish they'd stay this small, without the teeth."

"Personally, I can't wait for him to grow up."

She switched the baby to her other breast and he settled in comfortably. "Are you going to show him the stars? When he grows up?"

Clement pointed to the brass telescope on the back porch. "Perhaps from here. Maybe someday we'll take him to Kemmerine Station and to visit your parents on Shenghai. I'll tell him a few tall stories."

"I'm sure you will."

He reached over and kissed her—not as the mother of his children, but this time as his wife—with passion. "I love you, Mei. I think I did from the first time we met. It just took leaving the Navy for me to be able to express it."

"I know," she said. "Duty and honor and all that. But we're done with that, and if you keep kissing me like that little Cletus here is going to have a baby sister soon."

"I'll look forward to that," he said, then he kissed her again.

They sat together, hand in hand, gently swaying on the swing.

Contemplating the universe from their back porch.

**Master of Starfaring Adventure
and Military Science Fiction**

DAVE BARA

"Bara . . . ramp[s] up the depth and complexity of his world while retaining that sense of excitement, suspense, and adventure."   —*Barnes & Noble Sci Fi & Fantasy Blog*

TRINITY

TPB: 978-1-9821-2566-0 • $16.00 US / $22.00 CAN
MM: 978-1-9821-9222-8 • $9.99 US / $12.99 CAN

The Rim rebellion was glorious—and doomed from the start. Ten years later, Rim Confederation Navy spaceship captain Jared Clement regrets nothing, but would prefer to be left to his thoughts and drink. But humanity is on the brink of a new age, and everything depends on crusty starship captain Clement, his gritty crew, and the *Beauregard*, a ship that was never meant to wage war turned into a weapon-bristling battleship that will either propel humanity to ultimate destruction or into a new starfaring age of exploration and conflict. Along the way, Clement may finally get his revenge—and find his redemption.

TRINITY'S CHILDREN

TPB: 978-1-9821-9211-2 • $16.00 US / $22.00 CAN

Clement returns to Trinity as a 5 Suns Fleet Admiral. With his promotion comes increased responsibility: 30,000 settlers are leaving the dying planets of the Rim and resettling next to the natives of the planet Bellus. Clement is responsible for building a better future for them all, but when his migrant fleet arrives in the Trinity System, they are faced with enemies both old and new.

Available in bookstores everywhere.
Order e-books online at www.baen.com.

"SPACE OPERA IS ALIVE AND WELL"*

and *New York Times* best seller

DAVID WEBER

is the reigning king of the spaceways!

HONOR HARRINGTON NOVELS

On Basilisk Station   pb • 978-0-7434-3571-0 • $8.99
". . . an outstanding blend of military/technical writing balanced by superb character development and an excellent degree of human drama . . . very highly recommended."   —*Wilson Library Bulletin*

The Honor of the Queen   pb • 978-0-7434-3572-7 • $8.99
"Honor fights her way with fists, brains, and tactical genius through a tangle of politics, battles, and cultural differences. Although battered, she ends this book with her honor—and the Queen's—intact."—*Kliatt*

The Short Victorious War   pb • 978-0-7434-3573-4 • $8.99
"This remarkable story will appeal to readers interested in warfare, science, and technology of the future or just in interpersonal relationships, an important part of the story. Gratifying, especially to female readers, is the total equality of the sexes!"   —*Kliatt*

Field of Dishonor   pb • 978-0-7434-3574-1 • $8.99
"Great stuff...compelling combat combined with engaging characters for a great space opera adventure."   —*Locus*

Flag in Exile   pb • 978-0-7434-3575-8 • $7.99
"Packs enough punch to smash a starship to smithereens."
—*Publishers Weekly*

Honor Among Enemies   pb • 978-0-6718-7783-5 • $7.99
"Star Wars as it might have been written by C.S. Forester . . . fast-paced entertainment."   —*Booklist*

* *Starlog*

In Enemy Hands pb • 978-0-6715-7770-4 • $7.99
After being ambushed, Honor finds herself aboard an enemy cruiser, bound for her scheduled execution. But one lesson Honor has never learned is how to give up!

Echoes of Honor hc • 978-0-6718-7892-4 • $24.00
pb • 978-0-6715-7833-6 • $7.99
"Brilliant! Brilliant! Brilliant!" —Anne McCaffrey

Ashes of Victory pb • 978-0-6713-1977-9 • $7.99
Honor has escaped from the prison planet called Hell and returned to the Manticoran Alliance, to the heart of a furnace of new weapons, new strategies, new tactics, spies, diplomacy, and assassination.

War of Honor hc • 978-0-7434-3545-1 • $26.00
pb • 978-0-7434-7167-9 • $7.99
No one wanted another war. Neither the Republic of Haven, nor Manticore—and certainly not Honor Harrington. Unfortunately, what they wanted didn't matter.

At All Costs hc • 978-1-4165-0911-0 • $26.00
The war with the Republic of Haven has resumed. . . disastrously for the Star Kingdom of Manticore. The alternative to victory is total defeat, yet this time the cost of victory will be agonizingly high.

Mission of Honor hc • 978-1-4391-3361-3 • $27.00
The unstoppable juggernaut of the mighty Solarian League is on a collision course with Manticore. But if everything Honor Harrington loves is going down to destruction, it won't be going alone.

A Rising Thunder tpb • 978-1-4516-3871-4 • $15.00

Shadow of Freedom hc • 978-1-4516-3869-1 • $25.00
pb • 978-1-4767-8048-1 • $8.99
The survival of Manticore is at stake as Honor must battle not only the powerful Solarian League, but also the secret puppetmasters who plan to pick up all the pieces after galactic civilization is shattered.

Shadow of Victory pb • 978-1-4814-8288-2 • $10.99
"This latest Honor Harrington novel brings the saga to another crucial turning point. . . . Readers may feel confident that they will be Honored many more times and enjoy it every time." —*Booklist*

Uncompromising Honor hc • 978-1-4814-8350-6 • $28.00
pb • 978-1-9821-2413-7 $10.99
When the Manticoran Star Kingdom goes to war against the Solarian Empire, Honor Harrington leads the way. She'll take the fight to the enemy and end its menace forever.

HONORVERSE VOLUMES

Crown of Slaves pb • 978-0-7434-9899-9 • $7.99
(with Eric Flint)

Torch of Freedom hc • 978-1-4391-3305-7 • $26.00
(with Eric Flint)

Cauldron of Ghosts tpb • 9781476780382 • $15.00
(with Eric Flint)

To End in Fire hc • 978-1-9821-2564-6 • $27.00
(with Eric Flint)
Sent on a mission to keep Erewhon from breaking with Manticore, the Star Kingdom's most able agent and the Queen's niece may not even be able to escape with their lives . . .

House of Steel tpb • 978-1-4516-3893-6 • $15.00
(with Bu9) pb • 978-1-4767-3643-3 • $7.99

The Shadow of Saganami hc • 978-0-7434-8852-0 • $26.00

Storm From the Shadows hc • 978-1-4165-9147-4 • $27.00
pb • 978-1-4391-3354-5 • $8.99
As war erupts, a new generation of officers, trained by Honor Harrington, are ready to hit the front lines.

| *A Beautiful Friendship* | hc • 978-1-4516-3747-2 • $18.99 |
| | YA tpb • 978-1-4516-3826-4 • $9.00 |

| *Fire Season* | hc • 978-1-4516-3840-0 • $18.99 |
| (with Jane Lindskold) | |

| *Treecat Wars* | hc • 978-1-4516-3933-9 • $18.99 |
| (with Jane Lindskold) | |

"A stellar introduction to a new YA science-fiction series."
—*Booklist*, starred review

| *A Call to Duty* | hc • 978-1-4767-3684-6 • $25.00 |
| (with Timothy Zahn) | tpb • 978-1-4767-8081-8 • $15.00 |

| *A Call to Arms* | hc • 978-1-4767-8085-6 • $26.00 |
| (with Timothy Zahn & Thomas Pope) | pb • 978-1-4767-8156-3 • $9.99 |

| *A Call to Vengeance* | hc • 978-1-4767-8210-2 • $26.00 |
| (with Timothy Zahn & Thomas Pope) | |

| *A Call to Insurrection* | hc • 978-1-9821-2589-9 • $27.00 |
| (with Timothy Zahn & Thomas Pope) | pb • 978-1-9821-9237-2 • $9.99 |

The Royal Manticoran Navy rises as a new hero of the Honorverse answers the call!

ANTHOLOGIES EDITED BY WEBER

More Than Honor	pb • 978-0-6718-7857-3 • $7.99
Worlds of Honor	pb • 978-0-6715-7855-8 • $7.99
Changer of Worlds	pb • 978-0-7434-3520-8 • $7.99
The Service of the Sword	pb • 978-0-7434-8836-5 • $7.99
In Fire Forged	pb • 978-1-4516-3803-5 • $7.99
Beginnings	hc • 978-1-4516-3903-2 • $25.00

THE DAHAK SERIES

| *Mutineers' Moon* | pb • 978-0-6717-2085-8 • $7.99 |
| *Empire From the Ashes* | tpb • 978-1-4165-0993-2 • $16.00 |

Contains *Mutineers' Moon*, *The Armageddon Inheritance*, and *Heirs of Empire* in one volume.

THE BAHZELL SAGA

Oath of Swords	tpb • 978-1-4165-2086-3 • $15.00
	pb • 978-0-671-87642-5 • $7.99
The War God's Own	hc • 978-0-6718-7873-3 • $22.00
	pb • 978-0-6715-7792-6 • $7.99
Wind Rider's Oath	pb • 978-1-4165-0895-3 • $7.99
War Maid's Choice	pb • 978-1-4516-3901-8 • $7.99
The Sword of the South	hc • 978-1-4767-8084-9 • $27.00
	tpb • 978-1-4767-8127-3 • $18.00
	pb • 978-1-4814-8236-3 • $8.99

Bahzell Bahnakson of the hradani is no knight in shining armor and doesn't want to deal with anybody else's problems, let alone the War God's. The War God thinks otherwise.

OTHER NOVELS

The Excalibur Alternative   pb • 978-0-7434-3584-2 • $7.99
An English knight and an alien dragon join forces to overthrow the alien slavers who captured them. Set in the world of David Drake's Ranks of Bronze.

In Fury Born   tpb • 978-1-9821-2573-8 • $18.00
A greatly expanded new version of Path of the Fury, with almost twice the original wordage.

1633   pb • 978-0-7434-7155-8 • $7.99
(with Eric Flint)

1634: The Baltic War   pb • 978-1-4165-5588-9 • $7.99
(with Eric Flint)
American freedom and justice versus the tyrannies of the 17th century. Set in Flint's 1632 universe.

The Apocalypse Troll   tpb • 978-1-9821-2512-7• $16.00
After UFOs attack, a crippled alien lifeboat drifts down and homes in

on Richard Ashton's sailboat, leaving Navy man Ashton responsible for an unconscious, critically wounded, and impossibly human alien warrior—who also happens to be a gorgeous female.

THE STARFIRE SERIES WITH STEVE WHITE

The Stars at War   hc • 978-0-7434-8841-5 • $25.00
Rewritten *Insurrection* and *In Death Ground* in one massive volume.

The Stars at War II   hc • 978-0-7434-9912-5 • $27.00
The Shiva Option and *Crusade* in one massive volume.

PRINCE ROGER NOVELS WITH JOHN RINGO

"This is as good as military sf gets."   —*Booklist*

March Upcountry   pb • 978-0-7434-3538-3 • $7.99

March to the Sea   pb • 978-0-7434-3580-2 • $7.99

March to the Stars   pb • 978-0-7434-8818-1 • $7.99

Throne of Stars   omni tpb • 978-1-4767-3666-2 • $14.00
March to the Stars and *We Few* in one massive volume.

GORDIAN PROTOCOL SERIES WITH JACOB HOLO

The Gordian Protocol   pb • 978-1-9821-2459-5 • $8.99

The Valkyrie Protocol   hc • 978-1-9821-2490-8 • $27.00
      pb • 978-1-9821-2562-2 • $8.99
Untangling the complex web of the multiverse is not a job for the faint of heart. Navigating the paradoxes of time can be a killer task. But Agent Raibert Kaminski and the crew of the Transtemporal Vehicle *Kleio* won't go down without a fight, no matter where—or *when*—the threat to the multiverse arises!

Available in bookstores everywhere.
Order ebooks online at www.baen.com.

CHARLES E. GANNON
Alternate History, Space Opera, and Epic Fantasy on a Grand Scale

"Chuck Gannon is one of those marvelous finds—someone as comfortable with characters as he is with technology . . . . Imaginative, fun . . . his stories do not disappoint." —David Weber

THE CAINE RIORDAN SERIES

Fire with Fire   PB: 978-1-4767-3632-7 • $7.99
Nebula finalist! An agent for a spy organization uncovers an alien alliance that will soon involve humanity in politics and war on a galactic scale.

Trial by Fire   TPB: 978-1-4767-3664-8 • $15.00
Humanity's enemies are willing to do anything to stop interstellar war from breaking out once again—even if it means exterminating the human race.

Raising Caine   TPB: 978-1-4767-8093-1 • $17.00
A group of renegade aliens are out to stop humanity's hopes for peace. And to do so, they must find and kill Caine Riordan.

Caine's Mutiny   TPB: 978-1-4767-8219-5 $16.00
PB: 978-1-4814-8317-9 • $7.99
Caine Riordan finds himself at the center of a conflict that will determine the fate of humanity among the stars . . . or find him in front of a firing squad.

Marque of Caine   TPB: 978-1-4814-8409-1 • $16.00
PB: 978-1-9821-2467-0 • $8.99
Summoned to the collapsing world Dornaani, Caine Riordan hopes to find the mother of his child, Elena. But he may not have a chance. Dornaani's collapse is a prelude to a far more malign scheme: to clear a path for a foe bent on destroying Earth.

IN ERIC FLINT'S
RING OF FIRE SERIES

1635: The Papal Stakes
(with Eric Flint) PB: 978-1-4516-3920-9 • $7.99
Up to their necks in papal assassins, power politics, murder, and mayhem, the uptimers need help and they need it quickly.

1636: Commander Cantrell in the West Indies
(with Eric Flint) PB: 978-1-4767-8060-3 • $8.99
Oil. The Americas have it. The United States of Europe needs it. Commander Eddie Cantrell.

1636: The Vatican Sanction HC: 978-1-4814-8277-6 • $25.00
(with Eric Flint) PB: 978-1-4814-8386-5 • $7.99
Pope Urban has fled the Vatican and the traitor Borja. But assassins have followed him to France—and not only assassins! The Pope and his allies have fled right into the clutches of the vile Pedro Dolor.

1636: Calabar's War
(with Robert E. Waters) PB: 978-1-9821-2605-6 • $8.99
Once a military advisor to the Portuguese, Domingos Fernandes Calabar is now known as a "traitorous dog," helping the Dutch fleet strike at Portuguese and Spanish interests on land and sea.

IN JOHN RINGO'S
BLACK TIDE RISING SERIES

At the End of the World HC: 978-1-9821-2469-4 • $25.00
Six teenagers headed out on a senior summer cruise with a British captain who rarely smiles. What could go wrong? Zombies. Now the small ship they are sailing becomes their one hope for survival.